Sin With Me

A
SUGARLAND CREEK
NOVEL

BROOKE MONTGOMERY

Brooke M xo

Sugarland Creek series
Reading Order

Come With Me (Prequel)
Here With Me (#1)
Stay With Me (#2)
Fall With Me (#3)
Only With Me (#4)
Sin With Me (#5)

Each book can be read as a stand-alone and ends in a happily ever after. However, for the best reading experience, read in order.

Them winters wear on a cowboy
  And there's only so much you can do
  I was lonesome as leaves when the trees lay them down
  Then I looked up and laid eyes on you
  I needed a woman to hold me
  An angel to know me
  Girl even if it was just for a season
  It was you for a reason

-You For A Reason, **Warren Zeiders**

Playlist

Listen to the full *Sin With Me* playlist on Spotify

Wait For You | Myles Smith
Cowboys Cry Too | Kelsea Ballerini, Noah Kahan
Crazy Stupid Love | Blake Proehl
I Know Love | Tate McRae, The Kid LAROI
Devil You Know | Tyler Braden
Relapse | Warren Zeiders
Never Leave | Bailey Zimmerman
Easy | Camila Cabello
Intoxicated | Warren Zeiders
I Would, Would You | Kelsea Ballerini
Comfortably Numb | Abi Carter
You For A Reason | Warren Zeiders
Winning Streak | Jelly Roll
I Fall Apart | Post Malone
Indigo | Sam Barber, Avery Anna
Ordinary | Alex Warren
Forever & Again | The Kid LAROI

Welcome to

SUGARLAND CREEK

RANCH AND EQUINE RETREAT

SUGARLAND CREEK, TN

~Welcome to Sugarland Creek Ranch and Equine Retreat~

The town of Sugarland Creek is home to over two thousand residents and is surrounded by the beautiful Appalachian Mountains. We're only fifteen minutes from the downtown area, where you can shop at local boutiques, grab a latte, catch a movie, or simply enjoy the views.

We're an all-inclusive ranch. While we provide rustic lodging, each cabin is handicapped-accessible with ramps and smooth walking trails. If you need assistance with traveling between activities, we'll provide you with a staff member to pick you up in one of our handicapped-accessible vehicles at any time. Please request at the front desk or dial '0' on your room phone. We're here to help in any way we can.

To make your stay here the best experience, meet the family and learn about everything we have to offer at the retreat to ensure you have the vacation of a lifetime!

Meet the Hollis family:

Garrett & Dena Hollis

Mr. and Mrs. Hollis have been married for over thirty years and have five children. The Sugarland Creek Ranch has been home to over three Hollis generations. When the family officially took over twenty years ago, they added on the retreat to share their love of horses and the outdoors with the public.

Wilder and Waylon
Twin boys, the oldest

Landen
The middle child

Tripp
Youngest of the boys

Noah
The only girl and baby of the family

Whether you're here to relax and enjoy the views or you're ready to get your hands dirty, we have a variety of activities on the ranch for you to enjoy:

Horseback trail riding & tours
(10:00 a.m. and 4:00 p.m.)
Hiking, mountain biking, & fishing
(Maps available at The Lodge)
Family Game Nights
(Sundays and Wednesdays)
Karaoke & Square Dancing
(Friday and Saturday nights)
Kids Game Room
(Open 24/7)
Swimming
(Pool open 9:00 a.m. to 9:00 p.m. each day)
Bonfires with s'mores
(Fridays)
…and much more depending on the season!

The Lodge building is staffed 24 hours a day. It's home to our reception & guest services, The Sugarland Restaurant & Saloon, and activities sign-up.

Find all of our current information at sugarlandcreekranch.com.

We pride ourselves on serving authentic Southern food, so please let us know if you have any dietary restrictions or needs to better serve you. We offer brunch from 8:00 a.m. to 1:00 p.m. The restaurant is open for dinner from 5:00 p.m. to 9:00 p.m. If you wish to dine or find other activities off the ranch, we're less than an hour from Gatlinburg and are happy to provide you with suggestions.

Thank you so much for visiting us.
We hope you have the best time!

-The Hollis Family & Team Sugarland

See map on the next page!

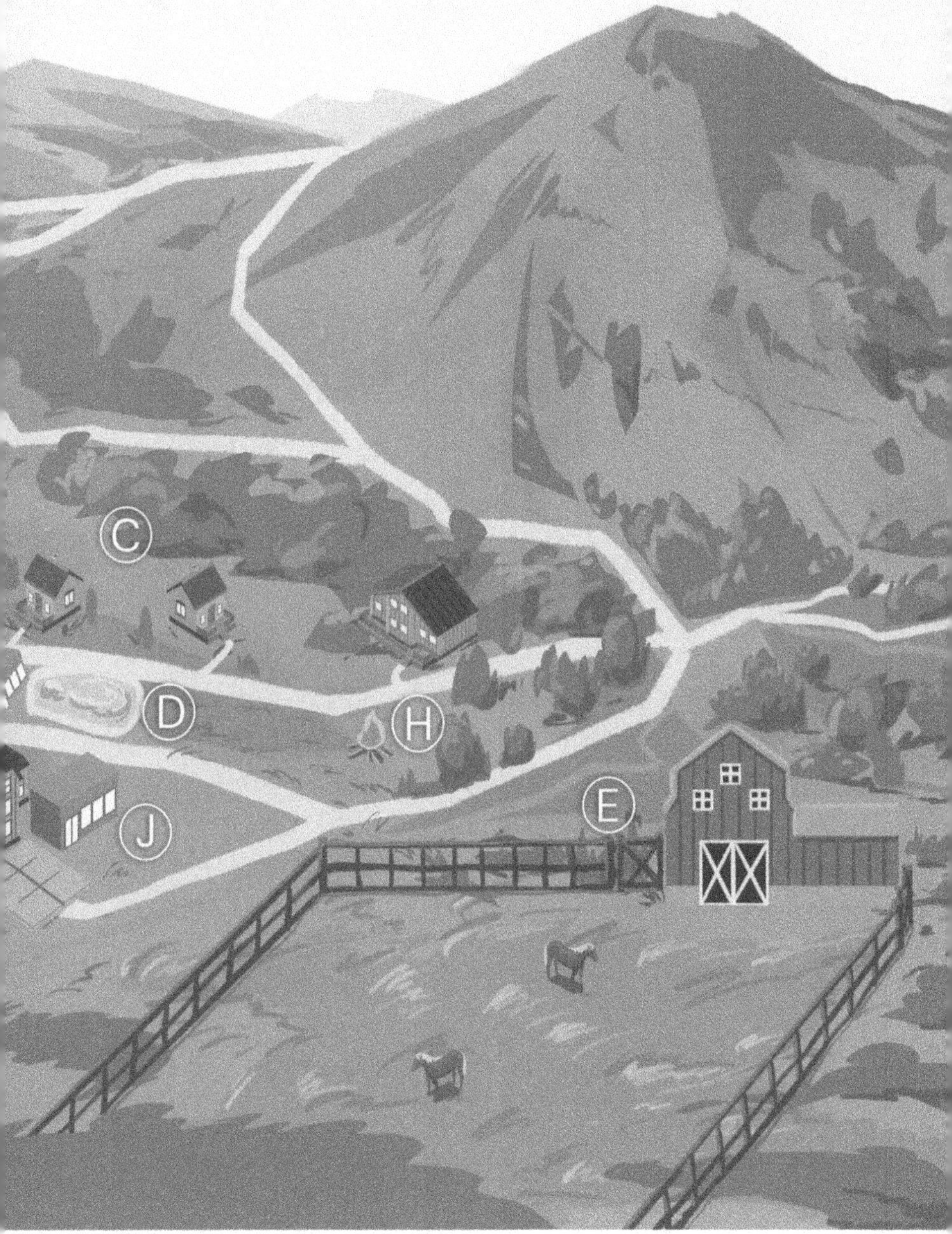

C

D

H

E

J

SUGARLAND CREEK

RANCH AND EQUINE RETREAT

SUGARLAND CREEK, TN

Author's Note

Sin With Me is book #5 in the Sugarland Creek series, and although each one can be read as standalones, this one is best read after book #4, *Only With Me*. The MCs are twin brothers and their stories intertwine, so for the best reading experience on a deeper understanding of Wilder's story, read this after you read Waylon's story. This one showcases Wilder's healing journey.

There are mentions and some details of past events that happen before this timeline begins in case you choose to read this on its own.

Content Warnings

Mentions and depictions of:
cutting, suicide, and substance abuse.

Mental health discussions surrounding grief, depression,
antidepressants, therapy, and panic attacks.

Mentions of a parent's death (not on page) and grief disorder.

Contains mentions of domestic violence but not graphic.

Prologue

Wilder

NINE YEARS AGO

"Hello, you reached the Haven Grace prayer crisis hotline. How can I assist you in prayer today?" a sweet female voice answers, and I swallow hard.

I've never called one of these hotlines before.

I don't know why I'm calling now.

Curiosity mostly.

Curious how it works and if it'd help.

When I looked up local crisis hotlines, this was the first one that popped up.

"Hi, are you there?" the sweet voice continues. "Do you need help?"

"Um…" I sigh, not sure what to say, not sure how to speak when I'm choking on my own guilt.

"I can wait till you're ready, but maybe you could tell me who I'm talkin' to, please?"

Tears well in the corner of my eyes, but I fight them back

and clear my throat. I try to say my name, but nothing comes out.

"I'm Delly," she says softly. "Do you need medical attention at the moment?"

I look down at my leg and wince at the blood running down my thigh. "No."

"Okay, good. How can I help you this evening?"

"I-I dunno. Not sure why I even called," I finally admit.

"That's okay, sir. I'm here to listen."

"*Sir*? No, I'm only twenty-four."

"Apologies, I was just being polite. Can you tell me your name?"

Hesitating, I lick my lips. I don't want anyone to know I called. Sugarland Creek, Tennessee is a small town and this is a *local* crisis hotline, so it's possible she'd recognize me if I told her my real name.

Shame. Guilt. Humiliation.

I feel enough of that. I don't need to feel that way with a stranger too.

Especially from a girl who sounds as graceful as she does.

"Uh…it's Luke."

The first name that pops into my head is the guy who I got into a fight with last night. My head's still throbbing from the hit he got on me after I decked him. But he deserved it when he asked if my little sister was of legal age yet so he could 'tap that ass.'

Motherfucker.

But now I wish I'd picked a different name because hearing her say *his* name makes me pissed off all over again.

"Okay, Luke. Are you a danger to yourself right now?"

"I…have a razor blade."

"It's in your hand now?"

I swallow hard, looking at it like a lifeline. My knuckles are white from how tight I'm gripping it. "Yes."

"Okay. Do you think you could set it down for me so we can talk?"

Shaking, I inhale a deep breath and then blow it out. "Sure, okay."

I set it down on the edge of the tub but keep my gaze locked on it.

"Good. Can you tell me where you are?"

"The bathroom."

"Have you harmed yourself before?"

"Yes." Leaning my head back against the tub, I exhale. "When I was sixteen and nineteen, I cut deep enough to lose consciousness and was hospitalized."

"Is there something makin' you want to again?"

I wouldn't even know where to begin explaining my thoughts. When I say them aloud, they sound stupid.

When I don't respond, she continues, "Do you struggle with depression often, Luke?"

I stifle a laugh. "That's what they tell me."

"Are you on medication for it?"

"Not anymore. I stopped takin' it when I turned eighteen."

"How come?"

"Because they wanted me to go to therapy, which I did for almost two years. Even sent me to a psychiatrist after the first hospitalization."

"Well, I'm no therapist or doctor, but considerin' you called tonight, I can safely assume you don't want to relapse and harm yourself."

"I'm tryin' hard not to, Delly…"

"But?"

"I'm in a lot of pain. Hell, I can barely remember a time when I haven't been. But tonight, I needed some relief from this doom feelin' that I haven't been able to escape in weeks. The urge to cut until I pass out is…strong," I confess, but if I were being totally honest, I'd tell her I've already made a cut on my upper thigh. Not deep, though. It only bled a little, but it didn't numb the pain either. It's why I didn't know when to stop the last time I landed in the hospital. I kept going until I felt that numbness and by then it was almost too late.

"Have you felt that urge since the last time you cut?"

"Yeah, a few times." Few *dozen*.

"And what stopped you those times?"

"Um, rememberin' the consequences and how the relief is only temporary. Thinkin' about my family. My brother, mostly. He's the one who found me in our parents' bathroom the first and second time."

"Does your brother live with you now?"

"Not exactly. He lives in the apartment below mine. We share a duplex."

"Is he home?"

"He's still workin'."

I asked Waylon to cover for me with the evening chores at the retreat barn so I could go home. Told him I wasn't feelin' well and he didn't ask any questions.

"What would he tell you if he knew you were strugglin' right now?"

He'd probably wanna punch me in the face.

"He'd tell me to think about our parents and what it'd do to them seein' me in the hospital again. How they'd worry. He'd remind me how scared he was last time and how losin' his twin brother would destroy him. He'd beg me to get help."

"You're twins?" she asks.

"Yep. And the oldest of five kids."

"Wow, so it sounds like you have a lot of people who love you and wouldn't want you to hurt yourself."

4

"You'd be correct."

"So thinkin' about them helped you stop last time?"

"Right, but it's not always enough." I blow out a shaky breath. "I already used the razor before I called you. But I stopped after the first cut."

"Are you bleedin', Luke?" The fear in her voice adds to my guilt. Without even knowing who she is, I hate hearing how concerned she sounds.

"No, ma'am. It stopped. But it's why I'm in the tub, so I didn't make a mess."

"For what it's worth, I'm proud of you for havin' the strength to stop when you did and for callin' here. I know that couldn't have been easy. But I need you to be straight with me. How many times have you cut tonight?"

"Just the one time, Delly. I promise," I say sincerely.

She blows out a breath I don't think she meant for me to hear because she quickly sucks in air to compose herself.

"Can you tell me why? Maybe we can talk it out."

I'd rather hang up than say the words aloud, but I say them anyway. I've already admitted this much. Might as well keep going.

I tell her about the pain, the sadness that overcomes me, and the darkness that consumes my thoughts. And how I sometimes need the relief to quiet the vile thoughts in my head and that relief comes from cutting my thighs until they bleed down my legs because that's when my mind clears. That's when I focus on the physical pain instead of the mental pain and all the negative thoughts disappear.

"It's a much-needed distraction from the depression, and even if it's temporary, the physical pain is more bearable than the mental pain."

And that barely scratches the surface.

"I'd like to say a prayer for you, Luke. Would that be okay?"

"Sure," I say, although I haven't prayed in years.

"It's okay if it's not your thing." Her voice is soft and nonjudgmental.

Then I squeeze my eyes closed as she says her little prayer.

"I pray for your strength so you can remind yourself why you fight. I pray for the courage to seek help if you find yourself in this same position tonight. And I pray you feel worthy enough to get treatment because you deserve to be happy."

"Thanks, Delly. I appreciate you takin' time out of your night to speak with me. I'm sure you have a lot better things to do."

"I volunteer at the church three evenings a week, so I assure you, it was no trouble."

"Three times a week? Wow. Are you some kinda saint?" I half laugh because I haven't been to church in years, even when my mom begs me to go.

"I enjoy helpin' people," she says without missing a beat. "And it was a pleasure to meet you even in these circumstances."

Goddamn, she's too sweet for her own good.

"How old are you, Delly?" I ask before hanging up.

"I'm almost twenty-three."

So she's about two years younger than me since I'll be twenty-five soon. That means she would've been a sophomore when I was a senior. Everyone knows everyone in our small town, but her name isn't ringing a bell. Not surprised, though, because in between dealing with my depressive episodes, I drank in high school...a lot. Shit, I still do. But also, I rarely paid attention to the underclassmen.

"And you're spendin' your Friday night answerin' crisis hotlines instead of a bar?"

"Yeah, because if I don't, who would've answered your call?"

"Hello, you reached the Haven Grace prayer crisis hotline. How can I assist you in prayer today?"

I smile when I hear her voice.

"Hi, Delly."

"Luke, is that you?"

"Yeah."

"Are you okay?"

"I am now."

"Whaddya mean?"

I lift a shoulder even though she can't see me. "It means... hearin' your voice is what I needed to clear my head."

She sighs happily as if she was expecting the worst. "Okay. What would you like to talk about, then?"

"I was feelin' down and had the urge to cut but didn't get out my blade this time."

"I'm happy to hear that, Luke. Did somethin' trigger you tonight?"

"Just a little self-deprecation."

"Talk me through what's goin' on in your mind."

And without hesitation, I do.

She's the first person I've ever felt comfortable enough to spill those secrets. And even though it's because she can't see me and has no idea who I am, it's still a weight off my chest to speak the words aloud to someone.

"You're a good listener, Delly..." I say when the silence between us gets too loud.

"Thank you for sharin' that with me." She sniffles a few times before clearing her throat. "Truly."

"Are you catchin' a cold?"

"Um...no." She sniffs again as if she's trying to control her emotions. "Just havin' a heavy night."

"You?" I stammer. "I don't like the sound of that. What's goin' on?"

She's quiet as if she's contemplating telling me.

"I had a caller before you that was quite challengin'." Her voice cracks, deepening with sorrow. "I had another volunteer call 911 while I kept him on the phone. Safe to say, I was relieved when I heard your voice because it..."

"It what?" I furrow my brows, wondering why she paused.

"It meant you were still alive and trusted me enough to call again."

My gut tightens at what she must've heard from the other caller. "Did the previous guy not make it?"

She swallows thickly. "I'm not sure. The operator disconnected when she confirmed paramedics were on the scene."

"What was his drug or weapon of choice?" I ask curiously.

"You know I can't share that confidential information."

Her sadness pours through the speaker and it breaks my heart.

"Okay, let's get your mind on somethin' happier," I suggest, hoping she'll take the bait so it takes my focus off my own tortured thoughts. "Tell me what you did today."

"We're supposed to be talkin' about you," she counters, her

voice back to sweet and tender. "Why don't you tell me about your day instead?"

"Only if you tell me about yours after?" I counter.

She sighs, but I hear the smile in that one calm breath. "Okay, fine."

"Hello, you reached the Haven Grace prayer crisis hotline. How can I assist you in prayer today?"

"Delly!" I cheer and then hiccup.

"Luke?"

"Mm-hmm. I'm so glad you picked up."

"Are you...*drunk*?"

"Eh, kinda."

Considering I'm slurring my words, it's no surprise she quickly caught on.

"How much have you had to drink?"

"Fuck, I dunno. Lost count."

"It's seven in the evening on a Wednesday."

"Okay, and?"

"How're you this drunk already?"

"I thought this was supposed to be a judge-free zone?" I quip stupidly.

She clears her throat. "This is, Luke. I'm just tryin' to figure out what happened to cause you to be this drunk so early. Did you harm yourself?"

"No...unless you count the substance abuse. I took a few fireball shots, too."

Which is still burning my stomach.

"Do you drink often?"

"Uh…yeah." I breathe out a laugh. "But it's better than cuttin' up my thigh, ain't it?"

"Are you at home?" she asks without responding.

"Yep. Why? You wanna come over?" I ask seductively.

"No, I wanna make sure you're not gonna drive drunk."

"Nah. My brother usually picks me up if I'm out drinkin', but tonight I stayed in. Just me and Mr. Jack Daniel's."

"Are you havin' thoughts about harmin' yourself?"

"Not anymore. That's why I'm drinkin', Delly. When I get close to passin' out, it numbs the sadness and thoughts. Can't be depressed if I'm drunk."

"So you traded in one vice for another."

"Alcohol has longer lastin' effects, too. You should be happy about that. Less blood," I muse.

"I'm happy you're safe at home but not that you're usin' alcohol as a copin' mechanism. There are many ways that being an alcoholic can lead to other issues."

"What other option do I have?"

"Therapy. Medication. Journaling. Support groups. Church. Praying."

"Yeah, I'm not doin' any of that," I scoff, looking up at my ceiling and realizing my bedroom is spinning.

"Why? Think it makes you weak or less of a man for needin' help?" she challenges.

Instead of responding, I hang up the phone and chuck it across my room.

"Hello, you reached the Haven Grace prayer crisis hotline. How can I assist you in prayer today?"

"Delly?" I ask pitifully like a dog with its tail between his legs.

"Hi, Luke."

Her soft voice instantly relaxes my shoulders, and I breathe out a sigh of relief.

"I'm so sorry for the other night. I feel like a jackass for callin' you when I was drunk like that."

"No need to apologize. That's why I'm here."

"Don't do that. You didn't deserve my drunken rambles or me makin' you worry. I shouldn't have treated you like that, and I'm sorry for callin' when I was in that condition."

"You needed to talk to someone, and I was happy to be that person, even if you *did* hang up on me."

The line stays silent, several seconds pass, and then minutes —and she doesn't rush me—before I finally speak up.

"I'm a coward."

"What?"

"I'm a coward," I repeat louder. "That's why I don't do those things you suggested."

"You can change that, ya know? Even if it's just baby steps. Callin' here was a good first step. You've shared a lot with me already. Maybe your next step could be seein' a professional?"

"It's easy to talk to you because you can't see me and have no idea who I am. I don't think I could face someone in person and tell 'em all the ways I've fucked up in life. I don't have to see the look of shame and pity on your probably beautiful face."

"*Probably beautiful?* Are you seriously hittin' on me?"

I gulp. Most girls melt into a puddle when I say sweet bullshit to them.

"Just payin' you a compliment. Based on the sound of your beautiful voice, I imagine the rest of you is, too."

She doesn't respond for several seconds.

"Well...as nice as that is, this ain't a datin' phone service, Luke."

"Probably a good thing. Based on my record, we wouldn't have talked again after the first conversation."

"Is that right?" she drawls, and I hear the amusement in her tone. "You're a hit-it-and-quit-it kinda guy?"

"Guess ya could say that," I admit sheepishly.

"One of your mechanisms to avoid rejection, shame, and guilt?"

I clear my throat, growing agitated that she's sounding a lot like my old therapist.

"It's easier not givin' them hope. I can't promise anythin' more than one night. I'm already a burden to my family. I don't wanna burden a partner, so might as well give 'em a good time for a night."

"Well, without the burden of proof, I don't believe your family feels that way. And you callin' here—more than once— is *proof* that deep down you know you're not. Your family loves you unconditionally."

"You're wrong."

I know I am.

I can see it in the way my brother looks at me. The way he follows me like a shadow because he doesn't trust I won't do something stupid or risky. And it's the way I let him because I don't trust myself either.

He hasn't even introduced me to his new girlfriend because he doesn't trust me not to fuck it up for him.

"Am I?" By the tone of her voice, I imagine her lifting a scolding brow at me. "If that's true, then you'd stop callin' me."

"Hello, you reached the Haven Grace prayer crisis hotline. How can I assist you in prayer today?"

"This is the fourth night you've volunteered this week."

"And this is the fourth night you've called this week." There's a hint of amusement in her voice but just a little to where it's not inappropriate to say to someone who's been calling a crisis hotline for two months.

It's actually the sixth night I've called. When she's not there, I hang up.

I have no interest in talking to someone new and starting over. But I also didn't want to scare her off by asking which nights she'd be there.

"The holidays are the most stressful time of the year," I say, only half-joking.

"Are you feelin' stressed or more worried than usual? Do you have the urge to —"

"No, no. I haven't felt that since I started talkin' to you."

"Oh. Really?" she asks as if that shocks her. Truthfully, it shocks me too.

"Yes, really. I look forward to talkin' to you. I'm finally not lettin' someone down for once."

"Whaddya mean?"

"I don't wanna disappoint you. I appreciate the way you listen to me without judgment, so the least I can do is make you proud."

It makes me think twice before grabbing my razor because I'll get to talk to her without feeling like a failure.

The line goes dead silent, and I worry we got disconnected. "Delly?"

"Ya know, that kinda sounds like somethin' a therapist would also do for you. Have you thought any more about seein' one?"

"Why do I need one when I have you? You've done more for me in two months than my psychiatrist did in two years."

"Because I won't be here forever and you'll still need someone."

"I'll magically be healed before that time comes."

"Is that so?" A laugh slips out of her mouth and it's the sweetest sound I've ever heard.

"Mm-hmm. Maybe you could be my sponsor. Then you'd have to gimme your number."

"You've tried that before, remember?"

"I'm nothin' if not persistent."

"So I've learned. But right now, we're supposed to be talkin' about you and your feelings."

I exhale through my nose because I hate doing that the most. I'd much rather just listen to her.

"Pass," I quip.

"Nice try," she says sternly. "How 'bout you start by tellin' me about your day?"

"Hello, you reached the Haven Grace prayer crisis hotline. How can I assist you in prayer today?"

"I need you to talk me off the ledge, Delly."

"Luke? Are you in danger?"

I hate how panicked she sounds but also grateful she picked up and recognized my voice. I almost didn't call because I didn't want to torture myself even more with her sweet voice.

"I'm really drunk." *Again.*

"Where're you right now?"

"Lyin' in my bathtub."

"Are you holdin' a razor blade?"

"Yeah…I don't think I'm gonna be able to stop tonight if I start," I admit.

"What happened? Talk me through it." The fear in her tone makes me regret calling her, but if I have any chance of stopping myself, I need to hear her voice.

"The sadness and dread are so fuckin' heavy. My chest burns. My heart's racin' so damn fast. My throat is dry and somehow wet at the same time. I'm sweatin' through my shirt. My mind is scrambled with thoughts. And…I just wanna make it stop."

"Luke, you're havin' a panic attack. I want you to put down the razor blade, close your eyes, and then listen to the sound of my voice."

"Alright."

After following her orders, I lean my head back against the cool porcelain and wait.

"I'm gonna count back from thirty. I want you to inhale a deep breath on the first five counts and then release it on the next five, and so on."

"Okay," I murmur.

"Deep inhale," she demands. "Twenty-nine, twenty-eight, twenty-seven, twenty-six and now exhale…"

I do as she says, listening to her counts and breathing in time with them. Clinging to her voice gives me something to focus on besides how foolish I feel for needing to be talked down.

When she gets to zero, my breathing goes back to normal.

"Good, Luke. How do you feel?"

"That tightness in my chest is a bit lighter," I tell her. The slow exhaling and deep breathing helped to release the tension locked in my ribs.

"Thank God. I'm glad to hear that." She releases a sigh of relief.

"But the sadness is still lurkin', taunting me to cut and release the pain so I can finally be free of it," I murmur honestly.

"That dread feelin' is *temporary*. It won't last forever and will eventually pass. Try to stay strong and fight through it the best you can so you don't give in to it. I'll stay on the phone with you as long as it takes. Think you can do that for me?"

"I dunno, Delly. I've been tryin' for three hours, but the urge is gettin' harder to resist."

Do it. Do it. Now. Do it.

The words have been on repeat.

A part of my brain knows it'll numb the pain and that's all it wants right now.

Fuck the consequences.

"Oh, Luke. Why didn't you call me sooner?"

I sigh, squeezing my eyes to hold back the scream I'm

tempted to release. "I didn't wanna hear the way you sound right now."

Disappointment. Worry. *Pity.*

"It's why I'm here. And for what it's worth, I'm proud of you for callin' before you hurt yourself."

"I'm a fuckin' mess, Delly. You deserve better than spendin' your night with me."

"Listen to me..." she says in the sternest tone I've ever heard from her. "I volunteer damn near every night so I don't risk missin' your call. And not just because I worry about your safety, but I need to hear your voice just as much as you need to hear mine."

"You do?" I whisper in disbelief, my eyes watering.

"Yes..." she says softly. "It brings me comfort to hear you breathin'. I could hear it for hours and never get bored."

"Like a dog pantin' in your ear? That does it for ya, huh?" My words come out more flirty than I intended, but she must find the humor in it because a laugh escapes from her mouth. Though I don't think she meant for me to hear it because she quickly clears her throat.

But it's too late because now that I've heard it, I want to hear it again and again.

"I'd stay on the line just to listen to you snore because it'd mean you're alive," she says, not humoring my dog panting comment.

"If I didn't know any better, Delly...you're getting attached to me, too."

My words are genuine even though I'm fighting a battle inside my head that feels as if I'll never win. It's armed and ready to pull the trigger, but the only defense I have is holding onto hope that I'm strong enough to resist.

"I think you're right, Luke. I am."

"Hello, you reached the Haven Grace prayer crisis hotline. How can I assist you in prayer today?" a sweet old lady's voice I don't recognize picks up.

"Uh, hello. Is Delly workin' tonight?"

"I'm sorry, honey. She's not. Is there somethin' I can help with?"

That's weird. She's been there every Friday night for the past six months. We spoke two nights ago, but I already miss her.

"No, thanks. Can you tell me when her next shift is?"

"I don't think she's comin' back, sweetie. Her little sister is in the hospital."

My heart drops into my stomach. She's told me a bit about her sister and how she's ten years younger than her, which would only make her thirteen.

"Oh my God. What happened?"

"I can't really say, but she's in critical condition. And with her dad's accident last year, I don't think she'll have time to volunteer anymore."

She never told me about her dad, so I don't know what happened, but now I'm worried about her and afraid I'll never get answers.

"I can't believe I finally get to meet this girlfriend of yours," I say, sliding my boots on.

"She was two years below us in high school, so you might recognize her once you see her, but please..." Waylon turns, his eyes pleading. "Don't be an ass. Or hit on her. Or —"

"Dude...why would I hit on her?"

It's possible I did back in school, considering I dated around...a lot.

He pierces me with a look. "Because I know you."

"I take offense to whatever the fuck that means!"

If we didn't look alike, you'd never know we're identical twins based on our different personalities. Waylon's quiet and reserved, my complete opposite, but in terms of relationships, we're pretty much the same in that we don't have them. So for him to let me meet her after all this time must mean they're getting serious.

"Just...don't be obnoxious. She's not much of a drinker and she's been goin' through a lot with her family the past few months."

I stand once my boots are tied. "Me, obnoxious?"

He stares at me, and I laugh at his deadpan expression.

"It took a lot of convincin' her to come out tonight, so don't make her regret it."

I snort. "Wow...she sounds like a ball of fun. No wonder she's datin' you."

"And now your ass is stayin' home."

"Oh, relax. I'll be nothin' less of a gentleman to Daphne."

"Delilah," he corrects.

"Right. Like the flower…"

"I guess." He shrugs, grabbing his wallet and keys. "Ready?"

Waylon drives us to the Twisted Bull. It's the best dance bar in town, with western decor and a mechanical bull. I've been trying to master it ever since my twenty-first birthday and I've yet to make it past four seconds.

Probably because I'm always wasted when I attempt to ride it, but it's still a fun time.

We walk in and make a beeline for the bar. Most of our high school friends who still live here also come out on the weekends—well, the ones who aren't married or have children. Most of the crowd is college-aged, but we still enjoy coming here.

"Here ya go." I turn around and hand Waylon his beer. We're almost shoulder to shoulder with how packed it is. "Is Landen meetin' us?"

"Yeah, he should be here soon," he tells me.

Our younger brother is twenty-two and usually parties with us. He's as wild as I am, which Waylon hates because then he's stuck babysitting both of us.

Tripp, our youngest brother, is only twenty and can't come out yet. Not sure he would even if he was allowed. After losing his best friend two years ago, he rarely does anything outside of work.

They both live with our parents and little sister, Noah, who's eighteen.

Mom kicked Waylon and me out at twenty-one because she got sick of hearing us stumble into the house at three in the morning. So now we live in the ranch hand duplexes on the property, which is way better anyway. We get our own spaces but are still close enough to everyone and our jobs at the equine retreat that's attached to the family horse ranch.

His gaze looks past me and his mouth twists into a wide smile. "Here she is."

Taking a pull of my beer, I turn and watch Waylon pull a blonde into his arms. Then he kisses her cheek before whispering something in her ear.

Probably warning her about me.

"Babe, this is Wilder," he tells her, then shifts his attention to me. "This is Delilah Fanning."

I hold out my hand and she takes it, smiling sweetly. "It's a pleasure to meet the woman brave enough to date my lookalike." I wink.

Her face tilts with scrunched eyebrows as if she can't believe how similar we look. "It's great to finally meet you, too. I've heard so much already."

"They're all lies, I swear," I quip.

"You're saved by the burden of proof." She smirks, but now I'm the one tilting my head because I've heard that exact phrase in that same sweet voice before.

One I've missed hearing.

And I do recognize her but not for the reason Waylon would assume.

Delilah...*Delly.* She gave me her nickname, not her full name.

Whenever the impulse to cut rushes through my mind, it's her voice in my head I focus on. It's not one I could ever forget.

I've called the hotline once a week since then to check if she'd returned.

It's been weeks since we talked, but I've continued fighting against touching a razor blade. When I get the urge to grab it, I hear her reminding me it'll pass. I hold my breath and exhale as I count down from thirty when my chest is tight. I remind myself of our conversations and hold onto them when I'm down.

I even threw out the blades because I hoped I'd get to speak to her again and wanted to make her proud. In fact, I was living for the possibility of hearing it in her voice —have been dying to hear it—and now she's standing in front of me and I can't even tell her what she's helped me accomplish.

"Sorry I can't say the same. He's only recently told me about your existence," I drawl, turning my focus to Waylon.

And I was right when I guessed she was beautiful.

Fucking *stunning.*

Long blond hair curled into waves down her back, bright blue eyes that I can't stop staring into, and luscious pink lips.

If she wasn't my type to a tee, I might find this a hilarious coincidence, but her dating my twin brother when she spent half a year talking to me on the phone isn't the kind of irony I expected.

I haven't stopped thinking about her since our first conversation. It's crazy to think how I'm not even that same person anymore, thanks to her.

If I believed in fate, I'd say that's what made me call the same night she was volunteering and made us meet. If someone else had picked up that night, the past six months would've gone differently.

Although I still struggle with depression and the urge to cut still lingers in my mind when it gets bad, she gave me the strength and confidence to fight through it instead of give in to it.

Go fucking figure, I finally meet her in person and can't even tell her it's me without admitting I gave her a fake name. Facing her after confessing all my dirty, dark secrets plus the times I called her drunk would be humiliating.

And I'd have to pretend my feelings for her didn't exist

because Waylon deserves to be happy. He has taken care of me most of our lives and I've never seen him look at a woman the way he's looking at her.

But worse, I don't want to see that look of pity and concern that'll inevitably flash across her face when I tell her. I get that enough from Waylon and my own reflection.

So I'll say nothing and pretend it never happened.

Even if it kills me.

Chapter One

Wilder

W hat's that condition where you're secretly obsessed with your twin's ex-girlfriend?

Because whatever that is, I have that.

But Delilah Fanning would never *ever* be interested in me.

For starters, she can hardly stand me.

By the tongue-lashing she just gave me, she wouldn't bat an eye if I got run over by a tractor attached to a manure spreader.

In fact, she'd be driving it.

Not that she hates me, per se, but she's definitely not a fan of my behavior.

Like right now…

"Wilder, I swear to God…" She pinches the bridge of her nose, leaning in closer so I can hear her over the loud music. The smell of her perfume—a mix of something sweet and floral —invades my senses.

25

People stand at the bar all around us, but when it's just me and her, they fade away.

"Pace yourself because if you throw up in my brand-new truck, I'll strip you naked and hogtie your balls until they fall off."

Jesus Christ.

My balls ache at the visual.

"Delly, *baby*…" I drawl. Her old nickname slips from my lips, but if she notices, she doesn't show it. "If you wanna get me naked, just ask."

"I've seen it all…I'm good," she deadpans, sliding a glass of ice water across the bar toward me.

"'Cuse me? You been spyin'?" I waggle my brows and she rolls her eyes.

"Against my will," she clarifies, tucking a loose strand behind her ear. "You tend to strip when you're drunk, and I've seen you drunk more times than I can count. So I'd be very careful the next time you show me your pierced dick because it might be the last."

A smug grin flashes across my face. "You've looked at my piercings, huh? You want a private viewin'?" I wink and then take a drink of the water to appease her when she scowls.

The three shots I took before this are barely affecting me. *Kinda.*

"Two weeks ago, you streaked through the ranch at four in the mornin' and then passed out in front of The Lodge. I had to drag your naked ass back to my truck and then lift you up into the seat. So yeah…I saw your piercings…up close and too personal."

"What about this one?" I flick out my tongue, showing off the piercing there.

"Mm-hmm. Also not impressive." She steals my water and drinks it as if she's bored.

26

"Wait, wait, wait…" I wave out my hands. "Are you callin' my piercings *not* impressive?"

Her gaze lowers to my groin before meeting my stare with an evil smirk, her tongue poking the inside of her cheek. "I'm sayin' the *whole* package ain't that impressive."

My jaw drops at her bald-faced lie. "Now I know you're full of shit. Women don't say they're *Wild for Wilder* for nothin'."

"Don't make me throw up." She pretends to gag.

I steal back the glass of water and chug the rest. It's the weekend before Thanksgiving and the Twisted Bull is packed with college-aged girls in mostly cropped tops and jean skirts. Most of the guys are in jeans, boots, and Stetson hats, playing the cowboy fantasy even though they've never worked on a ranch a day in their lives.

But it's why Delilah's glued to my hip because she's on *babysitting my ass* duty—her words, not mine. Waylon put her up to it. Anytime he can't come out, which has been more and more ever since he started dating Delilah's little sister, he puts her in charge of me.

I should be offended, considering I'm thirty-three years old, but I'd never drink and drive, so it's a good idea to have a DD. And well, there's been a few instances of fighting, so now anytime I go out, someone comes with me to make sure I get home safe. *And stay out of jail.*

I'm not even that drunk tonight, but considering how fucked up I got two weekends ago, it's best I take it easy. Especially since I don't even remember that night she's talking about.

And I don't want to see the look of disappointment on her face again.

Leaning in closer to her ear, I feel her shiver against me. "I'm ready to go if you are."

Her brows furrow as she cocks her head. "It's only midnight."

I shrug, not really in the mood to drink anymore.

This is when I should admit the new meds I started yesterday aren't supposed to be mixed with alcohol. Eight months ago, I started going to therapy and stopped having sex and drinking alcohol to get clean and focus on my mental health.

But then three months ago, I started drinking again when the pain got to be too much. It was either drink or cut, so I chose the lesser of two evils.

But I'm still abstinent, so that has to count for something, right?

The last woman I slept with was Jen—my on-again, off-again fling—who I haven't seen in almost a year. She caught me flirting with her friend, Bethany, who I didn't know was her friend at the time, and stormed off. She knew we weren't exclusive or serious and yet she acted like we were.

"I need an alcohol detox," I admit. "At least for a month."

That's how long my psychiatrist told me it'd take for the antidepressants to start working.

So I get to be sober *and* miserable until then.

I haven't told anyone that I'm trying them, not because I'm ashamed, but I don't want to hear their praises or how proud of me they are—at least not until I deserve to. Therapy has been great, and I consistently attend my appointments, but the sadness still tempts me to self-medicate with cutting and alcohol. When he suggested trying a low dose for the "seasonal depression" time of year, I agreed. At this point, I have nothing to lose but myself.

The last thing I want to continue being is a burden on my brother, who's always been there for me. He's happy for the first time in years, and I don't want to take that away from him.

Or anyone else.

"A *whole* month?" Delilah feigns shock, smacking a hand to her chest. "I'll be so bored not carryin' your drunken ass upstairs to your room. Whatever shall I do with all that free time?"

"Just admit you like hangin' out with me." I flash her a lopsided grin, but she doesn't fall for it.

"I might get a life of my own if I'm not always in charge of yours," she retorts.

And there it is.

Although her tone's teasing, there's truth to it.

The guilt wraps around my throat until it cuts off my windpipe, and I choke on it.

Not because she's wrong, but because Delilah has spent half her life taking care of people, and I hate that she's been liable for me for the past year. Even though I enjoy spending time with her, it's not the same if she feels obligated.

Before I stopped drinking the first time, she tagged along for a few months, and then when I started drinking again, she continued without complaint.

Though I'm not sure why.

She doesn't owe me anything.

But still, she took on the responsibility, and I should relieve her of that.

"Tonight's the last time you'll have to babysit me, I promise."

She arches a brow, genuinely curious. "You're serious?"

I nod, pulling out my wallet so I can pay the tab.

"At least until Vegas," I clarify jokingly. "Everyone else will be drinkin', so it'll be hard not to."

Landen's wife, Ellie, is competing at the National Finals Rodeo in the barrel racing competition in less than three weeks. My entire family is going for a few days, including Delilah, her sister, and their mom.

"But once we're back, I'll be sober, so you never have to take care of me again."

I wave to the bartender and grab her attention. "Ready for my tab, Rainy."

"So early?" she quips.

"Yep, gotta get home to the wife and kids."

Delilah nearly chokes on her saliva. "Now I know you're wasted when you make up a whole fake family."

I snort. "Oh, c'mon…couldn't you hear me sayin' that in twenty years?"

"*Twenty*? It's gonna take two more decades for you to settle down, huh?"

"Nah, I'll probably be single until the day I die." I shrug dismissively.

Who's going to want to take on my baggage anyway? I wouldn't want to give that to anyone. And according to everyone, I can hardly take care of myself, so what business do I have trying to take care of someone else?

"And why's that, Wilder?" She leans an elbow on the bar, but then some drunk guy crashes into her, spilling his beer on her.

"Oh my God," Delilah grits between her teeth, lifting her arms when the liquid falls down her low-cut top.

People around us spread out when his beer continues spilling on the floor.

"Hey, asshole," I shout, shoving him back since he has no concept of personal space. "Watch where you're goin'!"

"Wilder, stop," Delilah demands. "It was an accident."

Those are the last words I hear before the guy swings at me, knocking me square in the jaw.

That was no accident. *Motherfucker.*

With stars in my eyes, I shove my fist in his gut and he falls to his ass.

"Wilder!" Delilah grabs my arm, yanking me back.

"He hit me first!" I defend, rubbing over the spot he nailed me.

Someone helps the guy back to his feet and then he points a finger in my face, screaming at me. "Let's finish this outside, ya pussy. Now!"

"Pfft..." I bark out an amused laugh. "Like you know what a pussy looks like."

He cocks his brow, smirking like a smug son of a bitch. "I'm lookin' at one now."

Before I can deck him a second time, Delilah stands between us, and when I try moving her to the side, she jerks her elbow back into my gut.

"Shut the fuck up and get out of his face before I knee you in the dick," she shouts at him.

My brows pop up at her defending me. It wouldn't be the first time, but I haven't seen her this pissed in a hot minute.

"Got your little girlfriend to fight your battles for ya, huh?" He glares at me over her head. "How cute."

I should be furious at the way he's taunting me, but I can't help smiling at the way he called her my *girlfriend*.

Pfft. I fucking wish.

"She is cute, ain't she?" I roll my tongue piercing and lick my lips. "You should see how *cute* she looks when she's on her knees stuffed with my co—"

"Do *not* finish that sentence." Delilah shoots me a murderous glare over her shoulder, but I notice the blush covering her cheeks that wasn't there earlier.

"Why not, baby doll?" I wink, crossing my arms. She hates when I call her that, which is why I do it. I usually get some kind of reaction, but tonight she doesn't take the bait.

"Time to go," she tells me before facing the other guy. "Call me *cute* again and I'll jam my knee in your balls so hard, you'll choke from spitin' 'em out."

"Trust me, man. She'll do it," I say, stifling a chuckle when the guy finally gets the hint and walks away with his buddy.

"Pay your damn tab and meet me outside," Delilah orders, then walks toward the exit.

Yep, she's pissed.

I sign the receipt and give Rainy a big tip for dealing with my shit.

"You can't seriously be mad at me for self-defense?" I say once I open the passenger door of her truck. "That asshole hit me first. Granted I pushed him, but his drunk ass spilled beer on you! I was being chivalrous and standin' up for you. That's gotta at least earn me some brownie points."

Delilah doesn't respond or move. Her chest rapidly rises and falls as she white-knuckle-grips the steering wheel and stares out the windshield.

I wait for the inevitable scolding she's about to unleash on me.

"Del—" I whisper, reaching out to her. Neither of us has our seat belts on, so I inch closer, hoping it's enough to soften her. "I'm sorry for ruinin' your night. I meant what I said earlier. This is the last time. I'm freeing you of babysittin' me. I won't even drink in Vegas and will be your DD for once."

We won't be driving, but I'll be in charge of making sure she gets back to her room safely.

She continues ignoring my presence and words, making me feel even worse.

"I fucked up. How can I make it up to you? Please...I'll do anythin'." I grab her elbow that's as stiff as her fist.

Her lips twitch, but she remains silent.

"You want me to embarrass myself to prove how sorry I am? I'll streak down Main Street while shouting 'I have a teeny weeny' and will probably get my naked ass arrested, but for you, I'd do it." When she doesn't budge, I continue, "Do you wanna tie me up to the bumper so you can drag me all the way to the ranch? Knowin' how you drive, I'll probably die, but if that's what it takes to prove how badly I feel...I'll let ya do it."

I chuckle at the imagery of her hogtying my ankles and going eighty down the ranch's gravel road. She'd purposely fly over the speed bumps, too.

But still, *nothing*.

"Okay, fine. You wanna shoot me? Hell, I'll load the gun for ya. Just don't aim at the jewels, okay? Maybe the shoulder so I can still ride but not have to lift hay bales. Leave that bitch work to Waylon." I snort at the thought of him complaining and telling me I could still use my other arm.

"Delilah?" I brush a hand down her arm and it's as if my touch wakes her from a trance because she snaps her head toward me. "What's goin' on in that head of yours?"

Without a word, she yanks me toward her until our mouths collide.

I'm in so much shock, I freeze.

When her tongue slides between my lips, my brain finally catches up, and I sink into her.

What the hell is happening?

Fuck if I know, but I go along with it.

I've imagined kissing her for years—not exactly under these circumstances—but I'm not complaining.

Cupping her face, I groan and pull her closer. A mix of tequila and strawberries from her margarita floods my senses. She only had a couple of drinks before switching to Diet Coke, but I can still taste the sweetness on her tongue.

Delilah climbs over the center console without breaking contact and then straddles my thighs. It's a snug fit with her on top of me, but I quickly lower the seat back so her head doesn't smack the roof of the truck.

As she rocks against me, I dig my fingers into her hips and move her body faster over my erection.

Fingers weave through my hair as she grinds on me harder. When her tongue teases my piercing, I moan at how good it feels to have her like this.

I almost laugh at the irony of how less than twenty minutes ago she claimed my piercings and *whole package* weren't that impressive, but now she's in my lap, edging both of us.

My head can hardly keep up as my heart threatens to beat out of my chest because I've never felt anything like this.

This urgency.

This craving that only Delilah can satisfy.

This feeling of relief that's only ever been fulfilled from cutting—something I haven't done in years because of her—but you never forget the relief when the pain finally vanishes. It's a high that's too easy to get addicted to.

And now that I've discovered an alternate way to get that feeling, I'm never letting it go.

When she releases a throaty whimper, I nearly lose control. Kissing her isn't enough. I need to touch her.

My fingers brush the hem of her shirt, feeling the softness of her skin against my calluses as I explore her body. I slide a palm underneath her bra and glide my thumb over her peaked nipple.

Her head falls back when she gasps at the sensation. I kiss down her jawline, sucking on her neck and massaging her breast.

"Fuck, Delilah…" Groaning out her name, I lick over her pulse point and feel how fast her heart's beating.

"Touch me…" she begs, clinging tighter around my shoulders. "Lower."

I've never heard her voice so raspy, and I've never wanted to obey as urgently as I do now that I have.

My free hand pops the button of her jeans and then I lower the zipper until I feel the fabric of her panties. When I rub over her clit, she releases a needy moan, and I capture her lips again.

She fists my shirt as I tease her, moving from fast and hard to soft and slow.

"Wilder, more…I need — "

"Whaddya need, darlin'?" I prompt when she stops abruptly. "Tell me."

"Inside me…please."

Her desperate plea makes my cock so hard, I consider releasing myself just to relieve the ache.

"Lift slightly," I tell her.

She rises so I can slide my hand lower between her thighs. I glide a finger through her wet slit and when I find her opening, I sink a digit inside her.

"Oh my God," she breathes out, then rests her forehead against mine. "Gimme another one. I need more."

"You're so tight. I don't wanna hurt you."

Although she's plenty aroused, I don't know how long it's been since she's had sex and the thought of giving her any discomfort makes me hesitate.

"If I can shove a nine-inch dildo in my pussy, I can take two or three of your fingers," she spits out.

"Nine inches, huh?" I taunt with a devious smirk. "You've been preppin' for me."

"Get off your high horse and just make me come…unless you're unable to."

Delilah's feisty on a regular day, but this level of sass is making me hard as fuck.

Pulling my hand back slightly, I reenter with three fingers and grin when she cries out. The fit is tight with her panties and jeans still on, but I go as deep as I can with the room I do have.

"Oh, yes. Right there…" she breathes out with her eyes rolled back. Hanging onto my shoulders for support, she rocks against me and controls the speed.

I curl my fingers, hitting that deep spot that'll send her over the edge, and when it does, she pants and screams through her release. The column of her throat is exposed as she leans back and combined with the way her body vibrates against mine is the hottest thing I've ever witnessed.

With my hand drenched in her arousal, I slide out and then shove my fingers between my lips.

"Goddamn, you taste better than I imagined."

She watches as I lick between my fingers and her face flushes so beautifully.

"Next time I taste you, I'll be kneelin' between your legs."

"Do you have a condom in your wallet?" she blurts, ignoring my comment, and it throws me for a loop at how quickly she's moving.

"Um…" I scratch along my trimmed jawline, contemplating how to answer that. "Yes, but I'm not fuckin' you in the front seat of your truck."

"Why? No one's out here anyway."

Although that'd be a concern, it's not why I won't do it.

I grip her chin, forcing her eyes to lock on mine. "Thirty minutes ago, you could hardly stand me and now you want me to fuck you?"

She shrugs carelessly. "So? You have one-night stands all the time. What's the big deal?"

I flinch as if she'd slapped me in the face. "First off, I've not slept with anyone in a year. You should know that considerin'

I'm with you almost every weekend I go out. Secondly, you'd never be just a one-night stand to me."

"Ah." She pinches her lips and pushes out her cheek with her tongue as if she's trying to control her emotions. "You'll sleep with every other girl in town except me. Got it."

She goes to climb off me and settle back into the driver's seat, but I grab her before she can.

"Delilah, wait." I secure my hand around her wrist. "That's not it at all."

"No, it's fine." She yanks out of my grip, shifts across the center console, and sits behind the wheel.

I've been around women long enough to know she's in fact *not fine.*

"This was a mistake. I shouldn't have kissed you in the first place. It's a good thing you turned me down. I wasn't thinkin' straight."

I blink hard, grasping her words and how wrong they sound coming out of her mouth.

"I'm not rejectin' you because I don't want you," I clarify, facing her, but she won't look at me. "It wouldn't be just sex to me, so there's no reason to rush things."

She grabs her keys and turns the ignition, then jerks the truck into drive.

I've never seen her like this. It's as if there are a million thoughts in her head and she's picking the worst of them to project onto me.

Eight months of therapy taught me that.

Something I've been actively working on myself when it comes to my insecurities. Hard not to feel like you're a disappointment when all your siblings are married or in relationships, some with babies, too.

"I got hard the second you straddled me, so clearly, I want

you," I continue, hoping she'll be reasonable and finally talk to me about this.

"Wilder, drop it."

Not a chance in hell.

"If that's not enough proof, the second you kissed me, I didn't wanna stop. I rarely feel that way during sex, but I could hardly keep my mouth off you because I've wanted to kiss you for a long time."

"Forget it happened. I already have," she snaps, keeping her eyes glued to the road.

I open my mouth to speak, but I have no more words. Whatever just happened between us before I told her I wouldn't fuck her in here isn't the same Delilah I've come to know.

There's something she's not telling me, but I'm determined to find out what's haunting her so I can fix it.

Delilah Fanning is the only woman I've caught feelings for, and up until five minutes ago, considered off-limits.

But now that I've had a taste, I'm not giving up without a fight.

Chapter Two

Delilah

I shouldn't have kissed him.

I'd been doing a good job of pushing him away. Hell, I'd been doing it for years, so I should be a pro by now.

Pretend I'd never be interested and give him shit whenever we're together.

It was my protective armor.

But it's gotten harder over the past year when I became his weekend babysitter and watched women fall all over him — even though he hadn't taken any of them home. He'd paid more attention to me than them, and inevitably, my feelings have only grown.

When Waylon asked me to watch him on New Year's Eve, I agreed because I knew Waylon was burnt out. Although he's my ex-boyfriend, there's no bad blood between us.

And now that he's dating my little sister, Harlow, I consider him more as family than anything.

But Wilder's a different story.

He always has been and that's why I tried to stay away and act indifferent or annoyed with him when he was around me.

Sin With Me

It's not cute to crush on your ex's twin brother, who can't get his shit together and would never be able to give me what I need or be in a serious relationship. Wilder's a player, sleeps around, gets drunk every weekend, and doesn't take life too seriously. Knowing that and still getting involved would be asking for heartbreak.

And when he inevitably would, Waylon and Harlow would be put in the middle.

But he also makes my heart beat faster than any other guy I've tried to date.

A connection I've never felt before.

I've brushed it off for years. Focused on my trick riding career, my family, and my horse, Jasmine.

Tonight, something in me snapped.

When he said this would be the last time I'd have to babysit him, I needed to give him a reason to want to see me again.

Although I'd been giving him shit all night and even got frustrated with him a few times, the way he didn't think twice about getting in that guy's face made my stomach flutter.

Being the oldest daughter, who held a lot of responsibilities growing up—even more after my dad's work accident and Harlow's incident—and one who thrives on control, it's a foreign experience to have someone protective of me without a second thought.

It wasn't the first time he stood up to some drunken idiot, but it was the first time the fuse burning inside that kept me from acting on my feelings finally exploded.

I never expected him to reciprocate when I aggressively kissed him. If anything, I thought he'd push me away or laugh in my face. But I couldn't help myself. The need to know how his lips tasted and how it felt to have his tongue piercing in my mouth outweighed the possible embarrassment of his rejection.

He hasn't been with anyone in a while, so I figured his

erection was a normal response to being kissed. I didn't put too much stock in it, but when he got all flustered about me asking for a condom, my insecurities took over.

That and the habit of self-sabotaging whenever the waves of grief and guilt hit me.

Something I've learned from grief counseling.

Guilt for enjoying myself when I should be grieving my dad. Although he passed away ten months ago, my mom, sister, and I just celebrated his first birthday in heaven yesterday.

Maybe that's why I'm out of my mind and not thinking straight.

His unexpected death is still a lot to process and my mental health has been shit since we said goodbye to him.

No matter what I do, I can't get the image of him lying lifelessly in the hospital bed, looking at peace for the first time in years, and watching the doctor remove his life support.

I hadn't cried that hard since Harlow was fighting for her life in the ICU seven years prior.

Between his death and coming to terms that I'm a thirty-one-year-old single woman with nothing to show for it sent me down an emotional and mental spiral.

But throwing myself at Wilder and snapping at his rejection means I've officially hit rock bottom.

As I drive us through downtown toward Wilder's family ranch, a squirrel races out onto the street, and I quickly swerve so I don't hit it.

"Shit," I mutter under my breath, relieved no one was on the other side of the road. "Did he cross?"

"Uh, Del?" Wilder's hesitant voice grabs my attention, and I fear I didn't miss the squirrel after all. When I turn toward him, he tilts his head. "There's lights behind ya. You gotta pull over."

Glancing into my rearview window, I cuss again at the sheriff's SVU behind me. "Fuckin' great."

I lied...*this* might be rock bottom.

He's going to think I'm drunk.

Pulling over, I shift into park and then dig through my center console for my insurance card.

A tap on the window makes me jump and then I frown when I see it's one of Sheriff Wagner's deputies.

"Delilah Fanning," Wesley drawls, then peeks around me with his flashlight to see who my passenger is. "And Wilder Hollis. Interestin' choice."

"What seems to be the problem, *Deputy*?" Wilder asks in his smart-mouth tone that usually gets him into trouble.

Wesley snaps his gaze to mine, ignoring him. "License and proof of insurance?"

I grab my wallet and panic when I can't yank out my ID. *Why is it always so damn hard?* My fingers are sweating and not making it any easier.

"Sorry, here." I hand it over.

Wesley stares at it and then back at me as if we didn't go to the same high school.

"Is there a reason you were swervin'?" he asks.

"A squirrel ran out in front of me," I tell him. "I didn't wanna kill it."

"A squirrel, huh?" His deep voice echoes as if he doesn't believe me and then he wrinkles his nose. "Have you been drinkin', Miss Fanning?"

"I had a couple," I admit.

"*Hours* ago," Wilder interrupts. "Quit harassin' her."

"Shut up," I hiss at him under my breath. The more he talks, the more Wesley looks annoyed.

"And what about you, Mr. Hollis?" Wesley shines his flashlight directly into Wilder's eyes.

"What's it to ya? I'm not drivin'."

I blow out a frustrated breath.

"I'm gonna need you to step out of the vehicle," Wesley orders.

"Is that really necessary?" I panic at the thought of him arresting me.

"I smell beer on you, so yes."

"Someone spilled on me!" I quickly defend, but it's no use. He's already yanking the door handle.

"Dude, it's true. I saw it happen!" Wilder jumps out of his side, rounds the front, and makes the situation even worse.

"Get back in the truck!" Wesley orders, reaching for the taser on his belt.

"I'm not armed. Calm the fuck down. But don't harass her because you have beef with me."

Well, that's news to me.

Although I shouldn't be too surprised.

Wilder has beef with a lot of people.

"Ain't got nothin' to do with you unless you disobey. Get back in and let me do my job," Wesley demands.

"She was drivin' me home because I'm the one who was drinkin', not her."

"Don't make me arrest you for disorderly conduct."

"Oh, fuck off. You're just pissed because Sheriff Wagner called me a town hero. And I don't even wear a badge," he says smugly, crossing his arms.

I swallow hard at Wilder's taunting words that are sure to get him into even more trouble. The man was born without a filter.

Ten months ago, the same day my dad was found unresponsive, two men kidnapped Harlow. I called her at work and told her to get to the hospital as soon as she could. When she never showed up, I called Waylon. He drove to her work, but her manager claimed she'd left an hour ago. That's when I called her friend who obsessively tracked her location to check where she was.

Waylon and Wilder drove out to where it said she was—a ranch ten minutes out of town. One guy was guarding the barn doors with a paintball gun, so Wilder shot him in the shoulder to take him down. Waylon was able to go in to look for Harlow and then found her unconscious.

Sheriff Wagner declared them heroes for saving Harlow and discovering the kidnappers were two of the men from the robbery that forever changed our lives.

Three men broke into my parents' house that day and two had escaped.

My father shot the one who assaulted and put Harlow in the hospital, but even after his recovery and getting sentenced, he never disclosed his accomplices.

Thanks to the twins, the two idiots got to reunite with their friend behind bars.

"Wilder, stop it!" I shout at him for the third time tonight. "I'm fine. Get back in the truck."

"Yeah, Wilder," Wesley taunts. "Listen to your whore of the night and get your ass back—"

Wilder's fist cut off Wesley's words.

"Oh my God!" I squeal, jumping out of the way.

Wesley falls to the ground before he can defend himself, and I kneel beside him to make sure he's still breathing.

"He's out cold!" There's a pulse, but he's knocked out. "What the fuck were you thinkin'?"

Wilder shakes out his arm, eyes wide in disbelief that I'm pissed at him. "He called you a whore!"

"You assaulted an officer! You're gonna go to jail."

"Nah, Sheriff Wagner loves me. I'm a hero, remember?"

"You're delusional is what you are." I grab my phone from my truck and dial 911.

"What're you doin'?"

"Callin' for an ambulance. You probably gave him a concussion."

"Maybe he'll get amnesia and forget this happened?" Wilder quips.

"This ain't funny, Wilder!" I scold, and when the operator answers, I explain there's a deputy passed out who needs assistance.

"They'll be there in a few minutes," she tells me. "Hang tight."

This is a fucking nightmare.

"Wanna tell me why the hell you hit my deputy?" Sheriff Wagner crosses his arms, glaring at Wilder.

When he and the ambulance arrived, they put Wesley on a stretcher and sent him off to the hospital. He opened his eyes and spoke, but he's going to have one hell of headache tomorrow.

"He called Delilah a whore and that's completely out of line!" Wilder exclaims.

"Before or after he told you to get back in the truck?"

"After."

"Mm-hmm. And why did you get out in the first place?"

"He was gonna make Delilah do a field sobriety test because he smelled beer on her and we were explainin' that someone spilled theirs on her. I was the one who was drinkin', which is why she was drivin'."

"Well, he originally thought I was drinkin' because I swerved to avoid hittin' a squirrel."

"And had you been drinkin'?" the sheriff asks.

"I had a couple margaritas earlier in the night before switchin' to soda," I admit.

"Alright, I'm gonna give you a breathalyzer and then take Wilder down to the station."

"For what?" Wilder gapes.

The sheriff stares at him pointedly as if to say don't push his buttons with stupid questions. Wilder's lucky he's not in handcuffs as it is, but the Hollis family is basically town royalty around here. Sheriff Wagner also knows Wilder won't run or go anywhere, so he doesn't bother cuffing him.

I've never known anyone besides Wilder to get away with so much shit.

"You better pray the judge takes it easy on you or that Wesley doesn't press charges."

Oh shit. Considering they have history, there's no way he's *not* going to.

"He called her a whore," Wilder reminds him.

"And he'll be dealt with appropriately," Sheriff Wagner says. "Especially since I sent him home two hours ago."

"What?" Wilder and I exclaim simultaneously.

"He wasn't even on duty?" Wilder asks, sounding even more pissed off than before. "So he targeted us."

"I don't know until I get his statement. Regardless, you still assaulted an officer."

What the hell was Wesley doing for two hours after his shift?

After the breathalyzer proves I'm not over the legal

drinking limit, Sheriff Wagner tells me I'm free to go and then leads Wilder to the back of his SUV.

"Can I take him home after you book him or are you holdin' him?"

"As long as he cooperates, he'll get PR'd until he sees the judge on Monday."

So after they take his prints and mugshot, he'll be released from custody without having to post bail, with the promise he'll appear in court. The sheriff doesn't like keeping people over the weekend, especially if he knows they're not a flight risk.

But I'm sure there are other reasons, too.

"Sure ya wanna wait that long? It's gonna take a while since it's the weekend and now I have to deal with a deputy in the hospital." His aggravated tone and glare move toward Wilder.

"Yeah, I'm in charge of gettin' him home in one piece."

He shrugs. "Alright."

I return to my truck and start the engine. I'm already exhausted, but the adrenaline keeps me awake long enough to follow him to the station.

Once I arrive at the sheriff's office, I sit in the waiting room with a few other people and doze off against someone's shoulder. By the time I wake up, Wilder's carrying me bridal style.

"What're you doin'?" I ask, yawning.

"Figured you didn't wanna have a sleepover with the sheriff or the random guy you were snorin' on, so I'm takin' ya to my house."

He manages to open the passenger side door and then places me gently in the seat.

"I'm supposed to drive *you*," I complain, another yawn escaping me.

"I'd rather make it home in one piece, so I'm gonna take you to my place to sleep."

"I am not havin' sex with you!"

He laughs, reaches for my buckle, and then slides it across my body to click it in. "Don't recall askin' you. In fact, you're the one who was askin' me for a condom. Remember?"

I squeeze my eyes, mortified because for a few moments, I forgot about that.

After he closes my door, he hops into the driver's seat and takes us toward the ranch.

"You ever consider goin' to anger management for all the fights you get into?" I ask to break the silence but also curious. I know he suffers from depression, but he uses fighting as a resolution instead of walking away from the conflict, which has been an issue for longer than I've known him.

"Yeah, my therapist mentioned it a time or two." He scratches his cheek and his tongue pokes against it. "But I figure it's better than self-harmin', right? Fightin' releases adrenaline, endorphins, and dopamine—similar to what I feel when I cut and get relief from the pain."

I hate that for him—that in order to relieve himself from his inner turmoil and depressive episodes, he has to physically hurt himself. Waylon told me about his twin brother while we were dating, but I've noticed how Wilder tries to cover it up. He pretends he's fine or does whatever he can to repress it— drinking, one-night stands, fighting.

I was relieved when he admitted he was going to therapy. It won't "fix" his depression, but I can tell he's also trying to find healthier ways to cope.

But as someone who's been going to grief counseling for several months, not every week or even day is a good one, and sometimes all that progress goes out the window.

"Maybe you should join a gym. Do some kickboxin'? I heard that's a good outlet."

He glances at me, grinning. "Maybe I will. If you go with me?"

"Me?"

"Yeah...I think you need an outlet, too."

I sigh because he's right. After Dad died, I took the season off from trick riding, which usually kept my mind occupied. Now the only thing that keeps me busy is my store management job at Lacey's Lingerie. I enjoy it for the most part, but it doesn't compare to the rush I'd get from hanging upside down from a saddle or doing flips on Jasmine's back.

But I lost that passion I once felt about it—honestly, I lost my spark about most things in my life.

"Only if you teach me how to kick your ass," I retort.

He barks out a laugh. "Deal."

Chapter Three

Wilder

I stretch out my fist, feeling the ache in my fingers from punching Wesley in the face after I'd already hit the drunken idiot from the bar.

Tonight might be a new record for how much trouble I've gotten myself into in recent years.

Admittedly, I shouldn't have hit the bastard while he was in uniform, but he made my blood white-hot the moment he called Delilah a whore.

Fucker deserved it.

It's one thing to retaliate against me, but he knew what he was doing by setting me off at that moment.

He wanted me to hit him.

Once they take my fingerprints and mugshot, Sheriff Wagner has me writing down my full statement since Wesley isn't innocent in this either. Apparently, this is his third strike, so I'm not taking all the blame.

Still, considering what I did, I'm lucky the sheriff doesn't make me rot in a cell all weekend. Perks of him knowing my family helps. My parents are charitable when it comes to police fundraisers and to small businesses in town. Our ranch and retreat attract tourists, which helps bring in a lot of business to the local shops.

Even in small towns, it comes down to politics and money.

I'll see the judge on Monday, he'll give me a fine, and then tell me what the charges will be. Sheriff Wagner warned me to bring a lawyer, so now I have to tell my dad so he can call the family attorney and make sure he shows up on time.

That's going to be super fun.

Wesley could push for an assault and battery charge, but all they have to do is watch his body cam to know I'm telling the truth about his inappropriate name-calling.

The sheriff let it slip that their policy for field sobriety tests is to call for backup. And since he wasn't even supposed to be on duty, he never called it in or followed protocol.

So if he's smart, he won't dig himself into a deeper grave, but Wesley's proved he's not.

Either way, I'm not worrying about that now when I have Delilah in my bed.

"I woulda been fine to drive you and go back home so I could sleep in my own room," she mumbles when I tuck her underneath the covers.

With one eye open and the other fighting not to close, I snort at her delusion.

"But then we wouldn't be able to talk about that kiss," I taunt, sitting next to her.

Groaning, she buries her head in the pillow. "How about you tell me why you have beef with Wesley instead?"

I blow out a breath because I knew she'd eventually bring that up. "I slept with his wife."

Her eyes pop open, as does her mouth. "Jesus Christ. Why'd you do that?"

"I didn't know she was married!" I throw my arm up.

"She's not from here and wasn't wearin' a ring. Plus, it was like two years ago. Dude needs to let it go."

She rolls her eyes. "Would you be able to *let it go* if someone fucked your wife?"

I raise a brow at her question because did she not witness my response to someone calling her a horrible name? Or someone spilling beer on her? My reaction to someone sleeping with my *wife* would be ten times worse.

The guy would be in a coma needing a machine to push air into his lungs.

"We're not talkin' about hypotheticals here. Wesley puts the blame on me instead of where it should be." I smirk, then add, "Himself for not being able to properly please his woman."

"Just when I thought you were gonna say somethin' smart."

"Oh, c'mon. You can't tell me I'm wrong. Wesley's an arrogant douche and his wife pickin' me to cheat on him knocked his ego six feet under. Trust me, if she had slept with some average Joe from a coffee shop, he wouldn't be so pissed."

"Wow...the humbleness just floats off you."

"I am humble. But I'm also honest."

"Interestin' way to describe your ego but okay." She turns toward me on her side, folding her hands underneath her cheek. I can't resist grabbing the loose strand of hair that falls over her face and tucking it behind her ear.

"Now it's your turn to be honest. Why'd you kiss me and then freak out about me not wantin' to fuck you in the front seat of your truck?"

She squeezes her eyes and releases a deep sigh. "Considerin' everythin' that's happened tonight and how I waited four hours for you to get released, I'm gonna plead the fifth. I'm also not in the mood to talk about that right now."

Grinning, I nod. "Fair enough. Will you at least listen to

what I have to say then? You don't have to respond, just hear me out."

She lifts her shoulder. "Make it quick. You have two minutes before I fall asleep."

"I'm anythin' but quick, Delly..." Her nickname slips for the second time tonight and her gaze lowers to my lips when I say it.

I think she likes it.

"I'm not sure what enticed you to kiss me tonight or why you felt weird about it afterward, but I just wanna make it clear in case your brain is confused that I was in no way rejectin' you. But public sex ain't somethin' I'm tryin' to add to my rap sheet. I'm in enough trouble as it is..."

And *no random hookups* is what I promised my therapist.

Not that Delilah would ever be a random hookup, but it wouldn't have ended the way I'd want because she would've felt remorseful and ashamed as soon as it was over. And I know that because I'd feel those same things when I used sex as an outlet.

Dr. Branson wants me to challenge myself on making real connections with women before falling into bed with them. Instead of using sex as a distraction, he wants me to focus on getting to know someone and only getting intimate if feelings are involved.

So far, I've gone twelve months without it—a record since I started being sexually active back in high school.

Delilah giggles with a little snort and it's the cutest thing ever. I can tell she's exhausted and fighting sleep.

"It's good that you stopped us. I kissed you for the wrong reasons. I've not been myself lately, or rather, since my dad died. Between not ridin' as much as I used to and the grief suffocatin' me, I haven't been managin' my emotions in a healthy way."

"I know a thing or two about that." I lick my lips, wishing I could lean down and brush mine against hers. "Looks like we both need an outlet."

She arches a suspicious brow.

"A *healthy* one," I correct. Perhaps kickboxing would be a good activity to take up.

For her too.

I noticed a shift after her dad's death and should've figured that was the reason for her mood and behavior changes. There's no saying how I'd act out if I lost one of my parents or siblings. I'd probably lose my damn mind.

Delilah's close to her family and after watching her dad suffer for years, I'm sure she's feeling a mixture of emotions.

"I miss ridin', but I don't think I wanna trick ride professionally anymore. It's all I've known for the past seven years, and it kept my mind busy, but now I need to figure out who I am without it."

"I'm sure you will. That shit takes time, so give yourself some grace. You're allowed to grieve and just be in your feelings for a while. There's no rush."

"Yeah, but I feel guilty, too," she confesses. "Guilty that I wasn't home to help more or there to keep my dad company. Guilty that I feel so angry at him even though I knew he was sufferin' and is in a better place now. But mostly guilty that I'm still alive but not really livin' because of how lost and empty I feel. The hole in my heart gets bigger every day."

Tears fall down her cheeks and when she closes her eyes, I swipe the pad of my thumb underneath to catch them.

"I find some peace knowin' he's no longer in pain, but that doesn't always take away mine," she adds just above a whisper.

Mr. Fanning was in a wheelchair for the past eight years after a tractor accident took one of his legs. He suffered from chronic phantom limb pain. There's no cure, only temporary treatments, and he dealt with it daily. It fucked with his mental health. He spiraled into a deep depression and severe anxiety. As the years went on, he didn't even want to leave his house anymore.

One day, he couldn't bear it anymore and overdosed on pain meds.

By the time he got to the hospital, it was too late.

It was the wake-up call I needed to take my mental health seriously and seek therapy. After witnessing how distraught their family was and the aftereffects of his death, I knew I needed to make a change. Waylon begged me for years to get help, and I knew he was right but never wanted to admit it.

I didn't want my family to go through that kind of pain and grieve my self-inflicted death in the event I couldn't stop myself from cutting or taking an alternate way out. There's been a couple instances where I cut too deep and nearly bled out. I've had to get blood transfusions to save my life. When I get to that point, there's almost nothing to pull me out of it until I pass out.

Doing that to my family feels worse than horrific thoughts battling for my attention and I don't want them to have to go through that again.

I especially didn't want my twin brother to feel like he lost half his soul because that's exactly how I'd feel if I lost him.

Going to therapy and trying antidepressants is something I can control when for years I felt like I had none. It's not easy and doesn't "fix" everything, but it's helping me take the right steps to restrain from unhealthy coping mechanisms.

Tonight I've learned Delilah getting messed with or spoken to badly is a trigger for my anger.

Not that I'll apologize for reacting, but I can work on how fast my temper blows up and think about the consequences before I do something stupid.

Leaning down, I press my lips to her forehead and then rest

mine against hers. I love that she feels safe enough with me to let out her emotions and I want to keep it that way. I have a feeling being the oldest child, like me, she doesn't have many opportunities for someone to be there for her the way she's always there for others.

"You should get some sleep. We can talk some more tomorrow," I tell her.

The glow of the side table lamp casts over her beautiful face. Her eyes close and she hums out a response. "Mmkay."

But then her gaze finds mine again. "Wait, where're you sleepin'?"

"On the couch."

"Are you sure? I feel bad but also your bed is so comfy, so I don't feel *that* bad."

I chuckle as she sinks deeper into the mattress. "It's fine. I've crashed there hundreds of times."

Plus, I like that my bed will smell like her after she leaves.

My spare room is mostly random shit. I never got a bed for it because I never needed one.

"Good night, Delilah. Sweet dreams." Standing, I kiss her forehead again and then click off the lamp.

"Night," she murmurs softly.

"WILDER GARRETT HOLLIS!"

"Oh fuck," I mutter at the same time Waylon snaps his gaze to me. He's mucking the stall next to me.

"What the hell did you do?" he asks.

It's rare for our mother to scream at us, even more rare to drop our full names—it's usually Dad—but it was only a matter of time before she found out.

"You got arrested last night? When were you gonna tell me?" She stands in front of the stall gate with hands on her hips.

"Uh…now?" I flash her my boyish grin that usually gets me back into her good graces. Although I'm a fully grown man, Mom still sees me as a sixteen-year-old boy who can't stay out of trouble.

I glance at my twin, who looks less than amused. "I thought you were with Delilah?"

"She was there," I confirm.

"What'd you do?"

I don't get the chance to respond before Mom continues. "Betty Fields told Miss McWilliams that you beat up one of Sheriff Wagner's deputies and put him in the hospital!"

I roll my eyes at the exaggeration. Good ole rumor mills are already spreading misinformation.

He gapes. "You did *what*?"

"That's not entirely true…" I lean the rake against the stall. "I punched Wesley, only *once*, and he hit his head on the cement. He has a concussion, but he'll be fine."

Mom's eyes are wide with fury and her cheeks are bright red. "Have you lost your mind? Who raised you?"

Waylon snorts and then quickly hides his face when Mom scowls at him.

"He's gonna press charges!" she exclaims, crossing her arms. "Why on God's green earth would you hit a deputy?"

"He was harrassin' Delilah and then called her a whore! I knocked him out on his ass because he deserved it. Dad woulda done the same thing if any man spoke to you that way."

"You father would do it out of love, not spite."

Arching a brow, I stare at her in silence until it dawns on her.

"Oh, Wilder…" She sighs, resting a hand on her chest.

"What?" Waylon asks, clearly missing the obvious.

"Nothin'." I retrieve the rake and go back to work. "I'll go in front of a judge tomorrow and deal with the consequences. If Wesley wants to press charges, then he risks gettin' himself in more trouble too," I say without explaining all the details.

Sheriff Wagner can be a hard-ass on many things, but one thing's for sure—you talk badly to a woman in his town, he ain't letting you off the hook with only a slap on the wrist.

Considering the Fannings have a soft spot in his cold, black heart, I'd be surprised if he lets Wesley off the hook at all.

He was there when Mr. Fanning got hurt and saw him fighting for his life under that tractor that took his leg.

The following year, he was the first one to arrive at their house when Harlow was unconscious after being assaulted by one of the intruders. She had two broken legs, cracked ribs, and was put on life support due to swelling in her brain.

Then, on the day Harlow was kidnapped, he was the one who found the two guys in the barn after Waylon and I rescued her. Harlow took a bat and beat the living shit out of the one guy who was trying to kill her, and I shot the other, who was using a paintball gun to keep us out.

She was bruised and banged up but made a full recovery.

He knows their family has been through hell and back.

And Delilah had to witness most of it. She stayed home for years instead of getting her own place because her dad and sister needed her. Their mom's a nurse and works twelve-hour shifts, so someone always needed to be home.

With the full realization of how much their family has been through, I think a kickboxing class is just what Delilah needs. Or maybe a rage room where she can smash everything and anything she wants until all the weight of the stress and grief lifts off her chest.

"You're lucky the sheriff didn't lock you up all weekend," Mom says.

"Trust me, I know. Delilah waited while I got processed and then I drove us back to my place."

"She's there now?" Waylon asks.

"Yeah, she was exhausted. I didn't want her to take me home and then drive herself back to town that late."

Mom grins, then pats my arm. "See, now that's the Southern gentleman I raised, who makes sure a woman is safe."

"Safe in his *bed*…" Waylon muses under his breath, but I hear him.

"Thanks, Ma. I'm gonna check on her during my lunch break."

"Alright. Well, you better talk to your father afterward because he's not happy with you either. I'll call John so he meets you there in the mornin'."

Figured he wouldn't be.

"Will do. Thanks, Mom."

She leans in to hug me, and I wrap an arm around her, then kiss her cheek.

"Does she know?" Mom asks softly.

I lift my shoulder because it's more complicated than that.

"You should tell her before it's too late."

As if it's that easy.

"I'll try," I admit.

"See y'all at supper tonight," she says, waving at us while she walks out of the barn.

Every Sunday night, my siblings and I go to our parents' house for dinner. Everyone has busy schedules between their families and working on the ranch, so we use this time to catch up.

Sin With Me

My grandmother and younger cousin, Mallory, also live with my parents, which means when everyone's there — including my siblings' partners and kids — it's jam-packed. Mom sets up two large tables between the kitchen and dining room, but we still step on each other's feet with how crammed it is.

Gramma Grace loves to bake and cook with Mom, so they put on a whole feast. Afterward, they bring out scrapbooking supplies and everyone works on a few pages while they eat dessert.

Since Waylon and I have evening chores at the retreat barn, I don't usually stay after dinner, but at least once a month I try to stick around because it makes Mom happy.

Once my half of the stalls are mucked and water buckets refilled, I take my lunch break. Trail ride tours are usually at ten in the morning and four in the afternoon, but once it cools down, we only do them once per day at two.

I don't mind doing them twice a day during the summer since the trees provide shade throughout the trails, but during the winter, we have to bundle up to avoid freezing our asses.

But that means less work and more time to get shit done.

"Something goin' on between you and Delilah?" Waylon asks when I pull out my keys and walk toward my truck.

"Like what?" I play dumb because he doesn't need to know. I've gone this long without telling him about our past, it's easier at this point if the truth never comes out.

"I dunno. You tell me," he says, following me outside. "She's never slept over before, has she?"

I spin on my boots, facing him, and he nearly collides into me. "Not that it's any of your business, but no. And I slept on the couch, so you can stop lettin' your imagination run wild."

He shrugs, then folds his arms over his chest. "Alright, just checkin'."

"Why? You'd take issue if there were?" I fire back.

"I don't want her to get hurt. She's gone through a lot, especially this past year."

"I'm aware of that since I'm the one who's been with her almost every weekend. The last thing I wanna do is cause her more issues, which is why I told her I was done going out and set her free of babysittin' me."

Saying those words again causes my chest to tighten. I won't have any excuses to see her unless I make up a reason.

"Well, that was noble of you." He grins. "Harlow says she hardly hears from her and when they celebrated their dad's birthday, she barely spoke a word."

"She's grievin'," I remind him.

"Yeah, Harlow too. I hate that for 'em."

"I could tell somethin' was off last night even before the bar fight—"

"There was a bar fight, too?" he exclaims.

Shit. No one else knew about that.

"The asshole who spilled his beer on Delilah swung at me and I gut-punched him." I wave him off. "It's no biggie. He walked away with all his teeth and limbs."

Waylon snorts, rolling his eyes.

"Anyway…we're just friends. So you don't haveta worry about me doin' anything to her."

Even as I speak the words, they sound wrong coming out of my mouth.

Especially since she kissed and begged me to touch her, I want to be much more than *friends*.

Chapter Four

Delilah

Waking up in Wilder's bed isn't something I thought I'd ever experience.

But what's most surprising about it is that nothing happened between us in here.

I feel foolish for begging him to fuck me in my truck, and now I hope it's not awkward between us and that he'll never bring it up again.

"Hey, darlin'. How're you feelin'?"

My stomach flutters before my eyes peel open. Him calling me *that* in his gruff voice instead of Delly—which has always done something to me—has me dragging my bottom lip between my teeth.

He's called me Delly for years. It's what my high school friends called me, but I grew out of it after graduation. I don't even think he realizes he still calls me that, but it sounds different coming from him. Like a secret just between us.

Waylon and him were seniors when I was a sophomore and we ran in different social circles, but everyone knew of the

63

Hollis twins. You had to live under a rock not to know about them or think they weren't the hottest guys in school.

Wilder was always getting into trouble and Waylon was always bailing him out.

I was in the same class with their younger brother, Landen, who also got into a lot of shit. Pretty sure he dated most of the girls in our class.

Poor Mrs. Hollis was in the principal's office more in those years than when she attended.

Admittedly, when Waylon and I ran into each other years later, I was honored to get his attention. We had enough in common to enjoy each other's company and go on dates or hang out in between taking care of my dad and volunteering. But then my sister's incident happened only a couple months later.

He supported me through it as best as he could, but I couldn't juggle being in a relationship and a caregiver. Mom was working twelve-hour shifts at the hospital, so I was the only one who could stay home and help.

Inevitably, I told Waylon we needed to take a break so I'd stop feeling guilty for being a bad girlfriend. I couldn't give him the attention he deserved and needed time to dedicate to my family.

Waylon was hurt and assumed I was breaking up with him for good and ended up sleeping with someone else two weeks later.

I had hoped we'd eventually get back together once my sister recovered, but after that happened, I didn't see him the same way.

I was angry with him for a long time but eventually got over it. We both grew up and matured and got on friendly terms again. But then he fell in love with my little sister, who's ten years younger than me.

Sin With Me

Go figure.

"Woke up pissed that the floor didn't open up and swallow me whole," I respond to his question and then yank the covers higher to hide my face.

Wilder chuckles, deep and smooth, and it's such a rarity for it to be genuine that I'm almost taken aback by how much I love it.

And how much I want to hear it again and again.

Wilder is the epitome of someone who puts on a show that he's a happy-go-lucky, fun guy, but it's only surface-level because inside he's miserable.

He suffers from the type of depression where he can easily hide it by being the class clown and funny guy in group settings that if you didn't know his deepest, darkest secrets, you'd never know he used cutting, drinking, and sex as a coping device. One look at him and you'd think there's no way this good-looking and charming cowboy is miserable inside.

Wilder doesn't want to make anyone uncomfortable with his mental health issues, himself included, so he pretends he's fine.

He's a pro at it after all these years.

If Waylon hadn't told me ahead of time, I would've never guessed based on how he presented himself the first time we met in person.

"Wanna grab lunch at The Lodge before you go home?" he asks, sitting on the edge of the bed and slowly pulling down the covers to reveal my face.

"I don't have anything to wear. That guy spilled beer on my shirt, and I'm not wearin' that out in public."

"You can borrow somethin' of mine."

"I'll drown in anythin' of yours."

Although I like the thought of wearing one of his shirts, I wanna go home and shower. I probably look as rough as I feel.

It's my day off and all I wanna do is rot in my own bed until tomorrow morning.

"Nah, you can do that tuck 'n tie thing girls do…" He stands, walks to his closet, and goes through it.

"The what?" I murmur, pulling myself up into a sitting position in only my bra.

After Wilder tucked me in, I threw off my shirt and now I'm wishing I'd remembered to grab it before he returned.

His bed is actually super comfortable, so I slept like a rock, but I feel hungover. Not from alcohol, but from being up so late and mentally exhausted.

"Here, this should work." He holds up a black T-shirt with the ranch's white logo on the chest pocket. "Just tie it in a knot."

I lift a shoulder, giving in to the idea because I'm starving and can shower later. "Sure, fine. Do you have any headache meds?"

He stares at me before lowering his gaze down to my chest, and I wonder if he's remembering the way he touched my nipples last night. He clears his throat, then blinks a few times before he nods.

"Yeah, I'll grab you a couple and a glass of water." He hands me the shirt, then walks toward the kitchen like he can't leave the room fast enough.

Sin With Me

By the time we get to The Lodge, it's packed with guests and numerous Hollis family members.

It's the main building on the retreat where guests check in, sign up for activities, and where everyone eats when they stay here. The workers come in here during their breaks to take advantage of the brunch buffet. Considering their long hours and working in various weather conditions, it makes sense. I've only been here a handful of times, but I'm already glad I agreed to come.

The array of smells hits my nose as soon as we enter. One thing's for sure, Hollises don't mess around when it comes to Southern cuisine and their family recipes.

A few buffet-style tables line one wall with a dessert feast on the end, and I help myself to all of it.

Everyone stares when I bring my plate to the table and sit in between Wilder and Waylon. I know I look rough, but they're looking at me like I'm half-dead.

A zombie probably looks better than I do right now.

"Heard you had an entertainin' night," Waylon drawls.

"Guess you could call it that." I look around for the silverware, then realize I forgot to grab some.

Wilder takes a bite of his food before handing me his fork. "Here, take mine."

"Thanks," I say, then watch as he stands to grab a new one.

"You coulda called me so you didn't have to wait at the station," Waylon says.

"What for? I gave you my word I'd watch out for him and that's what I was doin'," I tell him. "Not like he punched a cop. Oh, wait—" I stop dramatically, and everyone's gaze flies toward Wilder as he sits next to me.

"Who'd you hit?" Landen asks, sitting across from us with Tripp to his left.

"Wesley," Wilder murmurs.

"How the hell are you not in jail?" Tripp asks the next question.

"Good fuckin' question." Waylon shakes his head.

"I already got my ass reamed by the sheriff and Mom. No need to add to it." Wilder digs into his pancakes and shoves a huge bite in his mouth, clearly not wanting to talk about it anymore.

"You slept here last night?" Noah asks from Landen's right. She's four years younger than me, but she's already married, with a three-year-old and a baby on the way. She's had her life figured out since before she could legally buy alcohol.

Makes me worried I'm behind in life being in my early thirties with neither a husband, kid, or career. But I don't blame her. I've wondered that more times this past year than ever before.

"Yep. After waitin' four hours for them to process him, I fell asleep, so Wilder drove us here," I tell her.

"Hm…interestin'." Noah grins around a sausage link, her eyes lingering over my face.

After lunch, I say goodbye to everyone and then Wilder walks me out to my truck.

"Do you want me to drive you back to the barn?" I ask, although it's just down the road.

Things are awkward now.

That's what I get for mauling him like a horny animal.

"Nah, it's a five-minute walk."

"You'll let me know how tomorrow goes?" I ask, jumping into the driver's seat.

"Yep…assumin' I don't get locked up right away. So if ya don't hear from me, bring bail money."

I start the engine, then roll down the window before closing the door.

"That's not funny," I deadpan. The Hollises have more than enough money to bail his dumb ass out, but I'd still hate to see him get jail time for something that involved me swerving in the first place.

"Don't worry. I'll sweet-talk my way outta it." He winks, leaning his elbows through the open window.

"That smug attitude is what gets you into trouble."

"So you shouldn't even be surprised at this point, right?"

That devilish smirk of his is why girls drop to their knees for him.

"I guess not. I'll talk to you tomorrow. Good luck."

His face is close to mine, almost too close, so I pull my seat belt over my chest and click it into place, then wait for him to get the hint to back away so I don't run over his boots.

"Delilah..." He rises on his feet and leans in further. "Don't think we aren't talkin' later about that kiss and you comin' on my fingers. But for now..." He brushes his lips against my cheek and presses them softly against my skin. "I'll see ya tomorrow."

I'm too shocked by his bold move that it takes me until I get home fifteen minutes later to process that he said he'd be *seeing* me tomorrow.

Not sure what he means by that considering I work all day. We don't normally see each other during the week either.

And I hate that a part of me gets excited about that thought.

"Girl, where the hell have you been and why do you look like you got railed all night long?" Matilda, my best friend since elementary school and roommate for the past few years, blurts the moment I walk into our apartment. She works at Lacey's with me and it's always a blast when we're scheduled together.

I drop my bag and keys on the table and then slide off my shoes. "Such a long-ass story. I need to shower and then I'll give you the CliffNotes."

"Screw that. I want the fully detailed story." She grins, curling up higher on the couch. "Especially wanna know who gave you that hickey."

"What?" I rush to the bathroom and scream when I look in the mirror.

That *motherfucker*. He didn't even tell me and no doubt he saw it.

No wonder Noah was grinning at me.

"Son of a bitch," I mutter, exiting the bathroom and shaking my head.

"So...who is he?" Mattie drawls.

"That's from a lapse of judgment from being horny and tipsy," I halfway lie, but she doesn't need to know the specifics.

"That doesn't answer my question of *who*..."

I grab a tumbler from the cabinet and fill it with ice and water before meeting her in the living room where she's eagerly waiting.

"You cannot freak out," I warn her. "But it was Wilder."

She dramatically smacks her hand down on the couch. "I fuckin' knew it! About goddamn time you two hooked up considerin' y'all go out so much."

"He stopped us before we could have sex, so don't get too excited."

"Wait...*he* stopped it?"

Sin With Me

"Hold on…we're gonna need somethin' much stronger than water." Standing, I go to the kitchen and find a bottle of white wine. All the glasses are dirty, so I unscrew the top and take a swig.

I might as well tell her everything and get it off my chest.

Chapter Five
Wilder

"Well…how'd it go? Are you behind bars? Do you need bail money? Or has some dude named Ralph made you his bitch already?"

Smirking, I replay Delilah's voice memo in my truck just to hear her voice and laughter again.

Holding up my phone, I take a selfie with my tongue sticking out and two fingers up.

"Not behind bars and no one's bitch…but I got a misdemeanor charge with a year probation—which means if I get into any more legal trouble before it's over, they'll send me to jail for the remainder of the time. There's a no contact order in place because Wesley's a little bitch who thinks I'll knock him out again. I have a hefty fine to pay, a hundred hours of community service, and then I have to take an anger management class. I'm almost wonderin' if you told 'em that. There'll be a review hearing in ninety days to check my progress."

Laughing at that last part, I send the voice memo and then

buckle in so I can get the hell out of here and back to the ranch.

DELILAH

Now that I know you're not behind bars, I can yell at you for giving me a hickey and then not telling me before we went to lunch with all your siblings!!!

I can't help the wide grin that spreads across my face when I read her text.

WILDER

Whoops...guess it slipped my mind.

Truthfully, I liked seeing it on her neck, fresh and purple, a memory that the night before happened regardless of her insisting we don't talk about it.

Tasting her for the first time is something I'll forever remember and never forget.

But I figured she'd see it in the mirror when she went to the bathroom. When she came back out and didn't say anything, I didn't either.

Once I'm parked in front of my place, I rush inside and change into my work clothes.

"Seriously, though, it sounds like you got lucky. Did Wesley show up? What did the judge say?"

Her next memo comes through and I debate calling her instead, but I'm already four hours behind my work schedule, so I quickly record another one while I get dressed.

"Yep, he sure did. Lookin' smug as hell too until the judge questioned him about patrollin' while off-duty. Apparently, he was parked at the Twisted Bull, *watching* someone he suspects is dealin' drugs and was waitin' to see them drive away so he

73

could follow. But he was *concerned*—which I call bullshit—when you stormed out of the bar and then five minutes later, I jumped into the passenger seat. When we left, he followed to make sure we weren't drinkin' and drivin'. But again, I call bullshit. Knowing Wesley, he wanted any reason to fuck with me and used you to do it."

I send the memo and then grab everything I need before rushing down to my truck.

Once it's started, I hit record again and drive toward the retreat.

"He probably saw us foolin' around and wanted to bust my balls because of the whole *sleepin' with his wife* thing. Anyway... the judge asked if he had documentation on this drug dealin' *suspect*, and when he said no, the judge basically discredited his excuse. Not sure what's gonna happen to him since he's already on suspended leave, but I'd avoid him to be safe."

She sends another memo as I park in front of the barn. "Well, I avoid most men, so it won't be an issue on my end."

I snort, then listen to her next one.

"I'm happy to hear you're not behind bars. But maybe for funsies, you stay out of trouble and keep your fists to yourself?"

WILDER

Just my fists?

DELILAH

Your mouth, too. It's what gets you into hot water most times because you're always running it.

WILDER

Pretty sure you liked my mouth on yours by the moaning and begging you were doing.

74

Sin With Me

I did not beg!

Grinning, I grab my Stetson hat and phone before exiting my truck, continuing the conversation about court. "John being there helped my case a lot. He argued about Wesley's unprofessionalism and provokin' me on purpose. The judge already saw the body cam footage, so he knew, and although he agreed that it was out of line, I still had to be punished for assaultin' an officer regardless if he was on duty or not. John talked him out of givin' me jail time since I wasn't a threat to the general public and was an asset needed on my family's ranch business. So he agreed with the probation and other stuff instead."

"An asset, huh?" She giggles in her next voice memo. "Don't tell your siblings. They'll give you shit for that one."

"Trust me, I know. But I'd rather they do that than have to serve time. I gotta get to work before Waylon kills me, but I'm pickin' you up at seven. Don't eat beforehand. I'm takin' you out to celebrate."

I pocket my phone without waiting for her response — since I'm sure she'll act defiant about it — and then find Waylon in one of the stalls.

"Well, well, well…" he drawls, and I already know he's going to be on my ass all day. "If it ain't the criminal."

"Save it. I'm here and gonna catch up," I tell him, grabbing one of the rakes and getting to work.

After we break for lunch, Waylon and I get the horses ready for the trail ride tour. Four people signed up for today, so we take out the horses assigned to them.

When guests check in, they can sign up for activities and when they choose trail riding, Tripp gives them a specific horse based on their experience and age. If they want to go more than once, they'll get the same horse each time.

Waylon usually leads the group and then I follow at the end to make sure no one gets left behind or a horse doesn't randomly take off. Sometimes we'll switch and then we each talk about the ranch's history and how Sugarland Creek became what it is today.

When the group is more playful or experienced with horses, I'll stand up in the stirrups and ride next to the other horses to get them to gallop faster. It usually makes the younger guests laugh and they get to experience the trails the fun way.

"Hey, everyone, welcome to the retreat! I'm Waylon and this is my brother Wilder, and we'll be your guides today. Has anyone been here before?"

Waylon continues with his usual welcoming speech as I lead two horses on each side of me toward the corral. It's where the guests will put on their saddles and get comfortable climbing on and off before we leave.

We'll check they're secure beforehand, but it's fun for them to learn about some of the aspects beforehand. When we return, they'll remove the saddles, and we'll talk them through grooming care.

"During this season, you're gonna get the most beautiful views from the mountains. Lots of colorful trees," I tell them once everyone's settled on their saddles. "We'll stop at the top so you can take pics if you want."

Before everything happened this past year, I was known to

be rowdy on the trails, sometimes even standing on my horse and taking bigger risks while riding. I wanted that adrenaline rush any way I could get it even if it meant falling on my ass or getting kicked off. And although I still do things that are considered reckless, I got a lot of perspective after Mr. Fanning's death and talking with a therapist.

The afternoon sun peeks through the trees as we give our usual spiel about the ranch and the Appalachian Mountains that surround it. A couple asks questions and then we stop to take photos for them.

Once we return from the tour and get the horses back in their stalls, the guests are free to explore, but they're usually with a group of people.

"Wilder, right?" One of the women from the tour taps me on the shoulder.

"Yep, that's me." I tip my cowboy hat with my usual lopsided grin.

"Hey, I'm Molly. I was wonderin' if I could get your number? Or I can give you mine?"

Her question takes me off guard because there were no signs she was interested in me that way. We'd talked a little, but there was no flirting, at least on my end.

"Unless you're married, of course." Her gaze falls to my left hand. "But I didn't notice a ring."

I lick my bottom lip, trying to figure out how to respond. The last thing I want to do is make her feel bad or ruin the rest of her vacation.

"Uh, no. Not married. But sorry, I don't have time to date right now either."

Unless she's five-foot-five, blond, and responds to Delly. Then I'd make all the time in the world for her.

Right now, she's currently blowing up my phone with

messages — probably insisting she can't go to dinner tonight for some bogus reason — but we have a strict no-phone policy when we're with the guests. I'll have to wait until I'm alone at the barn or in my truck to respond.

"Oh, because of the community service hours you have to do now?" she sasses.

I furrow my brows. How the hell does she know about that already? I only got out of court three hours ago. The small-town gossip mill is fast, but not *that* fast.

"Excuse me?"

Her entire demeanor changes and she whips out a recorder. "Could I get a statement for The Creek Chronicles about your charges? Perhaps shine some light on how you continually get away with breakin' the law?"

I step back, growing more pissed the longer she talks. "What're you talkin' about?"

"This is you, right?" She taps on her phone screen a few times and then holds it up for me. There are a couple old photos of me looking drunk and stupid, with her name printed below the headline:

Power and Privilege Prevail: Wilder Hollis Avoids Serious Punishment After Assaulting Officer, Sparks Public Outcry About Sugarland Creek's Popular Ranch & Equine Retreat

"You wrote this?" I grab her phone and scroll through the article. Paragraphs about the injustice from Judge Roberts about my "weak" punishment and how Officer Wesley Townsend is a victim who deserves justice. She even name drops Delilah as the witness who Wesley pulled over. Then it continues on about how my bad behavior and breaking the law are patterns and how I never have to pay any consequences. It encourages the public to boycott the ranch and retreat unless I get fired since I have a criminal record and should be in jail.

As if that's not bad enough, it praises Wesley as a heroic officer, but there's nothing about him getting suspended for his multiple issues—while in uniform.

"This is fuckin' bullshit." I smack her phone into her palm. "Ain't sayin' shit to you."

I walk in the other direction toward the barn.

"This is your chance to defend yourself…" She rushes to my side with the recorder in her grip. "Tell your side of the story."

"You his girlfriend or somethin'?" Because I know she's not his wife and only someone sleeping with him would believe a word that moron says.

"No, just a reporter after the truth."

"Pfft. Yeah, right. He knew his ass was already on the line, so now he's draggin' mine even though he's the one who started it." I huff, shaking my head at the ridiculousness. "Call my lawyer if you need a statement. For now, get off my property."

I nearly sprint to my truck so I can get the hell out of here. My parents are going to flip their shit when they read that.

"Wilder, wait!" She jumps on the running board and holds on to my door through the open window. I squeeze the shifter, ready to bolt. "Off the record…"

"What?" I grind out between my teeth, but I'm trying my damnedest to hold it together.

"Wesley's hired me and others to run a smear campaign to ruin your name and plant doubt in people's heads about supportin' the retreat. If you don't respond or share your version, he wins. And your family loses. Can you live with being the reason their business plummets?"

Fuck, she's shady.

But Wesley knows where to hit me for the biggest impact.

Screwing with me is one thing but bringing the retreat and my family into this is a low blow, and I'd love nothing more than to tell her about the true Wesley outside of the one the locals idolize.

However, one of the conditions of my parole was not talking to the press since Wesley's an officer and also being investigated for whatever shit he's been doing off the clock. So the fact he's doing this to me is comical. He knows pointing the finger at me will keep the attention off him when he inevitably gets busted.

And having the local reporter write it up as if she came up with the story makes him look innocent.

"Wesley's a piece of shit who deserved to get hit in the mouth because of what came out of it. He can try all he wants to fuck with me, but it's not gonna work. And you're no better for agreein' to work with him and bookin' a trail ride just to get my attention."

"I doubt I'm the first girl to do that. Considering your history with women, I'm sure you're used to it."

My blood boils at her baseless accusation. I've met women here who've given me their numbers, so I'm not denying it's happened, but he'd find a way to make it sound nonconsensual or inappropriate and that couldn't be further from the truth.

It's probably Wesley's next step in dragging me through the mud—find everyone I've slept with and come up with more lies. Or perhaps he's trying to push me over the edge and wants me to kick his ass so I break my parole conditions and get sent to jail.

Either way, it's not going to work.

"No, but you're the first one to use it against me."

"Well, maybe we could come up with an arrangement so the next thing written about you is on the positive side…"

Her devious tone tells me everything I need to know.

"You think I'm gonna pay you off to stop you from writin' more articles about me?" I arch a brow, tightening my grip on the steering wheel as my blood boils hotter. "Because I wouldn't trust you with a nickel, nevertheless savin' my reputation."

Her mouth falls open and her brows draw together in disbelief. "You think I'm lyin'?"

My gaze drops to her low-cut long-sleeved shirt and the outline of the recorder in between her breasts.

"Let's see, shall we?" Before she can react, I pull out the device and see that it's recording. "Off the record, my ass."

"Hey! Give that back!" She stretches out her arm through my truck, but I keep it out of her reach.

"It's mine now." I turn it off, then shove it into the glove compartment.

"That's stealin'!" She attempts to reach through the window again, but I could knock her down with one push if I needed to.

"Maybe, but I bet Sheriff Wagner will be interested in what else is on there."

"Give it back and I won't write another article about you."

"Remember what I said a moment ago about not trustin' you? That still applies."

"I swear! I'll even give you dirt on Wesley. I know his plans."

"Not interested," I deadpan. "But you have three minutes to leave or I'm callin' the sheriff to remove you for trespassin'. And don't think I won't just because you're an attractive woman."

Her lips curve into a seductive grin. "Attractive, huh?"

"That doesn't make you special, sweetheart." This time I do shove her just enough so she steps down from the running board.

"I thought you were too busy to date?"

"To date *you*," I correct. "And I was tryin' to be a gentleman. Heartless, connivin' women aren't my type."

She pouts and crosses her arms when I shift into reverse.

"And you can go ahead and put *that* in your next article about me."

Chapter Six

Delilah

"Have a lovely rest of your day, Mrs. Waters." I give her my well-practiced smile and hand her the bag of lingerie as if she didn't tell me what her romantic plans were for wearing it later tonight.

I didn't ask, but she was more than willing to tell me.

Though I don't usually mind small talk while helping customers, her husband is well-known in the community since he's the president of the town committee, so it feels wrong to know that he's not the one who's getting to see his wife in her new lingerie.

Mr. Waters has been visiting his family in Maine for the past week, and I know that because Mrs. Waters let it slip when she mentioned he wouldn't be home for another few days.

So who the hell is getting an early preview of her lingerie? I did not ask.

I get paid to be discreet, not nosy.

"Thanks, Delilah. See ya again soon." She winks, then sashays out the front door.

"Well...*that* was interestin'," Mattie murmurs as we both stare out into the street where Mrs. Waters gets into her Escalade.

"Uh, yeah...you could say that." I shake my head and visions of her cheating out of my mind. "Anyway...I'm gonna work on inventoryin' the new pieces now. Holler if you need me."

"Maybe you should buy one of those for yourself..." She gives me a taunting look. "I'm sure Wilder wouldn't mind."

I roll my eyes. "Very funny."

But once I'm in the backroom, looking at the new lavender lace garter set, I can't help wondering what his reaction would be. Even though he put a stop to things escalating between us, I felt his very large and thick reaction to me grinding on top of him.

Mondays aren't usually busy in the store, so it gives me more time to work on admin and manager duties while Mattie handles the floor. She does great in sales and earns commission on top of her hourly pay. Since I'm on salary, I like giving her the floor and it allows me to catch up on paperwork.

Before I clocked in, I talked to Wilder about how things went in court and was relieved to hear he didn't get jail time. He's damn lucky considering what he did, but now I hope it doesn't affect his mental health and all the progress he's made this past year. I'm still not sure what he meant by seeing me today, but a part of me can't deny I'm curious about his plans.

When I return from the bathroom, I hear Mattie tell someone up front in her customer service voice, "I'm afraid she's busy at the moment."

"It'd only take a few minutes. The article is scheduled to run in a couple hours and it'd be great gettin' her witness statement on the event."

Who the hell is she talking about?

"She's not talkin' to anyone without a lawyer, especially you."

"If she changes her mind, which I'm sure she will, here's my number."

Her harsh tone has me even more curious about who she is and what she wants, but I'm equally grateful Mattie dealt with her for me. Her father's an attorney and she's worked part-time at his office since she graduated from high school thirteen years ago. Although he wanted her to go to law school and follow in his footsteps, she didn't share the same passion. Mattie went to art school, but when her mom died a year after she graduated, Mattie returned to help her dad and hasn't pursued it since then.

We have a lot in common when it comes to putting our lives on hold for our loved ones and grew closer because of it. I was only twenty-two when Dad had his accident and then Harlow's incident happened a year later.

It was a big deal for both of us when we finally moved out of our childhood homes and rented an apartment together. We finally got to find independence and be on our own, although I felt guilty as hell about it. My parents nearly kicked me out and told me it was time I focus on myself.

I'm grateful they did, but I still wish I'd gone home more often to visit.

When I hear the bell on the door, I peek my head out toward the front.

"Uh...Mattie. Who was that?"

She turns toward me, grinning. "Some journalist after a story. She claims Wesley's been falsely criminalized while Wilder gets unlimited 'get out of jail free' cards. She wants to use your statement to make Wilder look bad. I told her to shove it where the sun don't shine."

I snort. "Spoken like a true attorney's daughter."

With a lazy shrug, she smirks. "Her card's up here if you want it, but I wouldn't speak to her without a lawyer."

"I'm not speakin' to anyone, so it won't be an issue on my end. Sheriff Wagner got my statement and that's all that needs to be said."

Once the new inventory is tracked and price tags have been added, I grab one in my size and hold it in the back.

It wouldn't hurt to have something sexy in my closet. Even if I'm the only one who sees it.

"You wanna go on your last break?" I ask Mattie. It's almost three and she gets done in a couple hours.

"Sure, I was gonna grab a smoothie from the café. Do you want one?" She grabs her bag from underneath the counter, then pulls out her phone and wallet.

"Yeah, that'd be great. Want some cash?"

"Nah, you can buy next time."

Once she leaves, a few customers enter and give me strange looks. They're pleasant as I help them find some new bras and panties, but there's a weird vibe.

"Delilah!" Mattie shouts the moment the back door swings open.

She's never this loud when there are potential customers in the store, so I rush to the back and make sure she's okay.

"What's wrong?"

She's staring at her phone with her mouth agape and wide eyes.

"That little bitch."

"Who?"

She shows me the screen, and I quickly take it so I can read the words.

"Oh my God!" I can't believe what I'm reading. "She's encouragin' people to boycott the retreat?"

"I knew she was a cunt," Mattie murmurs. "At the end, it

says she plans to reach out to the Hollis family for a statement, which means she might write more than one article. Might wanna warn Wilder."

"He'll never talk to her."

Wilder might do some stupid shit, but talking to a reporter? He'd know better than that.

"Maybe not willingly. She had a recorder. And isn't he one of the trail guides?"

"Yep." Groaning, I grab my phone from my bag and send him a text.

DELILAH

> Hey, a reporter came in a bit ago asking for my statement about you and Wesley. It looks like she wrote an article about y'all and is encouraging people to boycott the retreat. So just a heads-up, she might be coming to ask you for one too.

> Oh and she had a recorder, so be careful.

"What did she look like?" I ask Mattie. If I can give him as much information and details as possible, maybe it'll help him steer clear of her.

She gives me a description, and I repeat it to him.

DELILAH

> She's about five-foot-two, brown hair, and wearing a long-sleeved green shirt.

> Call or text me when you can!

"Ugh, he still hasn't responded." I pace the backroom after thirty minutes of silence. "What if she already got to him?"

A moment later, he finally responds.

WILDER

Sorry, I didn't see your texts until it was too late. I told her to fuck off, but I'm headed to my parents' now. They'll probably get the lawyer involved and it'll be another shitshow.

Thank you for looking out and trying to warn me. I appreciate it.

DELILAH

Of course. Let me know if there's anything I can do.

WILDER

Just be careful. I'm sure more vultures will come around.

DELILAH

Mattie put her in her place, but don't worry. I won't say a word.

WILDER

I'm sorry for getting you into this mess. I'll take care of it, I promise.

DELILAH

I'm not blaming you.

WILDER

You should. I fucked up and now your name is in the middle of it.

DELILAH

Stop worrying about it. Text me later if you have an update.

WILDER

I will. Sorry again, Delly.

"Well..." Mattie probes.

"He didn't say anythin' to her."

"Thank God. But this ain't just gonna go away."

I sigh. "Yeah, not in this small town."

With only five minutes left of my shift, I count my drawer and get ready to leave so Harper can take over for the night. She's the part-time manager who works evenings while she attends college during the day.

When the bell above the door dings, I expect her to walk in, but it's the man from the bar who spilled his beer on me.

For fuck's sake.

And I let Mattie leave already since the store was slow.

Could this day get any weirder?

"What're you doin' here?" I ask firmly before he gets any closer.

"I'm Jonah." He waves pitifully, looking less threatening than a moment ago. "I'm just here to apologize for the other night."

"How'd you find me?"

"I asked Rainy so I could apologize in person. I was quite drunk that night and very, very stupid. I shouldn't have said what I did or fought with Wilder. After hearing that me spillin' beer on you caused some issues when you got pulled over, I thought the least I could do is tell you how sorry I am."

"Oh." I hesitate bringing up the article, but it's obvious he read it. And probably heard plenty of gossip about it, too.

"Well, I appreciate your apology."

"Maybe we could start over, and I could buy you a drink? One that you won't have to wear?" he asks sheepishly. "Or even dinner. Maria's Kitchen has the best nachos. And I noticed you were drinkin' margaritas at the Twisted Bull. They make good ones there, too."

I stifle a laugh, finding his ramblings charming and genuine.

"You were watchin' me, huh?"

"It was impossible not to notice the most beautiful woman there. If I'm being honest, I came up with a game plan to go talk to you and my dumb ass tripped and that's when my beer went flyin'. I kinda got too drunk, so my plan went out the window."

"Yeah...that's a good way to put it." I grin. "While I appreciate the gesture, it's really not necessary. Things are a bit complicated in my life right now and—"

"We can go just as friends. No expectations, I swear. I just moved here to be closer to my sister, so I don't know many people."

Dammit. It can be tough coming into a tight-knit community of people who have lived here all our lives and not know anyone.

"Okay, sure. As friends," I reiterate.

Chapter Seven
Wilder

I haven't seen Gramma Grace this heated since I was a teenager and it not being directed at me for once is a nice change.

"I'm gonna figure out who Molly's mother and grandmother are and have myself a little chat with 'em about respect and *loyalty* in this town…" She paces the kitchen in her usual apron, aggressively stirring something in a big bowl. "And comin' onto the ranch…she must have balls of steel."

"I don't think she has balls, Gramma Grace," Noah muses from across the table from me.

"How did she even sign up for a tour?" Waylon asks. "That's only for registered guests."

"She made a reservation, got early check-in, and then signed up for a tour right away," Tripp explains. "It's not like she told us she was a journalist. We had no reason to be suspicious."

After I drove to the main house and told Mom what happened, she called an emergency family meeting. Dad's been on the phone with John, but there isn't much he can do since it's considered free speech and the court records are public.

But that doesn't mean the Hollises will go down without a fight.

"Alright…" Dad enters the kitchen, pocketing his phone. "The best we can do is damage control. Get ahead of it before it threatens the family or the business. Wilder, you're gonna stay away from the guests and retreat until this blows over. You'll switch jobs with Landen."

"*What*?" Landen and I exclaim simultaneously.

"He watches horses fuck and fondles their balls all day," I complain.

"Language," Mom scolds.

Landen manages the breeding operation. He takes care of our studs and the pregnant mares until they go home to their owners. He watches them mate all summer and then in the off-season, he collects their semen and sells it online.

"Doesn't sound much different than what you fondle in your room all night," Noah blurts.

I shoot her an unamused glare. "And how would you know?"

"I've heard stories."

"Kinda weird to be talkin' about your brother's balls…"

"Enough," Dad snaps. "Besides stayin' on the ranch side only, you will not leave the property unless you have an appointment, you're doing community service hours, or I say you can."

I roll my eyes, leaning my elbows on the table. "So I can go to therapy, but the grocery store is off-limits?"

"Correct. No talkin' to anyone who ain't family."

"Can I be exempt from that?" Noah raises her hand.

Tripp snorts.

"If you need anythin' in town, *Noah* will get it for you" Dad says, staring at her as he exaggerates her name.

"Oh, because I'm a woman, I should do his shoppin'?"

"That's sexist and buyin' into the patriarchal nonsense we've been stuck with for centuries," Mallory adds.

Dad pinches the bridge of his nose, then exhales through his mouth. "That ain't why I picked her to do it. She was being a smart-ass, but if you wanna volunteer, be my guest."

"Heck no." Mallory scoffs.

"She'd probably poison my food anyway."

She scoffs, leaning back casually in her chair. "I wouldn't waste my good Foxglove on you."

For only being seventeen, Mallory scares the shit out of me sometimes.

But I'd never admit that aloud.

"Am I still *allowed* to go to Vegas?" I ask Dad.

"That's three and a half weeks away, so we'll cross that bridge when we get closer," he says.

Not the answer I was hoping for, but at least it's not a definite no. I've been looking forward to that trip all year.

And that first beer I order when I get there will be the best sip of my life since I'm staying sober until then.

"For now, no one talks to the press, no one mentions anything in front of guests, and you go on as usual," Dad orders. "No matter what else is said. Do not retaliate or comment. Got it?"

He scans the room until his eyes lock on mine. He's warning me to stay out of trouble because if I get arrested while on probation, there's nothing anyone can do.

"Yes, sir," we respond.

Once the meeting is dismissed, everyone shuffles out the door to get back to work, but I stay put.

"Miss Tierney said she can get you registered to volunteer

at the shelter tomorrow at six. Think you can make it there on time? It's about forty-five minutes away."

"Sure, Mom. Not like I'm allowed to do anything else."

She pats my hand before moving toward the fridge to grab ingredients for dinner. Gramma Grace comes over and hands me a cookie. "Here, eat this. It'll make ya feel better."

"Oh? Is it a *special* cookie?" Grinning, I grab it and take a bite. Then I smell it.

When I glance up at her with a furrowed brow, she winks and then walks away.

Yep, she just gave me one of her pot cookies she takes for arthritis and nerve pain. I haven't had an edible in years.

This oughta be interesting.

Since I didn't get to surprise Delilah tonight like I wanted, I opted for the second-best option.

DELILAH

Did you send Chinese food and several bouquets of flowers to my apartment?

I lean back on the couch and kick my feet up on the coffee table until I'm comfortable. I've been waiting for her text since I placed the orders an hour ago.

After leaving my parents' house, I came up with the idea since I couldn't leave the property but still wanted her to know I was thinking about her. I hate that she ended up in this article drama with me.

Sin With Me

WILDER

Are there multiple suitors who'd send your favorite food and ten dozen flowers?

DELILAH

Oh yeah, there's a line out my door of men waiting to court me. Some even brought donkeys to trade for my love!

WILDER

Donkeys? Well, good thing I know more about you than they do.

DELILAH

Oh yeah? Such as...

WILDER

You hate donkeys, so immediate rejection.

DELILAH

...How do you know that?

WILDER

You got chased by one when you were twelve and have been deathly afraid of them ever since.

DELILAH

HOW DO YOU KNOW THAT?

WILDER

You think I don't listen when you talk but I'm always listening when it comes to you.

DELILAH

That's...kinda wholesome.

WILDER

Yeah?

DELILAH

But mostly creepy.

95

Brooke Montgomery

I roll my eyes even though she's giving me a hard time on purpose. Delilah's part-time job is finding ways to humble me.

WILDER

> Oh c'mon!

She replies with a silly tongue-out emoji.

I decide to add more, which she'll probably say is even more creepy, but at this point what do I have to lose? Besides my sanity, of course.

WILDER

> I also know how you prefer to eat at home than at a noisy restaurant because the music's always too loud and you hate the sound of other people's chewing. I know that you think buying flowers is a waste of money because they die so quickly but on the flip side you feel bad for the ones that don't get picked, which is why I asked the florist to send the rest of the flowers that didn't get sold today.

I've been observing Delilah for years, noticing all the little things about her, and learned even more about her over the past year. She just hadn't realized it or maybe she wasn't paying attention until now.

DELILAH

> Jesus. I'm not sure who's crazier. Me for thinking flowers have feelings or you for validating flowers have feelings.

WILDER

> At this rate, I think we're both crazy. But I think you've made me crazier than my normal crazy.

DELILAH

Pretty sure you're the one who's made ME crazy.

WILDER

Hopefully that means I get home field advantage from all those other losers lined up, right?

DELILAH

Or it means you're too cocky to realize you still have to practice for the big game.

WILDER

Wait...are we talking about sex or football?

She sends back an eye roll emoji with a bull's-eye. Now she's fucking with me.

WILDER

Truthfully, my plan was to take you out someplace quiet to celebrate not being behind bars, but I'm officially grounded to the property unless I have therapy or community service.

DELILAH

Your parents are pretty pissed, huh?

WILDER

Definitely not on the pleased with me side. But until this blows over, I have to stay away from the guests, which means I'm stuck on the ranch only side.

DELILAH

That's not too bad. At least you get to work and stay busy.

WILDER

Except they gave Landen my job, so now I'm doing his.

DELILAH

You mean...

She sends a squirting emoji with a hand gesture.

WILDER

Yep. FML.

DELILAH

Surely you're a pro at that by now?

WILDER

Jerking off horses? Strangely, no. That's beyond my personal experience.

DELILAH

What a time to be alive...

She sends a laughing emoji with an eggplant, making me laugh with her.

WILDER

Also, Gramma Grace gave me one of her pot cookies. So I might be a smidge high.

The effects of the cookie have fully set in, but it wasn't strong enough to do much besides make me super relaxed.

DELILAH

HAHAHA that explains everyyyyything.

WILDER

She's ready to kick Molly's ass.

Sin With Me

DELILAH

She can get in line because Mattie was ready to knock her out.

WILDER

The only silver lining is knowing Wesley's on suspension and probably driving his wife crazy.

DELILAH

Maybe she'll take one for the team and push him off their roof or something.

I bark out a laugh.

WILDER

Maybe she'll have him put up Christmas lights and he'll be Santa Claus'ed.

DELILAH

Hahaha slip and vanish into thin air. Poof!

WILDER

I must be high because now I wanna watch that movie.

DELILAH

Shoulda told me sooner and I would've brought this food over. It smells insane in here...literally. Chinese chicken and rice aroma in the kitchen and a floral shop in the living room.

WILDER

Guess that means we'll have to plan something for another night.

DELILAH

I was gonna come this weekend to ride Jasmine. Maybe we can go on a trail ride?

WILDER

I'd love that. Saturday at three?

DELILAH

Sounds good. Thank you for the food and the flowers. You really didn't have to go all out, but it made me smile after a hectic day.

WILDER

Good...then mission accomplished.

I send a saluting emoji with a red heart and she hearts the message in return.

I've flirted with Delilah plenty over the years without giving it much thought because I assumed she saw me as an annoying brother.

But after that hot make-out session where she came on my fingers and begged for more, I'm going to do whatever it takes to get out of the friend zone, even if it kills me.

Chapter Eight

Delilah

"So...how's life outside of prison?" My little sister makes herself at home behind the counter where she's not allowed to be. Ten minutes ago, she waltzed in, snacking on snap peas, and being overly obnoxious about it.

"I wasn't in prison..." I retort, shoving her toward the front of the checkout.

"You should hear the rumor mill swirlin'. Some chick asked if Wilder was allowed conjugal visits and where she could sign up for one." Harlow barks out a laugh.

I roll my eyes. "Doesn't anyone actually read? He's not in prison either."

"But it's hilarious to know that even if he was, chicks would still flock to him. Probably even harder than before."

"I wouldn't doubt it. He'd probably have thousands of pen pals too asking for marriage proposals and beggin' to have his babies."

I grab the pile of lingerie that needs to be entered into the system and focus on the computer screen.

"Someone sounds jealous…" She chomps on another snap pea.

"I'm not."

"Really? Your cheeks are flushed and your neck's all red. Pretty sure there's a hickey you're tryin' to hide with that bad cover-up job."

"Oh my God," I snap, slamming down the hangers. "Are you only here to get on my nerves?"

I immediately feel awful for yelling at her when she frowns, but then her mouth shifts into a shit-eating grin. "So the other rumors are true."

Furrowing my brows, I get back to scanning the items. "Which ones?"

"That you and Wilder hooked up."

"Who's sayin' that?"

"Uh…everyone."

Great.

"Well, they can fuck off. It's none of their business anyway."

"I'm your sister! Tell me."

"No! You didn't tell me when you were hookin' up with my *ex-boyfriend*…" I remind her. "In fact, I found out by walkin' in on you two makin' out in the tack room."

I mimic a gagging reaction.

"So now you're gettin' back at him by sleepin' with his twin brother? Bold. I like it." She snickers.

"It has nothin' to do with Waylon. Or you."

"You're really not gonna tell me?" she huffs, leaning against the counter and sticking out her lower lip. That used to work on me once upon a time.

But she's older now and I'm not buying it.

"Nope, but Wilder and I are just friends. He has enough

goin' on in his life, as do I, so I'm not lookin' to mess it up even more."

Which is mostly true.

But I also don't want to relive the embarrassment by telling her the story because as soon as I tell her we kissed, she'll want all the details the way Mattie did.

Wilder might have reciprocated the kiss and other stuff, but starting something between us would add a complication neither of us has time for—on top of what people are saying about the whole situation. The timing isn't right.

"Why would it get messy? I think you're just makin' excuses because you're scared."

"Okay, Miss Nosy…" I groan, grabbing the hangers of the lingerie pieces and walking out to put them on the racks.

"Tell me I'm wrong, then!"

I can't because she's somewhat right.

I'm not scared to be in a relationship, but I'm scared to get hurt. By him, especially. I'm scared that it'd ruin our friendship and then I'd miss what we had.

"I'm workin', Harlow," I singsong. "You need to go if you're not buyin' anything."

The store's been empty for the past hour, and I only have ten minutes left of my shift until Harper arrives.

"Ugh, you're not fun anymore. Is that what happens when you get into your thirties?" She aggressively chews and it makes my brain twitch.

"Very funny," I deadpan. She loves cracking jokes about my age since I'm so much older than her.

When the bell above the door goes off, we both look, and my eyes widen when Jonah walks in.

He's early.

And was supposed to meet me at the café, not here.

I didn't want to do dinner and drinks since I don't know him. That way if shit gets awkward, I can leave quickly.

"Hey," he greets, smiling wide. "I got here sooner than expected because I was worried I wouldn't find a parkin' spot. Guess that's not really an issue in this town."

"No, not usually." I smile awkwardly. "I'm almost done."

"No worries. I don't mind waitin'."

"And who are you?" Harlow stands in front of him, shifting her gaze up and down his body.

"I'm Jonah."

"Nice to meet you." Harlow holds out her hand. "I'm Delilah's sister, Harlow."

Jonah returns the pleasantries and shakes her hand.

"Where're y'all goin'?" Harlow asks.

"Grabbin' a coffee down the street. I owed her an apology for spillin' beer on her shirt."

"Ah…you're *that* guy."

I mentally smack myself in the face for telling her that part of the story.

"Yes, guilty as charged."

"So…" Harlow circles him with her arms behind her back like she's interrogating a suspect. "Is this a date?"

"Harlow!" I hiss, walking over to the counter.

"What? I'm just askin'."

It's most definitely *not* a date.

Sighing, I take my drawer to the backroom. I want to get out of here as soon as Harper arrives.

When I return to the front, Harlow and Jonah are laughing about something. Who knows what embarrassing thing she's said about me now, but I'm not about to ask in front of her.

Harper arrives, saving me from having to endure this awkwardness any longer, and I tell Harlow to get lost.

"When we see each other for Thanksgiving on Thursday,

I grind my teeth as she walks to her truck in the other direction.

"I'm so sorry about her…" I shake my head, my cheeks heating with embarrassment.

He leads us toward the café, which is only a few minutes away.

"Nah, it's fine. I have a little brother who acts the same."

"She's ten years younger than me and loves to taunt me as much as possible," I explain.

"Wow, that's a large gap. My brother's only two years younger but has always been a pain in my ass." He chuckles. "Do you have brothers?"

"Nope, just Harlow and me. One sister is enough." I giggle. "She's dating my ex-boyfriend."

I'm not sure why I blurt that out, but once I do, I can't take it back.

"Really? Ain't that awkward?"

"It was at first, but I got over it quickly when he saved her from a couple of guys who kidnapped her on the same day our dad died. So there wasn't much time to be mad about it."

His brows shoot toward the sky.

"Oh my God." I squeeze my eyes, mentally smacking myself in the forehead and realizing just how bad I am at having normal conversations. "I didn't mean to word vomit all that. I'm clearly not good at this."

Two dimples appear as he smiles wide and then opens the door to the café for me.

"It's fine. I wouldn't even know how to explain my family drama."

"Well, if you told me some, I'd feel better about blurtin' out mine."

He chuckles and it's a nice, deep sound. "Once we get our coffees, I'll tell ya about my sister, who threw up all over her weddin' dress ten minutes before she walked down the aisle."

My jaw drops. "Oh my God, my worst nightmare."

Once we arrive, Jonah opens the door for me and I walk in with him following close behind me. "Yeah…whatever you think about your family, I guarantee you, mine's ten times worse."

When we reach the counter, I order a drink and a muffin since I haven't eaten since noon. If I have coffee on an empty stomach, it'll make me queasy, and I've embarrassed myself enough for one day.

Jonah orders his next, and though I offer to pay for mine, he's adamant he owes me.

Two of the tables are taken, but the one by the window is empty, so we take it. He starts the conversation by talking about his family and how he moved across the state after college once he found a job.

"When my sister got married, she moved here to be with her husband, so we rarely saw each other. A few months ago, she announced her pregnancy, and I realized I didn't want to miss watching my nephew grow up. So I looked for a new job and moved here to be closer."

"Wow…that's really sweet of you. I'm sure she appreciates that." I take a bite of my muffin and then swallow it down with my iced latte. Although it'll probably keep me up later than usual, it's delicious and worth the insomnia.

"She does…her husband not so much."

"Oh…is that where some of the drama comes into play?"

He chuckles, taking a sip of his hot coffee. "You could say that. I'm pretty sure he was at the Twisted Bull last weekend spyin' on me. It was a rough week, so I got stupid drunk. More than I usually would."

"Wait…" Sitting up straighter in my chair, I think back to Wesley claiming he was there that night to follow a suspected drug dealer.

"What's your brother-in-law's name?" I ask hesitantly.

"Wesley Townsend. The deputy. I heard what happened and felt even worse about the incident."

Oh my God.

If Wesley's telling the truth, Jonah could be the guy he was watching.

He could be the drug dealer!

But Wesley could also be lying about the whole thing.

Either way, I shouldn't be sitting here with someone linked to him. Especially after Molly tried to weasel her way into talking to me.

It could be another trap for all I know.

"Sorry…" I stand abruptly with the latte in my hand. "I have to go."

"Wait, why?" He jumps to his feet, towering over me.

Before I can answer, the door of the café whips open and there stands Wilder looking sexy as fuck in his Stetson hat, dark Wranglers, and cowboy boots.

And the lethal glare he's shooting toward us tells me he's pissed as hell.

Chapter Nine
Wilder

MOM

Don't forget volunteer registration is at 6 tonight. Don't be late!

WILDER

I know and won't be.

MOM

Good. Drive safe.

WILDER

Thanks, Ma. I will.

M y first full day working the stud farm wasn't as bad as I expected. Our stud, Rocky, only tried to kick me once and luckily he missed or I'd be down a testicle.

Breeding season is over and the mares went back to their owners. The only thing for me to do besides take care of Rocky's needs is focus on online sales by collecting, evaluating, and processing his semen for shipment.

It's boring and weird as fuck—and definitely not my first choice of ranch duties—but hell, I've done worse.

The only thing that got me through the day was knowing I'd get to see Delilah, even if for a few minutes. She works till five, so I'll be cutting it close, but I'm hoping to catch her before she leaves the store.

Although she's not ready to discuss what happened between us this past weekend, I hope she will eventually. Until then, I'll play her little game of not talking about it.

Since it's a forty-five-minute drive to the shelter, I leave an hour early. By the time I get to the store, it's a few minutes past five, but her truck is still in the parking lot.

"Hi, welcome to Lacey's," one of the workers greets with a smile. "Lookin' for yourself or the misses?"

"Uh…" I scrub a hand over my jawline. "Is Delilah around?"

"That depends." She crosses her arms. "Are you a reporter?"

"No." I lift my Stetson so she can get a better view of my face. "I'm Wilder Hollis. A friend of hers."

"Ohh, right." She snaps her fingers. "The cop puncher."

I wince, waiting to see how she reacts.

"You just missed her," she continues. "She left with some guy."

My heart slams into my chest. "Who?"

She shrugs, messing around with random items behind the counter. "No idea. I came in for my shift and then they left."

"You don't know where they went?"

"She didn't say, but they took a right out the door, if that helps."

"Okay, thanks." I rush outside and debate if I should call her or not, but when I get down the block, I see her through the large café window.

She's sitting at a table with a man across from her. They each have a cup in front of them, smiling and laughing.

I growl, hating how jealous I am. As much as I want to barge in there and rip off the guy's head, I can't risk causing another scene that'll get me thrown in jail.

Getting closer, I continue watching him, vaguely recognizing him and trying to place from where.

And then it hits me.

You've gotta be fucking kidding me.

Why the hell would she go for coffee with the guy who spilled beer down her shirt and hit me?

That's fucked up.

Even more fucked up she didn't mention it to me when we texted this morning.

Before I can stop myself, I reach for the door and whip it open.

Delilah's already on her feet when I enter, staring at me like a deer in headlights.

My gaze shifts to the man behind her and my jaw clenches.

"Wilder." She steps closer, seemingly calm, but the grip on her iced coffee is tight as she holds it close to her body. "Let's talk outside."

"Delilah, wait—"

She spins around but inches back as he approaches.

"Don't," I warn him.

He holds up his palms in mock surrender. "Relax, I'm not gonna do anything."

"Sorry, Jonah. I have to go." The remorse in her voice has me even more confused.

Delilah turns and shoves me through the door. She stays silent as we walk toward the parking lot.

"Delilah...are you gonna say anything?" I ask before we approach her truck.

She finally looks at me. "What're you doing here? I thought you had registration."

"I was stoppin' in to see you quickly. Your coworker said you and some guy went downtown, so…"

She crosses her arms, leaning against the door. "So what?"

"I went to find you and see who you were with…" I shrug. "I was worried."

"Wilder, I can take care of myself."

"I'm aware, but why would you meet up with that guy of all people? He's the reason Wesley smelled beer on you."

She blows out a breath, dropping her arms. "He stopped by the store yesterday to apologize. When he asked to take me out, I suggested going for coffee instead. But it wasn't a date. We were going as friends."

I snort, lifting my hat to scrub a hand through my hair. "As friends? Did he know that?"

"Yes," she drawls, less than amused at my accusations. "You and I hang out as friends, so what's the big deal?"

"No…" I say firmly. "We're not friends. The moment your lips touched mine and I got a taste of you, we stopped being *just friends*."

"Wilder," she mutters softly, dropping her gaze.

"Yeah, I know you don't wanna talk about it, but I do."

"You're gonna be late."

I scoff. "I don't fuckin' care."

I'll apologize for it when I get there, but I'd rather stay here and talk this out if she's willing.

"It's part of your probation!" She shoves me lightly. "You need to go."

I grab her wrist before she pulls away, then lean in closer. "Gimme one good reason why we can't be more than friends."

Her gaze locks on mine as I tower over her. "We'd be toxic together."

Arching a brow, my spine straightens, and I release my hold on her. "Toxic how?"

"Our siblings are datin' and our lives are too intertwined. It'd make things awkward if we broke up. One or both of us will end up hurt. And it's not like we could avoid each other forever. Then what?"

"Who says we'd break up?"

"You've never been in a serious relationship, so what makes you think we could make one work with all the history between us?"

The history neither of us has ever brought up.

Stepping closer, I close the gap between us and rest my forehead against hers, defeated. With a deep sigh, I respond, "That's exactly how I know it would…but I guess you're not ready to have *that* conversation either."

My heart hammers so loud with anger and frustration, I wouldn't be shocked if she hears it when I storm away.

I arrive at the shelter five minutes late, but Miss Tierney waves me off when I apologize for my tardiness. She greets me with a smile and brings me back to the office.

"Even though this is part of your probation hours, we have rules we expect everyone to follow."

"Yes, ma'am. Whatever you need me to do. I'm not here to cause any trouble," I reassure her.

She furrows her brows when I call her ma'am, but she's probably in her late thirties, five to seven years older than me if I had to guess. But she knows my mom from the local 4-H program where Landen helps some of the kids with riding and roping lessons. She's one of the moms of a boy he's trained.

She goes through their rules and expectations. This is one of the larger shelters in the state and it's always at capacity. I'm ashamed to say I've never volunteered at one before, so even though this is for my community service mandate, I'm glad I'm here to help.

"You're gonna start in the back of the kitchen. Once you get a feel for things, you could get moved to the front. People who come here are in a vulnerable condition and are used to certain volunteers, so that's why it's a gradual change when we add in new people."

"No problem. I don't mind helpin' in the kitchen. Whatever you need," I say genuinely.

"Perfect!" she beams. "Fill out this paperwork and then I'll give you a tour."

Miss Tierney introduces me to some of the staff members as well as the volunteers who come on a regular basis. Most are older, in their sixties and seventies, but they glare at me like I'm in an orange jumpsuit and handcuffs.

Miss Tierney must've told them why I was coming ahead of time.

She shows me around the kitchen, gives me the basics on the tasks I'll be doing, and then she brings me back to the office.

"Me or another supervisor have to sign off on your hours after each shift. So make sure you find someone before you leave for the day. I know you work long hours at the ranch, so I scheduled you for Saturday and Sunday afternoons. You'll work through dinner prep and meal cleanup, then you're free to go."

Perhaps it's a good thing Dad made Landen and me switch

jobs since there's less work on the stud farm and I can take the weekends off to be here.

"Sounds good. I'll see you in four days, then."

Standing, she takes my hand and shakes it. "Regardless of the reason, I'm glad you'll be here. Your natural charm will make the women feel more comfortable around you."

I involuntarily blush and grin at her compliment. "Uh, thanks?"

Though I hadn't considered that a man working in a shelter for women and children would raise concerns, I can understand why. Who knows what they've gone through and the last thing I'd want to do is make any of them uneasy.

She snickers, patting my arm. "You're welcome. We'll see you Saturday at four."

When I get to my truck, I check my phone and am disappointed when I don't see any notifications from Delilah. Not that I expected her to text, but I hate how unresolved things feel between us, and I'd hoped she'd want to talk.

The forty-five-minute drive home helps clear my head some more, but I'm craving a beer while I process everything. I know it's one of my coping mechanisms, however, some days I need it to push the overwhelming thoughts roaming through my head.

Fortunately, or maybe unfortunately, there's no beer or liquor in my fridge. I stopped buying it regularly when I went sober the first time, and then only went back to social drinking when I started up again.

Too bad I don't have any of Gramma Grace's pot cookies.

Once I'm home, I hop in the shower since I didn't have time before registration. I changed out of my work clothes and cleaned up the best I could, but now I'm craving the scalding-hot water on my skin.

My therapist calls it a form of self-destructive behavior. It's an alternative to cutting but without the fear of bleeding out. It's a way for me to regulate my emotions while replicating the relief I used to get.

Sometimes I'll do ice-cold showers instead, usually if I'm hungover and have to go to work, but I'll stay under the water until my skin feels like it's frostbitten.

It's not a healthy mechanism, by any means, but it's the least damaging out of the others I've done.

Stepping in, I suck in a breath when the scorching water beads against my back, but I embrace the discomfort. Instead of feeding into the bad thoughts, my mind focuses on the pain while I wash my body and hair. When I change the spray pattern to a pulsating pressure, I let it drum hard against my chest until I can't take it any longer.

By the time I get out, steam consumes the bathroom. When I wipe the mirror, I examine my body before wrapping myself in a towel. The temperature isn't hot enough to cause scars but standing underneath it for more than ten minutes would do some temporary damage. After giving myself blisters a few years ago, I knew not to stay under it longer than that.

Since I didn't eat dinner and The Lodge is closing soon, I make a few ham and cheese sandwiches. It's pretty much the only thing I can 'cook' without setting off my smoke alarm.

I plop down on my couch in ripped lounge pants and set my paper plate of sandwiches on my bare stomach. With one foot propped up on my coffee table, game highlights playing on the TV, and a bottle of Coke next to me, I feel as pathetic as I must look.

Halfway through my second sandwich and doom scrolling on my phone, Delilah's name pops up with a text.

I hate how fast I click on it and how her messaging me first kicks up my heart rate.

DELILAH

How'd registration go?

Not wanting to come off too eager, I act indifferent that she's asking me.

WILDER

Fine.

DELILAH

When do you start?

WILDER

Saturday. I'll work every weekend until I hit my hours.

DELILAH

You're gonna stay busy.

WILDER

Seems that way.

DELILAH

You left before I could tell you…but you can't blow up and overreact.

What the fuck now?

Setting my plate down on the table, I sit up with my elbows on my knees.

WILDER

What is it?

DELILAH

Right before you arrived, I found out Jonah's sister is married to Wesley. Based on what Jonah told me, I think he's the one Wesley was watching at the Twisted Bull.

Sin With Me

Which means it's possible Jonah knows I'm the one who slept with his sister and could potentially use Delilah to get back at me.

DELILAH

If what Wesley said about the drugs is true, then he could be talking about Jonah. I didn't know if his true intention was to apologize or something else, so I told him I had to go.

I stare at the screen, my jaw locking and teeth grinding hard. That dipshit being related to Wesley makes this more twisted and fucked up. But I can't react with guns blazing so she doesn't know how heated this news makes me.

WILDER

You need to stay away from him.

DELILAH

Already planned on it. I'm not trusting anyone I don't know considering that damn article.

WILDER

Good.

I don't know what else to say at this point. Probably why it takes her a few minutes to reply.

DELILAH

Anyway…just wanted to tell you in case you saw him again. Better to be safe than sorry and keep your distance. The last thing you need is him antagonizing you on purpose.

WILDER

Duly noted.

If I see Jonah again, I'm putting my fist through his face for the ripple effect he caused.

Consequences be damned.

DELILAH

I was startled to see you at the cafe after I'd just found out, so I'm sorry for not telling you sooner.

WILDER

Not surprised since you don't wanna talk about a lot of things.

Yeah, I'm still butt hurt about it. Not because I can't take rejection, but she's the only woman I've caught feelings for, and I'm so goddamn tired of hiding them. The more I see and talk to her, the harder it gets to keep my distance.

But then getting to kiss and touch her? It's a miracle I haven't dropped to my knees to *beg* her to give me a chance. I understand why she's hesitant, but I wish she'd let me prove her wrong.

DELILAH

That's not fair. I already told you...I haven't felt like myself since my dad died and getting involved when I'm struggling this much wouldn't be fair to you. It wouldn't be a real shot. There'd be too much on the line if it went south. So for now, can you just forget it happened and go back to the way things were before that night?

Sin With Me

> I'm afraid I can't forget it, Delly. But I'll respect your decision and won't bring it up again unless you do. Maybe time apart will help me get over my feelings because seeing you only makes me remember that you want me too.

I hate how dramatic that sounds, especially for me. But after nine years of what I thought was one-sided pining, I can't go back to pretending my feelings don't exist.

DELILAH

> Time apart? What's that mean?

WILDER

> It means, the next time we'll see each other will be in Vegas...assuming I'm allowed to go.

DELILAH

> Are you sure that's necessary? That's not for three more weeks.

WILDER

> I have therapy and community service to focus on anyway.

Plus, I start anger management in two days and will have to go every Thursday for two months. Then it'll switch to every other Thursday until my review hearing.

It takes her a while to respond. The jumping dots appear and go away several times before she finally hits send.

DELILAH

> Fine. If that's what you want...

I roll my eyes because I knew she'd say that. It's a cop-out, but I didn't give her much room to argue anyway.

WILDER

It's not what I want but it's what I need to do.

I've been able to suppress my feelings for years because I never thought she'd return them. However, knowing she does but won't do anything about it means I need to try getting over her for good. I'll never be able to move on otherwise.

Chapter Ten
Delilah

*I*t's not what I want but it's what I need to do.

His message has been on repeat in my head for the past week.

Wilder and I originally had plans last Saturday to go on a trail ride, but he never showed up. I assume he had to go to the shelter, but I somewhat expected him to text me and let me know. It was a long shot after what he said, but I still held out hope he would.

My feelings for him are complicated and not black and white. There's a huge gray area of our past that we've never discussed. On top of everything else that concerns me about us being *more* than friends, I can't forget the countless one-night stands he's had over the years.

He's never shown any interest in having a relationship. That night at the bar, he even said he had another twenty years before he'd settle down. Even though he'd been drinking and talking shit, there's some truth to his words that he can't see himself being happy with one woman for the rest of his life.

So why would I assume I'm any different?

My attraction to him goes deeper than his looks. Even further than his ability to be charming and seductive. It's been there since before we met in person.

I should've said something years ago. But he was savoring his youth and clearly didn't want anything more than a booty call.

And I was fine with waiting if I had to. Trick riding consumed most of my free time and that was enough for me at the moment.

I figured when something finally happened between us, the timing would be right. Everything would fall into place and it'd feel as natural as it was talking on the phone for those six months.

But then Dad died and nothing's felt right since then.

The grief and pain of losing him hit me in random bursts. Seemingly out of nowhere and often inconvenient when it does.

It's why there are days I can barely get out of bed or clean my apartment and other days where I feel great and can finally catch up on laundry. If it gives me emotional whiplash, no doubt it'd do the same to a partner.

I'll never get over how he died or feel less guilty about it, but I'd like to be in a better headspace before I make another life change.

It doesn't help that he seems to want answers from me that I can't give him. I don't know when I'll be ready to discuss the elephant in the room. Even when we do, I'm hesitant to believe he's willing to give up his lifestyle permanently.

I'm proud of the work he's put in, and I can tell he's trying hard.

But that's why I think we both need to work through our personal shit before we're in a good place for someone else.

It's one of the things I've discussed with my grief counselor during my appointment yesterday. She can tell I've been struggling and when I mention Wilder and what happened between us, she doesn't immediately agree with my take.

However, she said if I'm not ready, then I need to listen to my gut and follow it.

After Wilder's message about wanting time apart to get over his feelings, my gut has been twisted in knots.

Feeling lost and needing fresh air, I drive to Dad's gravesite that's located behind the ranch hand quarters. Even though he was cremated, Mom wanted someplace special for us to visit him.

Waylon made a private garden and buried the leftover ashes we kept after spreading them on the farm he worked on for years before his accident.

There's a memorial bench, a Cherry blossom tree, and tons of flowers. Wilder found some old tractor tires and made a decorative display with straw bales, wildflowers, and some other old farm equipment.

I appreciate how much care and love they put into it, especially now when I could use my dad's advice more than ever.

"Hi, Daddy. I really miss you." I kneel in front of his gravestone, feeling guilty it's been a few weeks since I've been here. "Mom, Harlow, and I got through our first Thanksgiving without you. We ordered Chinese food and watched old Christmas movies, as usual, but it wasn't the same. Without realizing it, we ordered your favorite dish and ended up sharin' it so it didn't go to waste." I smile, remembering how confused we were when our order arrived and there was extra orange chicken and rice.

I pick one of the flowers and fidget with the stem between my fingers. My gaze lowers to the ground, remorse and grief hitting me hard in the chest.

"I've decided to officially retire from trick riding," I confess, wondering if he'd be disappointed in me for giving up something I love. "Still tryin' to figure out what I wanna do at thirty-one is kinda embarrassing, but I can't work at the lingerie shop forever. I mean…who's gonna buy a lacy teddy from a sixty-year-old?"

I smile to myself at the thought. Lacey, the owner, is in her fifties and mostly works behind the scenes. She does all the ordering and makes the schedules on top of all the business duties. She's nice, but I don't see her much.

"I think I'd enjoy helping people like when I volunteered at Haven Grace. That gave me a purpose." A very *specific* purpose.

If Harlow's accident hadn't happened when it did, I would've continued working there until it closed down two years ago.

"But I feel like I'm running out of time to decide. I never went to college at eighteen and thinkin' about going thirteen years later sounds so dauntin'. But I need to figure it out soon before it's too late, and I'm stuck. I'm not myself without a passion to focus on, and I'm afraid I've lost my spark for anything at this point."

Leaning back on my haunches, I look up at the sky and inhale the crisp air. Although the sun is brightly shining down on me, there's a chilly breeze that causes my cheeks to burn.

"It sucks not gettin' your input on this. You always gave the best advice and pep talks, and I took that for granted. I thought I'd always get to talk to you whenever I wanted. Now I'm stuck listenin' to my counselor, who's more of a *tough love* parent than I'm used to."

Admittedly, maybe that's what I need at this point.

Someone to keep me accountable so I don't become complacent and then never go after what I want in life.

Not everything can be easy and living with that mindset will only make me stumble longer. But fuck, some days I just don't have the mental or physical capacity to do anything more than getting out of bed.

Before I leave, I decide to tell him one more thing.

"Wilder knows, Daddy. He knows I'm the girl from the crisis hotline and he knows that I know. He keeps hintin' at wanting to talk about it and us being more than *just friends*, but I'm scared to relive that part of my life. It was a dark time for our family. He'll wanna know why I never said anything about it and discuss how he told me some of his deepest, darkest secrets. But more than that…" I inhale deeply, then close my eyes as I blow it out. "He wants more than I can give him right now. Even though I'm the one who's been waitin' this whole time, the timing is all wrong. How can I give someone my heart when it still feels like parts of it are missin'?"

I haven't stopped crying for the past five days. Unfortunately, I can't blame it on getting my period either.

But ever since I went to visit my dad and word vomited everything that's been on my mind, I've been sad, anxious, and lost.

Last night, I had dinner at Mom's with Waylon and Harlow. It's become a tradition since Dad died. Every Saturday, Mom makes a feast and then we play a few board games.

It's always a fun time and distracts me for a few hours. Even funnier when Harlow loses and pouts about it. When she'd play with our parents as a kid, they always let her win, but now as an adult, she has no idea how to strategize to win on her own.

She'll get there, *eventually*.

Mom could tell I'd been crying by my bloodshot and sunken eyes. Well, first she asked if I was high, and after reassuring her that I wasn't, she sat me down after they left.

I don't care how old I am, I'll never be too old to cry on my mom's shoulder until I'm a blubbering, snotty mess.

At the very least, it was therapeutic in a way I haven't felt in a long time. Crying into my pillow just isn't the same.

When I woke up this morning, I felt a hundred times better —like the dark cloud hovering above me had finally moved.

I showered for the first time in three days, put on makeup, and blew out my hair.

But then, as luck and my life would have it, one phone call ruined all of it.

"This is a collect call from Cocke County Jail…"

Chapter Eleven
Delilah

As I drive to the county jail, I debate with myself if this is the stupidest thing I've ever done, and before I even walk across the parking lot, I conclude that it is.

I've only ever been to the Sugarland Creek jail, which is really a two-person cell in the sheriff's office.

The county jail is bigger.

And scarier.

Saying that as someone who's not even the one behind bars is how I know this is a bad idea. But when he called—begging for my help, swearing he's innocent, and claiming he has no one else to call—I felt bad and caved.

Hearing Jonah's voice on the other line was unexpected and surprising after our last encounter.

Apparently, he got pulled over for speeding, though he claims he was only going five over the limit. They found an ounce of marijuana in the glove compartment and arrested him for drug possession.

He swears up and down it's not his and that Wesley planted it and then had one of his buddies follow him until they pulled him over. There's bad blood between them and he claims Wesley's trying to get him in trouble.

After finding out they're brothers-in-law and that Wesley was watching a suspect at the Twisted Bull, I assumed he was keeping an eye on Jonah. Otherwise, it's just a strange coincidence that he was there two hours after his shift to watch a suspect the same night his brother-in-law was there getting wasted.

But also, knowing Wesley and how shady he is, I don't believe a word he says either.

If Jonah's telling the truth, Wesley could be the one mixed up in drugs and that's how he had them planted in Jonah's truck in the first place.

However, my gut could be wrong, and I'm helping a drug dealer.

After his bail hearing, he called again to tell me it was set at two grand. He's lucky it wasn't more because otherwise, he would've had to get a bail bond to cover it. But since it's his first offense, he's not a flight risk and doesn't have a criminal record, they gave him leniency.

In a few days, he'll go to his arraignment and be formally charged. Then he'll have to figure it out on his own. Best-case scenario, he won't get jail time, but I only came to pay his bail and take him to his truck at the impound. I'm not getting involved more than that.

"Delilah…" He grabs my attention while I dazed out in the waiting room.

After I paid his bail, they directed me here, and I've been waiting for over two hours.

Standing, I greet him with a smile. "Hey. Glad they finally let you out."

"I can't thank you enough for comin'. Seriously, I owe you."

I snort, hauling my bag over my shoulder and across my chest. "Yeah, two thousand dollars and one heck of a favor."

He winces, and I know he feels bad. "I'll pay you back, I promise. And whatever else you need, consider it done. A liver? Kidneys? You can have both."

A laugh bubbles out of my mouth as I shake my head. He looks remorseful enough, so I don't add any more guilt to his plate. "Okay, let's go. It smells in here."

He chuckles, following me toward the exit. "You don't even wanna know what a cell smells like."

"Save me the trouble, please."

Once we get in my truck, he gives me directions to the impound lot. Apparently, they towed it after his arrest and now he has to pay to get it out.

"So how did they find the weed anyway?" I ask the burning question I've been wondering all day. "Did you give him permission to search your car?"

He scoffs. "Yeah, right. Officer Dickhead claimed I was actin' suspicious. But my lawyer's confident he can get the charges thrown out due to an unlawful search. After my arraignment, he'll file a motion to suppress due to lack of probable cause."

"How were you actin'?"

"Fuck if I know. I'd just worked a twelve-hour shift and was exhausted as hell. He said my eyes were bloodshot and that I'd been slurrin' my words, which I wasn't. When I tried to explain I was drivin' home after a long night, he demanded I get out and then proceeded to search my truck. I didn't argue because I knew I didn't have anythin' illegal, but when he waved a bag in my face, claimin' he found it in my glove compartment, I knew Wesley set me up. I don't smoke weed."

"Do you sell it?"

"Of course not! Wesley's the one who has access to drugs.

He's either usin', dealin' or both. Hell, he could've stolen evidence from another case or some shit."

"Does that actually happen in real life? Or have you been watchin' too many crime drama shows?"

He shrugs. "Well, it's the only thing that makes sense because it's not mine. And I'm not stupid enough to store it in a spot that's so easy to find."

"Where would you put it?" I ask because now I'm curious.

"Everyone knows you stuff it in your pants or between the cheeks."

Jesus Christ.

"Oh, of course…" I drawl sarcastically. "Right up the cooch too, right?"

He smirks. "So I've heard."

"Why does Wesley want you in jail so badly?"

"When Raven announced they were gettin' married, I spoke out against it. He's never treated her right and is a piece of shit who cheats on her. I'm the only one in my family who doesn't kiss his ass—the 'all-mighty' deputy…" He rolls his eyes. "So he finds any reason to fuck with me."

"Accordin' to Wilder, Raven cheated on him."

"They were separated at the time, but he denies it, so he accuses her of being unfaithful."

"Why'd they get back together?"

"Because he's a manipulative prick who gaslights her and makes empty promises to do better so she won't leave him."

"That makes me feel bad for Raven, who probably feels too trapped to get out. Wesley wouldn't make it easy on her if she tried," I admit. "There are programs who can help her get out safely."

"He's a cop, so she doesn't trust anyone not to take his side. It's a miracle I talked her into leavin' this last time."

"Do you have any other family she could stay with?"

"No, our parents live in a one-bedroom house two hours away and our mom isn't…" He chews his lip before continuing, "She's not well, mentally. It's why we don't always see eye to eye. My dad refuses to get her help because he claims she's just fine. Except *just fine* ain't bargin' into my room when I'm sixteen and pointin' a gun at my face because she thought I was an intruder."

My eyes widen in shock. "Oh my God."

"Yeah…that's not even the worst of it. So it wouldn't be a healthy environment for a pregnant woman hidin' out from her cop husband. They'd probably bring him right to her."

"Oh shit, I forgot she's pregnant too."

"Yep…it's why I was helpin' her pack when Wesley came home early and caught us. They had a fight the night before and he gave her a black eye. I told her she had to report it, and I'd put her up in my house until she could get a protective order in place."

"And him being a cop, he didn't like that…" I assume, shaking my head because I can tell where this is going.

"Nope. He punched me and then threw me into the wall, smashin' a handful of their picture frames in the process. Then he got in my face and said if he ever saw me in his house again, he'd make sure it was the last time."

"Fuckin' hell." My heart races just imagining what he put her through. "He sounds psychotic."

"Egomaniac, self-centered, power-hungry prick," he elaborates. "That was a few days before the Twisted Bull incident and why I was out with a co-worker gettin' wasted. I needed a night out."

Wesley must've been fuming by that point and used his pent-up anger on Wilder when he saw him get into my truck. Since Jonah hadn't come out of the bar, he followed me instead and waited for the right moment to pull us over. He blames

Wilder for sleeping with his wife and used me to antagonize him.

"So that's the real reason he was stakin' out in the parkin' lot?"

"Yeah, he probably hoped I'd lead him to where I stashed Raven or maybe try and run me off the road. Not that I planned on drivin' that night. Either way, he woulda fucked with me in some way if he'd gotten the chance."

"Oh, so you got her outta there? Thank God."

"Yep. One of her neighbors heard the fightin' and screamin' and called 911. I got the protection order for Raven and me, filed a police report for the assault, and then took her to a woman's shelter two towns over until I can find her an apartment. I refused to leave their house without her. Wesley was visibly pissed he couldn't come after me with the sheriff there."

That's why Sheriff Wagner said Wesley was already in hot water—the protection order and assaulting Jonah.

That would've been good information to have beforehand.

"Good for you. Now I'm glad Wilder knocked him out on his ass."

He chuckles. "At least he's suspended without pay."

"And I'm sure that pisses him off even more."

"Which is how I know this stunt is all his doing. I took his job and wife away and now he's tryin' to put me away. That's why I couldn't call Raven to help me. I wouldn't be surprised if he's nearby, hopin' she came to get me so he can follow her."

Well, that's an uncomfortable thought...

I look in my mirrors, checking for any suspicious drivers behind me.

"Don't worry, I've been keepin' an eye out," he tells me when he notices.

Knowing more about the details makes me thankful I came

because if I hadn't, he would've been stuck there for days, and his sister would've been left vulnerable.

"Too bad you didn't get pulled over in Sugarland Creek. Sheriff Wagner woulda known your history with Wesley and vouched for you."

"Wesley ain't that stupid, even if the rocks tumblin' in his brain say otherwise. I work an hour away, so he had one of his cop buddies from another town follow me. He did it that way on purpose."

I pull into the impound parking lot and stop in front of the office building.

"I'm sorry y'all are goin' through this, especially Raven. Please let me know if I can help her in some way. And I'm sorry I assumed the worst about you and bailed at the café."

"Don't be. I don't blame you considerin' the information you had at the time. I'm grateful you were willin' to come even when you thought I was a drug dealer."

I chuckle, my face heating with embarrassment for being so quick to judge.

"Well, for what it's worth, I'm glad to be proven wrong. Hope you get some sleep and be careful, okay?"

"I will. Wesley knows if he comes near me, he goes to jail, so he won't risk it. He'll try and find other ways to get back at me—like he did today."

He opens the door to get out but then glances over his shoulder. "Just to be safe, watch your back too, okay? No tellin' what Wesley will do to anyone in his way."

Chapter Twelve
Wilder

My blood boils over as I whip open the door of Delilah's store. She's behind the register and greets me in her customer service voice without looking up.

Rounding the counter, I grab her elbow and yank her into the backroom.

"What the—"

I spin her around until she faces me, my jaw clenched with fury.

"Wilder?" Her eyes widen when our gazes meet. "What the hell are you doin'?"

She yanks her arm out of my grip, but I'm tempted to reach out and touch her again. It's been a long two weeks without seeing or talking to her. Fortunately, or maybe unfortunately, I've been too busy to think too hard about it, but I miss her enough to keep me up at night.

Pretty sure I haven't slept for eight of those nights.

"Why the fuck would you bail out Jonah?"

She flinches and her body tenses as she crosses her arms. "How do you know about that?"

"Small town, remember? Just answer me."

Scowling, she takes a small step back. "It's none of your business."

"Oh really?"

"Jonah's just a friend. I was helpin' him in a pinch. What's the big deal?"

"The big deal is that now you've put a target on your back..."

"What're you talkin' about? His arraignment was this mornin'. They dismissed the charges."

"Yep, and Molly was front and center in the courtroom."

I pull out my phone and tap the screen a few times, then hand it over so she can read the article.

"Oh my God..." Her shoulders fall as she reads the headline and scrolls through paragraphs that Molly wrote about Jonah's drug possession and accuses him of being a dealer.

Judge's Ruling on Unlawful Search Sparks Public Outrage: 'Another Drug Dealer Walks Free'

She also name-drops Delilah as his accomplice who bailed him out. Then she rambles on about how even the Fanning name won't get her out of trouble if she's caught red-handed.

"There's no proof he's a dealer. How can she just spew this bullshit?" She hands back the phone, clearly angry and flustered about what she read.

"Freedom of the press," I tell her. "Not sure how she found out you bailed him out, though."

"Wesley," she states. "He must've seen us in the parking lot. After I picked up Jonah, I drove him to the impound to pick up his truck."

I straighten my spine and fold my arms across my chest again. "So are you gonna explain how you got involved?"

"Not that I *have* to explain anythin' to you, but Jonah called and begged me to help because he had no one else. He said Wesley set him up and that the weed wasn't his."

"Pfft. And you just took his word because drug dealers don't lie..."

"I believe him!" she shouts.

Luckily, there aren't any customers in the store or they'd hear everything.

"Why?" I ask, raising my voice. "Why would Wesley go after him?"

"Because he beats his pregnant wife! Wesley gave her a black eye, so Jonah begged her to finally leave him. Wesley walked in on them packin' up her stuff. He flipped out and threw Jonah into the wall. Ask the sheriff!" She shoves at my chest, but my feet stay planted to the floor, pissing her off even more. "They filed a protection order against him, which is why he was already in trouble the night he pulled me over. Wesley was at the Twisted Bull to spy on Jonah because he wants to find Raven."

That also explains why Wesley was so outraged that night and decided to take it out on me when he saw me get into Delilah's truck. He was looking for a fight and it didn't matter with who.

She blows out a frustrated breath when I don't respond.

"Believe me or not, but Wesley did this to get back at Jonah. He planted the drugs and made sure he got pulled over and searched. He was probably waitin' in the jail parkin' lot because he hoped Raven would pick him up, but then he saw me instead."

"I do believe you, but now that Jonah's put you in the middle of this, Wesley's gonna do anythin' he can to get back at you for helpin' him. He might even assume you know where his wife is."

She lifts her arms in a careless shrug. "Let him try. And it's not Jonah's fault. Wesley's a maniac!"

"You should talk to Sheriff Wagner and get a PO for yourself, too."

"If I do, will you get off my ass about it?"

I smirk, flicking my tongue ring and licking my lower lip. "Sure. For now."

She rolls her eyes. "People can say whatever they want, but the truth will come out. He breaks the PO with Raven or Wesley, he'll go to jail."

"He'll just use Molly again to make y'all look bad. And that's *if* he gets caught. I hope Raven's in a secure location."

Now that I'm not so heated, I'm thinking about Raven and what drastic measures Wesley would go to about finding her. Then if he does, what he'd do to her.

"She is. It's why Jonah couldn't call her for help and had to ask me."

Now I'm even more worried about Delilah's safety.

"You need to be extra careful. Watch your back. I can't work, go to anger management, therapy, volunteer, *and* watch you."

"I don't need you to watch me. I'm not a dog!"

I roll my eyes at her dramatics. "Fine, but for the love of God...if you're in any trouble or Jonah is, or if you're even suspicious Wesley's watchin' you, call me or the sheriff right away. Don't risk it."

"I will," she promises, sitting behind the small desk and logging into her computer. "I carry mace and a stun gun. I'm not afraid to use 'em."

After everything her family's been through, I don't blame her for having them, but I hate that she has to.

Brooke Montgomery

"And don't walk through the parkin' lot alone either. That's how they got Harlow."

"I know, and I won't. Mattie and I will stay together."

"Speakin' of Mattie, where is she?"

"I'm right here, lover boy," she calls from the front of the store.

I didn't even see her when I stormed in because I was laser-focused on finding Delilah.

"Did you hear what I said? Stay together," I call out.

"Sir, yes, sir!" she chants. "I will stand in front of the bathroom while she pees if I have to."

I snort. "Your own personal bodyguard."

Delilah cackles, turning to look at me. "You have no idea *how* personal."

Lifting a brow, I tilt the corner of my lips, intrigued.

"Like shove-her-hand-up-my-pussy-because-I-lost-a-tampon personal." Mattie enters the backroom with two handfuls of hangers. "It was that or go to the hospital, which woulda been humiliating. Luckily, Mrs. Fanning explained what to do over the phone so I didn't have to."

Delilah's mom is an ER nurse, so that checks out, but I'm still stuck on the whole *losing a tampon* thing.

"How in the world…" I hold up a hand, shaking my head. "Ya know what, never mind. I don't wanna know."

"You don't, trust me." Delilah shakes her head.

"Oh, like I wouldn't do it for you?" Mattie sasses. "In fact —"

"That's enough chitchat. Back to work," Delilah cuts her off.

Mattie laughs, hangs up the lingerie sets, and then grabs new ones. "Oh, c'mon…he was almost blushin'."

At the mention of it, my cheeks heat, and I lower my gaze to hide it.

138

"Aye, there we go." Mattie points at me before walking out to the front.

"She's...*something*."

"And that's before she's three margaritas deep. Which she will be in a couple hours."

"Where're y'all goin'?"

"Maria's Kitchen. We go every Thursday after work, have some drinks, chips and salsa, and then share a huge chimichanga."

"How're y'all gettin' home?"

"It's a mile from our apartment. We usually walk."

"No, you shouldn't be walkin' in the dark while tipsy. You'll be too vulnerable with Wesley out in the wind, so I don't think that's a good idea."

She sighs, her shoulders dropping in defeat. "Fine, we'll get an Uber. Happy?"

"That you're gonna listen to me for once? Yes. But I'd be happier if you'd stay home."

"I'm not gonna live my life in fear because of some asshole. Then he wins."

"It won't matter who wins or loses if he does somethin' to you."

"He won't. Have you seen Mattie? She can ride the mechanical bull in perfect form five-drinks deep. Unlike someone else I know..."

I scoff. "We'll just see about that the next time we go out."

She barks out a laugh, stands, and then pulls in her chair. "Sure, Wilder. The day you stay on it for eight seconds will be the day I marry you."

"Marry me?" Now that's an *interestin'* idea...

"Yeah, because both will never happen."

"You wound me, Mrs. Hollis." I sulk, placing a hand over my heart.

"That's not funny!" She playfully swats my chest.

I'm about to respond when she pulls out her phone from her back pocket.

"Oh my God..." she mutters, staring at the screen. "Jonah lost his job. They fired him because of the article!"

"Shit...I hope you don't lose yours."

"Lacey would never, but I can't believe they let him go."

"I can. He's a suspected drug dealer, or at the very least, was in the possession of drugs. Most companies aren't gonna be cool with that."

"Even though the charges were dropped? It wasn't his!"

I shrug, leaning against the wall. "Doesn't matter. Makes the company look bad and a liability they're not gonna take."

"Maybe he can work at the ranch? He's used to liftin' heavy shit and being out in the cold and heat."

"No."

"Wilder, c'mon!"

I don't even know where he worked. "What'd he do?"

"Construction."

"Of course he did..."

No wonder he's built like the Hulk.

"What's that mean?"

"Nothin', but I don't think it's a good idea with my name already makin' headlines. No way my dad's gonna hire him with all the bad press."

"No one has to know. He can work on the ranch side, like you."

"Who says he even wants to work on a ranch? Just because he did construction doesn't mean he's good with horses."

"So make him shovel shit or carry hay, I dunno. I'm sure he can do something."

"Shovel shit and carry hay?" I deadpan. "Is that all you think we do?"

She shrugs dramatically. "I'm usually there to ride and train. I don't pay attention to everythin' else."

I blow out a breath and scrub a hand through my hair. "I'm gonna be late for my class tonight, but fine…I'll talk to my dad."

"Thank you!" She wraps her arms around me so unexpectedly, I almost miss her touch before she pulls away.

"Text me when you're done at the restaurant. I'll come pick y'all up if I'm on my way home."

"Oh my God, it's a sexy cowboy! Over here! Come and get us!" Mattie whistles, waving her arm above her head like a lasso.

Jesus Christ, they're loaded.

"Do y'all usually get this drunk on a weekday?"

"Huh? We're not drunk." Delilah lifts herself up into the truck but then slips and falls face-first onto the passenger seat.

Mattie laughs uncontrollably behind her, then helps push her in.

"See? Totally sober."

"Yeah, we only had one margarita," Mattie adds, then burps. "Plus five."

Jonah walks up behind them, and I grind my molars. She didn't tell me he'd be tagging along.

"Sorry, man…they kept orderin' every time I wasn't lookin'."

Brooke Montgomery

I give a stiff nod and a forced close-mouthed smile. "Do you
need a ride, too?"

"Nah, I only had one beer when we first got here. I woulda
taken 'em home, but they said you were already on the way."

"I don't mind."

My anger management class is thirty minutes away and
lasts about forty-five minutes if I don't stick around for small
talk. As soon as she texted that they were on dessert, I booked
ass to get here before they left.

Once the girls are in, Jonah closes the door, then rounds
the front of my truck. "Delilah told me about what she asked
you. So I just wanted to say I appreciate it and no hard feelings
if it doesn't work out."

"It's fine. I called my dad already and he said he'd give you
a two-week trial run. But you're gonna be stuck doin' bitch
work."

He beams like the thought of that makes him happy. "That's
fine with me! Whatever it takes to support Raven."

I nod, feeling less worried about giving him a chance. "Be
there at six-thirty."

"You got it, boss."

"Don't call me that," I blurt. "Just…Wilder is fine."

He smirks. "I was just messin' with ya. Good luck with
those two."

"Yeah, thanks." I laugh.

The girls tell him goodbye and then I drive toward their
apartment.

"Aww…you two are buddies now!" Delilah taunts.

"Butt buddies!" Mattie shouts.

They both giggle, adding to my annoyance.

How did Waylon tolerate me being drunk for all those
years? Is this my punishment? I can't drink, so now I get to
deal with these drunks instead?

I'm sure he'd get a kick out of it too.

"You're gonna have the hottest threesome ever," Mattie tells Delilah. "Can I watch?"

"No!" Delilah scolds, but when Mattie whines, she adds, "Fine, you can listen. But no lookin' or touchin'."

"Deal! I'll use a toy anyway."

"The pink or black one?"

"Jesus fucking Christ. You two are *way* too fuckin' close," I mutter, shaking my head at how loud and obnoxious they're being.

"Ooh, should we tell him about your butt plug incident now?"

I damn near swerve off the road.

I've never seen Delilah this drunk before, probably because she was always taking care of my drunk ass, but holy shit. There's no filter on either of them.

"Nooo…that's embarrassing!"

"But it's sooo funny."

"Yeah, for you maybe. But you weren't the one who had it stuck inside you—*on vibrate*—and then lost the remote!"

I pinch the bridge of my nose, exhaling through my mouth. *Do not pop a boner.*

"Again…I don't wanna know, but how the hell does that happen?" I ask.

"She dared me to do it during a drinkin' game and then we got too drunk to remember where the remote was."

"And too drunk to figure out how to get it outta there," Mattie adds, tears streaming down her cheeks as she laughs. "I had to split her cheeks and slather her booty hole in baby oil."

"You weren't supposed to tell him that!" Delilah whisper-shouts.

"Why not? You have a nice ass. Big and round, with cute freckles on your cheeks."

And now I'm pitching a tent.

Delilah's face is beet red as she squeezes her eyes.

"If he ain't gonna tap it, someone else will…" Mattie taunts, and now *my* face is red.

"Okay, here we are…" I announce, pulling into a parking spot in front of their apartment building. "I'm gonna walk y'all inside."

"You wanna her freckles too, dontcha?" Mattie quips, nearly falling out of the truck as she opens the door.

"I wanna erase the last five minutes out of my memory," I mutter, getting out to help them.

They loop their arms together as they skip to their door, nearly tripping and face-planting the sidewalk.

"Gimme the keys," I say, grabbing them from Mattie's hand.

Once I unlock the door, I wait for them to get inside and then do a quick sweep through their place to make sure nothing looks suspicious. Besides the pile of laundry on the floor and the sink full of dishes, nothing looks out of the ordinary.

"Are we safe, detective cowboy?" Delilah plops on the couch, nearly falling off on her way down.

Mattie stumbles next to her. "If you're so worried, you can sleep in my bed tonight. I don't bite…but I do suck."

Delilah and her giggle, and now I know I owe Waylon the biggest apology for putting up with me over the years. Delilah too, but if this is payback, we're even now.

"I would rather drown in hot sauce…" I say under my breath.

Standing in front of Delilah, I grip her chin so she'll meet my gaze. "If you need anythin', please call me. Got it?"

"Yes, sir," she mocks with a salute.

Lord help me.

Chapter Thirteen
Delilah

With the Vegas trip this week, I've been packing and mentally preparing to see Wilder again. Although I saw him four days ago during my drunken escapade, I wasn't in my right mind to think too much about how we hadn't seen each other in two weeks before that.

I hate how much he made my heart flutter once he was done scolding me. Every time he flicked that stupid tongue piercing, I contemplated attacking his mouth again.

And the way he stormed in like a caveman, all angry and fired up, was a *little* bit hot.

But I'd never admit that aloud.

I didn't mean to get wasted at the Mexican restaurant with Mattie, but once we started drinking and my mind spiraled from the way he barged into the restaurant, I couldn't help ordering more to calm my racing thoughts.

I invited Jonah to meet us so I could tell him about the possibility of working at the ranch, assuming he'd even want to, and the more we talked, the more we drank.

Besides the morning after text asking how I was feeling and

him responding when I asked how Jonah was doing on his first day, we haven't talked. He replied with a quick: *he's fine.*

Jonah later told me Wilder was on his ass for ten hours straight and wouldn't make conversation with him besides giving him orders. Didn't even introduce him to the other ranch hands, so he did it himself.

He texted on his second day that some teenage girl threw him a dirty look for getting the four-wheeler stuck in the mud. And instead of helping, she walked away laughing.

After a few days of Jonah proving he's a hard worker, Wilder took it easier on him. He still makes him do bitch work, but Jonah's more than happy to do it for Raven's sake.

Since he's working long shifts, he gave Raven my number in case she ever needs anything and can't get ahold of him. She texted me once to thank me for helping Jonah get the job and I told her to contact me anytime.

After the article, neither of us has seen or heard from Wesley or Molly. I can only hope it stays that way because I'm sick of looking over my shoulder every time I leave my apartment. Getting out of town will be nice for that reason alone.

Wilder and I are on the same flight since Harlow and Waylon drove, but I'll be next to my mom so she's not alone.

I'm anxious to see how things will go between us after our "time apart." My biggest fear is things won't be the same between us. Either he'll say he's over it or he needs more space.

As much as I want things to go back to the way they were before I kissed him, it's not fair to ask him to do that. Not when I know he's had feelings for me and he knows I have them for him.

I hate that I can't get out of my grief and guilt enough to give in to those feelings and be what he deserves right now.

Although I've been talking to a counselor for the better part of the year, the impending one-year anniversary of my dad's death has me in a chokehold. This weird anticipation hangs over me like a deadline—if I make it to that date, I can say I survived the worst of it. The hardest year of my life will be over, and I can finally exhale.

But the reality will be that the hard days won't magically stop. And I still have to accept that.

"I can't believe you're goin' without me." Mattie pouts, body-slamming my bed and nearly crashing on top of my suitcase. "Can you at least bring me back a hot cowboy or cowgirl?"

"Why not one of each?" I tease.

She sits up, eyes bright and eager like a dog waiting for its bone. "Yes, please!"

I snort, grabbing more clothes.

"You should bring your new lavender lace set."

"For who?"

"Your future husband."

"And who's that?"

"Whichever hot piece of cowboy ass you find." She falls back against my pillows, sighing as she looks up dreamily.

"You're imaginin' guys in chaps and cowboy hats, aren't ya?"

"Just my type. Preferably shirtless and tattooed."

I chuckle, digging into my closet for the lingerie set I haven't even tried on.

"If I'm not ready to move forward with Wilder, what makes you think this will ever see the light of day?" I ask, holding it up against my body. It's teeny tiny compared to me.

"Maybe that'll give you the confidence you need to get outta that head of yours and finally be honest with yourself."

I groan and my eye twitches. "You sound like my therapist."

"Then we're both brilliant." She gloats.

"Mm-hmm." I drop the lingerie in my luggage because why the hell not.

"Send me a few selfies when you actually put that on…" She nods toward it. "So there's proof."

"Don't hold your breath."

I dig around for my favorite cowboy boots and add them to the pile. Then I look through my dresser for panties and socks. I don't know why I'm hyper-fixating on what I'm wearing underneath my clothes, but I'd rather overpack than somehow run out of underwear.

"Delilah?"

Mattie's booming voice grabs my attention, and I quickly spin toward her.

"What?" I ask, holding my items close to my chest.

"You okay?" She slides off the bed, then stands in front of me. "I said your name like three or four times. You completely dazed out."

Blinking a few times, I nod. "Yeah, I was focused on which pairs to bring, I guess." I let out a small chuckle. "Can never bring enough, right?"

"Yeah, I guess." Her hesitant voice tells me she's not buying it. "You don't have to go if you're havin' doubts. I'm sure Harlow would understand."

"It's not that…" I toss my items on the bed and sit. "Just anxious to be around Wilder in a different settin' and not know where his head is regardin' our…situation."

"I think you should go and try not to think about it. Just have fun and let loose. You're on vacation. It doesn't have to revolve around Wilder. Spend this time with your mom and sister. Wilder will wait or he'll find a way to talk to you if he wants to, but don't put any pressure on yourself. Plus, it's Vegas! Go experience it."

I nod, smiling wide. "You're right. It'll be nice to go have fun for a couple days."

"That's my girl!" She playfully smacks my knee. "Just don't come back pregnant. We promised to get knocked up together, and I'm not ready for that yet."

My head falls back, laughing at the pact we made when we were thirteen. "Okay, deal."

I haven't flown in several years, since Mattie and I went to Florida on a whim and spent the weekend in Key West. Most of it is a blur since we partied the whole time. But we had a blast and I'm hoping Vegas won't be any different.

Even though my nerves are on fire—for several reasons—I'm excited when I pick up my mom and see how amped up she is to be getting out of Sugarland Creek for a while.

Wilder's riding with Tripp and Magnolia to the airport, so I have an hour to clear my mind before we get there. Our flight doesn't leave for another three hours, so we should have plenty of time to get to our gate and wait to board.

"What would you think about goin' to the Hollises' for Christmas this year?"

My head snaps over to my mother in the passenger seat. "But we always eat at your house."

"Right, but it's the first one without your father, and I think it's time we make new traditions."

"We've made some," I counter. Like Saturday night game nights.

"I know, sweetheart. I guess it doesn't feel right havin' it at the house without him. Maybe eventually it will, but right now, I'd like to try somethin' new. Mrs. Hollis invited us."

"Oh…" My throat tightens, and I choke back tears. I should've realized how hard this would be on her too. "Okay, we can go."

"Thanks, honey." She reaches over and pats my hand. "Hopefully, you and Wilder make up by then."

"Huh? What makes you think we're fightin'?"

"I'm not blind, Delilah. You've been moppy the last two Saturdays, and I'm sure that article didn't help things. Was he mad about you helpin' Jonah?"

My shoulders tense, but she deserves an explanation. I've already told her about him and his sister and the shit with Wesley. But I didn't tell her the details with Wilder.

For the rest of the drive, I catch her up on everything. Hell, I basically word-vomit until my brain's empty. I even tell her the truth about the night I got pulled over and how Wilder and I made out.

And then how I freaked out and got pissed at him, which led to where we are now and why I'm anxious to see him again.

"You probably think I'm an emotional wreck, don't ya?"

When I glance at her, she's beaming. "Not at all."

"Why do you look so happy?"

"I've been wonderin' when you and Wilder were gonna finally get together." She shrugs bashfully. "Ever since you found out he was 'Luke' and then spent more time together, it was only a matter of time before your emotions spilled over."

I told my parents the Luke/Wilder story after Waylon and I had broken up two years later. When I asked Noah about training, I was hesitant at first. Not because of my past relationship with Waylon but because of Wilder.

"You heard the part where I freaked out on him, right?"

"Yes. And this whole takin' time apart business is a ploy."

"Whaddya mean?"

"He doesn't need time to get over you or move on. He's givin' you time to catch up because he knows the feelings are mutual."

"I don't think so, Mama. He was serious when he said it."

"I've always noticed the way he looked at you. Even drunk, he stared like you were his anchor. He held onto you to steady him and that's how I know he wouldn't give up that easily without a fight."

I never realized he looked at me a certain way.

"He knows I'm the girl from the crisis hotline," I tell her the same thing I told my father. "And he knows I know too."

"Doesn't surprise me. He felt safe with you. You got him through a hard period and he knew you'd never judge him the way he assumes everyone else does. You give him comfort and stability." She smiles so wide, it reaches her temples. "You're his safety pin."

My eyes fill with tears before I can stop them. I've never considered he saw me that way and even though I don't want to gloat and sound highly of myself, I can understand why.

Wilder and I spent weeks on the phone, discussing all his highs and lows. He shared so much with me—minus his real name and the truth about who he was—but I had his voice memorized and it was how I knew the first moment he spoke.

The rest clicked into place.

Twin brother. Oldest of five. Plus everything Waylon had told me about his mental health.

During those months we talked, I wondered who he was and eventually figured out he gave me a fake name when he nearly slipped during one of his story times. But I didn't push him to tell me because some people feel ashamed for calling into a crisis hotline, and I didn't want him to feel that way. I was proud he continued to call even when it was obvious it was only to talk to me. Hearing his voice was something I looked forward to hearing and missed when I had to leave abruptly.

"If you have feelings for him, tell him. Put that man out of his misery and yourself out of yours."

I wipe my cheek, sniffing back my emotions. "It ain't that easy, Mama."

"Love never is, sweetheart. Otherwise, there wouldn't be heartache."

Chapter Fourteen
Wilder

The anticipation of seeing Delilah again and spending the next few days in Vegas with her has me sweating through my shirt before we even walk into the airport. I hitched a ride with Tripp since Waylon and Harlow road-tripped it there and Noah's too pregnant to fly, so her husband, Fisher, drove them a few days ago. But Magnolia talked and sang to the radio during the entire drive so I couldn't even clear my mind before we arrived.

And I really need to because I've been spiraling. More than usual and it's brought me back to the days when I'd get so trapped in my head, I couldn't find a way out until I released the pain.

The overactive thoughts, the feeling of dread, the anxiety attacks.

Like I have no control of my life at the moment.

Some of this was my own doing, like hitting Wesley in the face, but I don't regret it. Every Thursday at anger management and every weekend at the shelter are worth it to have put him in his place.

Working with Jonah the past five days has kept me busier than usual, and although it's helped distract me a little, I'm still not a fan of him. Every time we took a break and he'd smile down at his phone while texting Delilah, I wanted to clock him.

She claims they're just friends, but if that's the case, what the hell does that make her and me?

Regardless, I'm looking forward to the break. Jonah's working under Ayden—the stables manager— and with the rest of the ranch hands that are staying behind, including Mallory and her boyfriend, Antonio.

This past summer, she begged Dad to let him work with her on the ranch after school and on the weekends. Originally he said no, but after some begging and crying that he needed to save money to buy his own horse for his future rodeo career, he caved.

Mallory's been learning how to barrel race so now she's on the ranch side more than normal and loves getting on my nerves.

After Landen began volunteering at the local 4-H Club two years ago, he started training Antonio on riding and roping skills and has since been practicing for when he can focus on it full-time after he graduates high school.

Which means the two of them are *always* around—touching and kissing—and grossing me out.

Admittedly, I don't like the little shithead. Haven't since I found them making out in the barn two years ago. When I saw his hand cupping a *certain* area, I pinned his ass to the wall and threatened his balls if he ever touched her again. I was ready to knock him out until Landen and Tripp showed up, demanding I let him go.

Mallory didn't speak to me for a month after that. She's never been afraid to express her opinions, and her anger toward me is no exception. Knowing how hotheaded she can be, I might find a little joy knowing Jonah's stuck there with them because I'm pretty sure she tolerates him less than I do.

Ruby, one of Noah's ranch hands, is already in Vegas with her husband, Levi, who's competing in the pro team roping events. The NFR takes place over ten days but since we couldn't take that much time off, we're arriving on day eight and will hopefully witness Ellie win the barrel racing championship on the final day.

"You only brought one bag?" Magnolia asks when I lift it onto the scale.

"Yeah? We're only going for a few days. How many did you bring?"

Tripp snorts. "Three. And one's just for shoes."

"Your boots are in there, too!" She swats his chest. "Plus, I needed clothes for the rodeo and some for the evenings when we go out."

"Oh yeah, me too," I mimic in a high-pitched voice. "My day shirts and my night shirts."

"Oh shut up." Magnolia laughs. "I'd be surprised if you remembered a change of underwear."

I snap my fingers. "Dammit, that's what I forgot."

Once we get through security, my palms sweat even more as we walk toward our gate. The moment I spot Delilah sitting next to her mom, my heart rate spikes.

"Hey! I'm so excited y'all are comin' too!" Magnolia wraps her arms around Delilah when she stands.

"Me too. Never been to Vegas before," Delilah says, avoiding my gaze.

"Oh my God, you're gonna love it. Last year was a blast. Watchin' Ellie win was an adrenaline rush I haven't felt since that day."

Delilah giggles. "Can't wait."

Magnolia drops her carry-on next to Tripp's seat. "Time to hit the bar."

"Dude, it's like eight in the mornin'," I mutter, wanting a moment with Delilah before she's pulled away.

"We're on airport time, which means it's never too early," Magnolia says over her shoulder.

"C'mon, Mom," Delilah tells her and she goes too.

"And y'all said I was bad." I snort.

The girls link arms, practically skipping away.

I sit next to Tripp and pull out my phone to check my messages.

Six from Mallory.

MALLORY

This guy is a bonehead.

Why'd you leave me here with him?

OMG he HUMS. He's a hummer! Red alert!

Even though it's the middle of the school week, she's stuck working a couple hours before class since we're not there. I wouldn't be surprised if she texts me every morning to complain until we return.

MALLORY

Oh and now he's whistling. I'm in hell.

I chuckle because I know how much she hates that.

MALLORY

Can I kill him, please?

I'll even clean up the blood.

Shaking my head, I type out my reply that she's gonna hate.

WILDER

Suck it up, buttercup. If I have to work with him ALL goddamn day, you can manage a few hours.

MALLORY

I didn't sign up for this! I was forced against my will!

I roll my eyes at her dramatics.

WILDER

Join the club.

When I hear Delilah laugh, I glance up and stare at her. "Doin' okay?" Tripp nudges my arm.

"Uh...yeah. Fine," I reply, keeping my gaze locked on her.

"Really?"

"Mm-hmm. Why?" I try reading her lips but I can't tell what she's staying.

"Because by that drool on your chin, I'd think you're in love..." he taunts, smacking my jaw.

I push him away, finally breaking my trance. "We haven't talked much lately."

"Well, go up and say somethin'."

"It's not that easy."

Tripp shifts toward me, inching closer. "Don't tell me after all these years dancin' around each other, you fucked her and then screwed it up..."

"No." I shift my gaze again. "She wanted to, but I shot her down."

Tripp furrows his brow, the corner of his lips tilting up in a mocking grin. "*You* shot *her* down? Ain't no way."

"Believe it or not, I haven't had sex in over a year. Part of my therapy and gettin' my head on straight was to stay celibate."

"Wow. I'm impressed." He smirks. "Who knew you could resist Delilah after all this time?"

"Trust me, it wasn't easy. She flipped out because she thought I was rejectin' her. But then she thanked me for stoppin' it because she claims the timing's all wrong and is still havin' a hard time with her dad's death."

"That's valid, especially since Harlow was kidnapped on the same day it happened. She's been through a lot."

"I didn't even know she wanted me like that, so I was surprised. All this time, I assumed she could hardly stand me. Turns out she's been fightin' her feelings just like I have."

"So what happened after?"

I scratch my cheek, contemplating how much to tell him.

"She asked me to forget about what we did that night and go back to being just friends, and I told her I couldn't. Then I said I needed some time apart to get over my feelings for her because being around her was too hard."

"Oh shit. You *really* like her." He widens his eyes. "I had no idea you were so down bad."

I roll my eyes at his Taylor Swift reference. The curse of being married to a Swiftie.

"No one did, really."

Since I never told my brothers how I called a crisis hotline and talked to her for six months before meeting her as Waylon's new girlfriend, there was no way to casually bring up why I've felt something for her all this time. Something deeper than attraction.

"Did the time apart work?"

I breathe out a humorless laugh. "Not even close. Actually, it made it worse. Not talkin' or seein' her made me want to talk and see her even more. When that article about Jonah came out, I asked her why she helped him and then we argued a little. Later that night, I picked her and Mattie up from the Mexican restaurant and they were drunk off their asses—with Jonah. I made sure they got home safely and texted her the next mornin' to check on her, but that's it."

"Sounds like you need to use the next few days to decide what you're gonna do. If you can't get over your feelings but you don't want to stop hangin' out, you're gonna have to learn how to suffer in silence. And trust me, I did that—for years. I had to watch Magnolia with her douchebag on-and-off again boyfriend and wait for the right moment."

"And what was the right moment for you?"

"It doesn't exist, man. There's no *one* right moment to tell the woman you're secretly in love with her that you love her. When I thought she was crushin' on some random dude, I snapped. Ask Landen. Nearly kicked his ass until he told me *I* was the dude she was crushin' on. That was the big *aha* moment. Not necessarily the right moment because I made a fool of myself for makin' assumptions, but it was *the* moment that made me realize if I didn't do somethin' now, I could lose her forever."

"But Magnolia jumped all in with you. How do I convince Delilah to at least give us a shot? Or a chance to prove myself?"

Tripp contemplates it for a moment. "You show her. She thinks she's not ready because she's scared and protectin' her heart. If she's been into you for a while, it's understandable why she's hesitant. She's had to watch you hook up with girls for years and never make a commitment. Prove to her you're ready by your actions."

"Okay." I nod, swallowing hard. "And how do I do that?"

Tripp grins, staring at Magnolia from across the gate. "Never give her a chance to doubt your intentions. Lay everythin' out so she knows exactly where you stand."

I'm stuck sitting next to someone I don't know since I'm the third-wheel. Delilah and Mrs. Fanning are a few rows in front of Tripp and Magnolia who are ahead of me. Less than two hours later, we land in Dallas for our layover.

And this time I'm determined to speak to her since I didn't get the chance to before we took off. Magnolia hogged her the entire time and then when we boarded, Delilah walked on with her mom.

"How were the airport cocktails?" I ask from behind while she stands in line for coffee. Mrs. Fanning is sitting at a table while Tripp and Magnolia walk around, so I take the opportunity to get her alone for a few minutes.

She turns until she faces me. "Expensive, but good. Definitely helped the pre-flight anxiety."

"Yeah, that was a bumpy ride."

When the plane hit turbulence, a chorus of gasps echoed throughout the cabin, and I had to hold onto the seat in front of me until it stopped.

"Shoulda had one with us," she says with a genuine smile, and I consider that a good sign. "Unless you're waitin' for Vegas before drinkin'?"

Stuffing my hands in my front pockets, I shrug. "Didn't wanna interrupt your girlfest."

With a snort, she turns and moves through the line. Her blue eyes meet mine over her shoulder. "Since when do you care about interruptin'? You love being the center of attention."

"That's not true..." With my arms pulled back behind me, I

draw closer. My lips brush the shell of her ear as my voice drops to a whisper, "I love being the center of *your* attention."

Her spine stiffens and the hair on the back of her neck prickles. But before she can respond, the cashier's voice cuts through the air, calling for the next person.

Delilah swallows hard and then walks until she's in front of the cashier.

After she orders, I move next to her and add in my drink, then pull out my wallet.

"I could've paid," she says softly, watching me.

"But then I couldn't call this a date." I wink, then hand the cashier my card.

A look of confusion spreads across her face. I probably shouldn't have said that before we had a chance to discuss the situation between us, but it's too late now.

Once we move to the end of the counter and wait for our drinks, we both start talking at the same time.

"Sorry, go ahead," I tell her.

"No, it's fine. You go."

I shift my weight uncomfortably, trying to come up with the words I want to say without scaring her away. Being in the middle of the airport where it's loud and chaotic isn't helping either.

"Uh, well..." Licking my lips, I scrub a hand across my jawline. "I wanted to tell you that takin' time apart didn't help me get over my feelings. Not that I truly thought it would but..."

I'm interrupted by the barista handing us our drinks. "Thank you."

Delilah grabs the two drinks for her and Mrs. Fanning, and I grab mine. Then I follow her to the table where her mom's waiting.

"Hi, Wilder." She smirks suspiciously at me, grabbing her coffee cup.

"Hello, Mrs. Fanning. How're you?"

"I'm lovely, thank you." She takes a sip of her chai tea, then shifts her gaze to Delilah. "I'm gonna walk around the gift shop and find a new book to read. I'll meet you back at our gate, sweetheart."

"Oh, are you sure?" Delilah looks panicked but her mom puts her at ease.

"Of course. That way you and Wilder can talk in private." She flashes her a wink before she leaves.

"That was...interestin'," I say, then bring the cup up to my lips to stop myself from asking if she talked to her mom about us.

"Very."

"I don't think I was supposed to see that little gesture she made, but I'm pretty sure she likes me." I waggle my brows and she rolls her eyes.

"Where do you wanna talk?" she asks.

"I'm sure there's an empty gate somewhere."

"Or we could find one of those private nursin' rooms and find out why they call it *breast feeding*..."

"Wilder Hollis!" She burst out laughing, playfully shoving my chest, but I don't budge. "You're not slick."

"What?" I feign innocence. "I can't be curious?"

"Mm-hmm...I'm sure you're *so* curious."

Chapter Fifteen
Delilah

It's a relief to smile and laugh around Wilder again. I wasn't sure how weird it'd be to face him, especially after he witnessed Mattie and I stumbling over ourselves and oversharing way too many details.

But if there's one thing he's good at, it's breaking the ice in awkward situations.

Even though I'm excited about this trip and watching Ellie race in the biggest competition of the year, I'm more psyched about getting this time with Wilder. I missed him and hate that I put up this barrier between us. Maybe it was what I needed to realize I'd rather push through my insecurities than risk losing him.

We walk for a few minutes until we find an empty gate and then take a seat in the back by the windows.

"How's volunteerin' and your anger management classes going?" I ask, then take a sip of my iced coffee.

He shifts in his seat until he's facing me, and I do the same. It's not comfortable but it's better than nothing.

"Honestly, it's goin' good. The anger classes have been eye-openin' to say the least. I went in with the mindset that I didn't need to be there because I had my emotions under control, but turns out identifyin' my triggers and understandin' my anger will help me find the right copin' mechanisms before I lash out. As much as I hate to admit it, I like going."

"That's so great, Wilder!" I beam with pride at him giving the classes an actual chance instead of not participating.

"The shelter has been enlightenin', too. I've met a lot of people and heard several of their stories. Tierney's a great mentor. Besides dealin' with an old ass dishwashin' system, it's been a good experience, and I feel good about being there. I wish I had volunteered there long before it was court ordered."

I smile at how genuine he sounds. It's good to see him like this—like he's found a purpose outside of being a rancher. "Sounds like it's been a great fit for you."

He nods.

"So, who's Tierney?" I've never heard that name before and now I'm skeptical because his face lit up when he said her name.

"She manages the staff and volunteers. Very nice. Gives a lot of guidance and resources to those who need it."

"Oh, gotcha." I nod along. "Is she an older woman?"

He flicks that tongue piercing that I swear has a direct-wire to my clit. "Maybe ten years older than me."

"She married?" I clear my throat when he catches me staring at his mouth. "I just mean, it sounds like she has a demandin' job. I wondered if her husband is as supportive of her as she is of other people."

Good save, moron. He saw right through that one.

"I'm not sure. Never asked her."

"Weddin' ring?" I prompt. "You were always a pro at lookin' out for those."

He rubs his hand along his scruffy jaw, one he hasn't shaved in a few days. "You're right. I haven't seen a ring."

"Hm. Well, I'm glad you get to spend your weekends with her. I mean, *there*. At the shelter. Helpin' people."

With an arched brow, his mouth curves into a smirk. "Are you...*jealous*?"

"Me? What? Pfft," I spit out so quickly, even I don't believe myself. "Of course not. Why would...er...should I be?"

"Then why're you so flustered?"

"I-I'm not. I was just curious, that's all."

"Alright, well..." He inches closer. "Just in case that curious mind of yours goes into overdrive, let me finish what I was sayin' earlier..."

Wilder leans in and brushes his lips against mine, slow and soft, but pulls away before I can react. "I've been wantin' to do that for the past several weeks, and I needed to taste you again before we have this conversation."

"Um..." I lick my lips, flustered. "You didn't give me a chance to kiss you back."

"That's because I was stealin' it," he says smugly. "But what I was sayin' before, about how time apart didn't help get over my feelings. I'd rather be friends than nothin' at all. It's never been about hopin' you'd like me back one day, but rather, how good I feel when I'm around you. I like that feelin', and if maybe one day I prove to you that I can be what you need, I'll be here and ready. Until then, I don't want space from you."

The corner of my eyes fill with tears, but I fight them back until I can get out my words. "I don't want space from you either," I confirm, seeing the creases of his eyes stretch with happiness. "But I want to be more than your friend."

He blinks. "Really?"

I suck in my lower lip to keep myself from bursting. "Yeah...I've waited for the day you told me your feelings matched mine, and now, I don't wanna let the fear of what-ifs get in the way of seein' where things go. However..."

He exhales deeply. "I knew there'd be a but."

I laugh, and he does too.

"It's not a but, it's a...stipulation. I want us to go slow. My mind is still playin' mental gymnastics that this is even happenin' and it needs time to catch up. I've not been in a relationship in a long time, and I'm afraid of screwin' this up."

"Darlin', if anyone's gonna screw it up, it's gonna be me." He tilts up my chin, inching closer again. "But I promise to take things slow, whatever you need, okay? There's no need to rush."

"You don't mind?"

"Nope." He presses his lips to my cheek, then lowers his voice in my ear, "In fact, I won't even kiss you on the mouth until you beg for it."

"Wilder!" I playfully push him away. "That's unfair."

"Oh, did you think I was gonna play fair just because you finally admitted you've wanted me all along?" He flicks that fucking tongue piercing that makes me squeeze my thighs. "Because you made me suffer for nine years. It's only *fair* I return the favor."

"Is that how it's gonna be?" I taunt, crossing my arms and straightening my spine. "Because two can play that game. If anyone's gonna beg, it'll be you when I climb on top of you in my new lavender lace lingerie set."

"You brought *lingerie* with you to Vegas?" He arches a suspicious brow, inching closer before he realizes it and then pulls back.

He can thank Mattie for encouraging me to bring it, but I'm not admitting that.

"Mm-hmm. I dare you to try and keep your hands off me. In fact, you'll be the one crawlin' to *me*..."

His gaze falls down my chest, the tip of his tongue peeking out as he examines every inch of my body. Then he noticeably adjusts himself and my eyes shoot down to his groin, remembering the first time I saw his *special* piercings. I had to look it up and was nearly blinded by what I found.

I'm not a prude but it looks painful and not just for him.

"You're doin' a horrible job at convincin' me you won't be the one beggin'," I tell him once I unglue my eyes from his crotch.

"I've restrained myself for years..."

"And so have I," I remind him. "Without random hookups and one-night-stands."

Not sure if that makes me look good or that no one else wanted to have sex with me. But between traveling for the rodeo, training, and doing my job at Lacey's, there wasn't time for dating. A few men were interested that I entertained for half a second but I haven't been serious with anyone since Waylon.

And isn't that a humbling thought.

Wilder tilts my chin, bringing his face half an inch from my lips. "A hundred bucks says you'll still be the first one to crack."

"Since we're goin' to Vegas, let's make it interestin'," I counter, pulling back until his grip loosens.

"Alright, what do you propose?"

"Five hundred dollars *and* the loser has to admit defeat by beggin' for a kiss."

"Oh, darlin'...you'll be beggin' for more than that." He winks, smirking so hard, I think he believes he's actually going to win.

"We'll see about that..."

"So, what're the rules?"

"None...not like you'd follow them anyway," I quip, then

167

take a long sip of my iced coffee to cool the sudden heat in my cheeks.

He feigns innocence with a playful scoff. "I only break the stupid ones."

"You can't afford to break *any* of them. You're lucky your dad and PO allowed you to leave the state as it is."

When I texted Harlow if she knew about Wilder being allowed to come, she told me what Waylon had said. Since this was a pre-planned trip and the ranch is sponsoring Ellie, his probation officer signed off on it—with the provision that he not get into any trouble while he's there.

She also told me that Waylon put me back on babysitting Wilder duty. Not that I mind, but I haven't exactly kept Harlow and Waylon updated, so I just sent back a salute-emoji.

"Trust me, I know. I had to get permission to miss my anger management class tomorrow night and skip my volunteer hours this weekend."

"Alright, so no gettin' shitfaced or punchin' people."

His tongue pokes against his cheek as if he's trying not to laugh. "Don't plan on it."

Once it's time to head back to our gate to catch our second flight, I can't stop smiling. Wilder and I being back to playful banter is enough to put me in a good mood for the rest of the month. Not talking or seeing him is torture. I'd rather go back to him rowdy and pissing me off than no contact at all.

But this time, I'm filled with nerves and butterflies.

Sin With Me

We didn't really label things between us, which is fine since he's been clear about his feelings, but I wish we had more time to talk and actually discuss what this means moving forward.

"Seems you and Wilder had a good chat," Mom says, leaning over toward me.

It only took her ten minutes after our plane took off to bring it up.

"Mm-hmm, we did," I say without giving anything away.

"And? What'd happen?"

"Are you being a gossip, Mama?" I taunt, knowing how much she hates the rumor mills.

"No! I'm sharin' an interest in my daughter's love life. I just wanna know if I'm lookin' at grandbabies in a few years...or like twenty."

"Mama!" I whisper-hiss, playfully scolding her. "You'll get them from Harlow before you get them from me."

"Okay, well then, maybe a weddin'?" she says all-too eagerly. "Nothin' big, just a sweet little outdoor ceremony and reception."

I gape at her like she's lost her mind. "Again, Harlow will beat me to the altar. You'll get your mother-of-the-bride moment with her soon enough."

"Why do you say that? Has Waylon said somethin' to you?"

And just like that, I'm no longer the topic of conversation. *Thank God.*

Over three hours of my mother talking my ear off means I had no time to process what happened during the layover. Encouraging a battle of who will crack first in kissing the other is literally the worst thing I could've agreed to since I was ready to jump him in the middle of the airport.

After we land, I text Mattie that we made it and give her a quick update.

MATTIE

OMG about fucking time!!!

DELILAH

Oh shush! I'm still mentally freaking out a little, but I'm trying not to let it get to me. He agreed to go slow, so that helps.

MATTIE

Slow?? Going slow is for teenagers and senior citizen couples! Put that sexy lingerie set on and rock his world to the moon and back.

DELILAH

Oh my God.

MATTIE

That's what you'll be screaming when he's spanking that ass and smashing it raw. You like it doggy style, don't you? He can hit all the right spots from that angle and with those piercings of his...you'll be squirting all over him.

Jesus fucking Christ.

I pinch the bridge of my nose because now I have that image in my head and beads of sweat form along my hairline at the very thought of that becoming a reality.

It's been a *long* damn time since I've had sex.

DELILAH

Maybe Wilder's right and we're a little bit too close...

MATTIE

To be fair, we're usually drunk when we talk about sex. Or play with toys.

DELILAH

Right, so clearly it's the alcohol's fault.

MATTIE

Exactly!

I snort, then pocket my phone so I can grab my carry-on and deplane.

"Whaddya wanna do first?" Magnolia comes to my side as we walk toward the baggage claim.

"Shower and eat," I quip. "And then find Harlow and Waylon."

"I wanna do the ziplinin' at Fremont Street Experience since I didn't get to last year."

"Over the street?" I confirm and she nods. "That might be above my adventure meter."

"You're a professional trick rider!" Magnolia nudges. "This should be right up your alley."

"It's not as scary as it sounds," Tripp adds.

I haven't told them that I'm not going back to the rodeo next season but don't feel like now is a good time to bring that up, so I just shrug it off.

"Maybe we could try those thrill rides or skyjump at The Strat?" Magnolia offers. "

"Oh, that sounds fun," Mom chimes in, and I look at her like she's grown a second head.

"You wanna jump off a hundred-something-floor building?" I ask, dumbfounded. "Aren't you always tellin' Harlow and me not to die doin' dumb shit?"

She's told us all kinds of horror stories of people coming into the ER after doing risky shit, so I'm shocked as hell she'd be on board for this.

"Well yeah, like...don't street race or jump off a cliff. These are meant to be *safe* thrillin' activities."

"Pretty sure you saw me in the ER twenty times when I

was in high school," Wilder says, walking next to my mom. "Because I did a *lot* of dumb shit."

"Oh, I remember." She laughs. "Pretty sure the nurses had a Bingo card and marked a square everytime you came in for being reckless. Only took a few months for someone to win."

Wilder's jaw drops and we all laugh. "That's because my parents made me go in for every little thing. Concussion, broken rib, leg injury..."

"Yeah, how dare Mom and Dad wanna keep you alive," Tripp deadpans, but I don't think he meant to say it like that because his face falls as soon as the words come out.

My heart jolts as Wilder's expression hardens with shame. He looks away, and I do too.

The conversation dies as we make our way through the airport. I take in all the bright lights and large screens featuring shows and casinos that Vegas has to offer. And I shouldn't be surprised, but I am when I see the rows of slot machines.

It takes almost thirty minutes for everyone to get their luggage. Since we're taking the shuttle to our hotel, we head outside to the pick-up area.

"I need a nap and a plateful of BBQ ribs," Mama says.

I laugh at the specific food she's craving. "I hear they have great buffets here."

"Oh they do," Wilder says, stepping up next to me. "Pretty sure I gained ten pounds before we left last year."

"Me too," Magnolia adds. "Just don't eat before goin' on the rides."

I laugh. "Wasn't plannin' to."

Wilder's hand brushes mine while we continue waiting. Mine are cold from standing outside in this weather, but as soon as he teases my fingers with his, my whole body overheats.

Then he casually leans in and brushes his mouth against my

ear. "I'll be alone in my room in case you wanna forfeit and give into what you really want me to do to you."

"You mean, what *you* wanna do to me," I retort quietly so no one else overhears.

"Potato, *potato*. Either way, you'll be beggin' for it."

Chapter Sixteen
Wilder

Looking out the window over the Vegas strip, I contemplate texting Delilah and asking her to come over. *God, I'm a simp.*

It's only been a couple hours since we made a deal to take things slow, but that quickly turned into a game of who will crack first, and fuck me, I'm ready to crack now.

I want to kiss those luscious lips of hers, suck on her neck, and feel those curves against my palms.

More importantly, I just want to spend time with her. Even if we're sitting and talking. I love being around her no matter what we're doing.

I miss that time when it's all we did, before we met in person, and nothing was off-limits. That hasn't been the focus of our friendship since then but it's what I crave the most.

...and edging her with my tongue until she comes all over my face.

But I promised to go at her pace, so until she's ready for more, I'll restrain myself.

Once we checked into the hotel, Delilah and her mom went to their room, Tripp and Magnolia went to theirs, and then I was left to go to mine alone. The NFR event started already, but everyone was too exhausted from traveling to go tonight.

Instead, we made plans to meet up tomorrow for brunch and then we'll go to the convention center for the NFR Experience—a free fan festival with live music, shopping, and an autograph session with rodeo stars. Magnolia's making us go since she didn't get to last year.

Once she's finished torturing us there, we'll go to the Thomas & Mack Center. The arena is massive, and although it'll be jam-packed, it's a fun experience.

Since I didn't want to eat out, I ordered room service and then took a hot shower. Now I'm bored out of my mind. I should go to bed and catch up on sleep, but I'm too wired. My brain won't shut off and when that happens, I usually find something to distract myself.

Grabbing my boots, I sit on the edge of the bed and slide them on. Then I put on my Stetson hat and grab my room key.

I haven't had a sip of alcohol in almost a month, so maybe a few beers will help relax me enough to pass out.

Except, when I open the door, I'm greeted by the very woman living rent-free in my head.

"Hey..." I blink to clear my vision to make sure she's really standing in front of me. "What're you doin' here? You okay?"

"Yeah, I'm fine." She notices my boots and hat. "You goin' somewhere?"

"I was bored." I shrug. "Was gonna go down to the casino and get a drink, maybe play some slots."

"Oh, okay." She takes a step back. "I don't want to interfere with your plans."

Fuck my plans.

"You wanna come in?" I ask, opening the door wider. "Because I'd much rather spend time with you."

"You would?"

"Yes," I laugh, motioning for her to enter. "I didn't text because I figured you were hangin' out with your mom or too tired to do anythin'."

I wait until she passes me, then close the door and follow her further into the room.

"We got food, showered, and then she went to bed. I tried going to sleep but..." She lifts her shoulders, then turns to face me. "My overactive brain wouldn't let me."

"That's the same issue I was havin'..." I stand in front of her and tilt up her chin until her eyes lock on mine. "What would you like to do?"

Her tongue peeks out and my entire body goes hot.

"We could...um," she mutters, then swallows hard. "Talk?"

I bite my lower lip to hold back my grin. Fuck, she's adorable when she's flustered.

"Sure, we can do that." I release my hold on her, then sit on the bed, and pat the open space next to me.

When she doesn't move, I arch a brow. "Delly?"

She sighs and then stands in between my legs. "I should've said somethin' to you a long time ago."

"About what?" Leaning back on my palms, I watch her expression change and worry what her next words will be.

"Our history. That I was the girl from the crisis hotline. And why I kept quiet."

Oh shit. She wants to have that conversation *now*? And here?

But I nod so she keeps going.

"I felt guilty for catchin' feelings for you while you were goin' through some of your darkest moments. And I felt somewhat silly about it because I only knew you by voice. When Waylon introduced us and I heard you speak, I was so conflicted on how to act. I recognized it right away and was partly in shock. Waylon had told me about some of your cuttin'

176

incidents, so it was easy to put the puzzle pieces together once we met in person."

"So you knew right away, too?" I sit up straighter, wanting to be closer to her.

"I wasn't sure when you figured it out."

"Right away. We talked for six months, sometimes up to five times a week. I heard your voice in my sleep. Every time I contemplated pickin' up a razor, I'd hear you tellin' me to put it down." I shake my head at the memories. "But I knew without a doubt it was you when you said I was saved by the *burden of proof* because you had said those same three words to me on the phone."

"I can't believe you remember that."

I set my hat down next to me and brush my fingers through my hair. "Fuck, I was so pissed he found you before I did. Just my goddamn luck, too. The one and only person I've ever connected with was the one makin' my brother happier than I'd ever seen him."

Her eyes soften and she lowers them, choking back tears.

"I never expected to find you. You gave me a fake name, so you could've been anyone."

Shit, I never realized she figured that out.

"But I was so happy to see how well you were doin'. Or at least, how well you wanted people to think you were doin'. I couldn't believe you were right in front of me, and I couldn't say a damn thing without violatin' the confidentiality agreement."

"Did you have feelings for me while datin' my brother?"

There would've been some crossover from our calls to when she started dating him, and I shouldn't ask, but selfishly want to know.

She winces, still not making eye contact. "Kinda, yeah. I really did like Waylon when we first reunited. He was a great boyfriend and supported me during one of the worst times of my life. But after Harlow's incident and my dad still needin' a lot of help, I couldn't put in the energy for a relationship."

"No one could blame you for needin' to take time away and focus on them. You're good at helpin' people, Delly. Your voice was always so soothin' to hear. It's why I called so much. I knew I sounded pathetic, but I didn't care as long as you picked up the phone."

She finally looks at me. "I was devastated knowin' you'd call in and have to hear I'd never be back. While I was cryin' over Harlow in the ICU, I was also cryin' for you. I worried so much that you'd relapse, and I wouldn't be there for you."

No longer able to keep my hands off her, I grip her hips and pull her onto my lap. She straddles my thighs, wrapping her arms around my neck, and it feels so good to be close to her like this.

It feels safe. Comforting. Like *home*.

"I called once a week askin' for you just in case you returned. Even though they said you weren't, I held onto hope that one day you'd be there and that was enough to keep me from cuttin'. I knew if I got to hear your voice again, I wanted to be able to tell you I didn't relapse. And because of you, I didn't."

Years later, I still haven't, but it's a daily struggle not to give into the pain and darkness when it cripples my mind.

"I wish you would've told me you knew who I was..." she whispers, leaning her forehead against mine, breathing harder than before. "So that I could've told you I knew, too."

"Would that have made a difference? I had the impression you wanted to avoid this conversation."

Her head pops up and she meets my eyes. "I-I dunno. I thought if I pretended there was nothin' between us, I'd eventually move on and wouldn't risk gettin' hurt. You weren't exactly...relationship material."

"That's true..." I nod, reaching up to brush loose strands of blonde hair behind her ear. "But that's because no one compared to you."

She leans into my touch, her eyelids fighting to stay open. "Do you really mean that?"

"A thousand percent. I've never felt that way with anyone else. It was a blessin' and a curse. I held onto that feelin' and chased it for years, hoping it'd come around again. Turns out, it's directly linked to you and only you."

"Wilder..." she breathes out barely above a whisper. "Will you kiss me, please?"

I cup the back of her neck, pushing us together, but stop before our lips can fully touch. "You sure, Delly? Once I kiss you, I won't be able to stop. So I need you to be aware of what you're askin' me."

"I'm sure..." she replies confidently. "*Please*, Wilder. Kiss me."

And that's all I need to hear before crashing our mouths together and sliding my tongue inside. She sucks on my piercing and moans when I tighten my arms around her waist, molding our bodies together.

Her fingers slide up into my hair, and I savor the feel of her mouth and hands on me.

Kissing her again like this, without the confusion of what's happening, makes it even better than the first time. It's never felt like this for me, kissing anyone else, but with Delilah—it's heart-pounding, thrilling, electric.

Intoxicating.

Her soft, tender lips caress mine in a way that has me moaning for more.

When my lips feather down her jaw, she rocks against my

erection, and I growl at how amazing it feels. Her head falls back when I make contact with her neck and suck the sweetness off her skin. My palms squeeze her ass, encouraging her to grind on me harder.

My cock swells and it's almost painful not to release it.

"Delly..." I whisper in her ear and she shivers. "I need to taste your pussy. Take off your clothes and sit on my face."

"*On* your face?" she asks when I brush my lips against hers.

"Mm-hmm. I've been dreamin' of it for far too long."

"I've never experienced that with a tongue piercin'..." she says, then hesitates. "Does it hurt?"

I smirk, sliding my palms underneath her shirt because I need to feel her bare skin, which is hot to the touch.

"Oh you're gonna love it, baby. Let me show you."

She climbs off my lap and keeps her gaze on mine while she removes her jeans and panties. I'm in disbelief that this is actually happening, but I can't move too fast. I told her we could take things slow, and I intend to keep that promise...after I make her come on my tongue.

Sliding up the bed, I lie back and then motion for her to climb up.

"All the way up, darlin'. Put that sweet cunt in my face," I demand when she hesitates where to go, then maneuvers herself up my body.

"This angle seems like it'd be unflatterin'..." She looks down at me.

"Not from where I'll be." I chuckle, waggling my brows.

Wrapping my hands around her thighs, I hoist her up even more until my tongue sticks out and I steal a taste. "Perfect. Now sit."

When she doesn't go low enough, I pull her down further. She squeals, quickly grabbing onto the headboard. She tries to lift, but I squeeze my fingers tighter and keep her right where I want her.

My tongue lashes at her clit, the piercing rubbing against her in a way she's never felt before, and by her squirming and moaning, she's enjoying it.

"Oh, God...that feels—" She releases another moan and the sound makes my dick harder.

Don't come in my pants. Don't come in my pants.

Sliding through her slit, I pierce her opening with tongue and devour her.

"Wilder, holy—" She gasps, her legs shaking next to my head. "Yes, right there."

She rides my tongue, panting and moaning through waves of pleasure. I switch between licking and sucking, and tease her clit until she screams through her release.

Groaning through my own, the vibrations against her pussy set her off again and soon she's screaming through it with my name on her lips.

Her sweet juices make a mess on my chin and mouth, but I love it.

"Fuck, that was..." She falls on the bed next to me, trying to catch her breath. "My brain forgot words."

Leaning up on my elbow, I roll toward her and cup her face.

"Hearin' you scream my name is a dream come true. You have no idea how long I've wanted to do that."

Bringing my mouth to hers, I sink my tongue between her lips and give her a taste.

"So fuckin' good," I murmur, threading my fingers through her hair and tightening my fist through the strands. Even though I want to bring her so much more pleasure, I hold back. "Christ, Delly. That was so worth the wait."

She sits up, then lowers her hand to my belt buckle. "Let me return the favor, cowboy."

Before she can unzip my jeans, I stop her. "Um...you don't need to do that. We're supposed to be goin' slow, remember?"

"You call what you just did to me *goin' slow*?"

"That was just a preview. I'm respectin' your wishes by not movin' too fast. Otherwise, I'd be nine-inches deep inside you by now."

"Jesus, Wilder!" She laughs, playfully shoving my chest. "What's the difference if we already did oral? You don't want me to go down on you? I've already seen *all* of you, if that's what you're concerned about."

"Uh, no..." I smirk, thinking about when she'll get to experience my *other* piercings. "But I may have gotten a little too excited while eatin' you out and hearin' you moan my name."

Her eyes widen and she sucks in her lips. "Oh."

"Don't laugh!" I poke her side and she nearly flies off the bed when I try tickling her.

"Didn't realize you had a *speedy* arrival time..." she muses, and I quickly roll on top of her.

Pushing her arms above her head, I pin her down with my hips and she wraps her thighs around mine. "I don't, but you have no idea how hot it is to tongue-fuck that sweet little cunt of yours. Add in all that squirmin' and moanin' you did and I couldn't help it."

Burying my face in her neck, I suck on the flesh underneath her ear, then slowly whisper, "And when I get the pleasure of being inside you, I'll make no apologies for how many times I make you come. Because I plan to edge you over and over until I can't hold back anymore. After I've thoroughly touched every inch of you, left my marks on your skin, and your throat is raw from screamin' will I let myself go."

Sin With Me

By the time I finish speaking, she's panting in my ear and lifting her hips into my groin.

I press my lips to her cheek. "But we're not doin' that tonight."

"Oh my God, you suck." She groans, throwing her head back.

I lift off her, grinning. "And you owe me five hundred bucks for being the first to crack."

Chapter Seventeen
Delilah

I wake up with the dumbest smile on my face.

After I got dressed and Wilder took a quick shower, we cuddled in bed and talked some more. We agreed to keep this between us for now, without the pressure from everyone else, and see where it goes before announcing it.

Well, besides Noah who noticed the hickey he gave me last month.

I'm still in disbelief that this is happening. For years, I've compartmentalized my feelings about him. The Wilder I met from the crisis hotline and the Wilder I knew in person. I didn't want to give away that I was aware of our history and that it had affected me. Not only did it feel wrong because he was my ex's twin brother but Wilder didn't date. He had flings and one-night-stands, and I wasn't stupid enough to think I'd be any different if we drunkenly hooked up.

So I kept my distance as much as I could until Waylon asked me to watch him.

That's when my walls started to crumble, and I knew my

feelings weren't just about the person he was nine years ago, but rather, how I felt being around him.

It's a risk, giving into these feelings, but if I've learned anything from what I've gone through, life's too short not to take it. And even though a part of me is cautioning I guard my heart, I'm following my gut that tells me to give it a chance.

"Mornin', sweetheart. How'd you sleep?" Mom asks when she exits the bathroom, dressed and ready to go down for brunch.

"Great!" I say a bit too eager, sitting at the desk and working on my makeup.

But it's true. After the most mind-blowing orgasms I've ever experienced, I slept like a baby.

When I woke up, I could still feel his tongue between my legs, and immediately wished I could climb back into his bed.

"How about you?" I ask.

"Pretty good. I was so exhausted, I nearly slept through my alarm."

"Six am was a bit early, Mama," I tease, but considering I didn't get into bed until two, hearing her alarm go off startled me awake. Luckily I was able to fall back asleep for a few more hours.

"That's what I'm used to. Any later and my whole day feels off."

I chuckle, then finish getting ready.

When my phone vibrates on the nightstand, Mom asks if I want it.

"Sure."

Before handing it over, she peeks at the screen and then raises her brows.

"What?" I ask, confused, and then I read what she saw.

WILDER

> Morning, beautiful. I loved falling asleep with the taste of you on my tongue. Might need a refresher later before it wears off completely.

"Oh my God." Squeezing my eyes closed, I smack my phone against my forehead. "That's...not what it sounds like."

"Mm-hmm," she sing-songs. "Then why're you blushin'?"

"Mama!" I squeal, meeting her eyes in the mirror in front of me. "Fine. But you're the one who told me to give him a chance."

"Glad to see you listened to me for once."

"We're not announcin' it yet. So—"

She zips her lips. "Don't worry. I'm not the gossip in the family."

We both laugh, knowing it's Harlow.

DELILAH

> My mom saw your message! So thanks for that...

WILDER

> Oops. Good thing she already loves me.

DELILAH

> Mm-hmm.

WILDER

> Are you going down for brunch?

DELILAH

> Yeah, we're about to leave now.

WILDER

> Okay, I'll go with you. Meet me in the hallway.

DELILAH

> Be right there.

Sin With Me

"Mom, we gotta go."

I slide on my purple cowboy boots that go with my outfit—a teal vintage boho long sleeve V neck with a purple belt around the waist. Magnolia said I had to *fit in* at the NFR and picked it out for me at Rodeo Belle, the store Harlow works at, and even made me pick out a new cowboy hat.

"Oh, sweetie. You look adorable."

I sigh, standing in front of the mirror. "Just what every woman in her thirties wants to hear."

Grabbing my bag, we walk to the door. When I open it, Wilder's leaning against the wall across from me with his arms crossed—looking all kinds of sexy in his tight Wranglers and boots.

He pushes off and drops his arms, lowering his gaze down my body. Licking his lips, he smirks when he meets my eyes.

"You..." He notices my mom next to me. "Both of you...look gorgeous."

"You're very handsome, Wilder," my mom says, then glances at me. "As always."

I roll my eyes at her being so obvious.

"Ready?" Wilder grins, holding out his arm for her, clearly enjoying her approval.

"Suck up," I mutter behind him.

We take the elevator down and find Tripp, Magnolia, Harlow, and Waylon already at the restaurant waiting for us. Moments later, Noah and Fisher join us.

"Landen and Ellie leave already?" I ask after we return from the buffet with full plates.

"Ellie had to be at the convention center by nine-thirty," Noah tells me. "By the time she gets home from the rodeo and back up to get ready for the day, she barely sleeps."

"She loves it though," Magnolia adds. "She's a champion."

I smile. "Can't wait to watch her tonight."

As we continue eating and talking, Wilder lowers his hand on my leg underneath the table and squeezes my knee. I try covering my face with my hand so no one notices the smile and blush consuming my face.

When everyone's distracted by their own conversations, he leans into my ear. "Excuse yourself to the bathroom in thirty seconds and meet me over there."

Before I can tell him no, he pushes his seat back and stands. "Nature calls. Be right back."

Noah watches him leave, and I know she's going to be suspicious if I follow.

Instead, I wait five minutes before excusing myself.

It's loud and chaotic, people are everywhere, and it's not even noon. I've not experienced anything like this before but it's somewhat comforting that so many are here for the NFR. I can tell because they're all dressed like me.

Wilder didn't bother telling me which bathroom to go into, so I don't know where I'm going.

Before I have to make a decision, I'm being pulled into a family single stall room.

"Wilder!" I whisper-hiss, recognizing his cologne.

He presses my back against his chest and quickly covers my mouth with his palm.

"I said thirty seconds," he murmurs in my ear, then drops his hand.

"That would've been too suspicious. Even now, they're going to wonder what's takin' you so long."

"I'll just tell them the food didn't agree with me."

I snort. "Gross."

He spins me around and crashes our mouths together before I have a moment to breathe.

"I couldn't wait to kiss you again," he says in between

sliding his tongue against mine. "Especially after I saw you in this dress that displays your tits like a piece of art."

"As sweet as that is...we're in a *bathroom*," I remind him. "Not sure this is the place we should be makin' out."

"I'll take what I can get." He walks me back into the door and then sucks on my neck. "Fuck, I want to mark you so all the horny men 'round here don't get any ideas."

"Horny men like you?" I quip, clinging to his biceps so I don't fall.

"Exactly. The worst kind..." He slides his tongue over my exposed collarbone, causing me to shiver at how turned on I am.

"We should get back before they notice," I tell him. "And before you give me another hickey!"

Pushing him away, I lower my gaze to his groin where his tight Wranglers are doing him no justice at hiding his erection.

"Don't come in your jeans again or you'll have to change," I tease, but it turns me on even more thinking about how aroused he got eating me out last night.

His palms flatten on the door beside my head, caging me in with his arms. Then he tips up my chin until our eyes meet. "You're the one who's gonna need new panties by the time I'm done with you..."

"Wha—"

He slides his hand underneath my dress and slips his fingers beneath my lace underwear. "And we're not leavin' here until you make a mess."

"We're gonna get caught," I whisper, but when he slides a digit inside, I lose the willpower to fight him.

"Then you better hurry up and come." He adds another, then curls them in deeper.

"Wilder," I breathe out, squeezing my eyes as I enjoy the intrusion.

"That's it, Delly. Fuck my fingers."

My hips rock against him, nails digging deeper into his arms as I ride his hand.

"You're so wet..." He presses his lips to my ear. "Come for me, baby. I want to suck your juices off my fingers and taste you again."

Warmth builds down my spine when he rubs the pad of his thumb over my clit and soon I'm losing myself in the pleasure. Not wanting to make a lot of noise, I clamp my hand over my mouth and moan through my release.

"*Fuuuck*," he groans in my neck.

I swallow hard, then try to catch my breath. There's no way his family won't know we were hooking up after being gone this long.

"We have to go back," I tell him, opening my eyes to meet his.

Wilder thrusts his fingers between his lips and slowly licks them clean, his piercing making an appearance as he does it. The way he moans, as if he can't get enough of the taste, has my pussy clenching all over again.

"You've turned me into an addict. One taste is all it took to get hooked. Now I'll be cravin' a fix every day." He winks, then flicks his tongue between the two digits and slides around them in a provocative way that isn't helping my need for him. "Just wait until I eat you from behind and taste *all* of you..."

"You have a dirty mouth," I whisper, still worried people are going to hear me.

He crashes his mouth to mine for a quick kiss. "You have no idea the *dirty* things I wanna do to you. Next time my face is between your thighs, I want them wrapped around my head while you're wearin' those boots—and only those boots."

His gaze falls to them and a devious smirk spreads over his handsome face.

And if I don't get out of here, I'll let him do all of those things to me right now.

"I'm leavin'," I whisper, shoving him. "Wait a minute and then come back to the table."

I take a quick look in the mirror and frown when I see how red my neck and chest are from his facial hair scratching the shit out of me. I comb my fingers through the ends of my hair, adjust my dress, and then unlock the door.

"Don't wait too long," I tell him, then peek out. Luckily, no one's waiting to use this room.

My heart pounds when I pull out my chair and rejoin the group.

Harlow meets my gaze and mouths, "You okay?"

"Yeah, long lines," I reply, waving her off.

Mom smiles at me, but it's one of those secret knowing smiles that only a mother can do. Like she knows exactly what took me so long.

Fucking great.

When I see Wilder out of my peripheral vision, I grab my glass and take a sip to hide the blush covering my cheeks. After what we just did, it's hard not to be hot and bothered at the sight of him.

Which is honestly ridiculous at my age, but I can't help it.

"I thought you got lost or died in the bathroom," Noah blurts when Wilder takes his seat next to me.

"Nah, just my IBS actin' up." He pats his stomach, and I choke on my water, spewing some down my chin.

"You okay?" Wilder asks, handing me a napkin.

"Mm-hmm, thanks." I take it from him and clean my face.

"If everyone's done, let's go!" Magnolia claps, overly eager for the festival.

It's only a mile away, so we decide to walk, and the closer we get, the larger the crowd gets. Wilder stays next to me, our fingers brushing while we make our way there—a constant reminder of where he was less than twenty minutes ago.

The convention center is massive with people coming and going in every direction. It's quite overwhelming, even for someone like me who travels to rodeos all summer long, but I've never been to something like this.

Which means the events tonight will be even more overstimulating.

"Wanna go find Ellie first?" Magnolia asks everyone. "She should be signin' autographs and takin' pictures."

Since she won the championship last year, she's at the barrel racing booth with other rodeo stars.

"Yes! I wanna get a picture with Tommy Graham," Harlow says, and the stars in her eyes make me laugh.

"Since when do you know about famous bull riders?" Waylon crosses his arms.

"Since it's all Antonio talks about. I told him I'd get an autograph for him," she explains, but by Waylon's expression, he's not convinced.

It takes over an hour to get to Ellie's booth since we stop at random vendors, lots of western clothing, cowboy boots, hats, buckles, and more. By the time we get through her line, it's another thirty minutes.

"Oh my God, hi!" Ellie squeals when she sees all of us.

She makes the rounds of giving everyone hugs and then has Landen take pictures.

"Y'all havin' fun so far?" he asks, nudging Wilder. "Surprised you're here."

"Why wouldn't I be?" he asks, sounding offended.

"No reason. Just doesn't seem like your thing."

"Hot fresh meat is definitely Wilder's thing," Waylon chimes in, apparently clueless to Wilder not leaving my side since we've arrived.

"Not really," Wilder snaps with no amusement on his face. I feel bad that his brothers will always see him as that person instead of the man he's become this past year. He's been working hard in therapy and getting his head on straight, despite the trouble he got in with Wesley.

"Well, not anymore..." Tripp adds, smacking his shoulder.

Landen shrugs. "Oh, alright."

"Where's Tommy?" Harlow asks, breaking the tension.

"You wanna meet him?" Ellie asks, her eyes widening with mischief. "He's even cuter in person."

"Excuse me?" Landen quickly asks.

"What? He is." Ellie gives no fucks, which is why I find her so hilarious. She spent four years hating Landen before they started dating, and even after getting married, still doesn't take his shit.

Landen pouts when Ellie grabs Harlow's hand and leads her over to another booth.

"Looks like you two lost your women," Wilder muses. "To a bull rider."

"Well...can you blame them?" Noah snickers, patting Fisher's chest who stands like a statue next to her. "Bull riders *are* pretty sexy."

Her husband's a retired bull rider, so of course she'd think that.

"And cocky motherfuckers." Fisher smirks, and I think that's the most I've heard him speak since we got here.

"Great," Landen and Waylon both mutter, then follow their girls.

Wilder takes the opportunity to lean into my ear since no one's paying attention. "After the rodeo and whatever else they drag us to, you're mine tonight. Got it?"

I fight the urge to smile. "We'll see about that, cowboy. Until then, behave yourself."

Chapter Eighteen
Wilder

"My feet are killin' me," Delilah complains when we leave the arena. "These boots were, in fact, not made for walkin'."

After three hours at the convention center, half of the group went back to the hotel to freshen up and change while the rest of us continued to explore Vegas. Delilah, her mom, and me stayed with Noah and Fisher, so we've been on our feet all damn day.

We ended up at a rooftop bar where I had my first beer in a month. Normally, I'd let myself indulge and have a few, but I wanted to stay alert and aware since we were surrounded by strangers in unfamiliar territory.

Delilah ordered Long Island Iced Tea's for her and her mom. But I'm certain she didn't realize how much alcohol they have because Mrs. Fanning was tipsy after her first one.

We were supposed to meet everyone at the hotel and go to the rodeo together, but the girls wanted to sober up beforehand and then ordered a variety of appetizers to soak up the alcohol.

Sin With Me

When the final event of the evening wrapped up, we booked ass out of there. Ellie did amazing, per usual, and came in second. But after nearly three hours of the girls screaming in my ear, I was more than ready to leave.

There are a bunch of NFR after parties happening on The Strip, but Mrs. Fanning is ready to tap out, so I offered to tag along with Delilah to take her back to the hotel while everyone else goes out.

"Want me to carry you?" I offer.

"Are you serious?"

I stand in front of her, then motion for her to get on my back.

She hesitates for a moment before finally doing it. I pull her up higher, then wrap my hands around her thighs to keep her in place.

"You're gonna pull a muscle with me up here." She wraps her arms around my neck, hanging on tight.

I turn my face toward her so she can hear me better. "Darlin', I lift shit twice as heavy as you for a livin', so stop doubtin' me."

"I wasn't, but I'm not exactly petite, either."

Mrs. Fanning nudges me. "She worries for nothin'. Her body is perfect."

I grin, looking at her. "That's what I've been sayin' for years."

Delilah snorts, squeezing her thighs around my waist tighter.

"It's usually you carryin' my drunk ass out," I tease, enjoying the way it feels to have her this close to me even if it's not sexual.

"I'm not *that* drunk..."

Halfway through the rodeo, we went to the concessions and

195

got a couple more drinks. That time she stuck to beer, but Delilah rarely has alcohol, so when she does, she's a lightweight.

Hence the night of too many margaritas with Mattie and Jonah.

It takes a bit longer to get to the hotel since the sidewalks are packed. But once we arrive, I set Delilah down before we get into the elevator.

"Are you kids gonna go out?" Mrs. Fanning asks as we make our way up to our floor.

Delilah glances at me before responding, "Yeah, probably. I'm gonna freshen up and change first. But I'm sure we'll find somethin' to do."

"I think Fisher and Landen were gonna hit up the casino downstairs. We could swing by them for a bit. I think the girls were gonna go to the bar while they waited."

"I heard someone talkin' about a strip club," Delilah blurts. "But it was for the ladies' if ya know what I mean."

"Ooh, like the Chippendales..." Mrs. Fanning smirks, and I chuckle at her suggestive tone.

"There's a great show called Thunder From Down Under," someone behind us chimes in, and we turn around. "Australian male dancers."

"Hmm...I vote for that one," Delilah quips.

Once we finally get to our floor, Mrs. Fanning and Delilah go to their room, and I go to mine.

Since we're heading out again, I decide to take a quick shower to rinse off the day. Time doesn't seem to exist in Vegas, especially with how bright-lit everything is and how many people walk around all night long.

A year ago, I would've indulged in the nightlife a lot more than I am now, and when I went last year, I definitely partied like I had nothing to lose.

But now I've learned I don't need to do that in order to have a good time or enjoy the company I'm with, especially when that company is Delilah.

And this time, I have *a lot* more to lose if I fuck up.

Grabbing a towel, I step out of the shower and dry off. The showers here are the best I've ever experienced, and I almost didn't want to get out. But I know Delilah will be ready soon.

Speaking of...

A knock at the door tells me she's here now.

I wrap the towel around my waist and then rush out of the bathroom to grab the door.

"Hey," I say, stepping back so she can enter.

She changed into another gorgeous dress, but this one's darker and more flowy.

"You look beautiful in this." I pluck the material between my fingers.

Ignoring me, she stares at my bare chest and then lowers her gaze to the towel resting on my hips. "You showered?"

"Yeah, I figured I had time," I tell her as the door closes behind her, bringing us closer. "It'll just take me a few minutes to get dressed. Did you decide where you wanna go?"

I walk toward my suitcase, but then her fingers wrap around my wrist and she yanks me toward her. "Actually..." Her other hand releases the knot on my towel and it falls to my feet. "I was thinkin' it was my turn to taste you."

Blinking in disbelief, I swallow hard. *"Now?"*

"Unless you'd rather I drag you to Magic Mike Live and let them give me a show instead." She bites down on her lower lip, looking up at me through her lashes.

If that's her version of trying to seduce me, it's working.

"Uh, definitely not." I tilt up her chin, stealing a kiss. "But you don't have to if—"

"Wilder, please...shut up for once." She wraps her palm

around my half-erect shaft, and I smirk at how adorable she sounds taking charge.

When she looks down at her hand and furrows her brows at my piercings, I know she's curious about them. I jerk my cock and she lets go as if a snake bit her.

"Oh my God." She scowls at me when I chuckle.

Wrapping my palm around myself, I give it a few tugs. "Am I allowed to talk now?"

She rolls her eyes at my smart-ass comment. "What's that kind of piercin' called?"

I hold up the tip to show her better. "A magic cross. Two barbells cross each other through the head. That's why there's four balls stickin' out."

"Jesus, that looks painful." She winces.

I put her hand back on me, then cover it with mine to show her what to do.

"It's not. You're not gonna hurt me, and dare I say, you're gonna enjoy it too."

She shifts her bashful gaze up to mine. "Tell me what you like."

It feels like I'm swallowing shards of glass because while I'm usually over-confident when it comes to sex, it's different with Delilah. I know it's been a while for her, but it has for me too.

"Get on your knees and open your mouth," I tell her.

She obeys, and once she's comfortable, I tighten my grip and pump myself.

"Stick out your tongue, Delly."

As soon as she does, I smack the tip on it a few times before sliding deeper.

Grabbing a fistful of her hair, I bring her face closer. "Good girl. Now suck..."

Sin With Me

She seals her lips around my cock, hollows her cheeks, and glides her tongue around my length. It's pure bliss.

"Fuck, that's it. Take as much of me as you can." My heart pounds at how fucking good it feels to have her mouth on me. Never in a million years did I think this would happen, and now that it is, I still can't believe it.

It doesn't take long for her to find a rhythm. Her mouth pops off and she strokes a few times before sliding her tongue underneath all the way back up to my piercings and enveloping them again.

"That's so good, baby. *Fuck* —" I'm at a loss for words because all I want to do is lift her up and devour that mouth.

She moans in between the delicious torture of her hand and mouth, swallowing me down and teasing me with her tongue. Her firm grip on my shaft while she plays with my piercings has me fighting back my release.

"Delly, I'm close...you might wanna —"

She frantically shakes her head, keeping her eyes locked on mine and digging her fingers into the backs of my thighs.

I can't keep my eyes off how stunning she looks stuffed with my cock and her lips swollen around the head of my cock. Every inch of my body shivers as my legs tense in anticipation.

Her loud sucking noises are my undoing, and I groan through the intensity of the climax. Delilah swallows me down like she can't get enough.

"Jesus Christ, you sucked me dry." I inhale sharply, trying to catch my breath.

"Guess that means I still got it," she quips, wiping her chin.

I chuckle, offering her my hand and helping her up.

Tilting her chin, I brush my lips against hers. "Your mouth on me will always feel amazin'. But *that* was fuckin' hot. Especially since I wasn't expectin' it."

"That seems to be the story of us, huh?" She grins. "Speaking of..."

Stepping back, she grabs the hem of her dress and yanks it over her head, revealing the lavender lingerie set she told me about earlier.

"Um..." I swallow my tongue, unable to form words as my eyes rake down her perfect body. A lacy corset top cups her breasts and a thong peeks beneath a garter set that sits over her curvy hips. "Fuck me. That's sexy as hell on you."

Without a second thought, I lift her up, and move us across the room. Then I push her up against the large floor to ceiling window and hold her up with my body when her thighs hug my waist.

"You bring that little vibratin' butt plug with you, too?" I taunt, cupping her ass.

"No, I lost the remote, remember?" She laughs and it makes me laugh too just thinking about Mattie oversharing while they were drunk.

"But I wouldn't mind gettin' a new one..." Her teeth drag across her bottom lip, and I swear my cock jumps at the thought of touching her back there.

"Someday soon," I promise.

If there was a cure for depression that didn't include talking about my feelings or taking medication, this would be it. This kind of heart racing, sweat-inducing, serotonin-boost is all I'd need for the rest of my life as long as it came in the form of being with Delilah.

When she yanks my mouth down to hers, I taste myself on her, and it makes me hard all over again. I grab her hand from around my neck and flatten it against the window above her head, pushing my erection against her stomach.

"I wanna tear this pretty little thing off you and fuck you against this window," I murmur when she pushes her hips into me. "But I promised to take things slow with you, so I'm not gonna do that."

"Wilder," she whines, and I kiss down her neck. "Fuck what I said."

Chuckling against her heated skin, I shake my head. "I didn't bring condoms, but even if I had one, it'd still be a bad idea to rush. I don't wanna screw this up."

"Are you sure I can't change your mind?" She lowers her free hand between us and grabs my cock, then rubs it over the lacy fabric barely concealing her pussy. "Because I can't stop thinkin' about how those piercings are gonna feel inside me."

She's literally trying to kill me.

"Delly..." I thrust into her grip, feeling her sweet juices rub over me. "You're testin' my willpower."

She pushes the fabric of her panties over just enough to tease the tip and piercings between her wet slit. "How 'bout now?"

"And here I thought I was the one corruptin' you." I rest my forehead on hers, fighting with my desire to say fuck it. "But unless you want me to fill this tight cunt with my cum and knock you up, you better not tempt me."

Before she can argue, I wrap my arms around her and toss her on the bed, then kneel between her thighs. Spreading them wide, I pull her panties to the side and feast on her like it's my last day on Earth.

Within minutes, she's arching her back and screaming my name, the taste of her arousal bursting on my tongue.

"Next time I wear this, you better have a condom," she says between catching her breath and leaning up on her elbows. "Or I'm using my vibrator."

"Oh, we'll definitely be using your vibrator..." I smirk, pressing a kiss to the inside of her thigh. "Just not tonight."

She falls back on a whimper, and I laugh at her dramatics.

"C'mon, time to get ready. Strip clubs and Long Island Ice Teas are waitin' for us."

And if I don't get us out of this room in the next ten minutes, I'll do exactly what I told her I wouldn't do and fuck her until my cum spills out of her.

Chapter Nineteen

Delilah

My legs feel like jelly, and not because of the two earth-shattering orgasms Wilder gave me earlier, but because I've never walked this much in cowboy boots before. My thighs are burning, nearly begging me to sit this one out, but I don't want to.

I want as much time with Wilder as I can get before we go back to the real world and things get messy again.

Between Jonah and Wesley's conflict with Raven in the middle and Molly's articles causing trouble, there's no telling what'll happen once we're home. Jonah texted a couple times, and as far as I know, nothing out of the ordinary has happened. Raven's still safe in the women's shelter and Wesley continues to be on mandatory leave.

Wilder and I ended up at some strip club, not the fun Magic Mike kind, but one that's crowded with half-naked gorgeous women and lots of alcohol. It's hard to see them flirting with him and even though he doesn't flirt back, it reminds me of the years he would without a second thought. He has a lot more sexual experience than I do, and I know it was all before we became more than friends, but it's hard not to compare myself to them.

I've been called pretty all my life. When guys hit on me at the bar, it's always *you're so beautiful* as they stare at my tits. And yeah sometimes that's a nice ego boost, but I'd rather be known as smart, talented, or hardworking. I'm more than my body and even more than my brains. It's a breath of fresh air when someone recognizes that and knows you better than you realize —something I've noticed Wilder does at the most unexpected times.

I'm also loyal to a fault. I give second, third, and sometimes fourth chances. I apologize even when I'm not in the wrong because keeping the peace is safer than starting a war.

I should probably talk to my therapist about that one.

But more than any of that, I'll always help someone in need, even when that person is a stranger throwing up on my shoes.

"Oh shit, I'm so sorry..." a girl I met in the bathroom line five minutes ago says. I could tell she wasn't going to make it much longer, so I grabbed her hand and cut in front of everyone else just in time for her to vomit in the trash can.

"It's okay. They're washable." I grab a few paper towels and get them wet before handing them to her.

"I don't usually drink this much, but my fiancé left me at the altar last weekend, so I took my bridesmaids on our honeymoon." She wipes her mouth and chin.

"Oh my God. I'm sorry to hear that. Sounds like you dodged a bullet if he couldn't even tell you before the ceremony." I grab more paper towels to clean off my ankle boots.

"That's what everyone keeps sayin' but he was the love of my life—or so I thought. I gave him seven years of my youth!"

My eyes widen as the plot thickens. "Seven years, huh? How long did it take for him to propose?"

"Five! But then we needed to save money and time to plan everything. Bastard had two years to tell me he changed his mind!" She washes her hands and then gargles her mouth with water. "That's what angers me the most. He wasted so much of my time and all the money we invested was *mine*! Pretty sure he was having an affair with his stepsister."

"His *what*?" Ain't no way this isn't the plot of some Lifetime movie. I'm trying to keep up with the storyline and then she hits me with *that*? "What makes you think that?"

She follows me out of the bathroom, and I apologize to everyone for cutting. I walk to the end of the line since I still need to pee, but I didn't want to butt in front of anyone.

"My little sister swears she saw them hugging a little too closely, if ya know what I mean..." She crosses her arms, waiting with me. "And they kiss on the mouth when they say goodbye. That's weird, right?"

I shrug, not sure what to think. "I'm from the South, so being overly friendly is normal where I'm from. But I'd never kiss my adult stepbrother on the mouth, especially if they were engaged."

"That's what I'm saying! It's suspicious at the very least. Anyway...my sister suggested we go on a girl's trip to Vegas, and well, here I am. Drinking my sorrows and apparently throwing up on complete strangers."

"I'm here with my sister, too. Well, she's not here but she's datin' my ex-boyfriend. So that's been...interestin'."

Her mouth falls open, and I laugh at her reaction. "Nah, it's not as weird as it sounds. We broke up years ago. But anyway, I came with a bunch of other people for the NFR. We decided to go out and explore since we're only here a few nights. My, uh...friend, came with me here while the rest went to the after parties."

"You mean that sexy-looking cowboy who couldn't keep his

hands and eyes off you? I saw you two earlier. You're telling me he's a *friend*?" She pins me with a disbelief stare.

I chuckle and step closer toward the stalls. "Okay yeah, we're datin'. But it's new and we haven't told anyone."

After all this time, calling it *dating* feels weird.

"Well, good luck. I hope it works out better than mine did."

"You're gonna find someone who'll treat you so well, you're gonna be grateful your engagement ended. Even if it's not right away or it ends up being the last person you expected, I have a really good feelin' about you."

"I think that's the sweetest thing anyone's ever said to me." She smiles appreciatively, and I notice the color coming back in her cheeks.

Even though the bathroom is loud and chaotic, it was nice meeting a stranger who I could make feel better, even if temporary.

Once I finish in the bathroom and wash my hands, I make my way back to the table where Wilder's sitting. He has another Long Island Iced Tea waiting for me and two shot glasses.

"What're these?" I ask, deciding to sit on his lap.

He wraps his arm around my waist and pulls me closer to his chest. "Tequila...thought we could play a little drinkin' game."

"You tryin' to get us wasted?" I grab my iced tea and take a sip, already well on my way there. If you told me these didn't have alcohol in them, I'd believe you, but considering I feel light as a feather, I know there has to be. "What's the game?"

"We take a shot everytime someone comes over and asks if my *wife* would like another. I've already been asked twice."

"Why would they assume I'm your wife?"

"Beats me, but two separate cocktail waitresses have asked while you were in the bathroom."

I snort, inhaling more of my sweet beverage. "Are you sure they weren't sayin' that so they could find out if you're single or not? They say *wife* and then wait for you to correct them so they know if you're available."

He brings his mouth to my ear. "Is it bad that I didn't wanna correct them?"

The vibration of his words against my earlobe make me shiver. "I think you've had too much to drink."

"Nah, I liked them assumin' I was your husband. Made me feel worthy of you."

"You already are," I reassure him, bringing my other hand up to his cheek. "Never thought otherwise."

He turns and kisses my palm. "Maybe one day I'll feel that way."

I grab one of the shots and shoot it down.

"You take the other one..." I hold it up for him, but instead of grabbing it, he opens his mouth and tilts his head back slightly.

Wilder holds my gaze intently while I pour it between his lips and then watch him swallow.

"Thanks, wifey."

I shoot him with a death glare. "Stop that."

"Why? It sounds good on you. Get you knocked up and then you'll be the sexiest MILF I've ever laid eyes on."

Laughing, I shake my head. "Now I know you're a goner."

"For you."

I roll my eyes at his corny one-liner. "I just met a girl in the bathroom who got dumped by her fiancé — of seven years — at the altar, so if that wasn't a sign, I dunno what is."

"A sign for what?"

"That marriage is a bad idea."

"No, he's just a coward, especially for makin' her wait so long. It took me seven seconds to realize I was into you."

I snort because he cannot be serious. "That's unrealistic."

"Nope. The moment I saw you and heard your voice, not only did I recognize you from the crisis hotline, but meetin' you also validated my feelings. You were the first person I met who knew about my past and still didn't treat me any differently. Waylon told you I was a mess—or somethin' along those lines—and still, you didn't smile at me with pity. You looked at me like I was just a person who needed someone to understand their pain."

My heart swells at his thoughtful words. After knowing him all these years, I've never heard such sweet things come out of his mouth until we became more than friends.

And I'm not gonna lie, I'm enjoying it—*a lot.*

Who knew Wilder had this tender side to him? He's always been so focused on pretending everything was fine when it wasn't that he never allowed himself to be okay when things were.

Cupping his cheek, I softly brush my lips against his—ones I still can't believe I get to kiss. "And in case you didn't know or need to hear it again, I'm proud of how far you've come. Especially durin' that time when it was really bad. Not everyone makes it out of the darkness and you fight like hell every day to stay out of it."

He rubs his nose against mine and it makes me laugh. "I don't think anyone's ever said somethin' so heartfelt to me. Thank you."

"You're welcome," I say as a woman approaches our table.

"Howdy." She smiles wide at Wilder's cowboy hat. "Would you or your wife like a dance?"

Wilder stares at me, his grin meeting his eyes. "No, thank you. But we'll take two more Tequila shots."

Before we left the arena, Waylon double checked with me that I was good to keep an eye on Wilder tonight. Not wanting to give anything away, I reassured him it was fine, but that he still owed me from New Year's Eve when he asked me to watch him.

I fear I might have overpromised my ability to keep an eye on his brother because after the strip club, we found a cowboy-themed bar with a mechanical bull, and Wilder's determined to make it the full eight seconds without falling off.

After each ride, successful or not, you get a free shot and Wilder's currently on his fifth attempt. Each time he got one, he bought me one too.

"Okay, this is the one. I can feel it!" he shouts over the music, holding me close to his side.

I shake my head and immediately regret it. It's already throbbing. "It better be because I can't drink anymore and neither should you."

"What, why? I'm sober as a goat."

"Huh?" When I stand on my tiptoes to hear him better, I stumble over my boots, and Wilder quickly catches me. "That doesn't even make sense."

"Sure it does! Because goats are always sober."

My brows furrow deeper and now I know I'm drunk because he makes a valid point.

"One more time, then we should go back to the hotel."

His brows furrow. "You're not havin' fun?"

"I'm still wearin' the lingerie underneath my dress," I

remind him. Just because we can't have sex, doesn't mean we can't do other things that involve stripping each other naked.

He smacks a kiss on my lips and then winks. "That was for luck."

The bar is crowded like the rest of Vegas, but I'm starting to get used to it. The music is different here though.

To mine and everyone else's surprise, Wilder manages to stay on for the full eight seconds and the crowd cheers for him. They've been waiting for him to make it, too.

And he doesn't even fall on his ass getting off. Either he's getting better at holding on or he has a higher tolerance than I remember.

Screaming, I jump up and down to celebrate with him. I know it's silly, but he's been trying to achieve this for years. It's not as easy as it looks and he's usually stumbling off of it.

Wilder engulfs me in his arms, picks me up and then spins me around. I hold tightly around his neck and laugh as he buries his face in my neck.

"Oh shit, that was a bad idea..." He finally stops and realizes how dizzy he made us.

"Yeah, I'm about to throw up."

Once he takes his free shot and I take one more with him, we find a booth.

"I should've been recordin' you so you could've showed your brothers," I say, realizing it far too late.

"That's okay. You're the only one I wanted to impress anyway." He winks and it sends butterflies to my stomach because I know it's not just a line, he's being truthful.

"Well then, consider me *very* impressed." I lean my head back on his shoulder, closing my eyes for a brief moment, and snuggling up to him. His cologne is as addicting as he is and I can't get enough of it.

"Remember when you said the day I stayed on it for eight

seconds will be the day you marry me?" he asks, and it takes me a minute to realize he's serious.

"Hmm...vaguely," I say, but I do because it was the same day Mattie and I got drunk on margaritas. "That was *before* though."

Wilder brushes his lips against my temple. "You wanna sin with me in Sin City, Delly?"

"Why does that sound like trouble comin' from you?" I look up at him and his devious smile reaches the creases of his eyes, which is all I need to know he's up to no good.

"Do you trust me?" he asks.

"Yes," I say without hesitation.

He cups the back of my neck and crashes his lips to mine and it's at this moment I know I'd do anything for him the way I know he would for me.

And that should probably scare me a lot more than it does.

But I blame my lack of inhibition.

It's not the first time Wilder's dragged me somewhere questionable while I was supposed to be watching over him. Over the summer when he went back to drinking for a few months, we ended up at a party in some random barn, and I swear we were the oldest people there. The worst part is the barn was home to pigs and it smelled so bad, I had to walk out several times for fresh air.

So in theory, as long as he doesn't take me to a pig barn, it can't be that bad.

However, there's always a chance to be proven wrong.

Chapter Twenty
Wilder

I wake up with the urge to piss and am so disoriented, I can't see where I am. Reaching for my phone on the nightstand, I'm confused when I can't find it like usual.

Shit, I must've lost it at some point last night, or rather, this morning when I stumbled into my room. *However long ago that was...*

The clock says it's after seven but I don't remember coming home last night.

Wouldn't be the first time.

Since I can't use my flashlight, I blindly crawl out of bed. I trip over random shit on the floor and smack my toe.

"Fuck..." Hopping on one leg, I keep going until I find a door.

My eyes are barely open but the bright light causes me to close them completely. I feel around for a lightswitch to turn it off but can't find one.

It's not until the door closes behind me, I realize I'm in the hallway. *A second too late.*

"Dammit." I smack the back of my head against the wood, but I still need to pee, so I walk to Waylon's room and knock.

Looking down, I notice I'm only in my boxers and knock again, desperately needing him to wake up before someone sees me.

But he always did sleep like the dead.

Exhaustion takes over, so I slide down the door and wait. They'll eventually have to get up for breakfast.

"What the fuck? Wilder!" Waylon's booming voice wakes me from my nap.

Opening my eyes, I smile in relief. "Hey...*finally.*"

"What the hell are you doin' out here?" he asks and then I notice Harlow standing next to him with a concerned look on her face. She's still in her pajamas, so I'm not sure how they knew I was out here if they weren't on their way out.

"I forgot my key," I explain, trying to get to my feet.

"This ain't your room," Waylon tells me, grabbing my hand and pulling me up "Where's your phone? It says your location is like on the roof or something."

"I dunno, I lost it," I mutter. "And I lost my key, so that's why I came here."

I have no idea where I put it last night because I have no memory after we left the cowboy-themed bar. We drank...a lot.

Oh fuck. Delilah. Where the hell is she?

"You wanna tell me about this?" Waylon grabs my left hand, revealing a brand-new wedding band on my ring finger.

"Oh shit..." My eyes widen, staring at it and wondering how the hell that got there. "Who'd I marry?"

If it's who I think it is —

"Jesus Christ," Waylon mutters, scrubbing a hand down his face. "My ex-girlfriend, you fucker."

Harlow snickers.

"Delilah?" I need to hear him confirm it because there's no way she'd agree to marry me if we were sober.

"Yep," he says.

"Fuck...she's gonna kill me, ain't she?" I scratch my head, contemplating what the hell I'm going to do now.

"Oh yeah..." Waylon shakes his head, crossing his arms. "I might as well start writin' your eulogy now."

Waylon finally lets me inside to use the bathroom.

"How'd y'all know I was out here?" I ask once I've washed my hands.

"Your *wife* called in a panic because she woke up and you were missin'," Waylon explains.

I can't help smiling at him calling her that.

"Get that dopey look off your face. She's gonna murder you."

"You don't even know if this is my fault. We were both wasted," I defend. "I just don't remember it."

"That doesn't explain why your location shows on the roof..." Waylon says, looking at his screen. "Oh wait, it moved."

Harlow glances over, tilting her head. "It's apparently flyin' over The Strip."

"Great." I blow out a frustrated breath. "Gonna need to go buy a new one before we leave."

Waylon's gaze lowers to my left hand. "I think you've got bigger problems than that right now."

My chest tightens. "Did she seem mad?"

"She's textin' me right now." Harlow's tense expression doesn't give me a good feeling. "She's waitin' for ya."

I suck in a deep breath and slowly blow it out. "Alright, tell her I'm comin'. Wish me luck."

"Good luck, brother-in-law!"

Waylon chuckles.

When I make the walk of shame to my room, Delilah's standing in front of the open door, blocking the entrance.

Her arms crossed tightly over her chest and the scowl etched on her face makes it painfully clear how pissed she is.

"Hi, *hubby*," she deadpans.

"Mornin'." I grin and then cup her face to lean in for a kiss, but she jerks back before I can touch her lips.

I step into the room, letting the door close behind me.

"If you're gonna yell at me, can you do it after I've slept a few more hours?"

She shoves me before I can pass her, then waves her left hand in my face. "How the hell did this happen?"

"I was hopin' you'd tell me..." I shrug, scrubbing a hand through my bedhead. "I don't remember anythin' after we left that cowboy bar. We took those last shots and then —"

"You asked if I trusted you and I stupidly said yes!"

"So why're you yellin' at me? For all I know, this was your idea."

She rolls her eyes, folding her arms again. "This has your name written all over it."

"Not gonna deny that but still, if we got married, you would've had to sign the license too. Are you sayin' I forced you to do that too?"

Her arms drop to her side. "No. I found that on the dresser."

Walking over, I grab it and read it over. Sure enough, two signatures.

"Oh shit, we went to the Little White Wedding Chapel." I breathe out an amused laugh.

Delilah stands next to me, reading it over again. "Oh God, I remember what else you said."

"Do I even wanna know?"

Sin With Me

"You asked if I wanted to sin with you in Sin City and then after we left the hotel, we walked to the chapel."

Oh fuck, she's right. I remember that now.

And then I told her to let me prove marriage wasn't a bad idea.

"Oh and here's the receipt." She picks it up from the floor and her brows raise as she scans over it. "Looks like you sprung for the deluxe package."

When she bursts out laughing, I'm taken off guard from the scowl she was just wearing.

"We picked out rings there..." She waves her left hand again, reading over the paper as she paces the room. "Pretty pricy ones too."

"Only the best for my wife."

Her smile drops, clearly not amused by me calling her that.

"Too bad we're returnin' them."

Before I have the chance to argue, she rushes to the bed and picks up her phone. "Wait, they gave us a link for the photos. I remember puttin' it in my notes app."

"Hold on. Go back. Why would we return the rings?"

"Um...because we're gettin' this annulled as soon as possible. I'm not keepin' a ring when we drunkenly got hitched."

I scratch along my jawline, trying to figure out how to slow her down and talk about this without freaking her out.

"Oh my God!" Her palm covers her mouth as she stares at her phone screen. "It should be illegal to allow people this drunk to get married."

Curious, I sit next to her and look. Sure enough, photo after photo of us posing with bloodshot eyes and dopey smiles. "Jesus Christ."

I can't help but laugh because it's clear as a cloudless sky we weren't in our right minds. But I don't remember feeling that drunk at the time. Those tequila shots must've caught up to me before I realized it.

"It's not like we didn't talk about marriage..." I begin, which by the look on her face, is a bad place to start. "Maybe we give it a shot before rushin' to get it annulled?"

"Are you outta your damn mind? You're still drunk, aren't you?" She looks more intently at me.

"No," I say offended. "We're datin', so it's not like—"

"We've been datin' for like two minutes! Wilder, you cannot be serious." She pins me with a look of disbelief. "We can't jump from being friends to havin' a few hot make-out sessions to then becomin' husband and wife. That's...*insanity*!"

"Why not?"

"*Why?*" she deadpans, then holds up a finger. "We haven't even had sex. We don't live together. We haven't even gone on a real date—unless you wanna count walkin' me down the aisle," she says dryly, continuing to put up more fingers. "We already have targets on our backs at home, so—"

"This'll give them somethin' else to talk about for a while." I shrug. "Who cares."

"I care, Wilder! Stayin' married when neither of us were ready in the first place is a recipe for disaster. Marriage isn't supposed to be temporary."

"Agreed, it's forever."

"We're not ready for that level of commitment."

"I am," I blurt.

"Wilder, be serious."

Instead of continuing to argue with her, I get down on one knee and grab her left hand.

"W-what're you doin'?" she stumbles over her words, and I grin at the faint blush covering her cheeks.

"Delly..." I begin, licking my lips while trying to calm my

racing heart. "I know this is quick, and you think we're going to fail, but if you give me thirty days to prove that I can be the husband you deserve, I promise not to let you down. If—for whatever reason—you still wanna get it annulled after that, then I won't fight you on it. But please, give me the chance first. Let me show you how great we can be together."

"Wilder..." she whispers my name, swallowing hard. "I don't wanna hurt you."

"Nothin' could top meetin' you for the first time and then havin' to see you with my twin brother. That's a level of pain I wouldn't wish on anyone."

Her eyes water, but she tries to hide it by closing her eyes and tilting her head back.

"It's only a month, baby. Move in with me and let's give this a real shot."

"Move in with you?" Her eyes pop open. "What about Mattie?"

"Well...as much as I like your roommate, I think squeezin' the three of us in my bed might be a bit snug."

She playfully swats my chest. "I don't wanna leave her hangin'. She relies on me for half the rent and bills."

"I wasn't gonna charge you to live with me, Delly."

"Why not? If we're married and livin' together, shouldn't I be responsible for half?"

"It comes outta my check before I even see it. Plus, even if that weren't the case, I wouldn't let you pay anyway. And just to further prove that I want this with you, I'll cover your expenses so Mattie doesn't have to worry. Hell, I'll pay for both of yours."

"You don't have to do that."

"I wouldn't mind either way. Whatever it takes for you to give me a chance..."

She bites her lower lip, contemplating in silence, and I wait while the carpet digs into my bare knee. But I'll stay here for as long as it takes for her to decide.

"One condition."

"Done."

"You haven't even heard it yet." She laughs. "We continue to *date* like normal. Just because we're married doesn't mean I'm expected to be in the kitchen cookin' dinner every night or doin' your laundry."

I smirk. "I've seen your apartment, so I wouldn't expect that anyway."

Her snarky glare has my smile widening.

"Yeah, well...it's been a rough year."

"I get it..." And I do. After losing her dad, I saw the spark leave her eyes. "Let me do those things for you. That should be my job, as your *husband*, to help you through your grief, make sure you're eatin' and have clean clothes, and whatever else you need me to do."

She looks at me skeptically. "You can barely do those things for yourself."

"But for the right person, I'd put in the time and effort to do it for them. And in case you've been livin' in a fish bowl for the past nine years, that person is you."

"You're really serious about this?"

I nod, squeezing her hand. "Yes. I wouldn't have asked you to sin with me if I wasn't."

Her eyes roll but the grin on her face tells me she loves it. "Okay."

"Okay?" I blurt loudly, needing to make sure I heard correctly.

She sighs, nodding. "I'll give you thirty days."

I jump to my feet and this time when I cup her face, I crash my mouth to hers and she doesn't push away.

"And you get *one* chance! One," she says firmly in between kissing me.

"That's all I need, baby."

Chapter Twenty-One
Delilah

"Mornin', sweetheart." Mom smiles when I walk into our room.

After agreeing to Wilder's thirty day marriage condition, I left to shower and change before going for breakfast and finding a gallon of coffee. It's going to be a rough day because I only slept for a few hours.

But now I have to tell my mom the news before we meet up with everyone else.

"Hey, Mom. How'd you sleep?" I ask, rummaging through my suitcase for clean clothes.

"Great. You? I was a bit surprised to wake up and see you weren't here."

I wince, slowly turning around to face her. "Yeah, I slept in Wilder's room."

She lifts a carefree shoulder. "I figured as much. Y'all have fun?"

"Uh...yeah. Guess you could say that." I bite the inside of my cheek, contemplating how to tell her. I need to just rip off the BandAid and get it over with before she sees the rock on my finger. "I have to tell you somethin' though."

I spin around to face her and she's already watching me. "What is it?"

"Um, well...Wilder and I drank *a lot* last night and kinda did somethin' stupid."

"Did he get arrested again?"

"No, thank God." I blow out a breath and brace for her reaction.

"Matchin' tattoos?" she guesses and when I shake my head, she continues, "Did you get somethin' *pierced...*" She points to my chest, and I snort.

"We...got hitched."

She tilts her head and crosses her arms, blinking a few times. "Uh...whaddya mean?"

Stepping closer, I hold out my left hand and show her the ring. "We went to one of those little chapels and got married."

"Delilah Fanning!" she scolds, then yanks my hand to take a better look. "Or is it *Hollis* now?"

"Mom!" I burst out laughing at her devious smile. "I blame those Long Island Iced Teas."

"Well..." She drops my hand. "They do taste good."

Grinning, I nod. "A bit *too* good."

"Is Wilder freakin' out?"

"Strangely, no. When I suggested we get an annulment, he begged me to give him thirty days to prove we can make this work. I'm a little skeptical, but I agreed to give him a chance."

"Good, I'm glad."

"You are?"

"Of course!" She opens her arms and wraps them around me. "Marriage is a beautiful commitment that only two people truly in love can experience the full benefits of what it has to offer."

223

"But we're not *in* love...we were drunk," I clarify.

"You will be. I have no doubt he already is."

"I'm not sure he knows what being in love feels like. He's never had a serious relationship. Plus, I haven't experienced it either." Waylon and I never said it to each other. "Neither of us have any business gettin' married this quickly."

"You've been in love with Wilder for years, you just never let yourself admit it. Once your head catches up to your heart, you'll feel it."

"Mama, that's impossible. How can you be in love with someone but not know it?"

The corner of her lips tilts up. "Our minds tend to protect us from gettin' hurt, so in order to do that, it blocks your ability to feel certain things. Wilder being emotionally unavailable and you keepin' your distance made it easier, but deep down, you fell for him a long time ago. But now you get to fall for the man he is today. A much better version of himself, as long as you open your heart *and* mind to it."

"Do you think you'll ever get married again?" I ask, needing a moment to think about what she said, because if she's right, I won't be able to walk away unscathed after thirty days.

"It's too soon to tell, but I doubt it."

"Maybe Daddy will send you someone," I tell her. "I know he'd want you to be happy."

"He'd want you to be, too, even if he can't be here and witness that happiness."

My eyes fill with tears as they have many times these past months. Anytime I think or talk about him, I get emotional.

"I miss him so much," I whisper, sitting on the edge of the bed.

"I do too, sweetie. There hasn't been a day I haven't thought about him." She sits next to me, wrapping her arm around my shoulders.

"I'm still strugglin' after almost a year and don't even live at home to see his things every day. I can't imagine how hard it must be for you being alone and surrounded by his chair, clothes, and books."

"It's comfortin'," she clarifies, her voice soothing. "Sometimes I trick my brain into thinkin' he's home with me and is takin' a nap. When I see his crossword puzzles, I'll do one and pretend he's tellin' me the answers. Makes me feel less lonely."

I choke back tears but they fall down my cheeks anyway. "I hate that you're alone now."

"Don't be, honey." She leans over and wipes my face. "My job keeps me plenty busy. I love my coworkers and helpin' all my patients. Losin' your dad reminds me why I work as hard as I do. I feel fulfilled at the end of the day knowin' I gave it my all."

"I wish I felt that level of passion," I admit. "I enjoy workin' at Lacey's but it's not satisfyin' like goin' to rodeos and performin'. I've decided not to return to trick ridin' next year but not sure what I wanna do."

"I kinda figured you wouldn't and that's okay. We all have to pivot to find what brings us joy. I have no doubt you'll figure it out, but it might not come easy."

"That's partly why I'm skeptical this marriage can work when I'm still figurin' out what I wanna do. And at my age, when most people are already married and having babies, I feel behind."

"Marriage is about growin' old with someone you love and havin' a partner to face the ups and downs. As long as you grow together and support each other, there's no reason you can't figure out what you want with him at your side."

Tears fill my eyes again, but for a different reason this time. My mom's been through a lot with my dad and she never left his side. She married the love of her life and stuck by him through every obstacle and never complained about it.

I want *that*.

"You don't think it's crazy we got married after datin' for like three days?"

"Of course." She laughs, and I do too. "But that doesn't mean you throw in the towel before givin' it a chance, especially when this was years in the makin'. I like Wilder, but even more, I like Wilder for you. If I had to pick a man for you, it'd be a man just like him. Sure, he doesn't have the best track record when it comes to relationships but the fact that he's askin' for a chance tells me he's ready. He's been waitin' for you."

I nod, then wrap my arms around her. "Thanks, Mom."

Once I've showered and dressed, Wilder and I go eat with his siblings who give us shit about being *newlyweds*. They seem happy enough for us, but I know they love teasing Wilder. Noah warned him their parents were going to flip but everyone agreed not to tell them until we could in person.

Another thing to worry about.

Since his phone went MIA, we find an Apple store so he can buy a new one. Then, he makes a show of changing my contact to MY WIFE.

I'd protest if that didn't sound so goddamn hot.

When I jokingly refuse to change his contact in my phone, he does it for me. Except he puts BABY DADDY.

"Not sure if you skipped biology, but without intercourse, there's a zero percent chance of that being true."

"You ever heard of *manifesting*? All I'm missin' is my lucky crystals and my plan to wed and bed you will be a success!"

I snort. "I'm startin' to wonder if you did do some voodoo afterall."

He winks. "I'll never tell."

He takes my hand, interconnecting our fingers as we make our way toward the arena. When he kisses my knuckles and gives me his infamous flirty grin, it gives me butterflies.

God, I sound like a teenage girl with her first boyfriend.

Since it's the final day of the NFR, it's more packed than yesterday, but we'll get to hopefully watch Ellie win the barrel racing championship for the second year in a row. We have an early flight tomorrow, so I won't be going to any after parties or getting drunk like we did last night.

Plus, I already need an eight hour nap.

"Think your parents really will flip out when we tell them?" I ask Wilder after thinking about what his siblings said at breakfast.

"After thirty-three years, they're pretty used to my antics. Not sure anythin' will shock them at this point." He grins. "Plus, it's not like I married a stranger. So that wins me brownie points."

I snort. "Silver linings."

Inhaling the sharp scent of leather mixed with dirt and musk, we sit in the arena with everyone and wait for the announcer to call Ellie's name. Being here brings me back to all the excitement of trick riding. The roar of the crowd, the loud music crackling through the air, and all the bright colors of the cowboy hats and boots hype me up.

I can only imagine the high it brings Ellie and all the other riders.

She's kicked ass every day, and I have no doubt she will today, too.

"I'm anxious, and I'm not even the one out there ridin'," I whisper to Wilder. "I dunno how she does it."

He leans in, squeezing my hand in his. "She's fierce. Never seen anythin' like it."

"Doesn't hurt that she trains with Noah screamin' at her," Magnolia says, and I laugh at her eavesdropping.

"I don't scream. I *cheer!*" Noah defends. "But it obviously helps because look how far she's come."

Landen turns and stares at Noah. "If that's what you call cheerin', then that must be what Ellie does in the bedroom when I have her—"

"Dude." Tripp kicks the back of his chair to stop him. "We don't wanna know."

"Speak for yourself..." Wilder waggles his brows at Landen just to rile him up.

"Do the newlyweds need some inspo?" Landen taunts, then shoots me a wicked grin. "Maybe try drawin' him pictures so he knows where to find *it*."

"Don't worry, his tongue piercin' found it just fine," I say, smirking at Wilder.

"Oh God..." Noah groans, her face twists in disgust.

"That's exactly what she screamed when I found it." He winks at me.

"Wilder!" My cheeks heat. "My mother is right next to me!"

"And your *sister*," Harlow adds.

Mom chuckles. "Nothin' I haven't heard before."

"As if I haven't had to hear you and my *brother* for the past year," Wilder reminds Harlow. His bedroom is above theirs and has complained about hearing them several times. "So just remember, pay back's a bitch."

"Wait a minute..." It dawns on me. Lowering my voice, I add, "I don't want them listenin'."

"Oh, they're gonna," he says proudly. "I'm determined to make sure they have to suffer the way they've made me."

"It's not my fault the ceilings and walls are thin!" Harlow shrugs. "That's why I got you headphones for your birthday."

"Just do what I do..." Waylon looks at Wilder over his shoulder. "When I know you're home and she gives me *the look*, I get in the shower. The water and fan drowns out the extra noise and you can't hear a thing upstairs."

"I beg your finest pardon?" Harlow looks horrified.

"You think I need to take three showers a day? I figured you knew." Waylon shrugs.

"We need to move out..." Harlow mutters, shaking her head.

Before Waylon can respond, we hear Ellie's name being announced and then she's flying out of the alleyway with her horse, Ranger.

The conversation is forgotten as we spring to our feet, cheering and screaming her name. Noah jumps up and down with a large sign, keeping with her tradition of inappropriate ones: *Round those barrels like you're being chased by a man!*

Ellie cleans all three barrels flawlessly and just as quickly as she entered, she's gone.

"Holy shit! That has to get her to first," Noah shouts, beaming with pride.

The rest of the crowd erupts when her time displays on the screen.

"Thirteen point one!" Magnolia shouts, raising her arms above her head. "That's one of her fastest times."

Once all the barrel racer's scores from the past ten days get added up, the top average time wins the championship. Racers can also win money and prizes each day and she's won a handful already.

After every racer has gone, they announce Ellie as the round ten winner and then we wait with baited breath for the overall results to display.

"Well folks, she's done it again. For the second year in a row, she proves why she's the Rodeo Princess! Congrats, Ellie Donovan and Ranger!"

1. Ellie Donovan - 13.3

"Holy shit, she did better than last year!" Noah jumps around, unable to contain herself, and then she takes off toward the exit. Landen's quick to follow her.

"Is she always this excited when Ellie wins?" I ask.

"Yes," Fisher, Wilder, Waylon, Tripp, and Magnolia answer in unison.

I laugh, sitting back in my seat so the people behind us can see the next event.

"What was her score last year?" I ask everyone.

"Thirteen point five. And even that was a record," Magnolia explains. "She trained hard this past year."

"It shows."

Wilder wraps his arm around me and I snuggle into his side with a smile on my face.

I love this for Ellie so much. Even though I don't know her super well, I can tell she loves this sport more than anything and has put everything she has into it. I want that type of passion. That feeling of accomplishment, knowing I worked hard for something and earned it.

I felt pride as a trick rider, but I lost my passion for it after

Dad died. That feeling of excitement was lost, and I'm not sure I'll ever feel it again.

But my goal is still finding a fulfilling career where I know I'm making a difference. Hopefully, I'll figure it out sooner rather than later.

Chapter Twenty-Two
Wilder

"Thank God you're home!" Mallory engulfs me in the biggest hug she's ever given me and when I glance over at Delilah, she's laughing at her dramatics. "If I had to work with that guy for one more day, I was gonna kill him."

Delilah and I flew back early this morning and after she dropped off her mom at home, she met me at my house so we could come up with a plan to tell my parents. Now we're here to tell them the news.

"Was he that bad?" Delilah asks once Mallory releases me.

"He acts like he's never worked on a ranch before." She blows out a frustrated breath. "I had to talk him through everythin' and then he'd ask me a hundred questions. I couldn't get any of my own stuff done. Eventually, I told Antonio to deal with him."

"He hasn't..." Delilah furrows her brows. "He did construction, not ranching."

Mallory tilts her head at me, glaring. "You told me he knew what he was doin'!"

"I trained him for a few days." I shrug, walking around her to go to the fridge.

"He probably just wanted someone to talk to," Delilah says. "He doesn't have a lot of friends here."

"Gee, I wonder why..." Mallory rolls her eyes, crossing her arms. "Well, either way...I'm tappin' out. He's your problem again."

I pour myself a glass of sweet tea and then one for Delilah. "You might have to deal with him for a few days next week."

Delilah's face twists as I hand her one of the glasses. I haven't told her I'm planning a mini honeymoon of sorts before Christmas, which doesn't give us much time, but I'm determined to make it work between our schedules. If I only have thirty days, I'm not wasting a single one.

"Wilder, you're home!" Mom enters the kitchen with Gramma Grace. She walks over with her arms open and wraps them around me. "Delilah? Hey, sweetheart."

Mom hugs her next. "How was y'alls flight?"

"Good," Delilah says, glancing at me over my mom's shoulder. I can tell she's panicking.

Gramma Grace comes over and gives me a little smack on the cheek. "What'd you do?"

I press my hand over where she hit. "What was that for?"

Her brows lift as her gaze finds my left hand. My smile is diabolical when I realize she's looking at my ring.

"Uh oh. What'd you do?" Mallory walks over, poking her nose between us.

I shove her away and stand next to Delilah.

"Is Dad home?" I ask my mom.

If I have to explain this, I'd rather only have to do it once.

"He's just gettin' outta the shower. He'll be down in a moment," Mom says. "Did y'all eat?"

"Not yet, but—"

"Mallory, set two more plates, please. There's enough roast for y'all. Take a seat," Mom demands, which means there's no room for arguing.

"You like strawberry cheesecake?" Gramma Grace asks Delilah once we sit.

"Yeah, that sounds delicious." Delilah smiles, but I can tell she's uneasy.

Bringing my hand to her leg, I give it a little squeeze and lean into her ear. "Relax. It's gonna be fine."

Her tight-lipped smile tells me she doesn't believe me.

While we wait for my father, we make small talk with Mallory and Gramma Grace. Apparently, they ran into Molly at the grocery store and Gramma Grace gave her an earful while Mallory warned her about dumping horseshit inside her car if she wrote another bad article about the family.

"Jesus Christ..." I crack a smile, shaking my head. "No wonder people call us the Southern mafia."

"Language." Mom snaps. "And who does?"

"*Everyone...*" I laugh, holding up my right hand and lifting a finger. "Craig died in the barn fire after threatenin' Noah's life." I bring up another finger. "Landen shot a drug dealer linked to Magnolia's baby daddy, who was also found dead in the trunk of said drug dealer." Another finger. "Tripp shot Ruby's ex-boyfriend who tried to kill her and then was found dead in the lake the followin' day." Another finger. "I shot the guy who kidnapped Harlow, who unfortunately, survived."

Delilah slowly glances at me, and I know exactly what she's thinking: *What the hell did I marry into?*

I'd burst out laughing if it wasn't so accurate.

"When you say it like that, we do sound a little mobish," Mallory winces.

"To be fair, those people deserved it." Gramma Grace

shrugs, stirring the gravy at the stovetop. "You protect the family at all costs."

"That's exactly what the mafia would say," I deadpan, taking a drink of my sweet tea.

"What's that?" Mallory points to my left hand.

Delilah keeps her head down, conveniently hiding her hands underneath the table.

"What's what?" Dad asks, finally entering the kitchen.

"She's askin' about my wedding band."

Delilah's head snaps up along with everyone else's.

"Why're you wearin' a wedding band on your ring finger?" Mallory asks, oblivious to the obvious.

"Because I got married in Vegas," I say calmly, watching and waiting for them to freak out.

"*Married*?" Dad's brows raise, crossing his arms as he stands at the head of the table. "To who?"

"Me," Delilah says timidly, holding up her left hand and revealing the rock I got her.

"I knew it!" Mallory shouts, pumping a fist in the air. "You owe me fifty bucks, Aunt Dena."

"Huh?" I shift my gaze from her to my mom.

"We bet that you two were secretly hookin' up. She thought I was crazy but—"

"We were drunk," I clarify, but mostly to burst her bubble.

"Still counts," Mallory argues.

"I—"

"Let me get this straight..." Dad holds up his palm, cutting me off. "You two..." He waves a finger between Delilah and me. "...got hitched in Vegas after gettin' wasted?"

"That's pretty much correct, yes."

I'm not about to admit there was a part of me that knew exactly what we were doing. Or that I don't regret it.

Mom stands next to Dad, rubbing her temples. "Are you...*together*?"

Grinning, I look at Delilah and squeeze her hand. "Yes."

"We just started datin'," Delilah clarifies. "Like three days ago."

"But when she screamed my first name, I couldn't resist givin' her my last." I wink at Delilah and her whole face beets red.

"Wilder!" she whisper-hisses, smacking her thigh into mine.

As if my parents aren't used to my oversharing big mouth.

"Oh I totally win the bet now," Mallory gloats, dancing in her seat. "I told y'all."

"I knew before everyone else," Gramma Grace gloats.

"Of course you did..." Mallory blows out a breath. "You always do."

I laugh because it's true.

"So now what?" Dad asks, grabbing a beer from the fridge.

"She's movin' in with me and we're seein' where it goes." I lift a shoulder because as simple as it sounds, it's true. Even though Delilah said thirty days, I have no doubt it's going to work long term.

"Well then..." Mom sets down the large dish with the roast in the middle of the table. "Welcome to the family, Delilah. I hope you know what you're doin'." She winks at her. "And you'll be expected at Sunday night suppers and stay for scrapbookin'."

Delilah's cheeks redden but her smile widens. "Yes, ma'am."

Sin With Me

"That wasn't so bad, was it?" I say, holding her hand as we walk to my truck.

"Better than I expected, honestly. But I feel like they're disappointed."

I open the passenger side door and help her in, but she angles toward me with her legs on either side of me. "Trust me, I've seen them disappointed, and that's not it. More like, concern. For you, not for me."

She chuckles. "After you've finished your volunteer hours at the shelter, you're gonna have to come to my parent's house for Saturday game nights. Especially if I'm comin' here every Sunday night."

"I might not be done with my hours in the next thirty days..." I tilt up her chin, bringing my mouth closer to hers, but not quite touching. "But if I'm still your husband when I've completed them, I'd be honored to go with you."

She closes the gap between us and brushes her lips against mine. "Deal, *hubby*."

"Fuck, don't make me hard." I adjust my cock in my jeans.

Laughing, she shakes her head. "You gonna tell me what you have up your sleeve for why you'll be missin' work?"

"Not yet. But prepare to need a few days off."

"I can't after takin' time off for Vegas."

"I'll talk to Lacey and Mattie. I'm sure—"

"You're not talkin' to my boss and coworker! That's oversteppin'."

"You're my *wife*—"

"Who doesn't need her *husband* to butt into her job."

I cup her face, leaning in close enough to rub my nose along her jawline and up to her ear. "We're goin' on a short honeymoon," I whisper. "I want a few days alone with my wife before the holidays."

She sucks in a breath. "Where?"

"Willow Branch Mountain. My aunt and uncle own a ranch and luxury resort up there. I texted my cousin, Warren, earlier and he found us a cabin to stay in. We leave Wednesday."

It's one of their older cabins that just got remodeled, so they hadn't had any bookings for it. They're usually scheduled out a year in advance, so I'm super grateful he's letting me use it.

"That's not enough time to find coverage for my shifts."

"Then, quit. I'll cover your bills and whatever else you need."

She shoves my chest, pushing me back. "You can't say stuff like that. I want to work and don't need you to take care of me."

"But what if I want to?"

"I know you're used to gettin' what you want and your family has tons of money, but I take pride in payin' my own way. Plus, I like my job."

"But it's not what you want to do long term."

"Correct, but until I figure out what I wanna do, I'm not quittin'."

"Okay, fine. But come Wednesday, you're mine through Saturday."

"What about your anger class and volunteerin'?"

"I'll go to my class on Thursday. It's only thirty minutes away from where we'll be. And I'll let Miss Tierney know I'll miss Saturday but will make it up during the holiday break."

The retreat closes Christmas Eve through New Year's Day, so Landen can take his job back at the stud farm since there won't be any trail rides for him to guide. Waylon can handle barn duties and I'll help wherever I'm needed when I'm not at the shelter.

She looks at me skeptically. "Okay...I'll figure out my schedule. But—" The smirk on her face grows as she sucks in her lower lip and bites it. "You better bring condoms this time."

Chapter Twenty-Three

Delilah

"Oh my God, finally!" Mattie screams when I walk into our apartment.

After dinner with the Hollises and Wilder convincing me to go with him next week, I drove home to tell Mattie the news.

I drop my suitcases when she hurls herself toward me, wrapping her arms around my neck.

"Jesus." I chuckle, grabbing onto her so we don't fall. "You act like I was gone for a month."

"You left me with Harper and Amanda at work..." She deadpans. "They couldn't find a clue even if they put their two brain cells together. I swear, if they weren't Lacey's nieces, they would've been fired by now."

I wince, feeling even more awful for what I'm about to tell her. "I'm sorry."

"I didn't hear from you very much. Did you have fun at least?"

She grabs one of my bags, and I take the other, bringing it to my bedroom. My heart hammers in my chest at what I need to tell her, but the sooner I spit it out, the better.

"Yeah, it was a good time. Lots of drinkin', which I haven't done in ages. Ellie kicked ass, so that was fun to watch."

"You and Wilder still going *slow*?" She raises her hands into air quotes. "Or did you finally jump on him like a bronc rider?"

I snort, tossing my suitcase on my bed and opening it. She reaches for the lavender lingerie set that's wrinkled into a ball.

"I knew it!" She holds it like an active bomb before tossing it into my laundry basket. "So...how was it?"

"We didn't have sex," I confirm, and then decide to just spill it. "But we did get married."

Her head falls back as laughter erupts from her throat. "Good one. So how big is his dick?" She holds her palms up, spreading them apart wider as if she's waiting for me to confirm.

"Mattie!" I chastise, then hold out my left hand to reveal my ring. "I'm being serious."

Her jaw drops and she freezes in place as her eyes narrow in on the rock.

"We were really drunk...like had seven shots too many drunk," I add. "I woke up to this on my finger, completely blackin' out on what we'd done the night before."

"What in the livin' fuck?" She yanks my hand, putting it two inches from her eyes. "This is *legal*?"

I chuckle. "Yep, I found the license and receipt to prove it. You should see the photos. We look outta our damn minds."

"When I said go experience Vegas, I didn't mean get hitched!"

"You said don't come back *pregnant*..." I teasingly remind her. "Which I'm not."

"So you're *legally* married but haven't done the horizontal tango?"

"We fooled around, but neither of us had a condom. However—" I give her my best *don't be mad at me* face. "We're goin' away this next week for a...honeymoon, of sorts? Up to his aunt and uncle's resort, so I need you to fill in for me at work."

"Please, no." Her face morphs into a frown. "I can't handle the Barbie twins anymore."

"I'll see if Lacey can take a couple of my shifts."

She hugs me. "Thank you! I don't mind workin' longer hours but I can't handle them."

"There's one more thing..."

Her shoulders drop. "Oh, God. What is it?"

"When I first realized what we'd done, I freaked out and told him we needed to get this annulled."

"Whew..." She releases a loud breath before I can finish. "So you did have a come to Jesus moment about how crazy this was?"

"Of course!" I throw the rest of my dirty laundry in the basket and then grab my other suitcase to unpack my toiletries. "He begged me to give him thirty days to prove we should stay married and wants me to move in with him during that time. Though, I told him I wasn't gonna become his maid or cook."

She snorts. "Good call."

"I'm nervous but after the talk I had with my mom, I think it's the right thing to do. If I don't give it a chance, I'll always wonder *what-if*. And I've lived with those long enough."

Mattie grabs my shoulder to stop me from pacing and meets my eyes. "I agree. You two deserve this shot and even though I'm sad as hell to be losin' you as a roommate, I want nothin' but happiness for you."

Tears well in the corner of my eyes and I pull her in for a hug. "Thank you. I love you."

"I love you, too." She pushes back slightly. "And I don't care that he's technically your husband, I still want details when y'all finally hook up."

I bellow out with laughter, shaking my head. "If you help me do laundry and re-pack, I'll tell you about his cock piercings."

"Oh hell yeah, deal!"

It feels weird being at work after five days off, but I'm happy to be back to a schedule, even if it's for a couple days. I let Lacey know I'll be leaving again and after some profuse begging and offering to work more over the holiday week, she gave me the time off.

Once I'm done with my shift, I'm going to Wilder's to "move in" for the next month. I'm still feeling weird about it, especially since I've never lived with a man besides my father, and Wilder's the last person I ever imagined as a roommate.

But I know I owe it to myself to try. Even though my instinct is to back out and go to my safe place hiding in my bed, I'm not letting myself.

I'm about to go on my lunch break when Jonah walks in, taking me by surprise.

"Hey!" I smile brightly. "What're doin' here?"

He scrubs a hand through his hair. "On my break and wanted to see you since it's been a while. I also have that two grand I owe ya."

"Perfect timin'. I'm takin' mine now. Wanna go to the café?" I grab my bag from the backroom and let Amanda know I'm heading out.

"Thank you again for bailin' me out." He hands me an envelope of cash.

"Of course." I stuff it into my purse and then loop my arm through his. "I'm dyin' to hear how things are goin' at the ranch."

He opens the door for me and then we walk out into the chilly air.

"I wanna hear about you gettin' hitched first..." He narrows his eyes at me.

"Heard about that, did ya?" I giggle.

"Wilder called you his *wife* about ten times this mornin' and I nearly choked on my tongue when I realized he was talkin' about you."

"Yeah, he sure loves sayin' that." My cheeks heat at the memories of hearing him call me that. "I'm still gettin' used to it myself."

When we arrive, he opens the door for me and then I walk in. Everyone's gazes shift and a dozen people stare at me.

"Guess everyone else heard by now, too," he says behind me.

"Great," I murmur.

"So how's Raven and the baby doin'?" I ask once we have our food and find a table.

"Good. I took her to a prenatal appointment on Friday and got to hear the heartbeat."

"Oh my gosh, that's so sweet. Does she know the gender?"

"She decided she wants it to be a surprise."

"Oh, love that! That takes a lot of restraint though. How's she doin' in the shelter?"

"They found her a remote job so it's a lot better now. Savin' up to get her an apartment."

"That's awesome! Well, I'd have to ask Mattie, but if she

wants to get outta there sooner, my room's available. Assumin' she doesn't mind livin' with someone else."

"Really? I think she'd love that. Guess that means you're movin' in with Wilder?"

"Yep, tonight actually. My furniture will be stayin' so Raven can use it and anythin' else I don't take with me."

"Well, if Mattie's cool with it, I'll ask Raven. I'm sure she'd love to have more space but room with another woman so she's not alone."

"And Mattie's hardcore, so anyone tries messin' with Raven, Mattie wouldn't think twice about kickin' their ass."

Jonah laughs, taking a bite of his food. "I appreciate that. I dunno what I would've done if I hadn't met you that night at the bar and then found you at Lacey's. You've been a really good friend to me and you had no reason to be."

I tilt my head and frown. "Everyone deserves a second chance. And I went with my gut, which told me you were a good person."

"Thanks, I appreciate that."

"You're welcome." I smile warmly. "Now, tell me about work. How're you likin' it?"

"Uh no...we're talkin' about you gettin' hitched in Vegas first to a guy I didn't even know you were datin'...."

I bark out a laugh and heat crawls up my neck thinking about Wilder. "Okay, fair."

Once I've confessed everything from start to finish, he finally tells me about working at the ranch.

"Besides takin' orders from a seventeen-year-old Satan, work has been fine. But goddamn, she's bossy and rude."

"If it makes ya feel any better, I think she gives Wilder a run for his money, too."

"I was huffin' and puffin' tryin' to get one of the horses to move—it was being a stubborn shit—and ya know what she said to me?"

"Not sure I even wanna know." I smirk around a French fry before eating it.

"If you wanna be a cry baby, go to daycare. Otherwise, suck it up and use those things you call muscles!"

The laugh that bubbles out of me has me quickly covering my mouth. "She's a savage."

"I wasn't even cryin'! Sweat got in my eyes."

"Oh my God, I'm dyin'." I take a drink before I choke on my food.

"She scares the shit outta me. And then she turns around and is all sweet to her little boyfriend."

"Well, of course." I snicker. "She's lived there since she was nine and was practically raised by the Hollises. She's gotta have thick skin to go through what she has in her short life, plus deal with four male cousins."

"I wondered about that...where are her parents?"

"Wilder didn't tell you?"

"No, he doesn't talk much. To me, at least."

"They died in a car accident. Dena and Garrett took her in."

"Oh damn. That's sad."

"I know. She's close to them and Gramma Grace. But I think she hides her pain from losin' them at such a young age."

"Which would be understandable. Guess that makes me a little less mad about how much she bosses me 'round."

I grin. "Maybe try talkin' to her about Raven and the baby. Find somethin' you can talk about that isn't work-related. I'm sure she'd love to hear about your sister and how brave she's been."

"Think so?"

"Yeah...doesn't hurt to try, at least."

"Alright, thanks. I will."

We finish our food and he walks me back to the store. I tell him about the honeymoon and that Wilder and I will be gone for a few days. Then, I promise to be better at staying in touch.

"Thanks for stoppin' in today. It was great catchin' up and seein' you."

He wraps me in a hug. "You too. Have a good rest of your day."

"Bye!" I wave once the door shuts.

"Who was that?" Amanda gushes as soon as he leaves.

"My friend, Jonah," I say, not making eye contact because I know what she's about to ask me next.

"Is Jonah single?"

"I fear you're not his type," I murmur, setting my purse in the backroom. "Sorry."

"What's that mean?"

I scratch my cheek, trying to come up with a quick lie. "He's into older women. That's why we've only stayed friends."

"Oh." She pouts, crossing her arms. "How old?"

"Like...at least fifty. I think his ex was fifty-two."

Her eyes widen and she drops her arms. "Oh. Never mind."

She spins on her heels and goes back into the front of the store.

Shaking my head, I mutter to myself, "You owe me one, Jonah. I just saved your ass."

Chapter Twenty-Four
Wilder

"Close your eyes," I tell Delilah once we park next to a tree.

"Is that really necessary?" she asks, unbuckling her belt.

"Yes." I hop out of my truck and round the front before opening her door. "It's a surprise."

She exhales with a grin on her beautiful face and finally obeys. "It better be good."

I chuckle, then reach in and pick her up.

"Wilder!" She quickly wraps her arms around my neck, tightly holding onto me. "What're you doin'?

"I didn't get to carry you over the threshold after we got hitched, so I'm doin' it here," I tell her, walking toward the deck of the cabin we'll be staying at for the next few nights.

She bellows out a laugh, burying her head in my neck. Her warm breath against my skin has me anxious to get us inside and strip her naked.

Ever since she officially moved in with me two days ago, we've shared my bed and fooled around some, but we both agreed to wait until we could be alone—without our siblings in the room beneath us—to go further.

But this honeymoon is so much more than that. It's about connection and spending quality time together without interruptions of work or other people. I'm taking the full opportunity of these next twenty-five days to prove to her how much we belong together.

"I think you've gone crazy," she says, giggling.

"Only for you, wifey."

She snorts. "I'm convinced the only reason you took us to that chapel is so you could call me that."

"And I'm convinced the only reason you brought that lingerie set to Vegas was to seduce me."

"Actually, that was Mattie's doing. However...puttin' it on underneath my dress was definitely my idea to tempt you."

I smile wide at her confession, reaching around to the doorknob and opening the door.

Stepping inside, I look around and beam at how great it looks. Warren undersold how nice the remodel turned out.

"Okay, settin' you down and then you can look."

Once I get her safely on her feet, I brush her long, blonde hair off to one shoulder and then whisper in her ear, "Open your eyes."

"Oh my gosh!" She steps forward and then spins around, taking it all in. "This is gorgeous."

"Isn't it?" I grin, then move to the kitchen counter where a large basket is waiting. "I think this is for us."

"From who?" She opens the card and reads it. "Congrats to the newlyweds! Hope you enjoy your stay at the Willow Branch Mountain Ranch and Resort. Please let us know if you need anything else. From..." She looks over at me before continuing, "Who're the Langstons?"

"Aunt Lindsey is my dad's sister and my mom's best friend. She married Grady Langston and they have five kids."

"Did you grow up with your cousins?" she asks, digging through the basket of goodies.

"Warren is the same age as Landen. They're pretty close. Growing up, we'd visit every summer and go zip lining, hiking, and cliff divin'. We always had a blast."

"Oh wow, that sounds fun." She pulls out a few items. "Face and eye masks! We're totally doin' these." Then she opens a jar of foaming milk bath. "Ooh, this smells good."

She holds it under my nose, and I inhale the lavender scent.

"My cousin, Posey, makes the goat soap here," I explain. "Check the label."

She flips it over and reads it. "Langston Soapworks. How cool. There's a couple books in here, too."

Holding up paperbacks, she scans the back. "Warren's wife, Maisie, is a literary agent. She usually includes books of her authors in the welcome baskets."

"Do I get to meet these cousins of yours?" she asks, setting them down and reaching for the bottle of champagne sitting in an ice bucket.

"Probably. They all live on the property and have various jobs on the ranch and resort. I'm sure we'll run into a couple of them."

"Well...what do ya wanna do first?" she asks, setting the champagne down.

I take her hand and pull her to my chest so I can press my lips to hers. "Lets take a tour and then I'll bring in our bags."

We walk through the living room, the bedrooms, and the massive bathroom. There's a deep soaking tub in front of a large scenic window next. You can see the trees and mountains in the distance as the sun starts to set.

"Sorry, but I'm spendin' our honeymoon in here." Delilah

steps inside the tub and slides down with the cutest grin on her face, then rests her arms on top as she leans back. "Mm...yeah, this'll do just fine."

"Looks big enough for two."

"Let's try it out. Bring the bubbly."

Smirking, I hold out my hand to help her out. "Champagne and a bubble bath. Who're you turnin' me into?"

"The man you were always meant to be." She wraps her arms around me and tilts her head up so I can press my mouth to hers. "And I get to put that sheet mask on your face."

I bark out a laugh, shaking my head. "We'll see."

After unpacking our bags, we raid the cupboards and check out what they stocked in the kitchen, which I know had to be Bellamy's doing. She helps with guest services but since she's the youngest, she gets stuck running all the errands and shopping. She's a few years younger than Noah and has a twin brother named Bodie, who mostly works at the ranch and takes care of the horses.

"Do you want me to make the steaks before or after the bath?" I ask, digging around for a pan. I'm not much of a cook, but I can fry some meat.

"After. I don't wanna be stuffed *and* naked," she says, sitting at the table and flipping through one of the books.

"Oh, you're gonna be stuffed and naked all right..." I smirk.

She smacks a palm to her forehead. "I walked right into that one, didn't I?"

"Sure did." I laugh, walking over and pulling her up. "Let's go."

She grabs a few items from the basket and then follows me to the bathroom.

While the hot water runs, I grab the bath items she picked and place them around the tub, then strip down. Delilah does the same and waits for me to get in first.

"Don't look at my stretch marks." She tries hiding her stomach, but I reach up and pull her arms down.

"I've seen all of you," I remind her. "And I love them."

She rolls her eyes, situating herself between my legs. "No one loves stretch marks on love handles."

"I disagree. Why else would they call them *love* handles?" I tease, wrapping my hands around her stomach and pulling her closer.

"A man probably named them," she deadpans.

I chuckle against her neck as I bury my face between her head and shoulder, inhaling the sweet scent of her shampoo.

She reaches for the milk bath and lathers it between her hands before covering her arms with it. When I take some, I rub it between my palms and then massage it over her breasts. I play with her nipples, softly brushing my lips underneath her ear.

I've never taken a bath with a woman before because of how intimate and sensual it is, so I'm glad I waited to experience this with her.

"Mm..." She hums, her head tilting to the side and giving me more access to her neck. "You keep doin' that, I'm gonna fall asleep."

"We can't have that..." I lower a hand down her body until I'm between her thighs. Sliding my fingers between her slit, I stop when I find her clit and rub slowly.

She gasps when the sensation builds and arches her back. "That feels so good."

"It's gonna feel even better when I'm inside you," I murmur in her ear, then glide two fingers between her folds until they're deep in her.

Her head falls back on my shoulder as her hands clamp around my thighs, squeezing hard.

"Please tell me you remembered condoms this time."

Chuckling, I nod. "Yes, but I did a rapid STI test two days ago and they emailed me the results this mornin'. In case you didn't wanna use one, I'm clear."

"You don't need me to take one?"

I add a third finger before impaling her again, enjoying how much she's moaning and squirming against me.

"I'm pretty sure you haven't had sex longer than me, so I trust you used protection too."

"Always, but that's a low blow."

Snickering, I capture her earlobe between my teeth. "It wasn't meant to be. But I know you well enough to know you haven't hooked up with a guy in a few years."

"How do you know that? I could've on the weekends I wasn't babysittin' your drunk ass."

"Hmm...well—" I contemplate how much to tell her but then remember she's my wife now, and I need to be honest with her, even if it pisses her off. "I might've been the reason guys didn't ask you out."

"W-what'd you mean?" Her tone drops but she stills moaning between her words.

"I...might've made it known around that you were off-limits and if I saw anyone checkin' you out, I'd give them my *if you think about touchin' her, I'll kill you* look. The locals knew, which is why I wasn't prepared for Jonah—the townie newbie—to come stumblin' through to grab your attention."

"Wait, back up—" She turns her face and meets my eyes. "You cockblocked me? For how long?"

Pinching my lips together, I act innocent with a small shrug. "I plead the fifth."

"Wilder Hollis!" She jerks her elbow back into my gut, causing me to let out a sharp *oof*.

"Okay, fine. After Barry Johnston kept flirtin' with you and you agreed to go on a date with him, I went to his job and told him to cancel it or I'd tell his boss he was sendin' dick pics to his wife."

"Oh my God!" Her jaw drops in horror. "*Why?*"

"Because he's a tool bag and you deserved better. But I knew you wouldn't listen to me. We were only casual friends back then, so I had to go about it in other ways."

"You're insane, you know that?"

"Only when it comes to you." I wink.

She rolls her eyes, situating herself against my body again. "So how did everyone else know not to ask me out?"

"Word travels quickly, especially when I'd go to some of the rodeos you'd be at, and make it known there, too."

"You're absolutely diabolical, you know that?"

"I warned ya that I was crazy about you."

"More like a stalker."

I chuckle, moving my attention to her clit. "Nothin' wrong with protectin' what I knew would be mine one day. I couldn't risk you findin' some moron who'd trick you into lovin' his bland ass."

She snickers, sucking in her lower lip. "You could've just told me you wanted me instead?"

My chest burns at the truth in her words because she's right. "I know, and I wish I would've, but I still had a lot of growin' up to do before I felt worthy. Still don't, but I couldn't wait any longer once you kissed me, and I knew the feelings weren't one-sided."

"Well, sorry to say, there's a couple guys who didn't get your memo." She purposely pushes her ass into my half-erect cock to taunt me. "I had some out-of-state rodeo events and a few too many drinks."

"Delly..." I growl, squeezing her breast harder.

"Hm?"

Her taunting tone tells me she knows exactly what she's doing.

"I don't wanna know."

"Why not? You made sure to scare as many of them away as you could. You don't wanna hear about the ones who —"

Grabbing her jaw, I crash my mouth down on hers and continue my movements between her legs. She moans when I swipe my tongue against hers and thrust deeper.

"It doesn't matter anymore because I plan to fuck any memory of them outta your mind as soon as I get inside you. You won't even remember their names after I'm done with you."

"Then what're you waitin' for, cowboy?"

I work my mouth down her jawline and neck. "Turn around and straddle me."

"Right now, in here?"

"I can't wait another second, Delly. Ride me so I can fill your sweet cunt," I nearly beg.

Luckily the tub is wide enough for her to kneel on top of my thighs, the sides of her legs hit against the porcelain, but there's enough room to stroke my shaft and slide between her legs.

She's a vision, looking so goddamn stunning on top of me. I can hardly believe this is *finally* happening.

"You ready?" I ask, gliding the tip of my cock between her slit.

"Is it gonna feel weird with your piercings?"

"Maybe at first, but it'll massage against your inner walls, which should be pleasurable," I explain, then gently grab her chin to look at me. "But if you're uncomfortable or in pain at any point, tell me. Okay?"

She nods. "I will."

Even though I can't see much beneath the water, I slowly guide my cock inside her, filling her inch by inch. Her rosy cheeks and sharp gasps hold my attention.

"Oh God..." Her eyes flutter closed as she tightens her grip on my shoulders.

"Doin' okay?"

She exhales, humming. "Mm-hmm."

"I'm gonna keep goin' then..."

"You're not all the way in?"

I hold back laughter, shaking my head. "Just breathe, baby. Relax your body for me."

She nods, dragging her bottom lip between her teeth.

With one hand on her hip and the other between us, I push her down and lift my hips until I'm fully seated inside her.

"Fuck, Delly..." I groan out her name, the feeling of being inside her so overwhelming, I forget to breathe.

"Can I move now?" she asks, holding onto my shoulders for leverage.

"God, yes."

The water around us splashes, spilling over the top ledge, and making a mess, but I don't have it in me to care. Delilah — *my wife* — feels so fucking good, I can't believe I've gone this long without her.

I grip her waist, helping her slide up and down my length, and as her tits bounce in my face, I lean in and taste them.

"It's so good," she whimpers, resting her forehead on mine. "Does it feel okay for you?"

Wrapping my hand behind her neck, I pull her lips closer. "You have no idea, baby."

It's a tight fit, in the tub and in her pussy, but I've never felt this type of high. Not even when I cut to release the pain and was close to passing out.

This isn't even comparable.

I shift her slightly so I can reach between us and thumb her clit. She continues riding me until she squeezes her eyes, throws her head back, and moans out her release—looking like the golden goddess as her wet hair splashes around us.

"You look so beautiful when you come," I tell her, teasing one of her nipples with my tongue. "I'm so close...but you feel too good. I don't wanna stop."

"Come inside me," she begs, and that's all it takes.

Arching my hips, I thrust a few more times before spilling inside her, filling her so full, I know she's going to leak the moment she stands.

"*Fuck*..." I bellow, leaning back against the tub, pulling her with me so her chest collides with mine. "That was a first for me."

"First what?" she asks, her chest rapidly moving as she resrts her head on my shoulder.

"First time without a condom. First time in a bathtub. First time feelin' this way."

"What way is that?" Her soft voice tells me she was hesitant to ask, but I'm glad she did.

It's hard to put into words, and I don't want to scare her away with the L word so quickly, but I want her to know how special this was and how special she is to me.

"For me, sex has always been physical—gettin' that euphoric feelin' and makin' sure my partner was satisfied. But once it was over, there was no desire for closeness. No emotions attached. But with you, I knew it'd be different. And it is. I've never had this fear of losin' someone or somethin' because no one and nothing's ever meant enough to be scared that I could somehow be without it. But when it comes to you, I'm terrified."

Delilah cups my cheeks, looks into my eyes, and then presses her soft lips to mine. I hold her against me like the lifeline she's always been.

"No one's ever expressed carin' about me that way," she whispers. "I hope you know I feel the same way. Even when I tried not to, you were always in the back of my mind. I never stopped thinkin' about you."

"Good...then let's hope it stays that way because now that I know what it feels to be inside you, there's no goin' back."

"Those piercings really do make a difference," she says, her cheeks flushing with heat.

I shake my head with laughter. "Just wait until I bend you over and hit even deeper."

"I don't think that's possible." She gives me a weary look.

"Oh, don't underestimate me." I play with the wet strands of her hair, brushing it behind her ear. "You'll be feelin' me in your throat by the time I sink into you."

"That's anatomically impossible, but I look forward to you provin' me wrong."

"You're such a smart-ass." I chuckle, pressing my lips to hers again because I can't stop tasting them.

"Who do you think I learned it from?" she murmurs, smirking against my mouth.

Wrapping my hand around her body, I slide down to her ass and give it a firm squeeze. "'Bout to teach you a lot more than that."

Chapter Twenty-Five
Delilah

After years of being a caregiver and the one to always help anyone in need, it's nice to be taken care of for once. But I never anticipated Wilder being the one doing it.

As we rinse off in the shower, he lathers soap over every inch of my body, slowly caressing his strong hands into my muscles and gently rubbing through the knots in my back and neck. The hot water streams down our bodies from the rainfall showerhead.

"I'm never leavin' this place," I murmur, moaning when he brings his hand between my legs to wash me there.

"Why do you think they book out a year in advance? Most of their bookings are returnin' customers."

"I'm ready to move in and never leave."

"I could remodel my bathroom like this for ya if you wanted," he says from behind me. "Although, I'd love to build a house on the ranch property like Landen and Ellie. Be close to the ranch while still havin' privacy."

"You've thought about stuff like that?"

"Of course. I don't wanna live in the ranch hand quarters

forever. They're nice enough for a bachelor but not nearly enough room for a family. I want my kids to have their own rooms and plenty of room for a swing set, trampoline, or sand box. Plus, the dogs will need a yard to roam free."

I blink my eyes open, double checking the man behind me is the same man I married.

"Why're you lookin' at me like you're surprised to hear I want kids and dogs?"

"Because I recall hearin' ya say you weren't settlin' down for another twenty years. Goin' from that to this is quite the extreme."

"That's before I knew being with you was an option." He faces me and winks, shifting the shower head so it doesn't spray in our faces. "And I know we're in this thirty day trial, but you should know, I'm all in with you and want everythin' you're willin' to give me. Babies, dogs, hell, cats too. And I'm happy to give you anythin' you want—deep tub included."

"I'm still not used to this open and sweet side of you," I admit bashfully. "Sometimes I forget you're the same man I've had to pull over on the side of the road for so you could throw up after drinkin' too much."

"That was a man buryin' his pain with alcohol." He closes the gap between us, cupping my face until our lips are inches apart. "Now the only pain I have is the thought of losin' you."

I lean in, bringing our mouths together for a brief kiss. "I share that same fear, Wilder. Since the moment I heard your voice and what you'd done to yourself, it consumed my thoughts. Even years later."

"I can promise you I'll never puttin' anyone through that trauma again. I work every day to fight those demons and they're not gonna win."

"I hate that you even have to."

He brushes wet strands off my forehead, looking more

vulnerable than I've ever seen him. "Therapy's been workin'
nicely. The antidepressants are still new and a low dose, so it's
too early to tell, but I'm hopeful for the first time in my life that
I'm on the right path."

"You're takin' medication? Since when?"

"A month ago." He shrugs. "I agreed to give them a shot,
but that's why I need to limit my alcohol. I gave myself a pass
for Vegas but now I want to stay clean to give them a chance to
work."

"I'm so proud of you for givin' yourself the best opportunity
at success. The Wilder I knew a year ago would've never done
this for himself."

"Your dad's death gave me a new perspective. After seeing
Harlow, your mom, and you distraught and heartbroken,
somethin' clicked in my mind that I needed to get help before it
was too late. Before I let the darkness consume me and win. I
knew I couldn't ignore it or drink the pain away for much
longer."

Tears well in the corner of my eyes. Dad's suicide affected
everyone, even if I could understand the chronic pain made
him take that path, I'm still conflicted about my anger and
sadness.

Wilder's thumbs wipe over my cheeks, catching the tears
before they fall.

"I'm so sick of cryin'," I whisper. "And feelin' sad."

"Let it out, baby. You don't need to hide your pain
from me."

He wraps his arms around me, pushing our bodies together,
when I bury my face against his chest, the tears continue to fall.

"Thanks for makin' me feel safe," I murmur once I'm all
cried out. "Not sure I've had that before."

Cupping my jaw, he presses a kiss to my forehead. "That's
my job—a privilege—and one I take seriously."

"These are the fluffiest robes I've ever worn." I beam, snuggling deeper into it while Wilder cooks our steaks, and I watch from the breakfast bar.

"They don't call it a luxury resort for nothin'." He grins. "Kinda cool to experience it as an adult, though. We usually camped out in the woods in tents and our trucks."

"I can see why couples come here. Gorgeous views, peaceful, and a romantic getaway with your partner."

"We always joked that it's the same model as the retreat, except ours focuses on families with kids, and theirs centers around couples only. Which, speakin' of, I have a couple's massage scheduled for us tomorrow before I have to go to my anger management class. Hope you don't mind I planned that."

My jaw's already on the floor before he finishes his sentence. "Are you kiddin'? That sounds amazin'."

"As long as they don't send a man to rub my wife, then it will be."

I roll my eyes, biting into a piece of the dark chocolate from the welcome basket. "Same goes for a woman rubbin' my husband, then."

"Say that again," he demands, his voice deeper than before.

"Which part?" I ask, confused.

"Where you called me your husband." He stalks over, turns my stool around so he can stand between my legs, and then cages me in with his arms against the counter behind me. "I wanna hear you call me that again."

"I shouldn't reward this caveman-like behavior..." I bite down on my lower lip when his gaze drops to my mouth.

He plucks my lip out, then rubs the pad of his thumb across it. "Please?"

"Well...since you asked so *nicely*," I taunt, bringing my hands up to his T-shirt and fisting the fabric to bring him closer. "I don't want another woman touchin' *my husband*."

His blue eyes darken and a raspy growl echoes from his throat before he slams his mouth down on mine. His tongue twists with mine, devouring me like he's waited his whole life to taste me.

The frying pan lid whistling grabs our attention and he rushes over to turn the burner down.

"Shit, I forgot about the steaks." He shakes his head, quickly flipping the meat. "You distracted me."

"*Me*? I was sittin' here mindin' my own business when you mauled me."

The side-eye he gives me makes me giggle.

I admire his shirtless back as he continues cooking, and even though I offer to help, he demands I stay put. Since he's not drinking, he told me to enjoy the champagne, so I pour myself a glass and drink it at the table while I wait.

"How many kids do you want?" I blurt when Wilder serves me my plate. A juicy steak with mushrooms and a baked potato stuffed with sour cream and cheese. I'm actually impressed with how well he did.

"Uh...maybe three."

"Boys or girls?" I cut into the meat and then dip it in the sauce before eating it.

"Doesn't matter to me, but one of each would be cool."

I nod as I finish chewing my food. "What kind of dog do you want?"

He furrows his brows, sticking his fork into a piece of meat. "I feel like I'm in a datin' interview."

"Well, kinda. Couples usually talk about this stuff during the datin' period and before they get married. Since we skipped all that, we're havin' it now."

"Okay...I think I'd like a Great Dane."

My eyes bulge out of my head. "Those are huge! Practically mini horses."

"I know. Big ole babies. What kind do you want?"

"I was thinkin' like a Bernese Mountain Dog. They're great farm and ranch dogs, plus they're amazin' with kids. Good work dog, good family dog. Win-win."

He nods along while chewing his food. "Okay, I can agree with that. What do you wanna name him?"

"Why do you assume we're gettin' a boy dog?"

"Oookay, what do ya wanna name *her*?"

"Depends which month she's born and time of year."

He gives me a weary look. "Why's that matter?"

"Because it'll determine if she gets a summer name or a winter name."

He smiles around his fork as if he's holding back from laughing at me. "Alright, let's say she's born in summer."

"Sunny, Daisy, Mango, Callie." Just to name a few.

"Cute. What if she's born in winter?"

"Ivy, Cocoa, Luna, Holly."

He arches a brow. "What if she's born in the fall?"

"Ah, trick question." I smirk, quickly thinking. "Belle, Willow, Ember, Hazel."

"How do you come up with these so fast?"

"I've been keepin' track of baby names I like since I was twelve."

"So you have our baby's names picked out too?"

I chuckle, lifting my shoulder slightly. "Maybe, maybe not."

"I'd like a Great Dane named Hank."

"Hank?" I snort, taking a sip of my champagne.

"Hank Hollis! Doesn't that sound badass?"

"Oh my God," I gasp, some of the liquid going up my nose.

"So how soon do you wanna have babies and dogs?" he asks, handing me a napkin for my face.

"Uh, well...accordin' to my OB and mother, I'm not gettin' any younger and neither are my eggs. I'll be considered high-risk when I'm thirty-five."

"That's still four years away."

"Right, but if we want three kids and each pregnancy takes nine months plus however long it takes to get pregnant, I should be pregnant with the first one..." I do the math in my head since I'll be thirty-two soon. "Within the next three months if I want to avoid the potential high-risk flag during my third pregnancy."

His Adam's Apple bobs when he swallows his food down. "Okay, then...well, I mean, after the thirty days are up, we should consider uh...makin' it happen within that timeframe."

I push my tongue into my cheek to keep from laughing at how flustered he sounds. "Are you sweatin'?"

"No, well, if I am, it's because I was in the hot kitchen. Not because we're talkin' about babies."

"Mm-hmm. Maybe we start with a dog, then?"

"I wasn't sweatin' over that," he urges.

When I arch my brow, he sits up straighter with determination.

"Don't believe me? I'll knock you up right now." He aims his thumb over his shoulder. "Let's go."

This time, I do laugh. "Stop worryin'. I think you'll make a great dad one day. When we're ready to take that step."

"You really think so?"

"Yes. I've seen you with Willow and Poppy, and even

Laken." Tripp and Magnolia's son is only a year old but he started walking three months ago and gives them a run for their money. "Not sayin' it'd be easy, but I've always wanted to be a mom."

"I can see that. You're gonna be an amazin' one, too."

"But a dog first...right?" I ask hesitantly because now I'm conflicted.

"Right, right. Like next week?"

I bellow out a laugh. "House, dog, and then babies."

"Okay, hold on..." He pulls out his phone. "Let me write this down."

I playfully kick him underneath the table. "It's okay if we let things happen how they happen. Not everythin' has to be planned out. Considerin' none of *this* was in the plan..." I wave my hand between us. "I kinda like not knowin' what's comin'."

"Good, because if there's one thing I've learned about life so far, it's that the unexpected parts are the most fun."

"I'll cheers to that." I hold up my glass and clank it with his sweet tea.

"Everythin' was delicious, by the way. You're not half bad in the kitchen," I tell him once we've cleared our plates.

"That's pretty much the limit on what I can do, so don't get too excited."

"It's more than I can do," I admit, rinsing the dishes in the sink.

He stands behind me, brushing my hair off to one shoulder. "There's ice cream in the freezer if you'd like some dessert."

"Hm...that sounds great."

"I think it'd taste even better suckin' it off this neck..." He slides his tongue underneath my ear, making me shiver.

"Stop fidgetin'..." I tell him for the third time, smacking his hand away from his face.

"Is it supposed to be so itchy?" He wiggles his nose, making the sheet mask move with it.

"That means it's workin'. Give it a few more minutes." I snuggle into the couch next to him, flipping through movies until we agree on one.

After dinner and eating dessert — in a bowl — I wanted to use some of the items from the gift basket and noticed there were two masks. He didn't find it as amusing as I did when I laughed at how it fit over his facial hair.

"It's cold," he complains.

"Aren't you supposed to be a rough 'n tough cowboy? Can't handle a little self care?"

"I get to pick the next activity," he says with a pout.

"Does it involve you being naked?"

"Well you definitely will be."

I nudge him with my elbow.

"But once I see that butt plug in your tight little ass, I'll be naked too."

"Wait, *what*?"

"You said you lost the remote to yours, so I had Mattie pick up a new one."

"Oh my God..." My head falls back on the cushion. "You told my best friend to buy me a new plug?"

"Trust me, she was more than happy to help."

"Why am I not even surprised?" I shake my head, cackling at the idea of them having a conversation about butt plugs.

We finally decide on what to watch after he vetoed all my romcoms and I rejected his action movies.

"We can take these off before we start it..." I jump to my feet and then pull him up with me.

"Thank God," he mutters.

"Don't think you're off the hook yet. Under eye masks are next."

"Under what? Why?"

"Because after thirty, we get eye bags, and these'll help."

Once we dry our faces, I get the eye masks out. "And they're cute."

"Just what I was hopin' for," he deadpans.

"You mock me, but one day you'll thank me when everyone else our age has baggy eyes but you don't."

He smirks. "Are you sayin' you won't love me if I do?"

My heart ticks up at the casual way he drops the L word. I'm not even sure he realizes he said it because he doesn't even flinch.

"No, but it'll keep us lookin' younger. And it's refreshin'." I grin, placing one underneath each of his eyes and rubbing my finger over it to make sure they stick. "There."

He glances in the mirror. "Of course they're pink and purple."

"I don't know what you're complainin' about. Purple is *so* your color," I tease, placing the other set under my eyes.

"Is it?" He purses his lips into a faux kissy pout and checks himself out in the mirror.

"Just remember..." I turn and go up on my tippy toes to bring our lips closer. "You married this."

He closes his arms around my waist, pulling me into his chest. "Sure did, and I'd do it again, sober or drunk."

"I think that's meant to be sweet, right?" I wrap my hands around his biceps, holding onto him.

He kisses the top of my nose. "That's correct, Mrs. Hollis."

Oh God, that's the first time he's called me that.

Besides the time he did it as a joke before we got hitched.

And while a part of me thinks that name is reserved for his mother, the other part is totally turned on by it.

"So…" I lick my lips. "Where did you say that butt plug is?"

Chapter Twenty-Six
Wilder

"Fuckin' *stunning.*" I smack her bare ass cheek, squeezing it after she wiggles her hips in front of me. Bent over on the bed, spread wide and naked, she's making me hard as fuck and testing every ounce of my willpower not to thrust into her right now.

Kneeling behind her, I dip my tongue between her slit and taste her wet pussy. Then I glide up between her cheeks and twirl my piercing along her crack, teasing the sensitive area.

"Oh God…" The plug soaking in her mouth muffles her words.

I fist my hand around a chunk of her hair and tug slightly before thrusting a finger deep inside her cunt. Once it's coated in her juices, I slide it up to where my tongue was and slowly push through the tight barrier.

"Relax, baby. Gonna go slow, but you can't tense up."

Leaning over, I press kisses along the soft skin of her lower back as my fingers play between her cheeks. She moans around the plug and then reaches between her thighs to rub her clit.

"You want me to fill you up, baby?" I bring my finger back to her tight hole and sink inside. "Fill all your pretty holes?"

She nods. "Yes, please."

Grabbing her hips, I pull her up until her back meets my chest. Then I remove the plug between her lips and quickly cover hers with mine.

"Hope you can keep up, darlin'. You've made me absolutely feral for you."

"Do your best, *hubby*." She licks her lips, smirking up at me. "I'm ready."

I bury my face in her neck and suck hard, needing to mark her. Then I kiss down her spine, tangling my fingers in her hair as I make my way down her back.

"Never thought I'd agree with Mattie, but she was right. You do have the cutest freckles on your ass."

She chuckles, but when I give her ass a hard smack, she yelps and nearly falls to her stomach. Luckily, she catches herself and props herself up with her palms.

"Fuck, Wilder."

Her scolding tone makes me smile with pride.

Grabbing the small bottle of lube Mattie also bought, I lather the plug and my fingers. Then I slide two inside, coating her with it as much as I can before pushing deeper inside.

"This okay?"

"Mm-hmm. You can put it in now," she urges.

Bringing the plug between her cheeks, I tease her hole before slowly twisting it in and securing it as deep as it'll go.

"How's that?"

"So good." She arches as low as she can go, giving me the perfect view of the red heart-shaped plug.

My cock throbs between us, and although I'm desperate to get inside her, I'm holding out as long as I can.

Grabbing the remote from the nightstand, I turn it on, and she immediately squeals at the sensation.

"Holy shit…" She buries her face in the pillow.

"Too much?" I ask, playing with the different vibration speeds.

Her moans muffle her reply, but she quickly shakes her head.

Setting the remote to the side, I pull her up and capture her mouth before lying back on the bed with her on top of me. Instead of straddling me, she slides down my naked body and grabs my shaft. She wraps her mouth around me and sucks me between her lips, using her tongue to slide around my pierced tip.

"Christ, Delly…that's so good." I lean back with my arms behind my head and watch as she takes every inch of me down her throat. "Just like that."

She peeks up at me, her mouth stuffed with my cock, and the sight has me ready to explode. Her palm slides up my abs and chest, and I lean in to capture a finger between my teeth.

Her mouth and hand work me so good, I have to stop her so I don't come.

With a few swift movements, I flip her over until she's bent over in front of me. Blond hair flies across her back and I twist the ends around my fist, then give it a quick tug.

"Hang on, my love."

I slide halfway into her and nearly lose my breath at how tight she squeezes me. Once I'm sure she's okay, I sink in deeper.

"*Fuck*," she says under her breath.

When I'm seated all the way, I pull out and then slam back in again. Her palms flatten against the headboard, but I reach up and pull her arms behind her back, then bind them with my hand.

"You feel nice and full, baby?"

"God, yes. Don't stop."

And I don't.

My fingers dig into her hip while my other hand continues holding her wrists in place. She's a breathless, sweaty mess by the time her body shakes with her first orgasm.

"Thatta girl." I release her arms, sit back on my haunches, and flip her over.

"Jesus." She gasps, situating her legs around my thighs before sliding back inside.

"How'd you like the piercings and plug from that angle?" I taunt, towering over her.

"That's the fastest I've ever come during sex before, so yeah, I'm a fan."

I chuckle at her honesty and then lift one of her legs, resting her ankle on my shoulder.

"Good, but now I wanna watch you come this way." I bring my mouth to hers, stretching her body with mine and feeling the tightness around me.

She wraps a hand around my neck, but I quickly pin it on the bed next to her, then suck underneath her ear.

"Use your other hand," I whisper. "Mark me."

Her nails dig into my skin, dragging down my back as far as she can go. It's the kind of pain I welcome and crave when it comes to her.

"Fuck, it's so good." I adjust my body with hers, wrapping her other leg around my waist until she lifts her hips and grinds against me. "Yes...do that again."

This time when she does, she throws her head back and screams through the built-up pleasure.

"So fuckin' beautiful," I tell her. "I can't get enough of you."

"Let me ride you," she begs.

I roll us over until she's positioned on top of me, her thighs straddling me and my arms pinned above my head with her hands.

"Don't move," she orders, and her taking control makes my cock twitch against her.

Instead of sliding down on my shaft like I expect, she presses her mouth to my chest and slowly kisses her way down my abdomen. Leaning up on my elbows, I watch as she makes her way to my cock, slowly sliding her tongue around the tip and piercings.

She smirks up at me, then spreads my legs farther apart so she can slide between them and starts kissing down one of my thighs. When she makes her way to the other one, I brace myself.

Her kisses soften as she slowly brushes her lips over the scar tissue as if she's purposely giving them extra attention. Her heated gaze meets mine, but when I see the tears in her eyes, my heart cracks in two.

"Delilah..." I reach for her, but she somberly shakes her head, then continues down my body.

I've never had a woman notice them the way she has, let alone get emotional over seeing them. Even though they're not as visible all these years later, she made an effort to seek them out and give them as much love and care as she did the rest of me.

When she finally climbs back up my body, I sit up and cup her face, crashing my mouth down on hers. She lifts up until she impales herself with my cock and we both gasp at the sensation.

"Goddamn, baby." I hold myself up with one hand behind me while the other cups her ass with a smack. "Take what you need from me."

"Mm, do that again."

I slap her ass harder this time and she yelps as I squeeze it in my grip.

"Again," she murmurs, rocking faster. "Harder."

"Jesus Christ…" I'm barely holding back as it is, but I give her exactly what she wants, making sure to leave a nice red handprint this time.

Her head falls back with a throaty moan, pushing her breasts out, and I quickly capture one in my palm.

"You like that, huh?" I taunt, pinching her nipple between my finger and thumb. "You're drivin' me crazy, Delly. I'm gonna fill you so fuckin' full."

"Yes, please…" she whimpers, nodding. "Come inside me."

My balls tighten up and she grinds down on me faster, holding on to my shoulders as our bodies move against each other.

"Play with your clit for me," I order. "I'm so close."

I somehow refrain until she comes once more, and then I bury my face in her neck and release inside her.

We end up a hot, tangled mess of limbs, heavy breathing, and hearts pounding.

With her body collapsed on top of me, I wrap my arms around her and roll us over to the side.

"You're so perfect," I whisper, brushing sweaty strands of hair off her face. "And so damn beautiful."

"I'm not perfect," she mutters, barely able to move.

My finger traces down her nose and around her cheek, memorizing every inch of her face.

"You're perfect *for me*. In every single way." I kiss the tip of her nose. "That's why I fell so hard for you before I even knew what you looked like. Then when we met, it only confirmed what I'd felt, and I knew no one else could ever compare. I was prepared to live the rest of my life without getting to act on my feelings, but as long as I got to be in yours in some capacity, I'd still die a happy man."

"Wilder…" She blinks, looking up at me with more tears in her eyes. "I don't need thirty days to know I want to stay married to you. No one has ever been so open about how they feel about me, and I'd be a fool to even think about lettin' you go when I've wanted you just as long."

My heart kicks up with shock and pure happiness. "Really?"

"Yes, really." She beams with laughter.

I roll on top of her, crashing my mouth down on hers, and she continues giggling when we nearly fall off the bed.

"Shit, we better go clean up before we make an even bigger mess."

Standing, I pull her up with me but can't stop smiling when she's in front of me.

"I'm still not doin' your laundry," she says firmly, poking me in the chest.

Grinning, I cup her cheeks and give her a quick peck on the lips. "Baby, I've been waitin' to take care of you for years, so stop worryin' about me. It's my turn to help you the way you helped me nine years ago."

Before she can respond, I lift her into my arms and take her into the shower. We clean each other and laugh about how it's our second of the day.

Once we dry off and change into comfy clothes, I make us popcorn and then we finally sit to watch the movie. Although truthfully, I hardly pay attention to it because mine is mostly on my wife and how gorgeous she is.

And how fucking happy she makes me.

Something I haven't genuinely felt in a long-ass time.

Halfway through, she falls asleep against me, so I carry her to bed and then clean up the kitchen before sliding in next to her. I don't remember ever feeling this level of happiness in my life before, and although I'm scared as hell to lose it, I'm putting everything I have into making sure I'm the best husband and partner for Delilah.

Not having to wake up for work at the ass crack of dawn is a nice change, but it means my body's still programmed to get up earlier than I need to be, which usually sucks.

But today, it means I get more time with my wife before I have to leave for anger management class.

Climbing out of bed, I head to the bathroom to freshen up, and then walk to the kitchen to figure out what I can make for breakfast.

There's a box of pancake mix in the pantry, fresh blueberries and bacon in the fridge, and a mini waffle maker on the counter. I've never made waffles before, but the directions on the box are simple enough, so I give it a try.

Thirty minutes later, I have two plates full of waffles, bacon, and scrambled eggs.

The rest of the kitchen — I'll deal with that later. It's a mess, but I got the job done.

Since Delilah hasn't woken up, I slide in next to her and feather kisses under her ear. "Baby, are you up? Breakfast is ready, so I hope you're hungry."

"Go away," she mutters, burying her face deeper in the pillow.

Chuckling, I slide my hand down her body and give her ass a little slap. "Don't make me wake you another way."

"Some of us prefer sleep."

"Is that so?" I challenge, sliding my hand beneath her shorts and discovering she's not wearing panties. When I brush a finger softly between her slit and rub over her clit, she moans quietly but doesn't move an inch.

"Hm...looks like I'm gonna need to go to plan B."

"As long as I don't have to move."

"Nope." Smirking, I slide underneath the covers and between her legs. Since she's not wearing underwear and the fabric of her shorts is thin, I bury my face between her thighs and moan against her pussy.

When she doesn't push me away or tell me off, I slowly slide her shorts down a few inches and start flicking my tongue against her clit. She squirms, arching her hips against my mouth, and then her fingers are tangling in my hair.

"Wilder?"

My head pops up, abruptly stopping. "Are you expectin' someone else down here?"

Her body shakes with laughter. "No, but I was half asleep."

"You can go back to sleep," I tease.

"Okay, but hurry up. I'm hungry."

"That's not funny," I deadpan.

Chuckling at my expression, she reaches down and pulls her shorts off, then spreads her legs around me. Repositioning myself between them, I wrap my hands around her thighs and drag her pussy closer to my mouth.

I thrust two fingers inside, feeling how wet she is, and then flatten my tongue up her slit before lathering her clit. She writhes underneath me, arching her back and pulling my hair —and I love every second of it. Bringing her to the edge and then pulling back before doing it again has her desperate and needy.

"Wilder, please...I'm so close," she whines, pushing my

head down against her core. "No more stoppin' or I swear to God—"

With a twist of my wrist, I hook my fingers in deeper, suck her clit harder, and then soon, she's falling over the edge. Her sweet juices explode on my tongue, and I lap them up before feather kisses along her thigh.

"Well…" Her chest rises and falls as she tries to catch her breath. "I'm awake now."

Chapter Twenty-Seven

Delilah

Waking up with Wilder's mouth between my thighs is something I could *definitely* get used to.

I knew he'd be good at *physical activities*, but it's so much more than that. When feelings this intense are involved, it makes everything he does ten times better.

The way my heart races when he kisses me and how butterflies invade my stomach whenever he touches me tells me I'm in *sooo* deep. Being down bad doesn't even scratch the surface of what I'm feeling because I've never felt this before.

And now I'm the one who's scared of losing it.

Because it feels too good to be true.

Wilder's breakfast spread is a nice surprise, but then we fight with the espresso maker that neither of us can seem to figure out. Instead of messing with it and breaking it, Wilder texts his cousin and a girl shows up with two coffees.

"Hi!" She beams when she enters the cabin. "I'm Bellamy Langston. You must be Delilah."

Ah…one of Wilder's cousins.

"Yes, I am. Thank you for bringin' these." I beam when she sets them down on the table.

She holds out her hand to shake mine. "My pleasure. Those machines can be tricky. Let me show ya how to use it."

Wilder's in the shower, so it's just me and her, but after a few minutes, I'm impressed with how quickly she got it to work.

"I'll give it a try tomorrow so we don't have to bother ya again," I say, hoping I can remember everything she showed me.

"Oh, it's no problem. This is my job. You'd be surprised how many times I walk in on half-naked couples." She purses her lips. "It's actually quite awkward."

"Hey, Bellamy!" Wilder calls from the hallway, approaching in only a towel.

"Yep, like that," she mutters.

I snort, shaking my head. Water drips down his hair and chest, making every inch look edible.

"Hey, how's the honeymoon goin' so far?"

"Great…" He smirks, waggling his brows at me. "We're gettin' a couples massage soon."

"Oh, you're gonna love that. Pedro and Felipe are literal gods and their hands are magic." She sighs, grinning. "Employees get free massages once a month and you better believe I request one of them every time."

"'Cuse me?" Wilder crosses his arms. "You have no female massage therapists?"

"Well, sure we do, but they're not workin' today."

"Looks like we're gonna have to cancel."

"Wilder!" I scold, rolling my eyes at him. "He's jokin'," I tell her.

"No, he's not," Wilder mimics.

"So did you like…marry him on purpose?" Bellamy jerks her head toward him.

"Drunk in Vegas…" I confirm.

"Ahh." She nods. "That makes sense."

"What's that supposed to mean?" Wilder grabs one of the coffees and takes a sip.

"She's too hot for you," Bellamy says bluntly. "Way outta your league."

My face heats, and I grab the other cup to hide the blush covering my cheeks.

"Now *that* I can agree with…" Wilder winks at me.

"That's not true. He's hot, too," I defend.

"Gross, strongly disagree." She claps her hands together. "If there's anythin' else y'all need, just text me."

"Thank you again for the coffee." I smile.

"You're welcome. Enjoy the rest of your honeymoon!" She walks toward the door, then quickly turns around. "But not too much. We've had to replace that table three times already."

"You sure you'll be okay while I'm gone?" Wilder asks me for the second time.

After our couples massage, I took a hot shower and haven't left the bed since. Felipe worked out every knot and kink in my body like some kind of magician. Bellamy wasn't lying.

I almost asked him to move in with us.

"Yes…" I snuggle deeper underneath the covers. "I'm

gonna catch up on sleep that you deprived me of and dream about Felipe's hands."

He swats my ass before sitting next to me on the mattress. I knew that'd rile him up.

"Just his hands!"

"Better be thinkin' of mine instead." He slides his palm under my shirt and squeezes my breast over my bra. "Gonna make you forget all about his hands when I get back later."

"Oh no...don't do that...how awful..." I drawl. "Whatever you do, don't rub them all over me with oil."

He palms an ass cheek again, squeezing it, then stands. "You're mouthy. Gonna have to deal with that later too." He winks, leaning in for a kiss. "Should be back in three hours."

"I'll be here, Pappi," I call out as he walks away, knowing that'll rile him up even more.

"Delilah! I *swear*..." He huffs.

Cackling at his frustration, I roll over and grab my phone from the nightstand so I can check in with Mattie.

DELILAH

I think I met your future husband. Big, strong hands. Dark, sultry eyes. An accent that'll cause you to leak down your thigh...

MATTIE

umm SOLD. When can I come pick him up?

DELILAH

He's one of the massage therapists at the resort. I think you'll have to move here.

MATTIE

Massage therapist? Say less. Surprised Wilder let another man touch you...unless this is where you tell me my future husband is down a hand?

Sin With Me

He wasn't a fan, but he sucked it up for the sake of knowing he'll get to twist me like a pretzel later.

MATTIE

You use the butt plug yet? 😈

I snort.

DELILAH

As a matter of fact, we did. Thanks for that, I guess?

MATTIE

Consider it my wedding gift to the horny couple!

Happy*

Oh wait, horny is probably more accurate.

I bellow out a laugh because she's definitely right.

DELILAH

And the wait was soooo worth it. That magic cross piercing gets an A+ from me. His tongue piercing does too, but the friction against the nerves feels so good.

MATTIE

Okay calm down, you're turning me on over here, and I didn't charge my vibrator.

DELILAH

Use your other one.

MATTIE

Oh good idea...if only they had pierced dildos.

DELILAH

New business idea...

MATTIE

Or maybe I need to get out and meet someone. Too bad all the men in this town give me the ick.

DELILAH

Maybe it's time to get out of Sugarland Creek and see what else is out there.

MATTIE

Probably more men who'll give me the ick.

DELILAH

Too bad all of Wilder's brothers are taken now.

MATTIE

Story of my life.

A knock on the door makes me jump. It's only been thirty minutes since Wilder left, so I have no idea who could be here.

After quickly putting on my leggings and sweatshirt, I walk hesitantly to the front and see a woman through the window. She smiles when she notices me and holds up what looks like a picnic basket.

"Hello?" I greet, cautiously opening the door.

"Hi. Delilah?"

"Yes."

"I'm Maisie, Warren's wife."

"Oh, hi. Come in." I step back to give her room to walk in. "Wilder's not here, though."

"He called and asked if I could bring you somethin' to eat because — his words, not mine — she'll starve if you don't feed her. She burns toast and will forget to turn on the stovetop when she boils water."

My mouth pops open, and I huff with my hands on my hips. "That was one time."

That's what I get for telling him embarrassing stories about myself.

Maisie laughs, setting the basket down on the table. "No judgment from me. When I went to college in New York, I lived off bagel runs and iced coffee. The second time I moved there, my apartment was too small to even have a full kitchen, so I rarely cooked."

"Wilder's told me a little about you being a literary agent. That sounds so cool."

"It can be..." She opens the basket and starts removing containers of food. "It's a lot of work and keeps me very busy. Not as much now since I hired a few agents, but in the beginning, it consumed my life day and night."

"I bet livin' in the city was a fun experience..." I grab two plates from the cupboard, unsure if she's staying or not, and bring them to the table.

"Yes and no. I'm glad I went because I learned a lot about myself, but now, I wouldn't leave this place if you paid me. This is where I grew up and it's home. Plus, comin' back and fallin' in love with Warren all over again was worth it."

"Aw...that sounds so sweet."

"It wasn't always sunshine and rainbows. When I first arrived, he slammed the door in my face."

My eyes widen, but now I'm fully locked in for the tea.

"Honestly, I don't blame him. We got married after I graduated college, but when I found a literary job in New York City, I moved back there even though I knew he wouldn't come with me. I hoped he'd change his mind, but years later, I met someone else. When he proposed, I came here to beg Warren to sign the divorce papers I sent him previously."

"Oh, shit." My jaw drops. "No wonder he slammed the door."

She laughs, nodding. "Yep, and it was a fight every second to get to where we are now. But it brought us back together, so I'm not too mad about it."

My stomach growls as she continues setting everything out. "This smells delicious."

"I can't take the credit. It's from the restaurant on the property here, but the chef is incredible. If y'all have time before you leave, stop in and have dinner. It's very romantic." She beams, piling beef tips and pasta on one of the plates.

"I'm sure we will, but if not, I'll make him bring me back." I grin. "Can you eat with me?"

"Are you sure? I was only intendin' to drop it off."

"Please, stay. I'd love to hear more about you and Warren, the resort, and your job."

"Okay, sure." She smiles. "But truthfully, I'm supposed to be gettin' information about you so I can tell the others about Wilder's mysterious new wife."

"Oh God…" I groan, chuckling. "It's a long story."

The corner of her lips curves up. "All the best ones are."

Maisie and I are curled up on the couch with wine glasses by the time Wilder walks in. He peeks into the living room and shakes his head when he sees she's still here.

"You were supposed to drop it off, remember?"

"She invited me," Maisie defends.

"What's wrong with her stayin' and keepin' me company?"
I ask.

Wilder kicks off his boots and walks over. "Because I know
Maisie has endless embarrassin' stories about me to tell."

"You mean like the time you ziplined through the resort
buck-ass naked?"

He points at her. "That's the one."

"I didn't realize y'all knew each other as teens too," I say to
Wilder. "You left that little part out, didn't ya?"

"Because I knew she had too much dirt on me."

"I really enjoyed the one where you bellyflopped off a cliff
and smacked the water so hard, your entire chest was bruised
for a month."

"Hey, that's better than the time I got drunk and jumped off
a twenty-foot quarry. Landen and Tripp had to give me CPR."

"That does not make me feel better, actually." I roll my eyes.
"No more cliff divin' for you."

"All the locals knew that when the Hollis siblings came over
the summer, there was gonna be trouble. There was either one
gettin' arrested or one being rushed to the ER."

I look at Wilder with a raised brow.

"Don't look at me like that. I wasn't the only one causin'
trouble…"

"I'm pretty sure most of the rules set in place here were
because of y'all," Maisie adds.

"Waylon never mentioned going while we dated. When did
y'all stop comin' here?"

"Uh…" Wilder scratches the back of his neck. "The year
Landen's friend died during their spring break."

"I don't think Waylon told me about that…" I try to think
back, but it's been years. I'm pretty sure I would've
remembered something like that, though.

"That's another long story," Wilder says, walking to the

kitchen, and then returns with a bottle of water moments later. "It involves Ellie's cousin, Angela."

"Oh…" Well, now I need to know.

"There's leftovers in the microwave for ya if you're hungry," Maisie tells him, getting to her feet. "I should get home before Warren comes lookin' for me."

"Thank you again for bringin' me dinner." I stand and give her a hug.

"You're so welcome. I'm glad we got to chat for a bit."

"Me too. Hope we can do it again soon."

We exchanged numbers before Wilder showed up, so we'll be able to text and keep in touch.

Maisie rounds the couch and stands in front of Wilder. "You picked a good one. Now don't fuck it up." She gives his chest a little smack.

His smile widens when he flicks his gaze over to me. "Don't plan on it."

He walks her to the door, thanks her again, and then returns to the living room.

"How was your class?" I ask, wrapping my arms around him. "Did ya miss me?"

"Good and abso-fucking-lutely I did." He leans down and presses his lips to mine.

"I'll warm up your plate if you're hungry," I offer.

"Sure, but then I'd like my dessert in bed." He cups my ass and squeezes.

"Okay, but it's self-serve only."

Chapter Twenty-Eight
Wilder

The past three days at Willow Branch Mountain have been some of the best days I've had in years. Spending them with Delilah, getting her *mostly* to myself, and learning new things about each other still has me in the best mood by the time I arrive at the shelter Sunday afternoon.

I hate that I'm missing another family dinner, but Delilah will be there, and if there's anyone I trust to handle my family's antics, it's her.

"Wilder!" Miss Tierney smiles wide, greeting me with a hug. "We've missed you 'round here."

"I'm glad to be back. Where do you need me tonight?"

It's the night before Christmas Eve, which means it's going to be packed. As sad as it is to think about so many people who aren't with their families this time of year, I'm glad I'm able to be here and help them have a holiday dinner.

"All hands on deck tonight, so you'll be servin' up front and then doin' dishes in the back. You might end up stayin' later than usual."

"No problem. I gave my wife a heads-up I'd be late tonight."

"*Wife*? When did that happen?"

She looks thoroughly shocked and my mind goes back to when Delilah asked a million questions about Miss Tierney and if she was married or not.

"A couple weeks ago."

She arches a brow, folding her arms. "When you were in Vegas?"

"Yep." I beam. "And then we took a mini honeymoon."

"Oh…" She plasters a smile on her face. "Well, congrats!"

"Thank you."

"Everyone's wearin' Santa hats or reindeer headbands, so feel free to pick one from my office."

"Sure, will do."

Then she's off making sure everything else is ready to go before the doors open.

Once the line of people enters, we stay busy for a solid two hours. The cooks bring out pan refills and then take back the empty ones I'll clean later.

Once the line comes to an end, I walk around and offer to clear their plates from the table. I enjoy this part of the night because it means I get a few seconds to chat with them and ask how they're doing.

One of the little boys comes up to me and hands me something wrapped in a white grocery bag.

"What's this?" I ask him.

"I made it at school."

"It's for me?"

He nods frantically, nearly jumping out of his shoes. "Yeah, open it!"

I unravel the tape and open the bag, then reach in to grab it.

"Oh my gosh, Sam." My jaw drops at the wooden photo frame decorated in red and green painted pasta noodles. But that's not what has my emotions in overdrive. Inside is a photo of us from my first weekend volunteering here.

I kneel in front of him, admiring how thoughtful this is. "This is absolutely precious. Thank you, bud."

As soon as I open my arms, he falls into them. "You're welcome."

"You have no idea how much this means to me."

He pulls back with a toothy grin on his face. "You like it?"

"I *love* it. I'm gonna display it on my kitchen counter so I see it every single day."

"Cool." He flashes a bashful smile.

I feel bad that I don't have anything to give him in return, so I pull off my Santa hat and put it on his head. "Here, you look much cuter in it than me."

He giggles. "Thanks."

"What're you hopin' Santa brings you this year?" I ask, wanting to give him something the next time I'm here. He's in second grade, so I assume he's into stuff like trucks and legos.

His gaze falls to the ground and he lifts a shoulder. "I didn't make a list."

"No? Why not?"

"Mama lost her job, and I didn't want her to feel sad."

My heart breaks in two, and I should've known better than to ask. "I'm sorry. I'll see what I can do for her, but in the meantime, what's somethin' you'd like?"

"Um...a bed?"

"What do you mean? Like new sheets?"

"No. I sleep on the couch because my little sister's crib takes up too much space in my mom's room. She has a bed we used to share, but she gets up a lot at night to feed Lily, so I sleep in the livin' room. But the couch ain't that comfortable."

I try not to show it on my face, but I'm devastated. It's not the first time I've heard their stories, and I always try to help when I can. Miss Tierney warned me not to get too emotionally attached, but when it comes to kids, there's no way I can't.

"Mom!" Sam calls, waving to her behind me.

"There ya are." She gives him a look, then glances at me. "Sorry, I went to change Lily and told him to stay put, but of course he ran off on me."

I stand, smiling at her. "No problem. He showed me the sweet photo frame he made for me."

"I thought you'd like it." She grins. "He talks about you all the time and gets so excited to see you on the weekends."

My chest aches, knowing he was probably let down at not seeing me yesterday or the weekend before.

I lower my voice so Sam can't overhear me. "I'd like to help with gettin' him something for Christmas, but I don't want to overstep. Please let me know what I can do. For you and Lily, too."

She looks uncomfortable at my offer.

"I know it's not easy accepting help, especially from someone you don't know that well, but I'd like to do somethin' if you're okay with it."

"Like what?" she asks just above a whisper.

"Sam says you're out of a job. We're lookin' for a receptionist at The Lodge in Sugarland Creek. Flexible hours, great pay, health benefits, and on-site childcare. The listin' hasn't even gone out yet, but if you want it, it's yours."

"You're serious?" she asks nervously, shifting Lily to her other hip.

"Absolutely."

She nods frantically, tears swelling in her eyes.

"Great." I smile wide. "I'll let them know to expect you on January second. Enjoy the holiday with your kids, and I'll make sure you have enough cash to cover your bills until then. I'll make sure Santa comes too…" I lean in and say softly.

"You really don't have to do that," she murmurs, on the verge of tears, but she quickly wipes her cheeks.

I look down at Sam and grin, seeing the sweetest kid I've ever met. "It'd be my honor to do it. Plus, I know my wife would love to as well."

Delilah and I have plans to go Christmas shopping tomorrow — on the busiest shopping day of the year, no less — but with everything else going on, we haven't had time.

"Here, program your number and address.," I hand her my phone. "I'll text you so we can swing by tomorrow night, if that's okay?"

"Yeah, we'll be home." She plugs in her name and information.

"Perfect." I kneel in front of Sam. "You better be good for your mom so Santa brings you lots of presents, okay?"

"Okay!" he squeals, jumping into my arms.

I laugh when he nearly tackles me to the floor.

"I gotta get back to the kitchen and clean up, but you guys have a good night. Thank you again for my gift. I'll treasure it forever." I wink.

"Is there a reason your grandmother would randomly put her hand on my belly and then walk away without so much as a word or explanation as to what she was doin'?" Delilah asks as she changes into her pajamas.

"Uh...beats me. Did she do it to anyone else?"

"No!" She stands in front of the full-length mirror and shifts to the side to look at herself. "Maybe I gained a few pounds. What'd you think?"

"Don't be silly. You look perfect." I stand in front of her. "Gramma Grace was probably just hintin' she wants more great-grandchildren. She likes to do weird voodoo shit like that."

"No, I do look bloated. It's all that salt in the food your mother makes me eat."

I chuckle, then lift her up and carry her over my shoulder.

"Wilder! Put me down." She smacks my back and tries kicking her feet.

Tossing her onto the bed, I tower over her with my hands on either side of her and my knees caging her legs in. "You're beautiful and nothin' you eat is gonna change that. Got it?"

She rolls her eyes, not taking me seriously. I grab her arms and pin them next to her head.

"Say it...say *I'm beautiful*," I demand.

She defiantly rolls her eyes. "I'm beautiful," she mutters, barely audible.

Leaning in, I bury my face in her neck and suck it—*hard*.

"No hickies!" She squirms beneath me.

"Then say it like you believe it," I warn, then continue sucking the same spot.

She shifts her head, trying to shove me off, but unlucky for her, I'm stronger.

"Fine, fine!" she shouts. "I'm beautiful!"

I smack one more kiss on her neck. "Perfect..." I lean back and smile at my handiwork. "As is that."

"I'm gonna kill you." She lifts her knee and nearly gets me right in the balls, but I'm quick to stop her.

"Tsk tsk, Mrs. Hollis. Is that any way to talk to your husband?"

"Payback's a bitch, ya know that?" She shoves at my chest.

I flash her a wicked grin, standing and pulling her up with me. "That's what I'm countin' on, baby."

She rolls her eyes again. "If you weren't the sweetest man ever, I'd seek revenge on you."

As soon as I got home, I told her about Sam and my plan to get him some gifts. She was immediately on board and even added that we should buy some things for his mom, too. Since she probably doesn't get to open anything, I loved the idea and also planned to find some gift cards.

"Feel free to seek revenge with you naked on top of me..." I tease, waggling my brows.

"I was thinkin' more along the lines of sittin' on your face until you can't breathe."

"Ooh, darlin'..." I cup her ass, pulling her closer. "Don't threaten me with a good time."

Chapter Twenty-Nine
Delilah

As expected, it's absolute chaos in downtown Sugarland Creek. Everyone's getting last-minute gifts or enjoying the festivities. There's a Santa display for kids to get their pictures taken, a hot cocoa station next to it with a massive Christmas tree, and carolers walking around.

But I haven't felt this kind of joy since before my dad died, so I'm doing my best to take it all in.

"Do you think he'd like this remote-control car?" Wilder's eyes light up like he's a ten-year-old boy again.

"Baby, you already got him so much. I'm not sure his mom will know where to even put everythin'."

We've had to bring bags of presents back to his truck three times already. He picked out the toys and I picked out more reasonable items such as clothes, shoes, socks. Then I went on a baby clothes binge for Lily. Since Wilder wasn't sure exactly how old she was, I grabbed a variety of sizes to hopefully last her longer. Then I grabbed boxes of diapers and wipes.

"Okay, last one. I promise!" He grabs it before I can stop him.

"Is this how you're gonna be when we have kids?" I halfway tease because I already know the answer to that.

"Oh, darlin', this is tame compared to what I'll do when we have babies. If I didn't already feel like I was overstepping Sam's mom, I'd be findin' her a new apartment with two or three bedrooms. But I don't wanna overwhelm her since she doesn't know me that well, so for now, I'll make sure Sam and Lily wake up to presents under their tree."

I look at my husband in awe as he continues to peruse the toy aisle. "You're really quite sweet, you know that?"

"You're just now figurin' that out?" He glances over at me and winks. "Maybe when she's more comfortable with me, I can offer to help her find a better place."

"Isn't one of the ranch hand duplexes available? If she's gonna work at the retreat anyway—"

"Yes!" He rushes over and cups my face, crashing his mouth to mine. "You're brilliant. That'd be perfect. She wouldn't have to travel for work, and I could hang out with Sam in between work. Plus, he'd have the other kids to play with, too. And you know how much Gramma Grace loves babies. She'd probably steal Lily."

I smile and laugh at how excited he is.

"Maybe let me talk to her so you don't scare her away."

"What's that mean?"

I lift a shoulder. "You're a big, scary man to some people."

After we checkout, we bring the rest of the bags back to his truck one final time. "Do you wanna swing by The Grindhouse? We can grab some wrappin' paper on the way there."

"Sure. I already told Mom and Mallory they were on wrappin' duty as soon as we got back."

"Your family is very nice to help on short notice." I beam.

They have their own family traditions but are willing to put some time aside to wrap gifts for another family.

Tomorrow's the big day at The Lodge, where my mom will come, and the rest of the Hollis siblings. I'm looking forward to it since it's the first Christmas since Dad died because I'm hoping it helps distract me enough so I don't cry the whole day.

"As are you." He tips up my chin. "Give yourself some credit."

I smile when he leans in and kisses me.

When we walk to the café, the line is nearly out the door. "I'll grab the wrappin' paper next door if you wanna wait in here?" I offer.

"Sure, you want your usual?"

"You *know* my usual?"

"Iced half-caf vanilla coffee with two creams and one sugar."

"I am so turned on right now…"

The blush that covers his face has me cackling. "I think that woman in front of us just heard you."

I shrug, then pull him in for a kiss. "Be right back."

Once I weave through the crowd on the sidewalk and make my way to the store next door, I'm relieved to see it's not as busy as the others.

There's a large variety for kids, so I kneel down and start browsing for ones I think Sam will like and ones for Lily. Then I find something more elegant for Sam's mom's gifts.

"Oh my God, did y'all see Wilder and his *new wife*?" A woman's grating voice grabs my attention from the next aisle. It's a voice I've heard before, but I can't quite place it.

I tilt my head and lean in closer to listen.

"Ya know she only married him for his money," another woman's voice adds.

"That or he knocked her up, so they had to have a shotgun weddin' before his mama found out."

A couple of them laugh before a third woman speaks up. "I doubt he'd marry someone just because she was pregnant. Knowin' Wilder, he woulda run in the other direction at the first glance of a positive pregnancy test."

They laugh again.

My hands tighten around the wrapping paper and my jaw tenses at how they're speaking about him. As if they know him, the *real* him—the only version I've known for nine years.

I want to speak up and bite their heads off for makin' half-ass assumptions, but what would I say? *Actually no, we were drunk and got hitched in Vegas.* It's no better than what they're saying.

"It's weird, though, out of all the women in this town, he marries *her*."

"Maybe it's fake. Like she had a life-savin' surgery and needed his health insurance. Or a Visa to stay in the country."

"She was born here, you idiot."

"Well, whatever..." She scoffs. "Delilah doesn't seem like his type at all."

What the fuck does that mean?

There were people staring at us in the other stores, but I thought it was because of the article Molly wrote about Wilder. This is the first time he's been out in public and everyone had their opinions about him and Wesley. It didn't help when the next article dropped about me bailing out a drug dealer.

I didn't realize they were staring at us because we got married.

Or rather, *judging.*

"Actually, she's very much my type." Wilder's booming voice in their aisle makes me jump. "And not that it's any of your business—especially not *yours*, Jen—but Delilah's ten times the woman you wish you could be. Keep my wife's name outta your mouth or I'll let her get in one good punch on you before I hold her back."

My eyes widen at his harshness, but I'd be lying if I said his words didn't do something to me.

Jen's his ex *fling* or whatever he called her. They stopped hooking up last year, and apparently, she didn't take it well.

"Ready to check out?" Wilder appears in my aisle with two coffees in his hands. Looking unfazed at what just happened, he smiles and winks at me.

"Yeah…" I echo loudly. "As long as you're payin' because I only married you for your money."

"I thought you married me for my big co—" I quickly cover his mouth with my palm.

"Jesus, Wilder," I whisper-hiss. "There are old ladies in here."

"What's that? The baby's cravin' ice cream?" he says purposely loud.

I glare at him, shaking my head. "Popcorn and M&M's, actually."

"Perfect, anythin' for my girls."

This time I do laugh because he's too good at playing the part.

After we check out, I carry the bags and stand taller as we walk past the women who were talking shit about me.

"Have the day you deserve, ladies." Wilder tips his hat to them, and I bite my lip to hold back laughter.

When he opens the door for me, I look at him with amusement. "Glad to see those anger management classes are payin' off."

We spend a couple hours at Wilder's parents' house and everyone chips in to wrap the gifts, well, besides the ones we got for them, which we'll have to do later.

Christmas music echoes throughout the house, Gramma Grace bakes several dozen cookies, and Mallory makes a show of her beautiful wrapping and bow-making skills. She invited her boyfriend, Antonio, and it was cute watching them together.

He held the ribbon in place while she tied it.

After she'd finished wrapping a gift, he'd set it aside next to the others and hand her the next one.

Then, when a fresh batch of cookies was done, he fed her one straight out of the oven and she nearly burned the top of her mouth. Which she laughed about and then he kissed the top of her nose.

At only seventeen, you can tell they really love each other.

Mr. Hollis helped Wilder load up his truck and then I accidentally caught a moment between them that had me in tears.

"I'm proud of you, son. You saw someone in need and didn't even hesitate to change your plans and help them. You've surprised me a lot this year, one being that you went and got married, but I've never seen you happier."

I didn't mean to eavesdrop, but a gift got left behind, and I was coming out to give it to them.

"Thanks, Dad. That means a lot to me."

"You've come a long way. I admit, I've spent countless

nights worryin' about you, but here you are being the prime example of a good man and husband."

"It's been eye-openin' how much life can change when you finally *decide* to make a change. It helps that you believed in me, too."

"Of course. I always knew you could. But as a parent, it's always bittersweet to see your kid on the right path and makin' smart choices."

"So...you're not mad I got hitched in Vegas?" Wilder prompts.

Mr. Hollis smirks. "Probably your smartest choice yet."

I nearly melt and then book it back into the house before they catch me.

Before we leave, Wilder texts Sam's mom to let her know we're on the way, and so we can sneak up there without Sam catching us. She informs us he fell asleep in her bed, so the coast is clear.

"You did a really good thing by helpin' this family," I tell him, squeezing his hand as he drives us out of town. "She's gonna be so grateful for your kindness."

He lifts our hands to his mouth and kisses my knuckles. "I was inspired by someone who helped me when I needed it."

When we arrive at their apartment, Sam's mom is waiting for us outside.

"Hi, I'm Delilah. It's so nice meetin' you."

"Amelia, and you too."

"We might've gone overboard..." Wilder rounds the truck, then opens the back.

Amelia stands frozen with watery eyes. "He's gonna be so surprised in the mornin'. I can't thank y'all enough."

"We're happy to do it," I tell her.

Wilder and I carry the gifts up to her apartment as quietly as we can and stack the gifts around the small tree. Her apartment is nice, but since it's only a one-bedroom, there's not a lot of extra room for toys.

"I hope this doesn't cross the line, but if you're okay with it, I'd like to move you guys to a duplex on the ranch. They have two bedrooms and a lot of open space. You'll be close to The Lodge then, too," Wilder says when we're done. "And the rent is cheap."

"I-I don't think I can accept that. You've already done enough with the gifts and the job…"

"It's just standin' there empty," I tell her. "And we'll come help you move so you don't have to do it alone."

"Why're you doin' this? I'm very grateful, but I don't feel worthy of it."

The sadness in her eyes breaks my heart.

"I know somethin' about feelin' that way, but I promise that you are. You're a good mom doin' the best she can for her kids and with what's been thrown at her. There's no shame in needin' help, especially when raising a family takes a village."

I beam at Wilder's response, knowing he meant it wholeheartedly.

"This is my first Christmas without my dad and if there's one thing I learned, it's how important community is. I know it's hard to accept help, whether it's from grief or pride, but my neighbors and friends really showed up after I lost him. And being able to give back to someone else the same way makes him being gone a little less sad."

Wilder's gaze meets mine and it's filled with tenderness and sorrow.

"Think about it, okay? You don't have to agree to anythin' you're not comfortable with, but it's yours if you want it," Wilder reassures her.

"Thank you. I will." She smiles, and this time, it reaches her eyes.

"Merry Christmas, Amelia. I hope you have the best day with your kids." I wrap an arm around her cautiously, not sure if she's a hugger, but then she fully embraces me.

"Thank you. So, so much."

After we quietly exit and walk back to the truck, Wilder pushes me up against the passenger door and cages me in with a devious look on his face.

"What're you doin'?" I step up on the curb so we're more at eye level.

"Can I give you an early Christmas gift?"

"I thought we weren't doin' that?"

We agreed not to exchange since we just had our honeymoon and neither of us needed anything.

"Well...there's one thing money can't buy."

I furrow my brows, confused. He tilts my chin and presses a soft kiss to my lips.

"Dr. Branson says I shouldn't keep things in or they'll eat at me."

"Right."

"And I don't think I can wait another day to say this before it eats at me."

"What is it?" My heart races with the possibilities.

"That I'm madly in love with you. I have been for a long fuckin' time and planned to wait until we made it to the thirty-day mark so I didn't freak you out by movin' too quickly. But I needed to tell you now because each day I get to wake up with you next to me is another day wasted not tellin' you."

My chest squeezes with joy, and I wrap my arms around him, crashing our mouths together.

"It's about goddamn time." I laugh against his lips. "I'm in love with you, too."

Smiling, he kisses me again. "Good, then I can give you this."

When he pulls something out of his pocket, I scowl at him buying me something anyway.

"You liar—"

He reveals a bright blue box I've only seen in movies.

"What's that?"

"Open it." He hands it to me, but I'm weary.

When I do, I gasp at the biggest ring I've ever seen. A princess cut with a diamond band. *It's stunning.*

"What's this for?"

"A weddin' ring you deserve and one I wanted you to have."

"What about the one we got in Vegas?"

"The one we were too drunk to even remember buyin'? That's fine when you're gonna get it annulled in a few weeks, but not somethin' you keep on your finger forever." He plucks the ring out and grabs my left hand, then slides it on my finger. "This is one you put on your *wife* that you're in love with."

I can't seem to lift my jaw off the ground. "I-I don't even know how you did this so fast. Isn't this company like...*really expensive?*" I whisper as if anyone's going to overhear when we're completely alone. But I'm too shocked to think straight.

He shrugs carelessly. "Only the best for my money-hungry, pregnant wife."

"Wilder!" I playfully shove him but then pull him back and kiss him hard on the mouth.

"When did you do this?" I ask.

I only told him I knew I didn't need thirty days or an annulment last week.

"When we got back from Vegas."

"We were still under the month-long trial."

"I was...hopeful."

Rolling my eyes at his overconfidence, I hold up my hand

but still can't believe it. "It's beyond beautiful. Thank you. I love it."

"Oh, and there's one more thing..."

I pinch my brows together when he gets down on one knee. "Will you marry me again?"

"Wait, whaddya mean?"

"Plan a ceremony. Dance at our reception. Get a weddin' dress. Say vows. The whole shebang."

"You really want all that?"

Wilder doesn't strike me as the type who'd want to fuss over wedding planning, but then again, I've been proven wrong before.

"I want that with *you*."

Just when I thought I was strong enough to hold back tears, they fall down my cheeks.

"Yes..." I nod profusely. "Yes, I'll marry you again!"

He swoops me up in his arms and then cups my face to kiss me.

"I can't wait to see you walkin' down the aisle to me. And then rippin' off that dress once we're alone." He winks, smirking like he's proud of himself.

"And there it is." I laugh but then wrap my arms around him. "Thank you for lovin' me durin' the hardest year of my life. This has already been the best Christmas when I'd been preparin' for it to be my worst."

He tilts my chin, gripping it tenderly. "I will love you through every storm—the same way you've done for me."

Chapter Thirty

Wilder

"Ooh, Mrs. Holhs…" I call out, removing my shirt and kicking off my boots.

After the day I've had, I've been anxious to get back home and to my wife.

"In here!" she shouts from the spare room.

She must be organizing it again. Ever since she moved in the rest of her stuff three weeks ago, she's been going through what to keep and what to get rid of.

Unbuttoning my jeans next, I slide them off until I'm left in my boxer briefs. I'm hoping to convince her to take a shower with me so we don't waste any time before we have to go to her mom's house for Saturday dinner and game night.

It'll be the first one I'm going to since I finished my hours at the shelter. I did the bulk of them over the holiday week and then did my final five hours last Sunday. Even though Miss Tierney signed off on them, I still vowed to come one weekend a month. Delilah signed on to come with me so she can help, too.

"Time to get naked, baby. We've got thirty minutes, and I

308

wanna spend twenty-five of those inside y—" I freeze when I walk into the room and find Amelia looking horrified.

"Wilder!" Delilah rushes toward me, quickly pushing me out into the hallway.

"I didn't know she was here!" I defend.

Her car's in the driveway, but it always is now that she moved in next door. She's been working here since the beginning of the month, but between our work schedules and everything else I have going on, I don't get to talk to her as much as Delilah does. But I do get to see her and Sam almost every day when I'm on my lunch break and he's at The Lodge eating with his mom.

"Yeah, well, now she's seen all of you." She pushes against my chest. "Get in the shower so we're not late."

"I was hopin' you'd join me…" I waggle my brows.

"I'm dressed and ready." She waves a hand down her body and my gaze follows, appreciating how good she looks. "I have a box of clothes I'm donatin' to the shelter but wanted to see if Amelia was interested in any of them first."

"That would've been nice to know about sixty seconds ago."

"Don't worry, I didn't see your *thing*!" Amelia calls out and Delilah's face reddens.

"Please go," Delilah says, defeated.

"Can I steal a kiss first?"

"Fine, but just one," she teases, puckering her lips.

I lean down and press my lips to hers, then steal a few extra kisses.

"Now hurry up."

Showering alone is now my least favorite activity when I've gotten used to having my wife in here with me. We've formed our own little routine in just the past few weeks, and I'm even more addicted to her than I was in Vegas.

Some might say it's a sickness.

But if so, then I never want to be cured.

"Is the coast clear?" I shout, poking my head through the bathroom door before I walk out in only a towel.

"Yes, Casanova. You have fifteen minutes," she singsongs from the living room.

"If it only takes me five to get dressed, can I use the other ten devourin' you?"

"Ew, I heard that!"

What the fuck?

"I thought you said Amelia wasn't here?" I rush toward the bedroom.

"She's not."

"But your sister-in-law is!" Harlow taunts.

"Jesus Christ."

"Don't worry, you don't have anythin' I haven't seen on your brother."

"Gross, Harlow!" Delilah scolds, but she laughs with her.

Delilah enters the bedroom as I finish getting dressed.

"We're carpoolin' with them, so we're just waitin' on Waylon to finish showerin' and then we'll go."

"Now has never been a better time to build our own house," I deadpan. "If it's not Amelia or Harlow I'm flashin', it's Mattie and Raven."

Raven moved into Delilah's old apartment a couple weeks ago since Wesley's been MIA. Sheriff's been on the lookout for him, but no one's seen him. That either means he took off to start over somewhere else or he's hidin' out. And if he's hidin' out, he eventually has to resurface.

But Mattie reassured everyone she's keeping an eye on her. Raven's job allows her to work from home, but since Mattie took on more hours at Lacey's, she invested in a good security system for when she's not home.

However, when they're not working, they're in my living room having girls' nights and watching movies.

"You shoulda known livin' with a girl came with her havin' girlfriends." Her adorable smirk makes it impossible to be mad.

"Mm-hmm." I capture her waist and press her body to mine. "As long as I get to fall asleep with you next to me and wake up with you in my arms, I'll live with it."

"Well, ain't that the sweetest thing I've ever heard."

"I think I've said sweeter things...usually when your mouth—"

"Stop," she blurts. "We don't have time for that and you'll only work yourself up by talkin' about it."

"How do you even know what I was gonna say?"

"Because you're my husband, and I know you."

I tip up her chin, inching my mouth closer to hers. "Now if anythin' was gonna make me horny, it's hearin' you call me that."

"Uno!" Harlow bellows out.

"Who taught you how to play this game?" Delilah pouts with her fan of cards taking up both hands.

"I've been practicin' with Willow and Poppy." She beams.

It's a running joke that their parents let Harlow win as a child, so she never learned strategy or how to follow the game rules. Looks like she's finally figured it out.

"Aren't they like three?" I ask.

"Three and a half, and they're actually quite good."

Delilah snorts, putting down her next card. "Well, now you can pick four."

"Y'all gangin' up on me ain't cute or good sportsmanship." Harlow reluctantly grabs her cards.

"Don't worry, baby. You're always a winner in my book," Waylon tells her, grinning. Even he knows she's not going to take the bait.

Mrs. Fanning stays quiet, but she's been smiling all night. With the one-year anniversary of her husband's death coming up at the end of the month, I worried she'd be spiraling or more upset, but she genuinely seems okay. Either that or she's even better at faking it than I give her credit for.

Delilah, on the other hand, has been putting her extra energy into decorating the apartment—since apparently it "lacked charm and homey vibes"—and cleaning every square inch. Considering her go-to strategy was wallowing in bed when she felt heavy sadness, I call it a win.

But I've already made plans that day so it can hopefully be remembered as a day of happiness instead.

"Uno," Mrs. Fanning says, surprising all of us because she's been on the quiet side tonight.

"How'd you get rid of all your cards?" Delilah gasps.

Mrs. Fanning shrugs with a secret grin on her face.

When it's my turn, I debate putting down a pick four color change card or a yellow one, which is the same color she needs to win. Since she's right next to me and she hasn't exactly been great at concealing her hand, I can see them.

Deciding that the faster this game ends, the faster I can take my wife home, I set down the yellow card.

Mrs. Fanning smirks over at me as if she knew I looked and puts hers on top.

"Noooo! I was so close!" Harlow pouts, slapping her cards on the table.

"And that's a wrap." I snicker, wrapping my arm around Delilah and pulling her closer. "Can we go home now? I want your pussy straddlin' my face within the next twenty minutes," I whisper in her ear.

"God, get a room," Harlow grumbles. "The newlywed stage is over."

"Speak for yourself," I mock.

"Do I need to remind you what I walked in on with you two?" Delilah scolds, raising a brow.

"One time!" Harlow throws her arms up. "And I live underneath you, so don't even pretend y'all are innocent."

Standing, I pick up my empty glass of sweet tea and round the table to take it into the kitchen. "In that case, I'm gonna have her screamin' extra loud tonight."

"Stop holdin' back...I know you can be louder than that."

We barely made it through the front door before I hauled her up and carried her into our room. The moment she was fully naked, I spread her out on the bed and feasted between her legs.

"Wilder...I don't *want* them to hear me," she whisper-hisses.

That sounds like a challenge to me.

I flatten my tongue and slide up her slit before sucking on her clit. With two fingers inside her pussy, I edge her closer and closer to the ledge but then abruptly stop before continuing my delicious torture.

"Wilder, I swear to God..." she hisses, pulling on my hair.

"Are you ready to scream for me, then?"

"Can I muffle it with a pillow?"

"Hell no. I want the people in the town over to hear you."

"That's not gonna happen, but they will hear *you* scream when I cut off your tongue for not finishin' the job."

"Don't even try to insult me."

I hook my fingers in deeper and smile in satisfaction when she gasps.

"I guess it's time for my plan B."

Propping one of her ankles up on my shoulder, I spread her legs farther apart and twist my wrist until I hit her sweet spot.

"Holy fuck." She arches her back, but I know she'll be saying a lot more than that in a few minutes.

I adjust my angle just a bit and then thrust my fingers in and out of her at rapid speed.

"Wilder, oh—" She fists the blankets as she tries to hold on, but when her body explodes, squirting all over my hand, she's unable to hold back. "Ohh my G-God."

She throws her head back and the sweetest moan releases from her throat.

"That's my good fuckin' girl."

I bring my fingers to my mouth and suck on them, tasting her on my tongue.

"How the hell did you do that?"

"I know your body better than you do, baby."

"No, that was some witchcraft hocus pocus shit. That's never happened before, like ever." She sits up on her elbows, still trying to catch her breath. "I think I made a mess on the bed."

I release her leg, slowly putting it back down so I can crawl up her body. "You did, which means I get to clean you off in the shower where I'll fuck you against the wall until you're squirtin' all over me again."

"You have a dirty mouth, Mr. Hollis," she taunts, her cheeks a beautiful shade of pink.

"That mouth is only for you, Mrs. Hollis." I wink, brushing my lips against hers.

"Forever?"

"For-fucking-ever, Delly."

Chapter Thirty-One
Delilah

The store has been slower than usual all month, which is quite common for January. Everyone spent their money before the holidays and no one's buying lingerie in the middle of winter. We mostly sell underwear and bras this time of year, but with fewer customers coming in, it makes the day drag on.

"You wanna take a second break?" I ask Mattie, sitting at my desk and twirling my pen. "No point in both of us bored off our asses."

"Sure, I could go for a smoothie. Want one?"

"No, thanks. I'm not hungry."

"You gotta eat, Delilah. I know you're tryin' to lose weight to fit into a weddin' gown, but one smoothie won't kill ya."

"I haven't even had time to look for a dress. Hopefully in a few weeks, though."

We've set a wedding date for the end of May, so now we have to get everythin' ordered and scheduled. The plan is to get a white tent and have it at the ranch, so we have to rent tables and chairs on top of it. Plus the DJ, catering, and everything else that comes with having a wedding.

Sin With Me

Although I'm already stressed thinking about it, it's been a nice distraction for my mom and me as we approach the anniversary of my dad's death.

"Did you let Jonah know we're meetin' at Milly's Diner tonight instead?" she asks, grabbing her coat and bag.

Since it's Thursday and Wilder has his anger management class tonight, we're going out for dinner and drinks, but I wasn't in the mood for Mexican, so we're going somewhere else. Raven meets us every week, too, so it's been fun going out with the four of us. Each week we try to come up with new baby name ideas and every time she vetoes them.

I'm determined to come up with one she actually likes. Otherwise, when she gives birth in a few weeks, her baby won't have one.

"He hasn't responded, but I'll try him again," I say, grabbing my phone.

"Okay, be back in a few."

When she leaves, I go to the front and stand behind the counter, then decide to text Jonah again.

DELILAH

> Hey, are you still up for dinner tonight? We're going to Milly's.

It shows that it was delivered, but he hasn't read any of my earlier texts. Even though he's at work and they're not supposed to be on their phones, I know they take breaks.

If anyone knows where he is, it should be Wilder.

DELILAH

> Can you tell Jonah to check his messages when he gets the chance? I want to make sure he sees where we're meeting tonight.

> Also, love you and miss you!

After a few minutes, he replies.

> WILDER
>
> No clue. Bastard didn't show up for work this morning and hasn't returned any of my texts or calls.

> DELILAH
>
> That's not like him. I'm gonna see if Raven has heard from him.

> WILDER
>
> Let me know or he's gonna get fired.

> DELILAH
>
> Just wait! There might be a legit reason.

> WILDER
>
>
>
> And I miss and love you too.

My heart still flutters when he says those three words.

Whether it be in the mornings before he takes off for work, when he gets home at night, or when we're naked in bed, I can't get enough of it.

> DELILAH
>
> Have you heard from your brother today? He didn't show up for work and hasn't responded to my texts. I'm worried about him.

But she doesn't reply to me either.

That's not out of the ordinary with her, though. Since she works remotely, they track her computer usage to make sure she's logged on during work hours, so she can only check her phone periodically.

When the bell above the door rings, I assume it's Mattie returning from the café, but when I glance up, I'm surprised to see it's Jonah.

"Hey!" I beam, tucking my phone into my pocket. "I've been—"

"I need you to walk out the back with me and get in my truck, Delilah," he says with his hands tucked in the pockets of his black coat.

I furrow my brows at his tone. "What?"

His demeanor is all wrong. He's tense and stiff, and his eyes are bloodshot.

"Go out the back door with me and get inside my truck," he repeats firmly.

"Jonah, I don't know what you're talkin' about, but I can't leave the store without someone here."

He removes one of his hands and reveals a gun. "Now, Delilah."

My eyes laser focus on the weapon pointed at me and then I can't breathe.

He wouldn't shoot me, would he?

We've spent countless hours hanging out, talking about personal shit, and growing closer.

This isn't like him.

"Move!" he shouts, causing me to jump out of my skin.

"Okay, I'm goin'…" I slowly walk backward, then turn around when we get to the back.

"Where're you takin' me?" I whisper.

"You'll find out. Just go. My truck's right outside."

I push open the door, fighting back my emotions because even though I know this isn't the Jonah I've come to think of as a brother, something is terribly wrong with him.

He opens the passenger side door, and I hesitate to comply. Maybe if I stall him, Mattie will return and distract him. Then I can smack the gun out of his hand and run.

But what if he uses it on Mattie instead?

I can't risk him hurting her because of me.

"C'mon, get in." He thrusts the barrel of the gun into my spine.

I jump in and he nods toward the belt. "Buckle in."

"Now what?" I snap once I'm secure.

"Don't move or try anythin', Delilah. I don't wanna have to hurt you."

"Then why're you doin' this?"

Instead of responding, he slams the door in my face and rushes around the front of the truck before jumping inside.

"This'll be over soon, I promise."

"That's not exactly reassurin' from someone who just kidnapped me at gunpoint."

He doesn't respond as he drives us out of the parking lot, but instead of driving through downtown where someone could see me, he takes the back roads out of Sugarland Creek.

I can't help thinking how confused and scared Mattie will be when she sees I'm not there.

My purse. My car. My jacket. *All left there.*

But I'll be nowhere to be found.

My phone...*is in my pocket?*

I quietly and slowly double-check it's still in there and breathe a half-sigh of relief when I feel that it is. Not that he won't notice me using it even if I were slick enough to send a text to Wilder or Mattie.

But if I slide it out and hide it underneath my thigh, maybe I can squeeze the two side buttons to trigger the emergency call pop-up.

I wait until his attention moves and once he looks to the left side at a four-way intersection, I shift my body just the slightest to where it looks like I'm readjusting. I manage to wiggle two fingers in my pocket and pull out my phone.

Sin With Me

I conceal it with my hand before gliding it halfway under my thigh.

"Sit still," he barks, making my heart stop.

Leaning back against the seat to avoid him paying attention to me, his gaze returns to the road.

Without moving, I look down and lift my leg just enough to get my fingers around my phone. I squeeze the two side buttons until the red bar appears and prompts me to swipe.

Without drawing attention to what I'm doing, I swipe the screen. Then I lower the volume so he doesn't hear them on the other line.

"Jonah, where are we?" I ask, hoping he'll give something away. I need to provide a landmark or something.

Assuming they can even hear me.

"I don't recognize this road," I say, hoping to prompt him to speak.

"Are we headin' out of state?" I try again, but the fear of that happening is real.

None of this makes sense.

What the hell does he want with me and why can't he tell me?

"No, it's only an hour away."

"An hour from Sugarland Creek?"

"Yeah."

"East or west?"

I didn't pay attention because I was too busy panicking and coming up with a plan to get my phone.

He turns and looks at me suspiciously. "East."

I nod, swallowing hard.

"Can you tell me why? Why're you takin' me an hour east?"

"Not yet."

I tap my foot, trying to come up with more questions to keep him talking and revealing where we're headed.

"Does Raven know you're doin' this?"

His fingers tighten around the steering wheel and he clicks his jaw.

"Just be quiet. No more talkin'."

I keep my mouth shut but manage to tap my screen to see if I'm still connected. With a sigh of relief, I can only hope they have a way to track my location or can overhear our conversation.

Sugarland Creek is already on the east side of the state, but he said we weren't leaving Tennessee, so it has to be close to the border.

A call from Mattie comes through and I contemplate answering it, but I don't want to hang up on 911, so I send it to voicemail.

Then a bunch of texts come through.

Fuck.

With one finger, I swipe over to my text messages and do my best to keep my head up while looking down and typing.

DELILAH

SOS.

Jonah.

Gun.

Then before I can send her my location, Jonah shouts at me.

"What're you doin'?"

Tucking the phone under my thigh, I sit up straighter. "Nothin'."

Keeping one hand on the steering wheel, he leans over and grabs my wrist. Then he rubs his hand along the seat and feels it.

I stretch out my leg, adding pressure to it, but he's stronger than me and pulls it out.

"Goddammit, Delilah." He rolls down his window and chucks it.

"Hey! What the fuck?"

"Quit playin' games," he hisses. "Just sit there and—"

Something comes over me and my fight-or-flight response finally triggers. Making sure there aren't any cars coming toward us, I grab the steering wheel and jerk it as hard as I can toward me, then brace for impact.

"Stop!" he shouts, trying to redirect the wheel, but I hold on with every ounce of strength I have.

The truck swerves into the other lane, but he slams on the brakes too late. We slide down a steep ditch and drive into a tree.

"He's gonna kill her!"

Those are the last words I hear before the airbags deploy and my body jerks back into the seat, causing my head to smack against the window.

And then it goes quiet and dark.

Chapter Thirty-Two
Wilder

"Has anyone seen Jonah?" I walk into the stables and call out toward Noah, Ruby, and Ayden.

"Why? You lost your boyfriend?" Noah taunts, walking toward me with one of the boarders.

"The motherfucker hasn't shown up."

"Uh-oh, trouble in paradise?" Ruby mocks, grabbing a bucket of feed and going into one of the stalls.

I roll my eyes. "If you see him, call me."

"Aye, aye, boss." She gives me a mock salute.

Scratching the back of my neck, I shake my head.

He's never been a no-call, no-show, so it's out of character for him.

I spend the rest of the morning mucking stalls and moving horses in and out of the pasture. I'm back working on the retreat side, but since we're still only doing one trail ride a day, I go back and forth with the ranch side since Jonah's working over there.

It's slow this time of year, but when the weather changes abruptly, things break and fences need fixing, so I usually get stuck on bitch duty—which is why it'd be nice if Jonah actually showed up so he could help me.

Needing a break and some water from my jug, I head back to my truck and find a text from Delilah waiting.

She hasn't seen or heard from Jonah either.

Meanwhile, she's probably worried about him, but I have a feeling he realized he's not cut out for working on a ranch. We've had a mix of rain and snow the past few days and he's bitched about it nonstop. With the Appalachian Mountains surrounding us, we get heavier snowfalls than the rest of the state and we're in that time of year where we have less sunlight during the day, so it gets cold as fuck toward the end of our shifts.

Although he previously did construction, he didn't have to deal with the weather while handling thousand-pound horses and walking through wet pastures.

Once the side of the fence I'm working on is done, I drive to the retreat barn and find Waylon fighting with one of the horses. Since the pastures are a mess, they're cooped up in their stalls and hate it.

"Need a hand?" I offer.

"Sure, but be careful. She's already kicked me once."

I chuckle, then grab another lead rope and help push her into the stall. When we can't take them out and need to clean their stall, we rotate them in and out of the grooming stall.

"Feisty today," I say, rubbing her neck to calm her down.

When I get a phone call, I walk into the aisle and although I don't recognize the number, I pick it up.

"Hello?"

"Wilder? Thank God."

"Mattie?"

"Yeah, hi. Have you heard from Delilah?"

"We were textin' about fifteen minutes ago. Why? Isn't she at work with you?"

"I left to get a smoothie and when I returned, there were a couple customers wanderin' around, but she wasn't up front. I assumed she was in the bathroom, so I helped them for a few minutes and then rang them up. As soon as they left, I went to check on her in the back, but she wasn't in there. Her truck's in the parkin' lot and her purse and coat are still here."

"Does she have her phone?"

"It's not in her bag, so she must have it."

"Did ya call her?"

"Yeah and texted."

"Is it possible she went to get somethin' to eat?"

"She'd never leave the store without one of us here. Plus, she said she wasn't hungry when I offered to get her a smoothie."

My heart races as I pace the barn. "Okay, let me try her—"

"Wait, she responded."

I blow out a relieved breath.

"SOS. Jonah. Gun."

"Huh?"

"Those were her messages! What the fuck does that mean?"

"Shit. Let me see if I can track her location."

We exchanged months ago when she was put on babysitting duty.

"What the hell?" I mutter, zooming in on where it says she is. "She's on a country back road...probably twenty minutes out."

"Jonah took her, didn't he?"

"And he has a gun."

The pieces come together.

"Motherfucker," I spit out. "I'm gonna head in that direction, but I'm at least thirty-five minutes away."

I wave and get Waylon's attention, then nod toward the barn doors as I walk in that direction. "Delilah's in trouble," I tell him.

"Want me to come?"

"Yeah, but I'm not gonna go the speed limit." I run to my truck and quickly get it started. Waylon jumps in after me and we take off.

"Should I call the sheriff and tell him?" Mattie asks.

"Yeah, maybe he can find his truck before I do. I'll keep an eye on her location—"

I refresh it and notice it stopped.

"Wait, she's not movin'."

"Where is she?"

"Somewhere off road."

"Oh my God, that can't be good."

"No…it's not."

We hang up so she can call Sheriff Wagner and then I catch Waylon up on what's going on. He calls our dad and informs him next.

"Do you have your rifle?" Dad asks on speakerphone.

"Yeah, underneath my seat."

The same one I shot Harlow's kidnapper with last year.

"Be careful. It's almost dark and there aren't any streetlights out there."

"I will." My jaw ticks with anger and my fist squeezes the steering wheel so tight, my knuckles throb.

"You have your flashlights?" he asks.

"In the back seat," I reassure him.

"Maybe they slid on some ice. Those roads get bad."

"I dunno, but if Jonah had anythin' to do with it or she's hurt because of him, I'm not promisin' I won't kill him."

"Don't do anythin' you'll regret, Wilder."

Too late. *I regret not kicking his ass when I had the chance.*

"Dad, the sheriff's callin' me."

Answering my phone, I put it on speaker so my dad and Waylon can listen. "Yeah?"

"We found Jonah's truck smashed into a tree and got him out."

"And Delilah?"

"She wasn't inside."

My stomach drops, and I feel like I'm going to throw up. "Are you sure?"

"The passenger airbag deployed, but the door was left open. She probably got out on her own and flagged someone down. I put out an APB. The surroundin' towns are keepin' an eye out and checkin' with their local hospitals."

"She coulda stumbled into the woods and got lost."

She'd be disoriented after a crash like that.

"Or worse, she *collapsed* and is out there freezing to death," I add.

"My guys are out searchin' the area now with K9s, but so far, they haven't found any indication that she's out there."

"Where's Jonah now?"

"Ambulance took him to the hospital. They think he has a concussion and most likely a few broken ribs."

Good, then he still has a few others I can break when I get my hands on him.

"Okay, I'm headin' there now." I quickly turn to head in that direction.

"You can't talk to him, Wilder."

"Why the hell not?"

"He'll be detained until we find her and find out what happened."

"He kidnapped her!"

"That's why he's currently in handcuffs."

"And I wanna know why the hell he took my wife and where he was takin' her!"

"I'm gonna question him as soon as they bring him back from his CT scan."

"Not good enough!"

"Wilder…" Waylon grabs my attention. He gives me a pointed look to calm down. But how can I when my wife is missing and no one knows where the fuck she is?

"Fine, I won't interfere, but then he better give us some answers."

We make it to the hospital in half the time and when we rush inside, we find Sheriff Wagner waiting for us.

"Any news?"

"He's back in his room, but he's not fully conscious. The pain med made him drowsy," he explains, and my blood boils. That bastard deserves to feel the pain.

"Then you better slap him awake and demand answers," I bark. "He's the only one who can give us answers."

Sheriff Wagner holds out his palm before putting it on my shoulder. "I will…but you need to let me do my job. I have over a dozen people searchin' for her, drivin' up and down the roads, and makin' calls. We're gonna find her."

His words should be reassuring, and they are somewhat knowing that he's put so much manpower into finding my wife, but my gut tells me something is terribly wrong.

"Did they find her phone?" I ask as calmly as I can make myself.

"Yes, it seems it was thrown before the crash site. But it's how we found her so fast. She made a 911 call and they were able to hear her givin' directions before the connection was lost."

My smart wife.

"Jonah probably tossed it when he saw her usin' it." My

hands ball into fists and I crack my neck. "He played us. Actin'
like he was her friend and—"

"Let's not make assumptions until we have more
information."

"What about his sister? Has anyone talked to her?" Waylon
asks.

"Mattie said she wasn't at their apartment, but her car is
there."

"Wait…" I blink. "Raven's missin' too?"

"Seems that way."

"Was she with Jonah, too? Could she have been in the back
seat?" Waylon asks.

"There was no indication of anyone else in the truck. With
how pregnant she is, I doubt she would've gotten out on her
own."

"Oh my God…" The realization hits me. "Wesley took her.
He has them both."

"What makes you think that?" Waylon asks.

I wrap my hands behind my head and pace in front of them.
"Wesley was after Raven, but with the PO, he had to keep his
distance. He must've found out where she was livin' and
somehow took her when Mattie was at work."

"Okay…and how does Delilah fit into that equation?"
Sheriff Wagner asks.

I blow out a breath, trying to organize my thoughts so I can
talk this out.

"I-I'm not one hundred percent certain…but it's too much
of a coincidence that they're both missin' at the same time and
their common links are Jonah and Wesley. We know Jonah
was plannin' to take Delilah somewhere…"

"Maybe he was bringin' her to Wesley in exchange for
Raven?" Waylon offers.

"But why would he want Delilah and not Raven?" Sheriff Wagner asks.

"To get back at me…or both of us. He blames us for ruinin' his career. He was officially terminated after Delilah got the PO against him. He knows takin' her will ruin my life."

"An eye for an eye…" Sheriff says, then grabs his radio and walks toward the doors.

"You really think he'd take Delilah to get back at you?" Waylon asks.

"I think he's lost his goddamn mind, so yeah, he's probably capable of anythin' right now. He knew he couldn't take Delilah without a fight, so he needed leverage to get Jonah to bring him to her instead.

"Raven for Delilah…" Waylon confirms.

"I could be way off base, but why else would Jonah flip a switch and threaten her with a gun? I'm not a fan of him in the first place, but he's too loyal to Raven to fuck up his life."

"You think Wesley would give up Raven, though?"

I snap my fingers as a light bulb goes off. "You're right…he probably wouldn't."

The sheriff returns. "I put out an APB on Wesley and Raven. The entire county is on alert."

We update the sheriff on our theory.

"I agree…he wouldn't give up his wife when she's the one he's been after the whole time." He nods, running a hand over his jawline. "He probably planned to kill Jonah."

"So where would he hide two women?" Waylon asks.

"I just had one of my guys check for any other properties in his name, but there's only his house and they were headed there now. But I'm not expectin' them to find much. If Jonah was takin' her outta town, he was plannin' to stash them somewhere else."

"What about in their parents' names?" I ask. "Or Jonah's?"

"Yeah, let me have them check." He pulls out his phone and texts someone. "They're out scoopin' every property and abandoned buildin' down that road and side roads. If he's hidin' out there, we'll find them."

I know he's trying to reassure me, but knowing she might be with Wesley has my guts in a knot.

"Excuse me, Sheriff Wagner?" a nurse grabs his attention. "He's awake if you wanna talk to him."

I go to walk past him, but he stops me. "Stay here. He's not gonna talk if you're in his face."

My chest vibrates with anger and frustration.

Waylon stands next to me and we watch as Sheriff Wagner goes down the hallway toward the deputy guarding one of the rooms. Then the sheriff glances at me briefly before going inside.

Waylon moves in front of me, blocking my view. "You should sit before your heart explodes."

"I'm gonna kill him."

"You can't do that unless you wanna spend the rest of your life behind bars because not even you are slick enough to get out of a murder charge."

"If he's the reason my wife dies, it'd be worth it."

"She's not dead," Waylon says gently. "Wesley needs her for a reason, so he'll keep her alive."

"That doesn't mean he won't hurt her."

"No, but you can't think like that."

"Why else would he take her?" I snap, pacing the room.

"To fuck with you?"

Before I can respond, the waiting room doors open and my family floods in with Mattie behind them.

"Wilder, I'm so sorry. It's my fault. I shouldn't have left her at the store alone."

I wrap my arms around her, knowing she's freaking out too.

"No, it's not. He was determined to get her and would've found a way eventually."

"My mom's on her way," Harlow tells me, and I can't help thinking about how much Mrs. Fanning has already gone through. It's been almost a year to the date since her husband died and Harlow was kidnapped.

And now it's happening all over again with Delilah.

I bring everyone up to date and what our theory is while we wait for the sheriff to return.

Finally, he does.

"We know where she is…"

Chapter Thirty-Three
Delilah

My body rolls into something and then the movement comes to a complete stop. When I open my eyes and try to look around, it's pitch black. I try to stretch my legs, but there isn't enough room.

I think I'm inside a trunk.

How did Jonah get me in here?

My throbbing head reminds me the truck crashed and then... I can't remember.

The trunk lid lifts and my breath hitches when I see the man towering over me.

Not Jonah.

"Wesley," I hiss, squinting at the blinding light above me.

"Rise 'n' shine. C'mon, let's go." He digs his fingers into my upper arm and pulls me out.

"Shit, my head." I press my fingers to my temple.

"I have meds in the loft." He digs what I can only assume is the barrel of a gun into my back. "Start walkin'."

"Where're we?" I ask, not recognizing the building as he

forces me through what looks like a dungeon but above ground.

It smells like oil and rust.

"That's not for you to worry about. Upstairs, go. Now."

"What's up here?" I ask, wary.

Nothing good, I'm sure.

"Stop askin' questions, Delilah. Raven needs you, so do as you're told, and no one gets hurt."

"Raven's here?"

A loud wailing in the distance answers my question.

"What'd you do to her?" I sprint up the stairs, not worrying about him behind me, and whip open the door.

A newly remodeled loft greets me. Although it's one large space, it's separated by designated rooms. A master bedroom, living room, kitchen, and bathroom.

But it's the room next to the bed that has me panicking.

A nursery.

Raven's on the bed, propped up on pillows, and she's sweating.

"Are you okay?" I grab her hand and scan her body for any injuries.

"My water broke," she explains, sounding terrified.

"Oh my God. She needs to go to the hospital," I tell Wesley. "The baby's early. She needs a doctor."

"No!" he roars behind me. "That's why you're here."

My head snaps toward him. "Are you crazy? I've never delivered a baby before. I haven't even been pregnant."

"Your mom's a nurse. I'm sure you know enough."

My eyes widen as I realize why he's brought me here.

"Wesley, no. Too much can go wrong. You should call an ambulance."

He shoves his gun against my cheek and my breath hitches.

"You get this baby out or you're both dead. Got it?"

I nod, drawing in a slow breath. "Okay."

"Good. Now tell me what you need."

Licking my lips, I scan the area. "Towels, dry and cold ones. Gloves. Baby blankets."

"Okay."

He heads to the kitchen area, and I kneel on the bed to wrap my arms around her.

"It's gonna be okay. Do you know how far apart your contractions are?"

"I-I think about four to five minutes."

"How'd you end up here?"

"I ordered food this mornin' and when I opened the door to grab it, he popped up outta nowhere and shoved me back into the apartment. Then he pressed his gun against my stomach and told me to go with him or he'd kill our baby. I was so stressed, my water broke an hour later."

"God, I'm so sorry, Raven." I lean in closer so he can't hear me. "We're gonna get outta here, I promise."

Her eyes fill with tears, but she nods with understanding.

"Okay, I'm sorry, but I have to look down there."

She nods, and I slide my body off the bed so I can uncover her legs. Then I remove her leggings and underwear.

"Looks like the baby dropped, so that's good at least."

"At my last appointment, my doctor said the baby was head down."

"Good! That helps."

I rack my brain for everything my mom's told me and what I've seen in movies.

"Let's get some pillows propped behind you so you're ready when it's time to push."

Wesley returns with the supplies I asked for. I wrap one of the cold towels around her neck and then put the dry towels underneath her butt and legs. Once I have the gloves on, I kneel between her thighs.

"I'm gonna check how far you're dilated." I hold up my hand. "I think four fingers is ten centimeters, so maybe it'll give us an idea how much further you have to go."

"Okay…" She nods.

"I'm sorry if I hurt you," I tell her ahead of time.

Although I don't really know what I'm doing, I want to sound confident for her sake.

"Alright, take a few deep breaths so I can…push in."

She blows out a breath and her thighs relax enough for me to slide inside. "I'd say three…and a half. I can almost get the fourth in there, so you're close."

She hisses and her body tenses as another contraction takes over.

"Do you have a heatin' pad?" I ask Wesley. "It might help her back pain."

"Yeah, one second."

I cover Raven up and readjust her pillows. "Do you want some ice to chew on?"

"Yes, please."

"I'll check the kitchen."

I walk to the fridge and open the freezer, then pull out the ice cube tray.

"What'd you think you're doin'?" Wesley pushes the barrel into the back of my head.

"She wants ice. You know you don't have to keep threatenin' me with that. I'm not goin' anywhere."

"Let's hope not. That'd be very stupid…for you and the baby."

"Do you have any Ziploc bags? I need to crush this."

"In the lower cupboard."

He backs up enough for me to open it and grab what I need. Then I pop the cubes inside and zip it.

"Anythin' firm I can use?"

"Here's a glass." He hands me one from the top cupboard.

I smack the bottom against the bag until the ice is crushed enough to eat. Then I bring it back to Raven and she shoves a handful in her mouth.

"Here's the heatin' pad." Wesley hands it to me, and I get it plugged in, then underneath Raven's body.

"How's that feel?"

"Perfect. Thank you."

"Have you picked a name?" I ask, hoping to distract her from this hellhole we're in. I also want to get her mind off the pain.

"I've narrowed it down to Bailey for a girl and Braden for a boy."

"We decided on Victor for a boy. After my grandpops," Wesley talks over her.

"Oh, right," Raven agrees, defeated.

Please, God. Let it be a girl.

"Oh shit, another one…" Her face pinches and when she can't take any more, she cries out.

Sitting on the bed next to her, I give her my hand and tell her to squeeze.

"That was a strong one." She falls back on the pillows when it passes. "It feels like they're gettin' closer."

"They probably are…" My heart races at the pressure of making sure she delivers this baby safely. "When they get about two to three minutes, I'll check you again, or if you feel the urge to push."

"I've been so scared about givin' birth…this isn't how it's supposed to be."

"I know, sweetie. But I'm here and we're gonna get through

this together." I move the cold towel up to her forehead and then wipe down her neck.

"Wesley said Jonah was supposed to bring you here. Have you seen him?" she whispers.

"Um…he forced me into his truck while I was at work and then he crashed his truck."

"Oh my God. Is he okay?"

"I-I dunno. I remember the airbags goin' off and then I woke up in Wesley's truck."

"You know he'd never hurt you," she says softly. "Wesley made him take you. He spent weeks buildin' the loft and then made a plan to take me. Me goin' into early labor fucked up his plan."

I nod, biting my lip. "Yeah, I pieced that together. He still scared the shit outta me."

"I'm sorry. This wouldn't be happenin' if—"

"Do not apologize for that man," I order.

"I still feel awful that you got dragged into this. Jonah didn't know I was in labor."

My brows pinch together. "Then what'd he think he was bringin' me here for?"

She looks over at the couch where Wesley's sitting and watching us. She swallows hard before lowering her voice. "Wesley told Jonah he took me, and that if he wanted me back, he had to bring you to him."

My jaw clenches.

If he wasn't bringing me here to help Raven, then… "He thought he was exchangin' us."

Lowering her eyes, she nods. "I know it sounds bad, but he was put in an impossible position."

Her life for mine.

I can't exactly fault him for wanting to save his pregnant

sister. But it doesn't make me any less furious that he was so willing to hand me over to Wesley.

"Do you think he's alive?"

Lifting a shoulder, I shake my head. "I dunno."

"They found him and took him to the hospital. Not sure if he made it, though," Wesley bellows, then lifts up a police scanner. "I heard them talkin' about a mysterious 911 call near the location Jonah would've been drivin' and sendin' someone out to investigate, so I took a little road trip to make sure he didn't get pulled over. Imagine my surprise when I found y'all in the ditch."

That confirms they could hear me. Too bad it ended up fucking me over.

"Moron didn't even check if you had your phone before takin' you." He tsks, shaking his head.

"How'd you know I didn't still have it on me?"

"Oh, I checked."

My body shivers at the thought of his hands on me.

Raven screams, and I grab her hand.

"Breathe...don't hold it in."

"Oh fuck, it hurts," she cries out, holding her stomach. "I think the baby's ready."

I jump to my feet. "You sure?"

"I dunno, but it feels like the head is right down there."

Removing the blankets, I lift her knees and drop them open. Then I feel around and fit four fingers easily inside this time.

"Yeah, I think you're fully dilated. Do you wanna try pushin'?"

She nods, tears streaming down her cheeks.

"Raven, look at me," I tell her. "When you feel the next contraction, bear down and push."

"Okay."

I stack the pillows behind her, making sure they keep her upright.

"You can do this, okay?"

"God, I hope you're right."

Less than two minutes later, her face squishes and I tell her to push.

Wesley stands next to me, and although I know she probably doesn't want him near her, I need his help.

"I need you to lift her leg and push it toward her chest."

"Me?"

"I can't deliver the baby and hold up her legs, so yeah, make yourself useful," I snap, no longer giving a shit that he has a gun. Raven's my priority at the moment.

"Raven, try to hold up your other leg. It'll give you better momentum."

She wraps her hand behind her knee and pulls it toward her.

"Good, keep pushin'."

Her body relaxes when the contraction stops and she releases the hold on her leg.

"Any chance you know how long it takes to push this baby out?"

"Everyone's different, but typically, the first pregnancy can take a while."

"How long is *a while?*" Wesley asks.

"My mom's had women push for upward of three hours."

"Oh, hell no." Raven's head falls back on the pillows. "I can't bear the pain that long. This shit hurts."

"Hopefully, that won't be your situation," I tell her, hopeful. Although it can help to have meds because then the mom doesn't tire out as quickly.

But I don't tell her that.

"Another one's comin'…" She repositions, lifting her leg.

"You're doin' great. I can see the head."

"You can?" Wesley sneaks a peek, and I push him away.

"This ain't a free show," I snap.

"That's still my baby, whether you like it or not."

"That doesn't give you a free pass to look at her while she's exposed. So be respectful."

He glares, his jaw locked in place, but doesn't argue. Returning to her leg, he continues holding it up.

"Keep pushin'…"

Raven cries out for the next hour and even though she's crowning, the baby doesn't move.

"I think something's wrong. The baby should be out more by now."

"Feel around and see if you touch anythin'," Raven suggests. "It said in one of the baby books I read, if the head doesn't descend, the cord could be wrapped around the neck. If that's the case, you should be able to put your fingers underneath and loosen it."

My eyes widen, thinking how the hell I'm going to do that.

"You want me to shove my hand that far up?"

"Just to feel for the cord. If you don't, then you shouldn't have to do anythin' else."

"I wish we had a heart monitor," I say, bracing myself to shove half my arm up her cooch.

"Oh shit, another contraction."

She tries pushing again, but there's no movement, and once it's over, I slide my hand up.

"Oh God, this is…there's a reason I'm not a nurse."

"What do you feel?"

"You don't wanna know…" I focus on feeling for the cord. "Okay, I think I found it. Feels like it's wrapped around the neck once."

"Slip two fingers underneath and then carefully lift it over the head."

"I hope I'm doin' this right," I murmur, gently doing what she said. Raven tries not to scream, but I know this can't be comfortable. "Okay, I think I did it."

"Thank God. That hurt like a bitch."

Sliding my hand out, I ask Wesley to get me some fresh gloves.

"The next contraction, you need to push as hard as you can," I tell her.

Wesley returns, and I quickly change out my gloves.

"Okay, get ready."

Wesley gets back into position, and I help Raven keep her other leg up with one hand. The head glides out and then the shoulders.

"Oh my God, keep pushin'!" I use both hands to hold it while the rest of the body comes out.

Raven pants and then finally breathes a sigh of relief.

"Towel," I call out, and when Wesley hands it to me, I wrap it around the baby.

"Why isn't it cryin'?" Wesley asks.

"I dunno. Gimme a second."

I wipe the face and eyes, then move down to the mouth and cheeks.

"What is it?" Raven asks. "Boy or girl?"

Oh shit, I didn't even look.

"Aw…it's a girl!" I announce.

"She's still not cryin'," Wesley says, staring down at me.

"C'mon, sweetie…" I pat her butt.

"Check her airway," Raven says.

"Oh wait, I remember this." I put her on my lap and open her mouth but don't see anything. Then I stimulate her chest for a few seconds before flipping her into a head-down position and let gravity do its job.

Moments later, she starts crying.

"There we go, sweet girl." I clean the rest of her off, then set her on Raven's chest with the blanket.

Raven cries and then mouths, "Thank you."

"You still need to deliver the placenta."

"What the hell is that?" Wesley asks.

I resist the urge to roll my eyes. "It's what is attached to the umbilical cord. It has to come out or Raven could hemorrhage."

"How does she do that?"

"It should come out naturally within a half hour after birth, otherwise I'll have to try to do it manually."

My mom told me a few horror stories, which I'm grateful for now.

"God, I hope not. You've been up my vagina enough for one day."

"Do you still feel contractions?"

"A little, yeah."

"That's good. It'll probably come on its own then."

I help Raven remove her shirt so she can do skin to skin. The baby's cries stop as soon as she feels her mama's warmth.

"She's so beautiful." I smile, looking at her.

Then I look at Wesley, who's watching them. "I think it'd be smart to get her checked out by a doctor."

"No," he snaps.

"She needs medical care. Shots. A birth certificate. You can't actually think you can keep her off-grid?"

Wesley holds up his gun, facing it at me. "You've done what I brought you here for."

"Wes, no!" Raven pleads. "Don't hurt her. The baby and I will stay here with you. Let her go."

"So she can go tell the police? I don't think so."

"Put me back in the trunk and drop me off somewhere. I have no idea where we are, so I won't be able to tell the location," I plead. "I won't say a word because I know if I do, Raven and the baby die."

He slowly lowers the gun. "It wouldn't just be them either. Jonah. Wilder. Your mom and sister."

My throat closes up at the mention of the people I love.

I nod in understanding. "I won't say anythin'. You have my word."

"Good. Because I'd hate for you to have to watch me kill your husband and then you next."

I know he's trying to get me to react, fall out of line so he can shove that gun in my face again, but it's not going to work.

"Understood," I say firmly.

We continue waiting for Raven's placenta to come out, and I breathe a sigh of relief that I didn't have to pull it out. Then we cut the cord.

I add another blanket over the baby and admire how happy Raven looks, even if it's temporary.

"Bailey looks like you," I whisper, then kiss her cheek and whisper in her ear, "Please be careful and remember what I promised."

She nods once. "You too."

"Alright, let's go." Wesley grabs my arm, pulling me back.

Then he holds up a set of handcuffs and grabs Raven's wrist.

"Is that necessary?" I scowl. "She just had a baby. It's not like she can run."

He snaps it into place and then attaches the other side to the headrail. "I'm not takin' any chances."

That's what he must've done when he left to find Jonah's truck.

Raven doesn't fight it and continues holding the baby with her other hand.

"Down the stairs, go," he orders.

With one more glance over my shoulder, I meet Raven's eyes, making sure she knows I'll be back for her.

When I get to the bottom of the stairs, I get a better look at what this building is.

"Was this a car repair shop?"

"Yeah, my grandpop was a mechanic years ago. He raised me and taught me everythin' I know about cars. I was the one who found him in his home garage, inside his truck with the engine runnin' and the windows down. He died of carbon monoxide poisoning."

"Oh God, that's horrible," I say as we continue walking through the building.

Wait a minute…

I wonder if that's around the time he started hitting Raven and—

"Sugarland Creek PD! Hands up!"

A dozen officers barge through the door with guns raised. Wesley moves behind me, wraps his arm tightly around my neck, then shoves his weapon into my skull.

"Wesley, put the gun down…" Sheriff Wagner calls out. "Let her go."

"No way. You're on private property. Get out!"

"You know we're not leavin' without the girls. Surrender and no one gets hurt."

"Wesley…" I whisper his name to get his attention. "Your grandpop wouldn't want you to do this. I think you're sufferin' from PTSD and grief disorder. You can get help for that."

I learned all about that in my grief counseling sessions. And now I'm kicking myself for not seeing the signs. I wish I'd known he'd recently lost someone close to him.

"He left me behind," he grits between his teeth.

"That doesn't mean he loved you any less. Or that you don't miss him."

"Shut up."

"Wesley..." Sheriff Wagner warns.

Next, we hear a helicopter flying ahead.

"Holy shit," I murmur.

It hits me that Wilder and my family are probably going out of their minds, worried about me. And I know my husband is losing his shit. I'm surprised he didn't demand to come out here.

However the hell they found us, I have no idea, but I do know Wilder is panicking.

"If I die, she dies with me..." He clicks off the safety.

Before anyone can move or say another word, Wesley jerks behind me and falls to the ground.

I scream when the weight of his body knocks me over and the officers rush over.

My heart's racing so hard, I can't breathe.

"Delilah, you're okay..." a female voice I don't recognize says, trying to lift me.

"I-I can't—" There's a piercing ring in my ears.

"Hang tight, sweetheart."

She places an oxygen mask over my mouth. "Inhale slowly."

I think I'm having a panic attack, but I've had those before and they've never felt like this.

My eyes struggle to stay open, losing the fight to see the woman in front of me.

And then the quiet and darkness surrounds me...again.

Chapter Thirty-Four

Wilder

The sight of Delilah in a hospital bed makes me sick to my stomach.

I want to rage, but at the same time, I want to curl up next to her and hold her.

And then never let her go.

They're pumping fluids and glucose in her while she sleeps off the benzodiazepines. She was so low on blood sugar, she passed out when she suffered from an acute panic attack.

Mattie mentioned she hadn't been eating because she wants to lose weight for the wedding, but I had no idea she was skipping meals.

"Wilder, hon…" Mrs. Fanning taps my arm. She and Harlow have been sitting in her room with me for the past few hours. "You should get some rest. Delilah will sleep through the night—"

"I'm not leavin' her."

She sighs, patting my shoulder. "I figured you wouldn't. But if you change your mind, you can sleep in one of the on-call rooms. It's just down the hall."

348

"Thanks, but I'm fine in here," I tell her.

"Okay. I'll be back in the mornin'." She kisses the top of my head and then tells Harlow goodbye.

"Will you text me if she wakes up before I come back?" Harlow stands, stretching her arms above her head.

Waylon's in the waiting room since we couldn't have more than three people in here, and I know they probably don't want to sleep here.

"Of course. Thanks for sittin' with me."

She takes me by surprise when she leans down and hugs me. "Thanks for being here for her and lovin' her so hard. You're good for her, Wilder."

My lips curve into a half-smile, and I nod. "Appreciate that, Harlow."

After she leaves, I scoot my chair closer and tighten my hand around hers. Then I rest my head down on her arm, needing to feel her warmth.

"Sir? Mr. Hollis?"

"Mm?" My head pops up, and I'm greeted with a grating headache.

"Sorry to wake you, but the doctor ordered an ultrasound, so I just need to lift up her gown so I can access her stomach."

I lean back, giving her room, and then watch as she puts gel on a wand and rolls it around Delilah's stomach.

"What are you checkin' exactly?" I ask after a few minutes.

As far as I know, Delilah didn't suffer from any internal injuries.

She smiles, then increases the volume of the fluttering noise. "Just checkin' the baby's heart rate. Except..."

Her face twists and then her wand's moving again.

"Yep, just what I thought...there are *two* heartbeats."

"Wait. Back up. She's pregnant?" I stand, no longer able to sit still.

"Y'all didn't know?"

"Um, no? T-this is the first time I'm hearin' about it…"

I'm so flustered, I can hardly speak.

"Oh, I'm so sorry. They took her blood when she first arrived, which is how we knew her blood sugar was low, but her hCG levels were high, so we tested for pregnancy."

"And?"

She glances at me, grinning. "And it was positive. It wasn't in her file and we weren't sure how far along she was, so that's why I'm doin' the ultrasound. We wanted to make sure the baby, or rather babies, are okay. She's still in early pregnancy, so you can't see much, but there are two sacs."

She points to two dark round spots on the screen.

I stare at where her finger is, but I'm still stuck on the her being pregnant part.

"First-time dad?" She smiles.

"Um, yeah…first-time husband, too."

She chuckles.

"How far along is she?"

"Without knowin' the first day of her last period, it's a bit hard to tell at this stage, but based on their measurements, probably six to seven weeks.

"We didn't have sex until our honeymoon…" I count the weeks in my head to when our honeymoon was. "Five weeks ago."

"Okay, so that's accurate then. Pregnancy's determined by the first day of her last period and since she would've ovulated in the middle of her cycle, about two weeks later, that'd line up with the conception timeframe."

"Huh?" I'm overwhelmed and have no idea what she just said.

"The babies' fetal age is five weeks, but their gestational age is seven weeks."

"Oh." So she definitely got knocked up during our honeymoon.

She wipes off the wand and then cleans Delilah's stomach before lowering her gown. "I'll print out a few pictures for you."

I cover Delilah back up with the blankets. "You're absolutely sure it's twins?"

"Yep, look here…" She holds up one of the images.

There's tiny text on it that reads BABY A and BABY B.

"Fraternal twins, two sacs."

"Oh my God." I blink at the photo. "Could that be why her blood sugar was low?"

"Possibly. A lot of women lose their appetite in the first trimester, so they forget to eat."

"Shouldn't there have been more signs or somethin'? She hasn't thrown up or said she was nauseous or anythin'."

"Not always. Some don't experience any symptoms, while others are sick the entire nine months."

Looking at the picture and then at my wife lying peacefully, I'm consumed with mixed feelings.

Rage — *Wesley almost killed my pregnant wife and caused her added distress.*

Anger — *Jonah kidnapped my pregnant wife and even though I know why he did it, I'm still angry about it.*

Grateful — *Delilah was found, mostly unharmed.*

Conflicted — *We talked about starting a family, but I didn't expect it to happen so quickly.*

Happy — *I'm going to be a dad and experience parenthood with the love of my life.*

I just hope she's as excited about it as I am.

"Delly, can you hear me?"

Delilah's eyes flutter open, looking around the room and then at me.

"Where's Raven and the baby?" she whispers.

I sit on her bed, leaning as close to her as I'm able to without squishing her. "They're safe in the maternity ward. Bailey is six pounds, ten ounces and nineteen inches long. She's strong and healthy, thanks to you."

When I first learned why Delilah was brought to the loft and what she'd done for Raven, I was in complete awe. I'm impressed by my wife on a normal day, but hearing what she did during a stressful situation, I was blown away.

"Thank God," she mutters. "What about Jonah and Wesley?"

"Jonah will live. Concussion and some broken ribs, but he's been arrested on kidnappin' charges."

She winces.

"Wesley got tased in the back and then detained. He's gettin' a handful of charges for what he did."

"They tased him? Oh my God, I thought they shot him."

"Probably thought it was too risky with you in front of him."

"Wow…"

I explain the full story from when I got the call from Mattie to Sheriff Wagner sending a whole SWAT team to the old auto body building. Then she tells me what she found out about

Wesley's grandfather. Regardless, he doesn't win any sympathy points from me.

"So wait, what happened to me? Why did they hospitalize me?"

"Low blood sugar mixed with a panic attack. You passed out and they gave you somethin' to calm your nerves," I explain, then add, "You can't be skippin' meals."

"I didn't on purpose, but nothin' sounded good to eat."

"Yeah, well..." I contemplate how to tell her, especially when she's still waking up. "That's probably due to the pregnancy hormones. Loss of appetite is a common symptom during the first trimester."

"Yeah, I know that...how do you know that? Wait—"

She digs her hands down into the bed and pulls herself up higher. I help and adjust her pillows so she's comfortable.

"I'm *pregnant*?"

Smiling, I trace a finger along her cheek before gently tucking loose strands behind her ear. "Yeah, darlin'. So much for waitin', huh?"

Her hands move to her stomach and she gasps. "I missed my appointment."

"Which one?"

"The one for my birth control shot I get every three months. I was due to get it the week we went to Vegas, and when I called to reschedule, they gave me an appointment for the following week. But then we went on our honeymoon, and I completely forgot to reschedule again."

"Baby, I'm not mad..." I tilt her chin. "And I should've asked if we needed protection for pregnancy. I only considered it for STI purposes."

"Ugh, I feel so dumb. It'd been so long since I was sexually active, it didn't even dawn on me that it would wear off not gettin' it renewed."

"It's not your fault, Delly. I was an active participant in the baby-makin' process…" I remind her, grinning. "If you don't want—"

"No, I do," she quickly answers. "I'm just in shock. But I'm happy. Are you?"

"More than I could've imagined, honestly. But there's somethin' else I should tell you…"

"What?"

"Um…they came and did an ultrasound when you were asleep, ya know, to make sure everythin' was okay and they found two heartbeats."

"You're kiddin'…no, you're messin' with me, right? Mattie tell you to say that?"

I burst out laughing, shaking my head. "Glad I'm not the only one who freaked out at first."

"Wilder!" She playfully swats my chest. "We're really havin' twins?"

Leaning in, I cup her chin and bring my lips to hers. "That's right, *Mama*. Twins."

"Holy fuck." She blinks a few times. "This is definitely your fault."

I chuckle. "Nope, fraternal twins are linked to the mother's side. And yes, I looked it up."

"But you *manifested* this with your damn crystals and puttin' your name in my phone as BABY DADDY," she reminds me, and I laugh at the memory.

"Might not be *all* my fault. I think Gramma Grace rubbed some potion on you and made it happen. She's witchy like that."

She rolls her eyes. "Maybe she knew already? That happened after the honeymoon, and I would've already been pregnant but didn't know it."

"Told you—she has a sixth sense for this shit."

"I'm startin' to believe it." She shakes her head, rubbing her palm over her stomach.

"Guess we'll be buildin' that house sooner rather than later." I wink. "Gotta make sure we have room for our babies. Plus, we agreed to have three, so we'll need extra bedrooms."

"Okay, slow down. I agreed to three babies and three pregnancies. Now we're getting a twofer and that changes things."

My cheeks hurt from smiling so wide, but I can't help it. "Okay, what about one pregnancy, two babies, and three dogs?"

Now she's the one laughing. "You have yourself a deal, *husband.*"

"See, now that" — I point at her — "is how you got knocked up in the first place."

She wraps an arm around me the best she can, pulling me closer. "I love you. And I love our babies. The shock has somewhat worn off, and I'm sure fear will come next, but right now, I'm so happy we're startin' a family."

"I am too, wife."

She brings his mouth to mine, stealing a kiss.

"I love you so much."

"Thank you for knockin' me up before I entered the high-risk danger zone."

"Jesus Christ." I chuckle. "Never in my life did I think I'd love hearin' those words directed at me."

Chapter Thirty-Five

Delilah

"S top wigglin'," Mattie scolds, tightening the ribbons on the back of my corset.

"I need to breathe!" I counter, hanging onto the kitchen counter for support. "No one wants to see a bride pass out before she makes it to her groom."

"Shoulda thought about that before lettin' him knock you up before your weddin' day."

"We're already married, thank you very much."

After finding out we were expecting, we moved the wedding date to early April so I didn't have to squeeze a six-month belly into a wedding dress. At twenty weeks, I'm more bloated than I've ever felt before.

And I look like I've enjoyed a few too many chimichangas.

But everything's gone smoothly so far. I've been fortunate not to experience too much sickness and once I hit the second trimester, my appetite came back in full force. We decided not to find out their genders, so we'll be surprised at their birth.

Although, the more I look at cute baby clothes, the more I want to know so I can buy more.

However, we start building our house on the property next month, which has been a nice distraction. It took a while to get permits and hire contractors, but I can't wait to furnish it and properly decorate.

Although it won't be done by the time the twins are born, they'll sleep in our room for the first few months anyway, so hopefully it'll be ready before they have to move into their nursery.

"Here, drink this…" Raven holds up a cup with a straw, and I take a long sip of water.

"Thanks. Who knew pregnancy hormones would make me sweat so much?"

Mom comes over with a handheld fan and turns it on toward me. "I'd sweat through my scrubs when I was pregnant with you and Harlow."

"Great, so I have that to look forward to for the next five months."

"Don't forget the engorged breasts and your bladder gettin' used like a trampoline," Raven adds.

Amelia chuckles. "And the stretchmarks and peein' every time you sneeze."

"I'm already experiencin' all of that." I groan.

Whoever said pregnancy was the most beautiful thing in the world had clearly never been pregnant before.

"Okay, all done. Can you walk?" Mattie asks after zipping me up.

"Doubt it." I groan but attempt to anyway.

My gown is loose-fitting and conceals my bump pretty well, but in order to tuck everything in, I added a corset underneath.

I turn around and show everyone.

"You look goooorgeous!" Amelia gushes.

"Stunnin'!" Harlow beams.

"I'd marry you," Mallory says.

"Very beautiful," Mom adds, and I can already see the tears welling in the corner of her eyes.

"Your tits are huge," Mattie blurts. "Maybe tuck them in."

"Where? They've grown two sizes already."

Mattie moves her hands around my chest. "I dunno, maybe push them into your armpits or somethin'."

Amelia snorts. "I don't think Wilder will complain."

No truer words have ever been spoken.

Ever since we found out I was pregnant, he hasn't been able to keep his hands off me. Not that I've minded, especially when I hit twelve weeks, and my hormones went into overdrive.

We spend the next two hours messing with my hair and makeup before Reagan, my photographer, tells me it's almost time for the first look. She's been in the apartment all morning taking pictures of us and then going down to Waylon's apartment, where Wilder and the other groomsmen are getting ready.

A part of me is sad Jonah isn't here. After he was charged with kidnapping, he got sentenced to two years in prison. He made one hell of a deal and agreed to testify against Wesley.

His trial is at the end of the summer, but until then, he's behind bars since he couldn't afford bail.

I'm not mad about what happened anymore. I'd rather preserve all my energy for my pregnancy and get things ready for the babies' arrival than stay angry. They're getting what they deserve, and even if Jonah did it to save his sister, he did put my life at risk.

But still, Raven and I visit Jonah once a month and will continue to while he's locked up. This way he still gets to see his niece even if he can't hold her. For now, we're working on rebuilding our friendship.

Everyone stays in the house as Reagan leads me outside

toward the trees next to the ranch hand quarters. Wilder's already there, waiting for me, but facing the opposite direction.

"Okay, I'm ready when you are…" She smiles, nodding at me to walk ahead.

"Hey, hubby. Whaddya think about marryin' your wife today?" I tap him on the shoulder, then step back so he can turn around and see me.

When he does, his eyes light up and his entire face splits in two.

"Holy hell…Delly!" His jaw's still on the ground when he reaches for me and pulls me to him. "You look…breathtakin'. Truly gorgeous."

"You don't look too bad yourself, cowboy." I slide my palm down his black tie that's concealed behind a vest and white button-up shirt.

Then I blush at his Stetson black hat.

My favorite.

"That hat is makin' me feral," I admit, groaning at how badly I want him right now.

"Save it for tonight, darlin'." He winks.

"I will."

"Good, because I've got some very dirty plans in store for you."

"Is that so, Mr. Hollis?"

"Hey, guys? You're supposed to look in love, not about to rip off each other's clothes," Reagan interrupts. "Not that I'm not enjoyin' this Rated R version, but your parents are gonna see these photos."

We burst out laughing because I forgot she was here.

Whoops.

After taking *appropriate* family-friendly photos, he kisses me before going off to meet with his father and groomsmen to walk to the altar.

Brooke Montgomery

The Hollises went all out, even more than I expected.

There's a large white tent decorated with lights and linens, with gorgeous centerpieces on the tables.

Lanterns and hay bales line the walkway toward the tent and to the barn where the ceremony is held. Once it's over, we'll go eat and dance the night away.

I left my hair down in beachy waves, with a purple floral crown on top of my head.

It matches Wilder's favorite purple boots that I'm wearing underneath my dress.

He asked Sam to be his ring bearer and he looks the cutest in his little bowtie and vest. It's been fun getting to hang out with him on the weekends when I watch him and Lily for a few hours so Amelia can catch up on housework or sleep. Wilder usually takes him to the barn and they go riding.

Willow and Poppy are my flower girls and do a fantastic job throwing petals everywhere.

It was a good use of day-old flowers.

Since Wilder knows my issue with buying fresh flowers, he made sure to buy the leftovers that didn't get sold the previous day.

My mom and Wilder's dad walk me down the aisle, and by the time we get to the front, I'm not sure who's choked up more —Mom or Mr. Hollis.

There's a chair in the front row with a photo of my dad and a bouquet of white roses. But if I look at it too long, I start crying, so I focus on Wilder instead.

As he shares his vows with me, tears stream down my cheeks and even though I just did my makeup, I don't care. He makes the most heartfelt promise to love me until the day he dies and to find me in every lifetime because we're soulmates and he can't imagine a world without me in it.

But what breaks the dam completely is when he credits me

for saving his life all those years ago when he was a broken man who didn't feel worthy of love, but how I proved he was because I loved him back.

When it's my turn, I can hardly speak through my emotions, but I clear my throat and push through.

I tell him he's the best thing that's ever happened to me and not only is he the love of my life but also my best friend. The person who makes me laugh every single day, the one who makes me feel safe and cherished even when I'm at my worst, and the man who shows up for me time and time again. Then I vow to love him till my dying breath and into eternity.

By the time we finish our vows, most people are dabbing tissues under their eyes.

Falling in love with Wilder and feeling so loved in return was the last thing I expected when I kissed him that night — only five months ago.

But I don't regret a single second because everything we went through brought us here to this moment where we vowed in front of our friends and family to love each other for the rest of our lives.

"Baby, come meet the rest of my cousins." He grabs my hand and leads me over to where I recognize a few from the Willow Branch Mountain resort.

"This is Aunt Lindsey and Uncle Grady Langston." Then he motions toward me. "Meet my wife, Delilah Hollis. And our soon-to-be twins." He rubs his hand over my belly, making it stand out.

"It's so nice to meet y'all," I tell them, but when I go to shake their hands, Lindsey pulls me into her arms.

She's a hugger. *Duly noted.*

"Congrats on the marriage and babies," she says. "You're glowin', by the way."

"Ooh, thank you. And I'm almost positive it's sweat."

She laughs.

Wilder directs me to the three cousins I met previously.

"And you know Maisie, Bellamy, and Posey from the honeymoon."

I give them all hugs and thank them for coming.

"Then my other cousins: Warren, Colton, and Bodie." He points to two of them—Bellamy and Bodie. "They're twins, too."

"I knew it! I don't care what science says. These twins are your fault."

Everyone chuckles.

"Maybe you'll get one of each like I did and get the best of both worlds for your first time," Lindsey says. "By the time I had mine, I already had three kids."

"*Three*? And you kept goin'...on purpose?"

Grady wraps his arm around his wife and pulls her closer. "She couldn't keep her hands off me."

"Ugh, Dad."

"Ew."

"Gross."

"We're in public!"

I snort at everyone's reactions because that's definitely how the Hollis siblings would react, too.

"You gonna introduce me to your bridesmaids?" Colton asks, nodding behind me.

When I turn and look, he's staring at Amelia.

"Uh…sure." I shrug.

"Who's the brunette?" Bodie asks.

"That's Raven. I suppose you want an introduction, too?"

"I mean…" He fidgets with his tie. "I wouldn't be opposed to it."

I bark out a laugh. "I can tell y'all are related."

After the dinner, speeches, and first dance as husband and wife, my feet officially tap out. Although the purple boots are cute and a homage to when I wore them in Vegas, my feet are swelling to twice their size. If I don't get them off soon, they're going to fuse right to the leather.

Amelia and Raven help remove them, and then we laugh at how it took the three of us to do it. I'm not even that big yet, and I'm already struggling at basic tasks — like bending over or touching my toes.

"It's time for the cake," Reagan tells me.

"Okay, but I'm doin' it barefoot."

"Don't worry, I can photoshop your feet out."

"And that's why I love you."

After we cut the cake his mom and Gramma Grace made and shove a piece of funfetti into each other's mouths, he's pulled away for the mother-son dance. I watch them and notice how proud she looks at him.

I am too, especially since he kept his promise to Miss Tierney about volunteering once a month. I went with him to the shelter up until a month ago when it became too much for me. Although I wasn't there as much as Wilder, I felt a tremendous amount of fulfillment getting to help and listen to their stories. He also finished his anger management hours and is officially off probation.

I'm still searching for that spark — something beyond sales that'll give me purpose in my career — but since I'll be a new mom soon, that'll be my priority. Perhaps one day when they're older or in school, I can pivot and find something new. For now, I'm excited for this upcoming journey and getting to raise a family.

Something I wasn't sure I'd get to do.

"Delilah…" Mr. Hollis grabs my attention from where I'm sitting. "I know you can't have a father-daughter dance, but if you're up for it, I'd love to dance with you."

Tears swell in my eyes and I nod, quickly wiping them before they fall. "I'd love that. Thank you."

It was Wilder's idea to ask him to walk me down with my mom, and I was thrilled when he agreed. Mr. and Mrs. Hollis have been nothing but kind and welcoming to me and Harlow, and being a part of their family is an honor.

He takes my hand and helps me up, then walks us out to the dance floor. The song changes to "My Girl" and then I full-on lose it.

"Your father would be so proud of the woman you've become this past year. He's watchin' over y'all. I can feel it."

I nod, swallowing glass as I try to talk through my tears. "I feel him, too."

He wraps me in a hug as we continue dancing, but before it ends, Wilder comes and takes over.

"You doin' okay?"

"Do I look like I'm doin' okay? God, these hormones have me so messed up."

He brushes the pads of his thumbs under my eyes, and I close them as I savor his touch. He holds me close and rocks me back and forth to the music.

When it reaches eleven o'clock, I'm ready for my bed. We do a final walk around and thank everyone again for coming. Then I spy a couple Langston cousins hanging around Raven and Amelia.

"I think there's matchmakin' in progress," I tell Wilder as he carries me to his truck.

"Nah, weddings are prime territory for one-night stands."

"Of course you'd know that," I deadpan.

"None of that, Mrs. Hollis. Especially when you're carryin' my babies." He sets me down on the passenger seat, then leans in for a kiss. "And am in love with only you, forever and ever."

"Okay, fine. I forgive you for being a slut before me."

He grins. "And now I'm only a slut for you."

"Hm…that gives me an idea. Tonight, it's your turn to crawl to me."

Considering I can't, because the minute I'm on my hands and knees, there's no way I'm getting back up.

"Fuck…" He adjusts his groin. "Second honeymoon here we come."

I laugh when he closes my door and sprints to the driver's side. Once he's buckled in, he takes my hand and presses his lips to my ring finger. "Thanks for marryin' me again."

Biting my lip, I beam at my husband. "I'll sin with you any day."

Epilogue
Wilder

"Welcome to the world, sweet babies." I stare at my son and daughter in awe as Delilah holds them against her bare chest.

I've never seen someone have so much strength and power while being in the most pain of their life, but if there's one thing about my wife, she's fearless and determined. When her water broke three weeks before their due date, I was scared shitless, but she stayed calm and reassured me it was normal for twins to come early.

Finley Beau and Luna Grace were born healthy and with a solid set of lungs.

And they look just like their mother.

"Can you believe we have two babies?" she whispers, gazing at them.

"No…" I chuckle softly. "And they're just gonna let us take them home?"

"I know! Without a manual or instruction pamphlet."

Scratching my cheek, I seriously wonder how we're going to juggle parenthood. I'm confident we'll figure it out, but I still haven't mastered how to change a diaper even after practicing on one of Willow's dolls.

"It's a good thing we have a big village of helpers."

Between Mattie and Harlow, I know we'll have a couple extra sets of hands, but we'll also need to figure it out ourselves and not depend on them.

"I didn't think I could love them any more than I already did, and then they were born, and now my heart is burstin' with how much I love them."

I smile at Delilah's words because she took them right out of my mouth.

"It's amazin', isn't it? Until you experience this kind of unconditional love, it's indescribable. But now I can't imagine life without it."

She looks up at me with tears in her eyes. "Thank you."

"For what? You're the one who carried them and gave birth. I just donated my DNA."

"Don't make me laugh…" She tries holding it in, then winces. "God, no one talks about how much it burns down there after childbirth."

I squeeze my legs just thinking about it.

"Anyway…" She licks her lips, then looks up at me again. "Thank you for helpin' me find my spark again. After my dad died, I wasn't sure I'd ever get it back. Then you entered my life in a way I never anticipated and now you've given me a family."

I tilt her chin and brush my lips against hers. "I think you're forgettin' you gave me a family, too. Something I didn't expect for another two decades."

She smirks, scrunching her nose. "And yet, we didn't even wait a year."

"When you know, there's no reason to wait. Especially when it's the love of your life. I let you go nine years ago, and I wasn't about to let you go again once you gave me the green light."

What we have is special, and I'll never deny that. A connection filled with respect, love, and loyalty.

"The timin' might not have felt right at the moment, but it's what we needed to realize we can't always control how the universe works," she says. "So deep in grief, I never imagined I'd be here less than a year later."

I brush my lips against hers once more. "Your dad would be so proud of how far you've come. And I just know he's beamin' with pride at his new grandkids."

"I wish he'd been able to meet them, but you're right. I like thinkin' that maybe he met them before we got to have them."

"That's a comfortin' thought," I tell her.

My therapist often talks about finding peace in your pain and figuring out coping mechanisms that can help pull you out of the darkness. I've had a couple episodes this past year, though I'm not sure where they came from, but they crept in out of nowhere. I felt down even when I had no reason to be.

But then I remembered what I'd learned in therapy and leaned on Delilah the way she told me to. She didn't tell me things would be okay or to stay strong because it'd eventually pass. She didn't force me to talk it out when I told her I didn't want to. Instead, she lay in bed with me and shared random stories. She kept my mind busy and comforted me without even realizing it.

It was an eye-opening experience because it reminded me of when we'd talk over the phone. She never pushed me to talk, just offered her company and made me feel normal for having very human emotions.

Thinking about how Wesley dealt with similar feelings as Delilah, it's a shame he let his grief take over his life instead of getting help because now he's missing out on his daughter's life.

He got his day in court, and although his defense leaned on his mental health for why he did what he did, the jury found him guilty on all counts. However, the judge gave him leniency for being a former police officer and his PTSD, so he sent him to a mental health clinic. Then once he completes their program, he'll finish out the rest of his ten-year sentence in prison.

"I love you." I trace a finger along her jawline. "So much."

Her brows pinch together. "I love you, too."

I smile at her confusion. "Just don't want you to forget."

"Never." She leans into my palm.

"How do you think Hank's gonna take havin' two cryin' infants in his house?"

"Probably wish he had a different family." She chuckles.

Delilah surprised me with a Great Dane puppy four months ago, and truthfully, it's been a wild fucking ride. Waylon got jealous, so we agreed to do joint custody.

Whenever he's at their place, we hear Harlow shouting at him for chewing up something of hers.

And then we laugh because he's at least not chewing something of ours.

"Well...our lives will be nothin' if not chaotic."

"That's for sure."

"Can we come in?" I hear my mom's soft voice with a soft knock on the door.

"Just go in! I wanna see my great-grandbabies." Gramma Grace barges in with my parents behind.

"She's doin' skin to skin," I explain.

"Nothin' I haven't seen before. Boobs are boobs." She goes to the sink and washes her hands. "Now which one can I hold?"

"Which one do you want?"

"The one who doesn't need a diaper change."

I chuckle, carefully picking up Luna and holding her against my chest before bringing her over to Gramma Grace on the couch.

"They're so tiny," Mom whispers.

"Trust me, they're not," Delilah argues. "Nearly ripped me in half."

My dad walks over and tenderly kisses her on the head. "Congrats. I heard you were a rock star."

"Someone had to be since your son wouldn't do it for me."

Dad smirks.

"Can I hold the other one?" Mom asks eagerly.

I pick up Finley next and bring him over where she sits next to Gramma Grace.

"He looks just like you did," Mom gushes. "Cutest button nose."

"Think so? Luna looks like Delilah, don't ya think?"

"No, she definitely has my features," Gramma Grace declares.

"Ma…" My mom nudges her softly.

"What?"

Delilah laughs. "It's okay. I think she looks like you, too."

"She'll probably be feisty like you," I say.

"Like who?" Gramma Grace raises a brow.

My parents spend the next hour hogging the babies, but when they start to fuss, I kick everyone out so Delilah can breastfeed.

Later, Mrs. Fanning and Harlow come, and then my siblings show up.

By the time everyone leaves, we're exhausted. After Delilah breastfeeds again, the nurse comes and takes the babies to the nursery for the night so Delilah can get some sleep.

"Can I tell you a secret?" I say, sitting in a chair next to her bed, rubbing my hand over hers.

"You're keepin' secrets from me?" she teases.

I smirk. "I'm glad you forgot to renew your birth control."

She glances at me with a suspicious grin. "Can I tell *you* a secret?"

Arching a brow, I scratch along my facial hair that I haven't shaved in five days. "What?"

The corner of her lips reaches her eyes. "I'm glad we got drunk in Vegas."

Bonus Epilogue
Delilah

TEN YEARS LATER

Looking out the kitchen window as I rinse dishes, I watch Finley and Luna on the trampoline with Hank barking up a storm and circling them. I hate that thing. It's dangerous, but Wilder and the kids *love* it.

Finley broke his arm last summer on it and Luna nearly sprained her ankle a month ago, but these kids are as reckless as their father.

After the twins were born, I became a stay-at-home mom. They kept me busy for years, so I could only volunteer at the shelter once a month when we could get someone to watch them for us. But I managed to go more often when they became more independent and eventually brought them with us to help, too.

We've gotten to know so many families, their stories, and help more people thanks to the nonprofit organization Wilder and I started: Hollis Hope Foundation. It focuses on helping people get back on their feet by finding them jobs, safe environments to live, and making sure they have everything they need from food to furniture. The Sugarland Creek Ranch & Retreat is our biggest donor next to the Willow Branch Mountain Ranch & Resort. The rest come from fundraisers and other state donors.

It took some time, but finally found that fulfillment I was searching for…that feeling of pride and satisfaction.

Bending down to put a plate in the dishwasher, I'm greeted with my husband behind me when I stand to grab the next dish. He wraps his arms around me and molds his body to mine.

"Good mornin', wife. Take off your clothes and meet me in the shower," he murmurs in my ear, sliding a hand between my thighs.

"After back-to-back ER visits, I'm not leavin' them out there unsupervised."

"They'll be out there for at least another half hour."

"Wilder…" I warn when his hand moves underneath my panties.

"Fine, I'll play with you right here. Don't move."

I scoff. "I was doin' the dishes."

"I'll finish them after I make you finish." He nips at my earlobe, dipping a finger inside me.

"Fuck," I breathe out, spreading my legs and grabbing the counter for support.

"That's my girl…" He sucks my neck, his tongue piercing dragging across my flesh and making my body vibrate with pleasure. "And don't you dare be quiet."

He works my clit as he sinks two fingers deeper. It doesn't take him long to set me off. He's a pro at it by now, but I still muffle my cries so the dog doesn't hear me and bark.

Belle, our Bernese Mountain Dog, is usually attached to my

hip, but she's napping in the other room. It wouldn't take much for her to hear us and wake up.

With a slap to my ass, he growls. "I told you not to hold back."

"They're comin' in." I arch my back, pushing him back with my ass.

Wilder turns on the sink and then washes his hands with soap, smirking at me over his shoulder.

"Mom!"

"What?"

"Finley pushed me," Luna whines.

"Finley! We don't push girls," Wilder scolds.

"She pushed me first!" he defends.

"Luna, is that true?"

She rolls her eyes. "That's part of the game."

"We don't have time for this. Go get dressed. We gotta leave the house in twenty minutes."

They shove each other as they race upstairs to their rooms.

Then I spin around toward Wilder and press my palms softly against his chest. "Are you sure you're gonna be okay today?"

A flash of sadness covers his face. "Yeah. I mean, I'm sad, of course. But Gramma Grace lived a long and happy life. I'm glad she went peacefully in her sleep instead of sufferin' with an illness or somethin' worse."

Nodding, I wrap my arms around him and squeeze him tight before releasing my hold. "She was such an important part of your life, even mine, and I'm gonna miss her."

"Me too. Sunday night dinners won't be the same without her baked goodies and scandalous stories."

"Let's get ready so we're not late. I have my dish ready to go in the oven."

They're hosting the luncheon at The Lodge and everyone's

bringing a dish to pass. She was cremated, per her wishes, so we're getting together for a memorial service. Then after we eat, everyone's supposed to stand up and share their favorite story about her.

My eyes are already watering thinking about it.

"You gonna be alright?" he asks, brushing his thumb over my cheek.

"I think so. Just thinkin' about all the fond memories we're gonna hear today."

He tilts my chin and then claims my mouth. "It's okay to cry. She was a very special woman and we were lucky enough to share part of our lives with her."

This time I let a tear fall. "Okay, I'm gonna get ready and put on waterproof mascara."

The size of the Hollis family has grown so much, we take up three large tables. The rest of the guests from the memorial fill up the rest.

The service was beautiful, and I'm not too ashamed to admit I cried through most of it. Mr. and Mrs. Hollis honored her life in such a respectful way. Photos covered the walls all the way from her childhood through her last days. There's a picture of her holding each grandchild and great-grandchild. She was a blessed woman and we were blessed to have her in our lives.

One of the last photos is with Ricky, Harlow and Waylon's second child, who was just born a few months ago.

The most recent one is from Christmas where we took a photo of everyone together. Mrs. Hollis blew it up and put it on display permanently at The Lodge.

I love that we'll get to see it every day and smile at the happy memories we made.

"If I can have everyone's attention..." Wilder's deep voice echoes through the room. "I'd like to start off with a story that I don't think many people know. But it's one of my favorites."

The room quiets down, and I scoot my chair closer to Luna, who's in front of me.

Wilder clears his throat and then looks down at his notes.

"I think most of us could relate to Gramma Grace's special *talent*, or sixth sense as some of us called it. Though it was often referred to as a witchcraft because she knew things before everyone else, sometimes even before we knew them about ourselves. But there was one instance where her voodoo led me on a path to meetin' my wife before I even knew who she was."

I listen intently, as does everyone else, but I have no idea where he's going with this story.

"Twenty years ago, I called a crisis hotline because I was in a dark place. I didn't know why I was callin' or what I expected, but I was pleasantly surprised by the woman who answered. She listened and talked me through a rough night. I didn't tell anyone that I had called. A part of me was ashamed, so I kept it to myself. The followin' day, I ran into Gramma Grace in the kitchen and she stared into my soul, which if you've experienced that, it can be kinda freaky."

The room erupts in laughter.

"When I asked her what was wrong, she said, 'stay happy.' I was so confused because I was the opposite of happy. Later that evening, I called the crisis hotline again and the same woman answered my call. And then it hit me that Gramma Grace was right—I was happy. Happy to feel seen and heard for the first time, but mostly happy to hear the voice on the other line being so happy to hear my voice too. There was somethin' about her I couldn't quite put my finger on, but I kept callin', and she kept answerin'. For six months."

He looks up and finds me in the crowd, then smiles wide.

"That voice on the other line was my future wife. I consider it fate that Gramma Grace made that one out-of-pocket comment, because without it, I'm not sure I would've had the nerve to call again."

Read Wilder & Delilah's bonus scene on my website
brookewritesromance.com/bonus-scenes

Curious about Warren & Maisie's story?
Find them next in *Take My Name,* book 1 of the Willow Branch Mountain series. You'll also get more Amelia and Raven in this series, so stay tuned for their upcoming books.

Take My Name

A second chance stand-alone from small-town romance author Brooke Montgomery about a literary agent from NYC who returns to her Southern hometown and the cowboy high school sweetheart she left behind...

About the Author

Brooke has been writing romance since 2013 under the *USA Today* Bestselling author pen names: Brooke Cumberland and Kennedy Fox, and now, **Brooke Montgomery** and **Brooke Fox**. She loves writing small town romance with big families and happily ever afters! She lives in the frozen tundra of Packer Nation with her husband, wild teenager, and four dogs. Brooke's addicted to iced coffee, leggings, and naps. She found her passion for telling stories during winter break one year in grad school—and she hasn't stopped since.

Find her on her website at
www.brookewritesromance.com
and follow her on social media:

facebook.com/brookemontgomeryauthor

instagram.com/brookewritesromance

amazon.com/author/brookemontgomery

tiktok.com/@brookewritesromance

goodreads.com/brookemontgomery

bookbub.com/authors/brooke-montgomery

threads.net/@brookewritesromance

bsky.app/profile/brookemontgomery.bsky.social